HEART Broken

SATAN'S DEVILS #5

COPYRIGHT

Published 2017 by Trish Haill Associates
Copyright Manda Mellett

ISBN: 978-1-912288-07-6

Cover Design by Lia Rees at Free Your Words
(www.freeyourwords.com)

Formatted and re-edited by Maggie Kern @ Ms.K Edits

www.mandamellett.com

Disclaimer
This is a work of fiction. Names, characters, businesses, places, events and incidents are either the products of the author's imagination or used in a fictitious manner. Any resemblance to actual persons, living or dead, or actual events is purely coincidental.

Warning

This book is dark in places and contains content of a sexual, abusive and violent nature. It is not suitable for persons under the age of 18.

AUTHOR'S NOTE

Heart Broken is the fifth in the Satan's Devils MC Series.

While this book can be read as a standalone, it concludes Heart's story which began in *Slick Running,* and continued in *Targeting Dart.* To get the full benefit, I advise you to read books 3, 4, and 5 in the right order.

If you're new to MC books, you may find there are terms that you haven't heard before, so I've included a glossary to help along the way. I hope you get drawn into this mysterious and dark world in the same way I have done–there will be further books in the Satan's Devils series which I hope you'll want to follow.

If you've picked this book up because, like me, you read anything MC, I hope you'll enjoy it for what it is, a fictional insight into the underground culture of alpha men and their bikes.

CAST OF CHARACTERS - ARIZONA

Officers
Drummer – President
Wraith – Vice President
Heart – Secretary
Dollar – Treasurer
Peg – Sergeant-at-arms
Blade – Enforcer
Mouse – Computer Expert
Joker - Road Captain

Patched Members
Beef
Bullet
Lady
Marvel
Paladin
Road
Rock
Slick
Shooter
Tongue

Viper

Prospects
Fergus
Hyde
Jekyll

Old Ladies & Children
Carmen (Bullet's)
Sandy (Viper's)
Crystal (Heart's): Amy
Sophie (Wraith's): Olivia
Sam (Drummer's): Elijah
Ella (Slick's)

Sweet Butts
Allie
Diva
Jill
Paige
Pussy

Members who've moved on
Dart - transferred

Deceased Members
Adam
Buster
Hank

SATAN'S DEVILS MC

PROLOGUE

*H*eart…

The change in tempo causes me to glance across to the bar, seeing, as expected, Peg's in charge of the music again. I raise my eyebrows toward Wraith, and we give almost identical shakes of our heads. When the sergeant-at-arms is in one of his moods, who knows what he's going to put on, and it would be useless to object to the playlist he's chosen for the night.

Out of the corner of my eye I see Crystal, my old lady, my soulmate, the love of my life. She's standing over by the bar, her hands gently supporting Amy, our three-year-old daughter, who's perched on a stool. As she looks over and gives a little wave of her fingers and one of her brilliant full-of-love smiles, the song starting to play sends me back to when I first met her, and soon I'm losing myself, listening as the words of *Main Street* take me back in time.

She wasn't a dancer, and it wasn't a club downtown, but a bar where she worked as a barista. And yeah, I was walking past the first time I caught a glimpse of her through the window, her beauty and vivaciousness clear through the glass.

It was nearly closing time, and fuck knows why, but I stopped and waited, smoking cigarette after cigarette until, eventually, I saw her come out. She was walking up that lonely street, frowning. Worried how vulnerable she'd seemed, I'd followed her at a distance to make sure she was safe. It was only a block to the parking lot where she had left her car, but seeing her, such a beautiful woman and all alone, made my heart skip a beat. She shouldn't be walking the streets in the dark. *Not without someone to watch out for her.*

I couldn't explain what drew me there, but the next night I returned to the same bar, and staying outside, peered in and watched her work. Her tables seemed to fill quickly, patrons being drawn to the girl in bright coloured clothes who always had a smile on her face and a friendly comment for everyone. People sitting in her area looked happier than those at other tables, as though just being close to her lightened their moods. Her obvious joy in life was infectious.

I'd been a full member of the Satan's Devils MC for just over six months, and like any newly patched brother, made full use of the sweet butts whose services had been denied to me while I'd been prospecting. But from that first night that I saw her, I turned them all away. She didn't know it, but she was already mine.

Not being modest, I know I'm good looking—shoulder-length blond hair, and blue eyes that seem to draw attention from the women I meet. A big burly tattooed biker, men tremble in front of me while their women flutter their eyelids from behind, trying to capture my eye. I'm not afraid of anyone or anything, except I'm nervous of approaching this woman who's drawn me in. Almost scared of this inexplicable attraction that wipes all other women from my mind. What's keeping me from getting close and taking what I want?

It's the fear of rejection that's holding me back. The concern she might just treat me like any other one of the numerous advances she must have. That I'd be dismissed in the same polite way she's clearly declining suggestions from other men. I've watched her enough to know she's an expert at turning them down, somehow leaving them wearing a smile even as she rebuffs them.

I'm walking too close, I know it, but can't stop myself closing the gap just to watch her long auburn hair swing around that heart-shaped ass. Her tight leggings do nothing to hide her figure as she strides confidently to her car. Suddenly she stops and turns, coming face-to-face with me, a rugged biker.

"Are you following me?" Her voice is musical, her tone half-amused, as if it's an everyday occurrence to have a man just trying to be near her. And it probably is.

"What? No. I'm just walking to my bike." Which happens to be parked in the same parking lot as her car. "It's in the lot up the street."

"Mine too." I already know that. It's no coincidence.

"Then shall we walk together? It's not safe for a woman to be walking alone." Not one like you, who any man would lust after.

She shrugs and awards me one of her heart-stopping smiles. "Seems I don't have a choice if we're going the same way."

There's so much I want to ask her, such as would she like to spend the night in my bed? But I feel strangely tongue-tied and awkward. Silence descends as we go to our separate vehicles. I don't get her number, or try to take up any more of her time.

She drives away and, after a moment, I follow her to the exit, but peel off in the other direction. Going back to the club, and straight to my bed, I relieve my cock with my hand.

A pep talk to myself, and the very next day I pluck up the courage, and instead of stalking her from outside, go and take the last table in her section. Recognising me, she comes over, hands me a menu, and then, fuck me, she takes the seat opposite. Elbows on the table, she rests her chin on her hands and studies me as I pretend to read the specials for the day. My mouth unable to form any sensible words, I stutter my order, not really caring what I'm going to be served.

"What's your name, biker boy?" she asks as she jots down what I've asked for.

"Dale," I reply.

Her head tilts to one side. "Thought you bikers had road names."

I shrug. "Not been give one yet."

Her eyes shine, her gorgeous mouth turns up at the corner, then she gets up and puts her hand on my shoulder in passing. "Right, I'll get on and get this for you."

Even through the leather of my cut, my skin burns where she's touched me, as though with that one action she's marked me as hers. She leaves me feeling like a schoolboy with a crush, unable to say what I really want. My food's delivered. I couldn't say what I ate. When she brings me the bill, I shoot out my hand and rest it on her wrist. "Wanna get together sometime?"

"I thought you'd never ask."

I treated her like porcelain, careful not to frighten off the woman who captured my heart from the first time I saw her. I wined her, dined her, and eventually took her to the clubhouse, the first biker on the new compound to get serious about a woman. I was nervous about how she'd fit in with my brothers, but I needn't have had any concerns. The very first step she took over the threshold, she walked in and owned that place—and them—from the start.

They'd laughed at me, the rough biker brought to his knees by a woman, and she teased me along with them. When she started to say I had a big heart, it caught on quickly and became my road name. She captured me, she was it for me. She named me, and I knew I'd be forever hers.

The Bob Seger song ends, and I realise she's standing beside me, a hand on my shoulder. She squeezes her fingers and asks in her soft, sweet voice, "What were you thinking about? You were miles away."

I cover her hand with my own and give her the honest answer. "About how much I love you." I stand and pull her close, feeling our hearts beating in time. "And how you're the only woman and old lady I'll ever want, or have."

CHAPTER ONE

*H*eart…

Taking my pack of cigarettes from my cut, I tap one out, put it in my mouth and light it, inhaling the smoke deep into my lungs. Accepting part of the reason I took up smoking again is just one more way I hope to rid myself of the body I'm trapped in. I'd kicked the habit when my wife, Crystal, got pregnant, but now that she's no longer breathing, I couldn't care less what happens to me. A nicotine fix is a poor substitution for the object of my main addiction, which I'll never be able to indulge in again.

Taking another drag, my mind flits to my daughter, Amy. The three-year-old little imp that is, was, fuck, I don't know what tense to use, the second love of my life. Close, but not right up there with Crystal. I blow out smoke, seeing the vapour swirl like fog as the warm air from my mouth meets the cold of this autumn day. Amy. Too great a reminder of just what I've lost, and left behind in the safe hands and care of my president, or rather, ex-prez and his old lady. They'll look after her as though she was their own, and better than I ever could. Of course I miss her, but can do nothing for her. I know I'll never play the role of her father again. I've no intention of ever going back.

Still astride my bike, I wait for my leg to stop throbbing enough to let me put my foot to the ground. I shiver, a visible sign of how much lower the temperature is here, a sharp contrast to the warm balmy day I'd left in Tucson. Cold. Like my soul.

When the pain's eased sufficiently, I still pause before throwing my leg over the seat, taking a moment to consider my surroundings, knowing I've been lucky to arrive in Flagstaff just before the first of the winter snows. The tops of the mountains glow white in the last of the day's sun, as if a warning that if I want to carry on, I can't linger here long. Not unless I want to be trapped here for the winter. Bikes and snow do not mix.

My leg protests, shooting pains stabbing up to my groin as I attempt to put weight on it, leaving me in no doubt the four-hour ride combined with the noticeable drop in temperature was far from the best thing I could have attempted. A sensible person wouldn't even be riding yet, but I hadn't left my brothers much choice, and I wasn't going to constrict myself in a cage. The timing of my journey determined by the wrong I'd done to my club. The pick of destination had been mine, an unconscious decision, an undeniable urge to start on this pilgrimage originally planned with my wife before she was so cruelly snatched away from me.

I'd managed to cover the miles by gritting my teeth through the gear changes, and once in top kept it there as long as I could. The Harley beneath me forgiving, continuing on while the grunt from the engine let its protests be known as I attempted to drive without shifting down. It's not that I don't care about the Low Rider, I've no desire to damage it, but it doesn't belong to me. Drummer letting me borrow it was the quickest way to get me off the compound. There was no one who wanted me hanging around.

Not that Adam, its rightful owner, would have much to say about it—seeing as he's been dead for going on six months. While I might not be religious and don't believe in life after death, there's a part of me wondering if somehow he knows and is looking down, grimacing each time I grind through the gears. *Sorry, Brother, I'm doing the best that I can.*

Finished with my smoke, I pull the key from the ignition and stand and stretch before entering the restaurant that's next to the motel I'll be holing up in for a few days. I'm as weak as any human, not having the strength to neglect the burning in my stomach reminding me that, just like my bike, I need fuel.

The bell above the door tinkles as I step inside, and the sight in front of me makes me come to an abrupt halt. *Fuck. Crystal would have loved this shit.*

Crystal, my wife. My soulmate. Killed just two months ago. Not that I'd known she was gone until she'd been dead for four weeks. The accident that took her had left me in a coma, and she'd been buried and placed deep underground before I came to. Accident? It certainly wasn't that. Cold-blooded murder that was supposed to kill me as well.

Every second, every minute, every hour of every day, I wish that it had.

Whether it's a masochistic action, or in reverence to her memory, I can't stop my hand reaching out and reverently touching some of the Christmas ornaments on sale, remembering how each year Crystal would buy a new one for the tree we'd put up at home. I would laugh at her, joking she seemed to go for the gaudiest she could find. Last year it had been a Santa riding a motorbike. And the year before that, Micky Mouse dressed in red and white—for Amy she said.

I've become a bastard, selfish. Not giving a damn about my life or the people around me. Caring more for the dead than for the living. I have nothing to offer my daughter. She's better off with people who can give her what I can't anymore. There's no love left inside me. Crystal took all of that with her. That emotion, my heart and my soul, left me when Crystal took her last breath.

Heart. That's my fucking handle, that's who I am. That's what the accident took away from me. Thrown away from my body just as I was tossed off my bike. There might be the organ of that name still pumping blood around my body, but I only curse it for keeping me alive. The cold in the air outside has nothing on the chill deep inside me. I don't give a damn for anything anymore.

Which one would you like, Crystal? My fingers touch a snowflake globe. In the scene, Santa's landed his sleigh on a roof, the reindeer looking impatient to get going again. It's cheesy, and just what she'd go for. *Shall we get this one?* But what's the point? This year there'll be no tree in the house that we shared, and which has lain empty and abandoned since the last day she was alive. Without her, I have no home. There's no place for me in this world anymore.

For a second I swear I feel a hand on my shoulder, fingers pressing in in a barely there caress. I look around, but there's no one behind me. Only the storekeeper eyeing me strangely, the biker transfixed by Christmas ornaments, a look of suspicion on his face as though I'll steal it away. Something that costs just a few dollars, but which would have brought my dead wife so much joy.

"You gonna buy that, son?"

Son? I haven't been anyone's son for a very long time, but I won't pull him up on it. He must be sixty if he's a day, almost double my age.

Without knowing what I'm doing, or why, I slide the ornament off the rack and take it across to the counter, passing over the dollars and rejecting the change. He puts the five cents in a collection box for orphans. Apt. My Amy is now without either of her parents. *But Drummer and Sam will give her the love that I can't.*

Having made my senseless purchase, I proceed into the restaurant, order something and attempt to eat it, my hand automatically lifting my fork, unable to distinguish the different flavours. I could be eating a gourmet meal or a bowl of leftovers. I snap at the waitress when she attempts to be friendly, glad when she has the sense not to bother me again. I've not been able to make polite conversation since the day I woke up from my coma and the doctors delivered the news.

At last my plate's empty and my attention is caught by the weather forecast on the television. The sound is turned down, so I'm forced to read the captions. Snow is forecasted for the day after next. Unless I want to spend more time than I'd like in Flagstaff, it's time for me to get moving again.

Returning to the motel, I prepare for bed like an automaton, undressing and sliding under the covers, going through the same mechanical routine born simply from habit. As usual, sleep evades me. I spend the night planning the next stage of my journey, accepting my mind no longer knows how to switch off, allowing me no respite from my thoughts. Crystal might be gone from the physical world, but I'm never going to let her leave me. I feel her presence so strongly. My hands twitch, unable to understand why I can't reach out and touch her. Oh, how I ache to be able hold her. My arms feel so empty, my heart broken completely.

Crystal. I love you. Like a clock that's stopped working, hands frozen in time, I can't move past this, can't acknowledge I'm never going to hold or see her again, or smell the sweet perfume that was all hers.

Another sleepless night passes, and I rise early. After a smoke, I refuel both my bike and myself, stuffing down a breakfast that tastes like cardboard, simply to get myself moving again, knowing I've another long journey in front of me. *Vegas, Crystal. Are you ready for that?*

That's my next destination, the second stop on my itinerary. One place I know I'll avoid, the Sin City's Satan's Devils chapter. I doubt I'd be welcome after the trouble I'd caused back in Tucson, and it's far too early for me to see any man I used to call *Brother* again. I'm busting to fight, to argue, to mock... Which is all I've been doing since I woke up. If I started that shit in Red's chapter, word would get back to Drummer, who wouldn't hesitate in carrying out his threat to kill me. The idea is tempting.

I'm burning inside and unable to see a time when this anger will leave me. Accepting I'll be gone before it has a chance to morph into another emotion, the chances are good that I won't stay long breathing. I'm a lone biker, out on the road, unprotected, no one to watch my back. It's the rightly deserved punishment I had handed to me.

Drummer, the president of the Satan's Devils Tucson chapter, the mother chapter for the club, let me off lightly. He could have burned the tattoo from my back, and I'm still not sure why he didn't. Instead, he sent me out to roam as a Ronin. Six solitary months on the road. Automatically my hand rubs my bare cut, stripped of all Satan's Devils' patches, but having gained a new one denoting what I now am. I'm just an anonymous biker out on his own, unable to call any man, *Brother*, but carrying a token that will maybe ease my passage through areas controlled by different clubs, respect being mutually given where due. Unless I fuck up.

If I can't control my temper, I'll be disrespecting Drummer. Although I've no intention to return and again wear the Satan's Devils' patch on my cut, there's a part of me inside that doesn't want my behaviour to reflect on my club. I can't take the risk of lashing out at any brother. It's been an easy decision to steer well clear of the Las Vegas chapter.

My hand lingers on my wallet and the business card inside. *My token.* Then it lingers on the one patch I wear on my sleeve. *Ronin.* Everything happened so quickly, it still hasn't completely sunk in that I'm now solitarily roaming, just like the legendary samurai of old, with no master to serve and no one to pay allegiance to.

I feel no sense of urgency, no place to be or appointment to attend. My thoughts continue churning as I put the key in the ignition of my borrowed bike. Just another sign of how much I'd blown it. While I'd been injured, the club had offered to buy me a replacement for my smashed-up sled, but how could I think of a cold metal beast when I was in mourning? I'd turned down their offer, and not pleasantly or with thanks. In fact, I remember clearly telling whoever suggested it to me to fuck off. And that wasn't the worst of the shit I'd pulled back in Tucson. If I still had a heart, I'd hate myself for what I did.

But a biker can't go on the road without a bike. When Drummer had banished me, he'd brought Adam's bike out of storage. Yesterday morning, as it was wheeled in front of me, I had a pang, a worry that after my accident I wouldn't be able to ride. But having no recollection of being shunted off the road, I found being back on a bike didn't concern me. Memory muscle had taken over and, like my head, my body seemed unable to recall the terror of those final minutes before we'd landed shiny side down. If I'd seen Crystal's broken body, it's one mercy I can't recall it.

Adam's bike suits me down to the ground—a long-range tank on a Low Rider, chain-drive replacing the belt for added speed, and the best thing? Adam, a confirmed bachelor, had had a single seat fitted. Never again would anyone ride up behind me, that place reserved only for my wife.

Ghost arms come around me and a chin rests on my shoulder. *Okay, babe. Let's get this show moving.* I take the one final item I need to carefully pack in the saddlebags, holding it in my hand for a second. The Christmas snow globe wrapped carefully in tissue paper. I slide it down between my clothes for safe keeping.

Pressing start, the engine roars to life. A single snowflake flutters to the ground, and as I watch it melt on the asphalt, recognise the sign it's too late to linger. My indicators flash, then I'm leaving the parking lot, the motel, and then Flagstaff in my rear view.

Did it live up to your expectations, babe? There's no reply, not even in my head, just a light touch to my shoulder.

Another four-hour ride lies ahead. I'd planned to stay longer at my first stop to give my body a chance to rest, but the weather had had other ideas and had chased me away. My leg, the most serious reminder of the accident I can't remember and now bolted together with steel pins, starts complaining before I've gone more than a few miles. As I did yesterday, I ignore it and just push on through, only stopping when the pain gets too bad to go on. A smoke, a piss, then popping a painkiller, I'm on my way again, this time wearing a helmet, knowing the law in Nevada is stricter than Arizona, which I'd just left.

As the near-freezing temperatures give way to gentle heat, my muscles stop tensing. The warmth and painkillers kick in. I'm feeling almost normal as in the mid-afternoon I approach Vegas, the city that never sleeps appearing in front of me, rising up from the desert. Before finding somewhere to make my base, I take a leisurely ride along the strip, turning my head this way and that to gaze at the casinos I've only before seen on television and in films. *Excalibur*, shaped like a castle, then almost opposite, the *MGM Grand*. Then *Bellagio* and *Aladdin* and *Paris. Venetian* and *Treasure Island*. Taking them all in until I come to *Sahara* and *Stratosphere* at the other end.

Is it what you expected, Crystal? Larger than life, isn't it, babe?

Again, I feel hands squeeze my waist, making me appreciate how excited she would have been to ride down the strip. I can picture her laughing, her hair flowing back with the breeze. Giggling with anticipation, joking she was going to win our fortune at the tables tonight. Me grumbling I expect, it more likely she'd lose all my money instead.

Turning off the strip, I explore the back streets. I draw up at the first cheap looking place I find, dump my saddlebags onto the bed, and place my head in my hands. Then I stand and slam my fists into the wall, beating them until I break the skin. *Why did you leave me? Why?* The burning rage all but consumes me as I fail to understand why this world took the love of my life away from me. She should be here, by my side, enjoying Vegas. Not in a cold grave.

I concentrate on my breathing, taking breaths in and out. Ranting at the world isn't going to bring her back. The only thing I can do is go through the motions. For her. Until we're together again.

When I finally have myself under control, I go to revisit the strip, this time on foot.

It's the noise that gets to me. Music playing, machines ringing bells or playing sequences of notes to attract you to take your chances, to get rich quick. Occasionally there's a rattling of coins as they pay out, followed by shouting and cheering, but more often groans, as yet more dollars are lost. Croupiers are calling, and all around people are talking loudly. My head starts to pound with the cacophony of sound.

I'm approached as I walk along the pavement, leaflets shoved into my hand showing scantily clad girls offering a menu of their services, but none interest me. I crumple them up and throw them into the already overflowing bins. My cock hasn't stirred since I lost my wife. Not one twitch, solidifying my perception that while I might still be breathing, inside I'm already dead, just waiting for the grim reaper to creep alongside and catch up.

That evening in Tucson when I attacked Tinker, I wouldn't have been capable of rape, even though I'm not surprised that thought was my intention. I was angry, incensed that a sweet woman like her was stripping to earn money, ignoring the fact she didn't have any other choice. I was trying to show her what a man would think she was offering. I'd been out of my mind with rage and grief, not knowing what I was doing, just wanting to lash out, and she bore the brunt.

No, even an erection is now beyond me. I might be only thirty-four years old, but I'm beginning to think Viagra's in my future if I ever want to have sex. But as that's the last thing on my mind, I'm not worried. It's one less thing to think about. I'll be faithful to Crystal for the rest of my hopefully short life.

I make myself stay a few days in Vegas, owing it to my dead wife, experiencing the things she's missing out on. But one day I can't make myself leave the hotel, justifying it that I'm taking the opportunity to pop painkillers to give my leg a rest. The bones might have healed, but the muscles needed more time than I'd been able to give them.

Then my restlessness, my desire to put an end to all this, my growing hatred of the discordance of sound I can't seem to escape, drives me to leave before I lose what little remains of my mind. I pack my saddlebags, making sure that Christmas ornament is stored carefully, and take off for somewhere quieter. A few hours later, and I arrive at Stovepipe Wells in the centre of Death Valley.

Sauntering into the motel, unable to hide my limp, I toss a glare at the clerk behind the reception desk, recognising I look out of place alongside the vacationers who are taking advantage of exploring the area in the lower temperatures of late autumn.

"We've no vacancy." She throws me and my leathers a look of disdain, and then a glance of distrust at my face.

But I'd pre-empted this disappointment. Knowing this time of year the valley would be busy, I'd pre-booked a room before I left Vegas. I show her my phone and my booking.

Faced with the evidence, she sighs, then gives in and points me to a room at the end of a row, keeping the biker well out of sight of the rest of the guests.

"Mr Norman." She checks my driver's license. "How long do you intend to be with us?"

I tap the booking still showing on my phone. "A week, as I told you. I'm here to rest, recover." I make a show of rubbing my sore leg. "I'll be sleeping a lot, so I won't need the room serviced."

I ignore her suspicious glance, only registering her nod. I don't care what anyone thinks of me anymore. I'm only thinking of the seven days of privacy while people would think I am hidden away, licking my physical and mental wounds. One hundred and sixty-eight hours when no one would think of looking or trying to find me.

Taking my key, avoiding her guarded half-smile, I ride down the row and park my bike. As I cut the engine, I notice immediately how quiet and peaceful it is. Such a stark contrast to Vegas, the silence causing a ringing in my ears.

Collecting my saddlebags, I enter the room that's been assigned to me and close the door, shutting out the world. I take off my cut and lie on the double bed, leaving the right-hand side empty, as always. My hand rubs over the comforter, feeling her absence, missing the warm body lying next to me.

I hadn't lied when I said my leg needed time to recuperate. I'm sure the surgeons would have conniptions if they knew how little I cared for all the hard work that they'd done. I lie, waiting for the painkillers to work, and only when the throbbing in my leg begins to ease, take a shower to wash away the dust of the road. When I clear steam from the glass and glance in the mirror, I barely recognise the face looking back at me. There's no point fussing over my appearance, there's no one to care. My hair is the same as when I awoke from my dream and stepped into my nightmare. One side half shaved and the other side long. The hair on my left side not as stubbly as it first was, now starting to grow back, but not long enough to hide my unbalanced appearance—just the right look for an unbalanced man.

I need to eat, so as I'm entering polite society, quickly shave away my five o'clock shadow, but that's the most I bother to do before I rejoin civilisation.

Walking into the restaurant next to the motel, I get the strange looks that I've become used to, but am quickly seated and left all alone. Not surprisingly, no one wants to share a table with a biker whose face is fixed in a scowl. I order a steak, fitting for a man's last meal, but the succulent meat is as tasteless as anything I've recently put into my mouth.

As soon as my plate's empty, I walk back to my room, noticing, to my surprise, coyotes wandering around the forecourt of the gas station and small convenience store on the other side of the road. I hadn't expected that, and I pause a moment to watch them scavenging. *Fuck, Crystal. You'd have loved this shit. Are you with me, babe? You seeing this?*

The timing is wrong, as autumn is coming to an end in the valley, and it's not perhaps the best time to do what I intend. But having checked, tomorrow's forecast is predicting unseasonal temperatures that might reach the forties. Enough for an unfit biker to carry out his plan.

I'm tired and exhausted from days, months of no real sleep. I don't even get undressed, just lie fully clothed, letting my thoughts torture me until I'm ready to start on my final journey. Hours of thinking there's nothing left. Only the hope of joining my wife in her rest, where there'll be no more pain and no memories to haunt me. *Wait for me, Crystal. I'm coming.*

When only the sounds of the night can be heard—the crying of coyotes, hooting of night-hunting birds, nothing to suggest humans are still stirring—I slip on my cut, open my door, and start walking.

The night air is cool, which will allow me to put sufficient distance between myself and the motel. Come morning, I'll be too far, too weak, in too much pain, and too exhausted to turn back in the dry, debilitating heat.

CHAPTER TWO

*M*arc…

After rubbing it over my greasy hands to clean them, I throw the now filthy cloth onto the workbench and take my vibrating phone out of my pocket, glancing down at the caller display. A small smile plays at my lips as I answer.

"Hey, Les. It's been a while. What's up?"

"Just checking in. Seeing how you're getting on, down in desert land."

Thinking it's nice to hear a friendly voice for a change, I sink down onto the floor and draw up my knees, getting comfortable. "I'm doing okay." It's good to hear from my old fuck buddy, it's been a few weeks since we last spoke. We're friends, nothing more, only ever finding solace in each other's bodies, little more than working off excess energy and satisfying a joint need. Just how I like it. I never get close to people, or allow them to get close to me. That way I can never get hurt when they leave.

"Bike get there okay?"

"Only because I trailered it." I let the frustration show in my voice. "Lucky I didn't try to ride it here. Took it out the other day, and the darn engine went. Black smoke billowing everywhere. It's finished, Les."

"Worth the money you paid for it then." A chuckle comes down the line.

My lips curl. I'd paid nothing. An old unwanted bike, a going-away present for me. "I suppose it was, though I think you should have given me money to take it away."

"You gonna scrap it?"

My eyes fall on the currently useless machine. "I haven't decided. If I can find a replacement engine, I might try to get it back on the road." As I speak, eyeing up what other people would think is a piece of crap, I think it's too soon to send it to its grave. An early 1990s Suzuki GSXR 750 now with a blown engine. The broken heap stands next to my bright green Kawasaki Ninja. For some reason though, it's currently a metal frame missing its major part. I'm still fond of it, and have no regrets that Les offloaded it on me. Fixing it would be a challenge, and being friendless in this new environment, something to occupy me.

"Let me know how you get on. Are you coming back this way soon?"

I'd landed in Tucson having gotten a transfer and promotion. Having left, I've no desire to return to South Carolina again. I'd only stayed there long enough to jumpstart my career. Apart from Les, I've no friends there and nothing to go back for. A new start, a clean break. That's what I was after.

"I'm not sure, Les." I let the doubt in my voice show. Not a definite negative, but I don't want to give him hope.

There's a sigh. Before I'd left, I'd given no promise that I'd ever return, considering we owe nothing to each other, just shared the occasional fuck to scratch our mutual itch. On my side, it was never anything more than that.

"But I'm really grateful to you for letting me have the Suzuki." My words are only to fill the awkward silence.

"Doesn't sound like I did you much of a favour. In fact, it was more the other way around. Needed to clear space in my garage."

"I'll let you know how I get on with it."

Another sigh, a brief period of silence, then, "I don't think I can do this, Marc. I know we just had fun together, but I would have wanted more if you hadn't moved a few states away."

Now it's my time to take some space before replying. I'd suspected there were feelings growing I'd be unable to return. "Long-distance relationships don't work, Les."

"And certainly not physical ones like ours."

"Are you saying we're not friends?"

Now I hear a long drawn-out sigh. "I don't know what I'm saying. Just that it's hard hearing your voice when you're never going to come back. Look, if you need anything, I'm here. If not…"

Don't ring. That's what he's saying. Just another person I've pushed away.

We end the call awkwardly, with no promises to keep in touch. As I replace my phone in my pocket, I realise that instead of the phone call cheering me up, it had proved to be the opposite. A shit start to what will probably be a shit day.

Time's getting on. Going into my house, I shower and change into smart dress pants and a plain, pale-blue button-up shirt, then slip on my holster and gun. Finally, sliding into my leather jacket and placing my protective helmet on my head, I take out the only roadworthy mode of transportation I've got, my Kawasaki, and soar my way through the streets to the precinct where I work. All too soon I'm swapping my leather for a light linen jacket.

I've only just exited the locker room when I hear an expected shout.

"Sergeant Reynolds wants you."

I knew it was coming, just hoped I'd have a little more time to prepare. I let out a deep sigh and pull back my shoulders. *Might as well man up and face things head-on.*

Without even time to get a coffee inside me, only minutes later I'm sitting in front of my immediate superior. His face is dark and his mouth twists as he spits out without preamble, "This report's rubbish! Nothing more than conjecture. You're maligning a police officer, and one who's given his life in the line of duty, with no facts to back it up."

I open my mouth, but Sergeant Reynolds holds up his hand.

"I expected more of you than this. You came to Tucson with a glowing recommendation. You apparently cracked a case when no one else could, but now I've seen your incompetence first hand, I have to wonder whether that was sheer luck." He glares and then shakes his head. "Oh, you got a prosecution in that case —your evidence enough to convince a jury—but if it was no better than the work you've been doing lately, I'd be worried you put the wrong man in jail."

I bristle. There's no way I did. The man I was responsible for putting behind bars was as guilty as they come, only no one else had managed to join the dots and point their finger at him. Once we had a name, it had all fallen into place. That's how I got my relatively early promotion to detective.

Trying to be reasonable, I sit back, clasp my hands in my lap, and take a less combative stance. "Archer was identified as having rented the truck that knocked Dale and Crystal Norman off the road."

"Show some respect. It's a dodgy identification at best."

There was definitely something suspicious about it, but I'd discovered it was the police process that was suspect. "*Detective* Archer," I start again, and say with emphasis, "rented the truck. When I questioned the rental agency, they were quite certain of that."

"Where's the evidence that he was driving it?" Hmm. He's stopped refuting that he rented it. Has he conceded that point and moved on? *Score one to me if he has.*

But as my shoulders rise and lower, I know I can't tell him I've found anything to prove Archer was behind the wheel when the truck ran the biker and his wife off the road. I only have my thoughts putting together the clues. The truck was found burned out and forensics found nothing, no fingerprints or anything else. Clearly an expert job by someone who knew what he was doing.

I'd only gotten the receptionist at the rental agency to confirm it was indeed Archer who had rented the truck when I'd gone back myself to ask. Other officers had been there before me and had come back with nothing. Now I reckon I'm a pretty good detective, but even I wouldn't say it was because of my prowess in my job that I got them to talk. Something tells me those that proceeded me hadn't bothered to ask, or buried the truth once they found it. *Which would mean more dirty cops.* Oh, I know who my prime suspects are, but am biding my time. You don't make accusations against fellow officers without just cause. Quickest way to finding yourself unemployed.

"And so what if he's a distant relation to the Herreras? Or that his body was found in that house? There's nothing to link him with the grooming of girls, nothing to say that activity was going on in that house at the time he was there and was killed." Reynolds pauses, and I swear his eyes glow as he raises his voice. "And if there was, Detective Archer was probably present to make an arrest. You clearly haven't thought about that. There are other options—he could simply have been visiting family. One of the bodies was identified as his cousin, Lucas Herrera."

Second cousin, I correct, but don't say that out loud. "The house has been linked—"

"No proof. There's only the word of an unreliable kid. As far as I see it, Detective Archer lost his life in the pursuit of his duties and should be given a hero's funeral. We can't ask him about renting the truck—fuck, if he did rent it, it could have been to move some furniture or scrap, and it could have been stolen from him. We can't ask why he was in the house. He's fucking dead!" Spit flies out of my sergeant's mouth.

If the truck had been stolen, why hadn't he reported it? Well I'm one person who won't be attending his funeral, or at least, not to pay my respects. There are too many things which don't stack up. If he'd been at that house owned by Lucas Herrera to make an arrest, why was there no paper, or rather computer trail, showing what he was doing? Anything put forward to prove Archer's innocence in my opinion seems to be a white-wash. I might be new to the grade of detective, but that doesn't mean I'm stupid.

The sergeant glowers again. "And you say he was helping Susie Clyde get custody of her granddaughter." He holds up his hand as I go to speak. "I'll give you that a druggie is no person to look after a young kid, but let's give the detective the benefit of the doubt. He might not have known about her habit."

But the only thing that makes sense to me is that he did. And working on behalf of the Herreras, was going to take little Amy Norman in payment for her grandma's debts. Why else would he offer his assistance to the unpleasant, strung-out woman? Unable to suppress a shudder at the fate that little girl had luckily escaped when her father had come back from the dead, I draw another look of contempt from my boss.

He picks up the folder and chucks it across the desk. "I don't want you wasting anymore time trying to malign a dead colleague. And as for the biker's accident? It's not worth spending taxpayers' money on the likes of him. Most probably it was a rival gang trying to take them out."

I can't prove it wasn't, but I'd like to try. Anyone, whatever their status in life, deserves justice in my view. "A young woman died."

"A woman who'd taken up with outlaws. She would have known the risks."

He hadn't had to interview the biker in the hospital, seen the predictable grief and rage that his wife had been killed. Dale and Crystal Norman deserve more than simply to be dismissed because of the lifestyle they chose.

There's more to this case, I know—a tangled dark web of intrigue. But even I'm not crazy enough to keep flogging a dead horse, at least, not officially. For one reason or another, Sergeant

Reynolds has made up his mind. I pick up the file, stand, and turn to leave.

"One last thing, Detective. If you want to keep that promotion, don't go against my wishes. This case is closed, we've far more important things to be working on."

My shoulders shoot back. It's totally unreasonable of him to threaten my position. He can tell me what cases to work, but can't prevent my doing what I want on my own time. As I leave his office my nose twitches. It wouldn't be the first time I've followed my gut feeling when something didn't smell right. I'll just have to keep whatever I do under the radar until I can come up with some cast-iron evidence.

I leave it a couple of days until my next rest day, then take a chance and visit with Susie Clyde, Crystal Norman's mother, an utterly nasty piece of work. When Dale came out of his coma, it was to find she'd already buried his wife, on the grounds that as he couldn't speak for her, she was the closest next of kin. And before that, again while he was still unconscious, aided by my ex-partner Archer, she'd started a custody battle for care of his young daughter, not expecting Dale to wake up.

As I approach the front door, I can't help wondering where the little girl is now. Maybe still being looked after by Drummer, the president of the Satan's Devils, and his old lady, Sam. I knew Dale hadn't returned immediately to the club, but it is possible that he's back now and has taken over his parenting role. I lost track of him after he'd been discharged from the hospital. Maybe I should call him, bring him up to date with the case? Yeah, but what can I tell him? Only that we've reached a dead end.

It seems to take Clyde a very long time to answer the door. Just as I'm about to give up, I hear someone moving about inside, and then the latch sliding back.

She glares at me, instant recognition in her eyes. "What d'ya want, Detective?" She clearly doesn't welcome the intrusion.

"Can I come inside and talk to you for a moment?" I keep my voice light. Entering her house is the last thing I want to do from the unpleasant aromas wafting out from behind the open door, but something I can't escape if I want to give the biker some answers, and to ensure there's no continuing risk to his daughter.

"Ain't got nothing to talk to you about."

It's all in a day's work. Suppressing my sigh, I try again. "There are just some details I'd like to go over with you, if I may?"

"Ask your questions. You don't need to come in."

The hand holding the door is trembling, but whether she's scared I'm here or anxious for her next fix, it's hard to tell. I try to test the waters by throwing out, "Mrs? Ms?" When she nods at the second, I continue, "Ms Clyde. You remember my partner, Detective Archer? I don't know if you've heard, he died in service." The last I say through gritted teeth. "I'm investigating his death." Well, it sounds plausible to me. "Could you tell me when you first met him?" I'm after something to link him with her prior to their first ostensibly formal meeting.

Her eyes flick to the left before coming back to mine. "At those bastards' clubhouse. The ones that took my grandbaby from me."

Hmm. That was the first time I know she'd officially met him, but somehow my gut tells me they'd come across each other before. He'd been so quick to offer to help her, *too* quick, and acting out of character. I might not have been working with him long, but it had only taken a minute to pick up on his lack of empathy with the people we encountered on the job, both perpetrators and victims. I try again. "And what is your involvement with the Herreras? Can you give me the name of your drug dealer?"

She freezes, and I give myself a mental kick. It's more than her life's work to give that kind of information to me. *Rookie error. Pushing too hard too fast.*

I try to recover it. "Okay, so Archer was helping you get custody of Amy Norman—until her father came out of the hospital—" Her spit on the ground interrupts me, and I take a step back. She'd missed my toes by inches. "When did you first discuss custody with Detective Archer?"

"When he first… when I went to the biker gangs' compound."

Interesting choice of words. Law enforcement tend to call them gangs, they call themselves clubs. Her daughter would surely have set her right on that, and she almost slipped up. *Has someone schooled her?*

She's starting to shut the door in my face. I'm not here officially and can't risk her making a complaint, so knowing I've gotten all I can for today, it's only served to confirm the suspicions I already had. "Well, thank you, Ms Clyde. I'll be back in touch if I need to."

"Don't see why you would. My daughter's dead. Left me nothing, the lazy good for nothing…"

Ignoring her rant, I ask one last question. "Oh, just one more thing. Are you still in debt to the Herreras?"

She's not going to tell me, but I wait for the flicker of fear to cross her face to tell me she is. When it doesn't appear, the answer is obvious. *She's been paid off.* As my sergeant would say, I'm relying on assumptions here, but I'm extremely good about reading body language. Non-verbal communication often gives away far more than words. *What's she got to offer for the Herreras to clear what she owes?* There's only one answer that I can think of. *Amy.* Is that little girl still at risk?

The door slams in front of me while I remain lost in my thoughts.

A dead end? I don't think so. My nose is twitching like a dog who's picked up a scent. But unfortunately, my olfactory endings are not quite so well-tuned, and I'll have to use my brain to sniff out where the odour's coming from. The Herrera family, *the* crime family in Tucson, is the obvious place to start, but if I tackle them head-on, I suspect I'd end up like Archer, in so many pieces no one could be sure if every part of him was in the right coffin. I'd be questioning them about a family member, and one who's very dead now, along with several other members of that family who all died mysteriously on the same night.

And why is Clyde still alive? Herreras aren't known for having compassion. Do they think she'll be able to get her hands on Amy for them? But they can't, not while her father is still alive. Now I feel a trickle of fear for his life. *Perhaps I should warn him.*

As I walk away from the house, I leave the subject of Susie Clyde for the moment and focus instead on my strange interview with my sergeant this morning. While I'd been dropped subtle hints that my report wasn't going down well, I didn't expect him to blast it out of the water in the way that he had. I'm a good cop. I don't deserve the criticism I'd received, nor the rebuke. Nor the allegation that back in South Carolina I might have put the wrong man in prison. I know it's never easy joining a new team, but surely this is taking that to the limits.

What caused Sergeant Reynolds to react so strongly to the suggestion of any stain on Archer's character? Is he scared of the Herreras? Is that why he's trying to put a stop to the investigation? Or could it be something else? *That he's working for them.* The thought is obnoxious to me. I play things straight down the line, and up to now, where I worked previously, my colleagues had been the same. Or, as far as I could tell. But here I've already been thinking I smelled something that wasn't right, and while I'd been casting suspicious eyes sideways, I hadn't looked above me as yet.

Going back to my bike, I sit astride, but don't drive off. Dirty cops. Is that what I'm dealing with here, or am I just seeing things that aren't there?

I tap the handlebars and go to press start, then pause. There's something else niggling at me. I can't rid myself of the lurking suspicion that Drummer, the president of the Satan's Devils MC, knows a lot more about Archer's demise than he's letting on. But it would be a waste of time to confront him. Even if I was given entrance into the compound, Drummer's never going to admit any involvement, whether there was any or not.

I know how bikers work, retribution is swift. If they knew who was behind Dale's accident, they'll have dealt with it themselves. No waiting for a trial, they'd have been both judge and jury if they had come to the same conclusion as myself. It's highly likely they were behind the explosion that killed my ex-partner. Another waft in the air, but this time I don't think it's such a bad smell. If Archer had indeed played any part in the biker's accident, I'd have felt like murdering him myself. But of course I wouldn't, I'd have done it all properly. He'd have been arrested and gone through the courts like any other criminal. Unless the department protected him when he was alive the same way as they're protecting him now that he's dead. A possibility that makes me feel nauseous.

When I finally start the engine and kick down into first, another thought comes into my head. Maybe the Herreras aren't involved. *Could the Satan's Devils be the ones buying cops?* Certainly not something to dismiss—in which case I have to tread very carefully. But it seems unlikely. Unless… Oh, for heaven's sake. All I'm doing is thinking around in circles. Enough of this, I'll be convincing myself the sky's pink in a moment.

Thoughts still keep going around my head during work the next day. I go through the motions, but this time I'm watching my colleagues around me, listening for things they might let drop that could give me a clue as to whether they're on the take. It's a horrible feeling not knowing who to trust. In my last precinct, I was certain every man and woman would have had my back. Here, I can almost feel daggers being sharpened in preparation.

At last I get a reprieve and get out of the office when I'm needed to go and investigate a burglary. That takes most of the afternoon, and by the time I return, I'm relieved to find I'm at the end of my shift. Parking my official car back at the precinct, I go inside to my locker to put on my leathers and grab my helmet, glad to get out of the claustrophobic vehicle and onto my preferred method of travel. I'm looking forward to the ride home, as the breeze will help to shake off the shackles of the day.

Autumn is a great time for riding—the monsoons of summer have gone, and what rain Tucson has is not so torrential. Even if it's wet, I prefer to be out in the elements. I learned long ago I don't melt. Summoning up the feeling of freedom that being on my bike gives me, I place my hand on the tank as if communicating with a pet. Then, just as I'm about to fire up the Kawasaki, already anticipating the pleasure of the open road, a man comes to stand in front of me, his long legs straddling the front wheel, his hands on the handlebars preventing any forward motion.

Oh, for fuck's sake. My fingers still hovering over the ignition, I sigh. "What do you want, Garza? I'm off duty and on my way home."

The man blocking my escape chews his gum, his mouth visibly working, then smacks it loudly, making me cringe. "Reynolds tell you you've got a new partner?"

No, he didn't. He must have omitted that gem during the meeting the other day. I tilt my head on one side and wait. Garza's a terrible gossip. Want everyone to know your business? You just tell it to him and you're done.

"Me."

For a second what he's telling me doesn't register. And when it does, my heart drops and I have to query to make sure I heard right. "You? But you've already got a partner." *Please don't let this be true.*

"Yeah, but Terry's on sick leave. Got a hernia or something. Reynolds thought he'd pair us up for a spell." He chews and pops that gum again.

Jesus Christ! If I had to pick one person I didn't want to be stuck with day after day, this man would be it. He's lazy, careless, and has a reputation for cutting corners. Certainly not someone I could confide my suspicions to.

"Knew you'd be happy." He laughs, then sneaks a look under

the jacket I've yet to zip up. Yup, there's more than one reason why I dislike the man.

I don't trust the right words to come out of my mouth, so I restrict myself to a nod and am answered by yet another smack of that gum.

Needing to get out of here, I switch on the engine. He leers, waits, then when he sees I know it's in his time and not mine, at last steps away from the bike. Resisting the urge to stick up one finger, I put it into first, twist the throttle, and I'm off, leaving the precinct and Garza behind me.

Soon I'm enjoying the fresh air, which helps to clear away some of the stench I smelled around the station, but it doesn't banish thoughts from my head.

As I step into my apartment, it feels like it's been a very long week, and not for the first time I'm starting to regret ever moving to Tucson. Being called out by my sergeant, my concerns about not knowing who's for or against me, and finally, those worries partly confirmed by Garza being appointed my partner, who'll be holding me back from everything I want to do. Christ, everything's going to hell in a handbasket.

I place my helmet and gloves on my hall table and hang my jacket up behind the door, then take a second to look around my sparse apartment, furnished with just the necessities. I could make the excuse I've not been in Tucson long, but in truth it's just like anywhere I've ever stayed. I don't have photos I want to display, and nothing I want to keep around to remind me of my past. I don't put down roots, preferring to move around. I nod in satisfaction. This isn't home, it's just a place to exist. It's my penance for being alive.

Going into the kitchen, I place a TV dinner for one in the microwave, eat it without really tasting it, then take myself off to bed.

But sleep doesn't come easily. Thoughts of the past haunting me in the normal way, together with the dissatisfaction I'm no closer to being able to give the biker closure, and that I seem even further away from discovering the truth. I've so much sympathy for him, knowing only too well how hard it is to cope with a loss, especially when you don't have answers as to why such a devastating event happened.

I find myself hoping Dale's been reunited with his daughter, and that he's leaning on the support offered by his biker family. He'll need what I've seen is a close-knit group helping him as he goes through the stages of grief. I can personally attest to that being a long and difficult journey.

I give up on trying to sleep when the sun starts to rise in the sky, hating that we're leaving a man hanging, possibly never to know the reason why his wife died. During the small hours, I'd come to a decision. I might be risking my career, but I'm going to give him what updates I can.

And of course, I can justify that I'm making contact to sneakily try and discover whether the Satan's Devils know more about Archer's death than they've admitted. Reynolds told me I hadn't considered any alternative options. It's a tenuous excuse, but something at least.

Not checking the time, having convinced myself I'm justified in making contact, I pick up my phone. Yeah, that's why I'm calling. If I offer him information, it's in the hope that in return he might let something slip.

CHAPTER THREE

*H*eart...

Dawn's approaching, the sun rising into the cloudless sky, throwing the mountains into relief and gradually illuminating my way. Pain blasts through me with every step. When I'd stumbled in the darkness, I'd put my left foot down hard.

I'm dragging my leg. It's becoming harder to ignore the bolts of agony slicing through me with each forward motion, barely able to put weight on it at all now. I try swallowing some painkillers, but without anything to wash them down, they stick in my dry throat. For that sole reason, I regret not bringing water with me, not wanting pain to force me to stop. My brain keeps instructing that I must keep on moving, knowing at some point my sense of self-preservation will make it hard to resist turning back. But I won't be doing that. There's nothing left for me now, nothing to live for. I'm ready to die.

Of course, it would have been easier to swallow all my tablets at once and simply pass away in my sleep, but something prevented me from taking the coward's way out. A part of me doesn't want my brothers to learn I'd given up, that I'd taken my own life. I don't want them to bear any blame for sending me away. In my twisted mind it makes perfect sense that doing it this way, I'll either never be found, or it would be assumed I'd simply got lost and died an unfortunate death.

Forced to pause when I take another uneven step, I check the phone to see the time, noting there's no phone signal here at all, the realisation bringing a small frown to my face. I've no way of calling for help, there's now no way for me to be located in time. *But that's what I wanted.*

Pushing on in the same direction, I take another step, and then another, cursing my throbbing leg, not sure how much longer I can carry on, and hoping I'm even now far enough away. Spying some rocks up ahead of me, I decide it's a good enough spot to wait up for a moment. I might not have traversed the distance I wanted, but from here it would be the devil's own job getting back, dragging my limb so badly injured in the crash.

At last at the rocks, I find a comfortable perch and start massaging my weak, barely healed muscles. I'm thirsty, tired, and starting to get hungry, and for the first time I wonder how long this will take. Will dehydration and heat exhaustion make me start hallucinating? Or can I just curl up into a ball and wait for my life to fade, my final thoughts of my wife.

I sit, my head full of Crystal, remembering the good times we had, knowing it's impossible to go on without her. The sun starts to appear over the mountains, and as the day brightens, my thoughts grow dark.

I startle when the phone starts vibrating in my pocket, then I laugh, thinking the delirium has started. *I've got no signal, I've already checked that.* Knowing there's no point answering a phantom call, I ignore it until it rings off. *What a strange delusion to have.* Then it chimes and shakes again, and again, until it eventually stops. And then once more. Part of me is still hardwired to think it might be important, part of me is amused, as why should I give a damn at this point? And as there's no signal, it can't be a real call.

A couple of minutes pass, then it rings and vibrates once more.

Do ghosts contact you by phone? Is there some mystical signal they can tap into? I wish it would stop, the interruption is disturbing the serenity of my surroundings. Someone's insistent, and it's starting to annoy me. *Why can't I just die in peace?* I glance at the caller id, but it's from a number I don't recognise—well of course not, it's not really ringing… That's when I see I somehow have got some signal, though it's only one bar. A few steps on and even that might disappear. My hand hovers for a moment, then my innate brain takes over and I find without having a fucking clue as to why, that I'm accepting the call.

"Good morning, Mr Norman. I'm sorry for interrupting you this early."

My real name. Not many people call me that. I take the phone away from my ear and regard it with annoyance, tempted just to press the red key, but I find myself holding it close once again and asking, "And you are?" My voice sounds gravelly, dry and unused.

"I'm the detective handling your accident and your wife's death."

"She was murdered." Saying it aloud and so starkly with all the harsh nature around me sounds right. Someone took her life, and now I'm going to give mine to join her.

"I'm aware of that. But we've just found some evidence that moves the case on."

I say nothing to prompt more, I know all I need to. My brothers had my back. While I'd lain unconscious, the man responsible for killing Crystal was killed. All the cops can do now is catch up. And as they do so, hopefully they'll find nothing to link his death to my club. My chest tightens as I realise somewhere deep inside I still care and don't want to bring trouble down on the men that I'd left behind.

"Mr Norman, we've managed to discover who rented the truck that ran you off the road." There's a sound like a clearing of a throat. "It was..." There's a pause as if the words are hard to say. "It was… a man named Archer."

Again, I say nothing. I already know *Detective* Archer was responsible for running us off the road. Do I say I know who Archer was? Or wait to be told—if this detective will come clean and admit it?

"Mr Norman, we don't know much more at the moment. Archer was connected to the Herrera family, and it would help me to know if you've come up against them at all? We all know they don't like to be crossed."

I'm thinking hard, remembering not to let on what I know, wondering whether Drummer needs to know the police aren't letting the case drop.

"Mr Norman? Are you still there?"

"I'm here. So you're going to be questioning Archer?" They can't. He's dead. But I'll pretend and play along as I should.

"That's my other news. There's nothing to prove he was driving the truck, just that he rented it. But the other thing is, there was a house explosion in Tucson a couple of months back. Set by an expert, as the whole place was incinerated."

That would be Slick. A small smile fleetingly comes to my lips. He knows his trade.

"We've only just managed to put the pieces together, and one of the bodies, well, body parts that is, we've identified as belonging to Archer."

What do they know? Here it comes. Here's where I learn if there's anything pointing back to the Satan's Devils. If there is, I'll need to get the information to Drummer. Thank fuck I've got some kind of signal here, or at least, for the moment.

"Was it an accident or deliberate?" I ask, thinking to find out info that might help Prez and my brothers. "And if deliberate, who took him out?" I'm holding my breath as I wait for the answer.

Another clearing of a throat. "I'm afraid I can't tell you that."

I sigh, looking out into the barren land around me, not a sign of civilisation in sight. Nothing for Drummer, no information. I can go on without calling him, my conscience clear and my endeavour undisturbed.

"Look, Mr Norman, I'd like to meet up with you so we can go over what we know and try to piece everything together. You still have no memory of the accident, I suppose?"

"It wasn't an accident," I growl. "And no, I don't." I don't remember losing control and killing my wife. Oh, Archer might have been driving the truck, but obviously I hadn't seen the threat coming, and that's down to me. I hadn't corrected the bike, I hadn't... *Oh fuck, Crystal, I'm so fucking sorry.* Making an effort, I try to suppress my sob.

"Where are you now, Mr Norman? Can you come into the precinct today, or meet me somewhere in town?" The voice sounds anxious, obviously I hadn't been successful in hiding my grief.

But no is the answer. I'll never be putting in an appearance. "I'm not in Tucson. I'm in California."

"When will you be back?" the detective asks sharply.

"I can't tell you that." When they find my dead body, someone might care enough to take it home, or the vultures might pick my bones clean, leaving nothing to find.

Maybe the tone of my voice gives something away, but the next question surprises me. "Mr Norman, Dale. Is it all right to call you that?"

For some unknown reason, I don't want the last name I'm called to be that of a man I haven't been for so many years. I want to hear the name that I earned after I was given my patch, the name my wife gave me. "Heart. Call me Heart."

"Heart..." There's a pause. "Are you alright?"

No, I'm really not. I'm as far from alright as it's possible to get. "My fuckin' wife's dead," I spit out. "How do you fuckin' think I'm feeling?"

The other end of the phone goes quiet, and I'm about to hang up when more comes, "Heart. Don't give up." I'm about to blast a sneering reply when words come down the line, tumbling out one after the other in a rush. "Never give up. I know it's no consolation, but I've been where you are, and it is possible to move forward, though I can't lie and say it's not fucking hard every step of the way. Sometimes the only thing we can do for someone we've lost is to keep them alive by living ourselves. You give up on yourself, you give up on Crystal."

"I'm not giving up." *I'm giving in to my pain.*

"You're in the middle of Death Valley and not close to a road."

Fuck! The fucking cop's traced my cell. The first thought going through my head is fear that I might not be allowed to die today, and that's followed by one that takes me by surprise. *Maybe this isn't my time.*

How, I've no fucking idea, but the detective seems to have put it together. "Believe me, Heart. It's not easy, but you can move past this. You've lost your wife and you can't see a way out of your pain. I understand that. It will never go away completely, but you can learn to live with it. I know, Heart. I know."

There's something about the tone of voice, sympathetic, but not the forced compassion from someone who hasn't a fucking clue what I'm going through.

"How do you know?" *Is it possible to be able to go on?* It seems so much easier simply to give up.

"I've been where you are." Something in the way the words said before are repeated makes me believe them. There's a depth of emotion in the tone.

I look around at the barren landscape around me, as desolate as my broken heart. "There's nothing left," I whisper. "Nothing at all." Part of me wonders why I'm still talking to the cop. All I need to do is end the call then switch off my phone. Throw it away, shatter it against the rocks so I can never be disturbed or traced again, but for some reason my hand is gripping it tight.

"She's gone, Heart. She's gone. And however much you want to, you can't join her."

I can. It's easy. I just won't go back. I'll keep to my plan.

"What would she have wanted you to do, Heart? Would she have wanted you to just give up and stop living? Or carry on? Keeping her memory alive."

I slam my hand down on the rock beside me. Why the fuck am I still on this call? Why am I being made to think of things I want to avoid? *What would Crystal have said?* I stand, kicking at the rock with my steel-toe boot. *Shit!*

"Heart?"

I didn't need to have this conversation. Not today.

"I can get a team out to you if you can't get back by yourself."

How the fuck does this detective know what I was planning to do? I didn't realise I'd asked the question out loud until I'm given the answer.

"Because, and I know I'm repeating it, but I understand how you're feeling. And while you can't see how it's possible, you can survive."

Christ, it's getting hot in the sun. I stand facing the direction I had been walking and, without warning, a lone coyote appears, running across left to right in front of me. The hair on the back of my neck rises as something bugs me at the edge of my consciousness, a conversation I once had with Mouse. The substance disappears before I can take hold of it.

Then without realising I've turned, I'm now facing the other way with the words the detective said going through my head. *Crystal wouldn't have wanted me to go like this.* As I wipe the sweat off my brow, I realise subconsciously I've already made a decision. I'll try and get back. If I can't, well, I'll have made the attempt. What am I wasting but time? I can always change my mind. A few more days of suffering, there'll be another chance around the corner. I give the cop something. "I'm not returning to Tucson." Then, in case I'm misunderstood, add, "I'm on a road trip."

There's a sigh on the phone, then a brief period of silence. The detective appears to know I've been talked down from the ledge. For now. "Where are you heading to next?" is asked in a conversational tone.

I suppress my normal reaction to say nothing to the cops. It doesn't bother me now that I'm no longer part of the club. It's my business, not club business, and the answer is easy. I've already started on the route Crystal and I had planned, for when Amy was old enough to be left. We talked about it for months, years even. Crystal hadn't had a good upbringing, her mom usually too doped up to care for her. Vacations and even days out just didn't happen. I'd promised her we'd see as much of the country as we could, starting with a road trip through Nevada and California. And that fatal trip to Tucson had been just the first planned to take her to the more local sites.

There's nothing to stop me sharing. "Yosemite," I answer.

"I've never been, but I've heard how beautiful it is. You hoping to get there before the snow?"

I'm thinking logically now. If I want to go over Tioga Pass as we'd planned, I'll need to check out the weather conditions first. You can put snow chains on a car, but not on a bike. I'll have to stock up on more warm clothes. I'm amazed how quickly my brain's latched on to the practicalities.

"Is it alright if I call again to keep you updated?"

Yeah. Because anything useful I learn I can feed back to Drum. Maybe there's still something for me to do before I leave this life. The thought solidifies my resolve that I won't, if I can help it, be dying today. *Wait a little longer, Crystal.*

"Don't take risks, Heart. I didn't know Crystal, but if I know anything about women, she'd want you to keep living."

I'm not sure I'm doing much more than existing, but I am living her dream. Seeing the things she'd set her heart on. Experiencing the life she ought to still have.

I try to sound nonchalant. "Yeah, keep in touch."

"You can ring to check up… On the case if you want."

Nah, I'll be deleting this number after the call.

I end the connection and check my phone. Would you fucking believe it? Even with all the shit in my head, it's still got twenty percent battery. Par for the course. Over the past couple of months, I've been doing everything on autopilot. Having a signal for now, I call up the GPS and check my position, then turn to limp back in the direction I'd come.

One last moment of hesitation, a few seconds to reconsider if I'm making the right decision. Living is hard, dying out here not much easier. As I stand, undecided, I feel that hand on my shoulder, and a slight pressure toward Stovepipe Wells. In a gesture of long practice, I raise my arm to place my fingers over those touching me, feeling nothing but the sun-warmed leather of my cut underneath.

Not sure if I can do this without you, babe.

A wind blows up out of nowhere, tumbleweeds blowing past my feet, turning over and over in the direction I'm facing as if it's a sign from a ghost that I'm doing the right thing.

Until Crystal died, I've never believed in God, or a hereafter, always accepting that when you're dead, you're dead and you're not coming back. But even given my beliefs, I can't imagine a world without something of Crystal in it, and pray there's a part of her left that knows that every mile I'm travelling, every step I'm taking, it's all for her.

Don't leave me, babe.

I'm not sure I can even do this. My feet sore and tired, my leg giving me nothing but pain, and my skin burned red by the sun, placing one foot in front of the other is almost too much of an effort. I'm about to give up, this time not because of any suicidal desire, but from sheer exhaustion. My vision is blurred, but not enough that I don't see the coyotes dogging my steps as if waiting for me to succumb. Is that the way I'll end up? A meal for the pack? The thought they might not wait until I'm dead spurs me to make one last effort. My head is swimming, my thoughts jumbled and erratic.

A coyote comes alongside me. I eye him up, looking directly into his sea-green eyes, which seem to glow with satisfaction. Fuck this, I must be far gone.

The spirits are waiting.

I stagger and fall, the coyote comes up alongside.

You're already a dead man walking.

Yeah, well I'm not going to lay down and die so you can have me for dinner, Mr Coyote. And if you can speak, why do you tell me what I already know?

Christ, I'm in a bad way if I'm imagining voices, and touch, sensation. A prod on my back that feels like a human hand.

Unsteadily, I stand and get moving again, one foot unevenly in front of the other. I cover the last mile slowly, relieved when the motel eventually comes into sight.

I arrive back in early evening, pausing only to grab the courtesy bottle of water from the fridge before collapsing on the bed, drinking it all, but not before using it to wash down a handful of painkillers. The last distance I'd covered only on pure desperation, that hand on my back making me unwilling to give up. I have no appetite, no desire to drink or even to smoke. My body's exhausted and my mind, for once, too drained to think. I settle back to enjoy another restless night, but as soon as my head hits the pillow I'm out like a light, sleeping dreamlessly for the first time in weeks, and for twenty-four hours straight.

I end up spending the remainder of the week in Stovepipe Wells, the original time I'd booked the room for, but not the purpose I'd planned, letting my body and mind recover from my self-imposed ordeal in the desert.

My dreams full of tumbleweeds and coyotes, making me remember Mouse and the time he went on what he called a vision quest to commune with nature. He'd departed uptight and tense, and had returned relaxed. Though he hadn't shared the details, I'd known he'd seen visions and claimed they had cleansed his mind. I'm ashamed to recall how I'd mocked him, said it was the starvation he'd put himself through that made him hallucinate. But after that day in the desert, I'm no longer certain.

I'd felt Crystal's presence, and saw signs she wanted me to continue.

Maybe it's not time to join her yet. Not until I've seen everything she wanted to see.

Up until now I've relied on room service, but on my last day I decide to venture into the restaurant again, the first time I'd been outside since I'd returned. Leaving my room, I find a coyote waiting, having a remarkable resemblance to the one who'd spoken to me in the desert. It walks alongside until the light of the building floods out over the ground. I pause as it steps away, seeming nervous to step onto the illuminated ground. The last thing I see before it's swallowed up in the darkness are its yellow eyes reflecting the light and focused on me.

The spirits are waiting.

The coldly delivered words send a shiver down my spine.

Fuck. I must be in a bad way if I'm hearing animals talk when I'm stone-cold sober and not suffering exhaustion.

CHAPTER FOUR

*M*arc…

My day off, and I'm spending it going around scrap metal yards in Tucson, seeking that elusive animal, a 750 cc engine for the Suzuki, and so far with no luck. As I ride the Kawasaki into the fifth yard I've tried, I'm heartened to see there are a number of bike parts scattered around. Maybe I'll have more luck at this location.

I'm only just throwing my leg over the seat when a man approaches me. He's broad, about my height, covered with tattoos and an unlit cigarette is tucked behind his ear. When he speaks his voice is gruff and rough, just like his appearance. He looks me up and down and then sneers. "I take it you don't want to scrap that." He points at my bike.

"God, no." I laugh, and without bothering to exchange pleasantries, explain what I'm after.

His eyes sharpen as he realises I'm here to buy, not to sell. "Got any experience putting in an engine?"

"I can do it," I assure him. There are YouTube videos for that.

A half-smile plays on his lips as though he's got doubts, but not wanting to turn down a sale, he waves toward an office, a ramshackle hut that's seen better days. "Well, come with me and I'll see what I've got."

I follow him and stand while he sits at a grubby computer. Large fingers tap slowly and deliberately at the keyboard.

As he shakes his head, I prepare to be disappointed. "Hmm, don't have nothing listed."

I sigh deeply, thinking of going to the next place on my list, starting to think I'll never find what I'm after.

"But let's go take a look. Sometimes stock doesn't all get entered."

What's it going to take? Just a few more moments out of my precious day off when I don't have to put up with Garza popping his gum. "Thank you," I say politely.

"Suzuki GSXR? 750 you say?"

I nod. What was he looking for if he needed to confirm that again?

The smile turns into a grin. "Got something you might be interested in. Depends on whether you've got guts or not."

Now that's got me interested. "What are you thinking?"

For an answer, he shakes his head. "This way." I'm following him out into the sunshine again.

He leads me around the shells of cars, old washing machines, and other scrapped metal until we come to a couple of bike engines. He moves the one in front, then points to the block behind. I lean forward to look. A bubble of excitement billows up inside me. I cock my eyebrow as I realise what he's thinking. "7/11?" Those bikes have intrigued me before. The seven-hundred-fifty engine swapped out for an eleven hundred, giving rise to the name.

He laughs and slaps my back. "Didn't know if you'd recognise it. But yeah, that's my thought."

I think about it for a moment. Putting an eleven hundred cc engine into the Suzuki would make it one hell of a beast. *Take off the fairing…* A perfect rat bike.

Then I frown. I'm a cop. It's hard enough to keep to the speed limits with my Kawasaki. Something like this… *They'd never catch me.* I can't help it. I grin at him, thinking of the excitement it would inject into my life, and make the decision on the spot. "I'll take it."

Having arranged the price, he agrees to get it delivered, and I promise to come back and show him the finished result. Money changes hands, and I walk off, already planning to add a turbo to the beast I'll be creating, while wondering why a law-abiding person like me is so enamoured by the thought of building a supercharged rat bike.

The engine arrives the next morning, my second day off. I waste no time getting started. Soon I'm up to my elbows in grease and oil, my knuckles grazed as though I've been in a fight. It was almost too heavy for me to handle, but by the end of the day the engines are swapped out. Now I love my Kawasaki, but I get a thrill deep inside me just looking at what I've ended up with. *I'll have to tell Les.* It will make him laugh. Then I remember I can't. For a moment, a sense of loss washes through me before I realise cutting him out of my life was for the best. *Before I started to care.* But I'm sad for a moment that there's no one I can share my new pride and joy with.

A test drive, a quick burn up the highway, and I'm almost overwhelmed by the speed of my new 7/11. Stripping it down by not replacing the fairing means I've got a very light bike with a powerful engine. Something totally unexpected for a person like me. A burst of power causes an unexpected wheelie, and I back off the throttle fast to get that front wheel back down, laughing with exhilaration. *Now this* is *a bike.*

A couple of showers, a bucket-load of degreaser, and somehow I manage to remove all the muck from my skin by the time I walk into the precinct the following morning. While I've left the rat at home, I'm still ramped up by my achievement.

"What's got you fucking smiling?"

And just like that, my good mood disappears. My new partner wouldn't understand yesterday's triumph—that I've managed to build myself a new ride. I limit myself to, "Just had a good couple of days off."

He's not interested in probing further, which suits me fine. I start to walk to my desk, but he puts his hand on my arm. "Already got a case."

My gut churns as I feel his fingers on my bare skin where I've rolled up my shirt sleeves, but as I'm already walking on thin ice in this department, I don't protest the inappropriate touch. Shrugging off his hand, I ask wearily, "What's that?"

He grins before popping that gum. "Someone's been snatching wallets at one of the malls. We're going to go watch and see if we can spot him."

"Or her," I add automatically. "Have they checked CCTV?" I would have thought that was the best place to start.

"Oh, come on now. Staking the place out is better than sitting watching tapes all day."

It seems strange to me, but his reasoning becomes clear when Garza finds a coffee shop and takes up residence there. Okay, he's got a place by the window, but it's me who takes to my feet and starts milling around.

I keep checking back, but Garza doesn't move from his seat, reading a paper and drinking one drink after another. I'm not surprised when I ask to find he hasn't seen anything—pretty hard to do with your nose in the news.

We stay there all day, no perpetrator or victim to be seen. My feet are aching at the end of my shift and, as I ruefully rub my sore toes, I realise I've successfully been kept away from computers and paperwork, allowing me no chance to continue my investigation. I've wasted my time on a wild goose chase.

When I get back to the precinct, I've already had enough. Whether there was a valid reason to spend the day at the mall, Garza only proved once again how lazy and ineffective he is. Buoyed up by my frustration and without thinking it through, I go immediately to see Sergeant Reynolds, who isn't impressed by my request for a new partner.

"What reason can you possibly have? I teamed you up with one of our most experienced officers. Something I did deliberately, as you don't seem to have a clue about how a real detective works." He stares at me, unblinking. "Now give me one good damn reason why I should reassign you."

Because he's lazy as hell? Leaves me to do all the work? Pops his gum disgustingly? Realising he's not going to listen to anything I say, I manage to thank Reynolds for his time and leave.

Exiting his office, I stop and rest my head against the wall, wondering if it's already time to move on from Tucson. Before I can come to any conclusion, a man appears at the end of the corridor, and I watch Garza approaching. He walks past and pauses with his hand on Reynolds' door. The snide look he gives me lets me know the conversation I've just had is going to be reported back to the very man I was complaining about.

Well, fuck them. Fuck them all. I give him a sharp nod, not trusting myself to say anything. Not for the first time, I regret coming to this city.

The only thing that stops me looking for a new place to work is my concern about the department's lack of desire to continue investigating Heart's accident. If no one else is going to look into it, I will. And if I can't officially work on the case by day, then I'll spend my spare time doing it. There's no way I'm going to let the murder of a woman drop, not even if my boss thinks she's the scum of society.

Too frustrated after the fruitless day, I don't go straight home, but detour via the gym, planting my fist on that punching bag time after time while visualising Garza's face. Then I drop into a martial arts class, at last with a clear enough head to hold my own.

Finally feeling slightly better, I go back to my house, eat, then pour myself a drink and open my laptop. While I'm waiting for it to boot up, I remember the time I had to go to the Satan's Devils' compound and met Drummer and the other bikers. They might be considered outlaws, but it was easy to see how much they cared for each other and were looking out for Heart's little daughter. And unlike my ex-partner, doing all that they could to keep her out of the hands of her obnoxious grandmother. If I had to choose, I'd take any of them over the repulsive gum-smacking Garza any day.

Thinking of the Satan's Devils puts me in a mind to call Heart. There was no doubt he'd had a death wish when I'd last spoken to him, and I hoped I'd said enough to make him rethink. I've got no connection to him other than I'm a cop looking into his wife's death, but a niggling feeling inside me wants to make sure he's okay.

As I place the call, half of me wonders if he'll answer, the other half if he's already given up.

I hold my breath as the phone rings and rings, and just when I'm despairing it will ever be answered, I hear a voice.

"Yo."

"Heart, it's—"

"I know who you are, Detective. Got news for me?"

"No, I'm sorry. Nothing's moved on."

"So why you bothering me?" I hear the snap in his tone.

I've no excuse I can give him, other than to be honest. "I wanted to check you're okay." I expect him to end the call with something dismissive, but instead, after a pause, he starts talking to me.

"I'm at Yosemite. Will be staying here a few days."

He'd told me he was on a road trip, a ride planned with his wife up behind him. I know he can only be torturing himself being alone on the road. He needs support. "Why don't you come back to Tucson, Heart? You shouldn't be on your own right now. You need your friends."

I hear an abrupt mirthless laugh. "Burned my bridges there, Detective."

"What do you mean?"

A pause. "Won't go into details, but I'm no longer welcome

as a member of the club. Not until I get my head sorted. Can't go back for six months."

I don't question why he's apparently been banned for that period of time because I read something into what he hasn't quite said. "You don't intend ever to go back, do you?" I say quietly.

When he finally answers in the negative, it's obvious he doesn't mean he's going to be looking for another club. He wasn't just acting on impulse in Death Valley. Somehow, Heart is determined to join his wife.

Should I alert the authorities in the area that they should be looking for a suicidal biker? Or should I try to do something about it myself? I say the first thing that comes into my mind. "Hey, while you've been living it up in the mountains, take a guess at what I've been doing."

I hear the snick of a lighter and an indrawn breath. Then, "Well, I'm not going anywhere. You wanna tell me, I'm listening."

Well that sounds like progress. "I've built myself a Suzuki 7/11."

"A rat bike? Didn't even know you fuckin' ride." A chuckle bursts out of him. "What the fuck made you do that?"

Having been given an opening, I tell him the story of the bike I brought with me. How I'd gotten it for free. How the engine blew up, and the search for a new one. His voice gradually loses some of the tension as we talk performance, and he actually chuckles at the thought of a cop catching it for speeding.

While he's an out-and-out Harley enthusiast, he's not averse to discussing plastic rockets, and we spend some time discussing different models. At the end of the call, I'm convinced he's sounding more relaxed.

At last, when we ring off, Heart doesn't protest when I tell him I'll call again.

CHAPTER FIVE

*H*eart…

For some reason, one of the highlights of our trip as far as Crystal had been concerned was going to be Yosemite National Park. She'd been full of plans for what she'd wanted to do and see there, in the place so different from her Arizona place of birth. As I'm delaying joining her, I'll try and do everything she had planned. It helps to keep her beside me and alive in my mind.

She's with me as I ride, her arms around my waist, and as we approach the place she'd so longed to see, the wind carries snippets of her voice and laughter.

It's not excellent timing with winter just around the corner, a summer trip would have allowed me to do more. As it is, I need to make this visit to the highest parts short to get out before the snow falls and makes the roads impassable by bike. Taking advantage of the dry weather, when I reach the park, I don't stop, riding on until I reach Tuolumne Meadows.

I'd left Stovepipe Wells this morning with its elevation of just ten feet above sea level. When I reach my destination, I've risen over eight thousand feet higher. Unprepared for the change in altitude, my head hurts like a bitch with the worst sinus headache I've ever experienced. While I do my best to take in the majestic scenery, doing my best to see it through my old lady's eyes, I find the air thin and hard to breathe, and have overlooked how out of shape I am. Before the thin air completely incapacitates me, I make my way back down to lower levels, feeling the pressure ease the further down I ride.

Summer is the best time to visit the park, and unlike Death Valley where the cooler season is the busiest time of the year, the lack of tourists at least means I don't have any difficulty getting a room at a lodge, even though this time I hadn't thought to book ahead. I don't bother examining the room that I've been given. It's just another place to lay my head, just another location where I have no distractions or relief from the deep pain inside me. Even the scenery surrounding the lodge reminds me of what I've lost. *Crystal, you'd have loved this place.* It would have fulfilled all your expectations.

When I didn't expect to return from Death Valley, I didn't bother about how I was going to survive. But now I'll be around at least a little longer, and I begin to consider that a man has to pay for places to stay. He needs money for food. For the first time the realities of my position come into my head. *How long can I afford to go from place to place?* I take out my phone and check my bank balance, and as I stare in disbelief, one side of my mouth turns up. *You didn't need to do that, Drummer.* My payment has gone in as usual, my share of the profits from the club. He's keeping me on the payroll even though I'm no longer contributing. And as I spent nothing during my weeks laid up, my funds are actually looking healthy.

Relieved, and surprised Drummer's still got my back, for now money will not be an issue. I'm about to put my phone away when it vibrates in my hand.

"Yo."

It's the detective.

I find myself relaxing as she talks, a strange reaction, and one I've certainly never had before when talking to a cop. But after

I'm told there's no further progress, and that they're no closer to finding who caused Crystal's death, I'm surprised when the conversation turns personal, and suddenly I'm hearing shit about building a rat bike. Stunned, I chuckle for the first time in weeks. When I put down the phone, I am still grinning, amused at the thought of a cop being caught riding something as fast as that.

Normally I'd stay the fuck away from anything to do with the police. I'm still in two minds how I feel about the detective's part in saving my life in Death Valley, but instead of resenting it, the call's been a welcome interruption. I go to bed with a smile on my face, thoughts of the cop doing wheelies on that Suzuki strangely helping to push some of the more painful memories out of my head.

Yosemite draws me in, and I end up spending a couple of weeks here, driving to visit the locations Crystal had longed to see. I hike and take in the Giant Sequoia trees towering two hundred feet or so above me, along with waterfalls and lakes, and along the way, take time to appreciate the views that change with every few steps I take. I'm doing everything my wife and I had discussed. Every memory I'm storing up is for her.

But along with satisfying a dead woman's dream comes unexpected side effects. All the hiking is making me fitter. As I'm exercising gently and taking things slowly, I can feel muscles developing on my injured leg.

Her ghost keeps me company every step of the way. Every vista I stop at I share with my wife, her touch to my shoulder reminding me she's with me. But I no longer turn my head to find her, her tactile presence reassuring, but however hard I try, I never see her.

Today, after a longer hike, my leg is protesting. I have room service deliver instead of going to the restaurant, popping painkillers washed down with beer. As I'm lying back on the bed, regretting how much I'd overdone it, I start to grow cold. Goosebumps arise on my skin and the hairs stand up on the back of my neck. There seems to be no reason I've become uneasy until I hear a tap on the window.

My heartbeat increases as I look up to see an owl perched on a branch outside. At other times it would be an interesting sight, but with a feeling of premonition, I'm viewing it not a cute object of nature, but a harbinger of doom instead.

I try to stare it down, but don't have a chance. Its unblinking eyes putting me increasingly on edge, its unwavering glower looking like it's trying to communicate. The knowledge creeps up on me that I wouldn't like what it has to say.

Whether it's real or a figment of my imagination, I swing my legs off the bed, get to my feet and pull the curtains shut, locking out the owl from view. It reminds me of the darn coyote I'd seen, and the words it said to me. Or did it? Animals don't talk. *The spirits are waiting.* That darn owl's put that thought again in my head.

Suddenly I wonder about the ghost that accompanies me. Is it really Crystal? And are those touches I feel really the hands of my dead wife? *Of course they are. She's never going to leave me.* Unless grief is slowly driving me mad.

The phone rings, and for once I welcome the interruption, something so ordinary banishing my fears of the unknown. I huff a laugh, shake my head, and try to pull myself together. It must be down to spending so long alone on the road.

I haven't set the detective up as a contact, but I'm starting to recognise the number.

"Mr… Er, Heart?"

Who else would be answering my phone? I stay quiet, already recognising the voice at the other end, while words echo in my head, my previous thoughts still disturbing me. Do I want the spirits to wait for me? Am I already a dead man walking? Fuck it. If I try to join Crystal, she could be in one place and I'll be headed in the other direction. A shudder goes through me as I try to focus on the call, grasping the offered anchor to bring me back to the land of the living.

Again I'm told there's no new information, but I don't need to hear any progress the police have made. I know exactly who caused my wife's death. And while I'd had preferred to deliver retribution myself, my brothers had carried that out for me. Another thing to add to the list of frustrations. I have no one to direct my anger upon.

"Heart? Are you there? Can you hear me?"

"I'm here," I say gruffly.

"I'm, er, just ringing to give you an update."

"Go ahead." This time I can summon up a little more interest, remembering to find out what I can and, if necessary, feed it back to the club.

There's quiet, a clearing of a throat, and then, "I'm going out on a limb, here, Heart. I can't keep this to myself anymore, and I shouldn't be speaking to you."

"So why are you calling?" But the words have piqued my interest.

There's a brief pause, and then I hear frustration in the tone. "Because I don't have anyone else to speak to. Things don't add up or make sense."

I'm not a sounding board, nor would be even if I was in a better headspace. "Surely you've got a partner to bounce ideas off?" Ignoring the non-smoking sign, I pull a cigarette out of my pack and light it. *I'll open the window in a moment.* And just hope that owl's not still there.

Not really interested—I won't be helping her solve a case which was sorted some time ago now—I let the voice wash over me as I take in a drag.

"That's part of the problem. Yes, I have a new partner." While finished, the sentence seems to hang in the air.

"But?" A prompt seems necessary.

"He's the laziest motherfucker in the whole department. Who always seems to have more change in his pocket than he should."

"He on the take?" It wouldn't surprise me.

Silence. Then, "It may be that I'm paranoid."

Paranoid? "He's checking up on you?"

"That's what I believe. And it goes further than that. I didn't tell you this, but my sergeant threw out my report on Archer."

"What did the report say?" My ears perk. Ah, perhaps here's something for the club. Something to give credence to my extended time on this earth.

A sigh, a pause. "This is only conjecture, and Archer's dead, otherwise I wouldn't be telling you this, but I believe it was Archer who ran you off the road."

The cops, or at least this one, has gotten there at last. But have they found any links to the club? I sit up and run the last two sentences back through my head. "Did he?" I try to inject surprise into my voice. "That's what you think? But clearly your sergeant doesn't agree."

"No. He's trying to convince everyone Archer died a hero."

What the fuck for? "Perhaps you've got it all wrong." I consider how to continue this conversation. Really, I should put a stop to it, but I'm wondering how far she's gotten putting things together. "What reason could there be for a cop to run me and Crystal off the road?"

There's no delay in getting to the point. "Money, I suspect. And possibly because Archer's got a link to the Herreras. I suspect my sergeant's covering for him."

The sergeant as well as the partner? If he was involved, maybe there's someone I can take down after all. "Who's paying them?"

"I don't know. But I want to find out." A clearing of a throat and a slight delay before the clarification. "It could be the Herreras, or it could be your club."

I slap that down fast. "Satan's Devils don't have cops in their pockets. Assure you of that." Now this is the reason I'm still talking to the cop—to knock any idea of that sort on the head. I'm not even stretching the truth. Oh, I know some of our other chapters have police on the take, but not in Tucson. There's a good reason why we haven't. *We don't trust them.* Not even the bad apples.

"I'm not leaning the Satan's Devils way, or not at the moment. Look, Heart, if they were paying my partner and sergeant, or any other cop, I'm not stupid, and I know you wouldn't admit it. But something tells me that's not the line I should be taking for now."

But might in the future. I can't forget it's a cop I'm talking to. I've not exercised my brain cells for a very long time. "Why are you telling me this? What the fuck has it got to do with me?" I've got to take a step back. *From the cop.* Drummer would kill me if he knew I was even having this conversation.

Another sigh. "Because I don't think it's over. Whatever Archer was involved in? Well, it's still going on. I've been looking into the paper trails and files on the computer. Records have been changed. I've spoken to Crystal's mother and don't like that she's still walking free."

But Prez and the boys took out everyone involved who was grooming those kids. Didn't they? Then as I add two and two together, the dire thought slams into my head, the reason why this cop's ringing me. "Are you saying Amy's still in danger?"

"I can't tell you she is, but I can't assure you she's not. There's unfinished business, of that I'm certain. But I think she's safe at the compound. Drummer will be able to protect her. And I might be completely wrong, Heart. It might be something else altogether. Or nothing at all. All I know is I've been threatened with demotion if I keep digging around."

And from the sound of it, she won't be putting that shovel down yet. "You should stop." *Leave it to the Satan's Devils.*

"I can't. Not until I've gotten to the bottom of what's going on. I'm not made that way, Heart."

I breathe in deeply through my nose. "As far as I'm concerned, it's over and done with." And even if it isn't, I don't want anyone else doing my work for me.

"Well I don't give up. I'm going to talk to Leonardo Herrera."

Now that's just dangerous. He's the head of the largest crime family in Tucson. "I wouldn't fuckin' go there. Especially if you don't have backup." If I wasn't so far away, and essentially kicked out of the club for the next few months, I could have involved Drummer. He might have provided someone to have this cop's back. But on second thought, that would never work. He wouldn't want to side with anyone connected to law enforcement, however much they were going out on a limb or for what.

"Heart, I can't give up. And what about you? Don't you want to know the truth? Don't you want to get all the bastards who played their part in the death of your wife?"

A week or so ago I was ready to give up, and maybe I still am. Perhaps the reason I'm still breathing is to discover the whys and wherefores of what happened. "Maybe," I tentatively reply. "But I can't see what I can do." I'm nearly eight-hundred miles away and not allowed to go back, even if I wanted to. I made a bargain with Drummer, and I'm going to keep to it.

A sigh. "I can't talk to anyone else. It helps that you're there and listening, I need that."

Strangely, I find I'm smiling. "You gonna keep calling?"

A pause. "I'd like to do that, if you don't mind. And Heart, you need to stay in the land of the living. Nothing makes sense if you're not around to learn all the facts."

Two weeks ago I thought that was impossible. "Why are you bothering? Wouldn't it be easier for you to let everything drop?"

"I've been where you are, Heart. I know what you're going through." There's a rustle as though the cop's getting comfortable. *Maybe lying on a bed?* Then, "It's called survivor's guilt."

Hmm. That was mentioned to me before. For the first time in a long while I find I'm interested in someone else. Perhaps there might be a magic solution to what I'm going through, but I sincerely doubt it. Can't hurt to ask. I ease my way over to my own bed and sit down. "What happened to you?"

"I... I lost someone too, Heart. Let's just leave it at that."

"How long ago?" *How long does it take to start to come back?*

A sigh, then, "Eight years."

Eight years. Eight years of grieving. Eight long fucking years finding it hard to put one step in front of the other. Can it be done? "Does… does it get easier?" I'm not sure why I'm asking, or whether I'm bothered about the answer. The next eight days will be hard enough.

"Yeah. Yes, eventually it does. Have you heard about the stages of grief, Heart? Well, the last one's acceptance. You won't be the same, you won't forget your wife, but it will become easier to think about her, and you'll learn to live with your loss."

I'm shaking my head as I just can't see that happening. As we've moved into personal territory, I suddenly have the desire to know who I'm talking to. "What do I call you?" I don't want to say "Detective" every time the phone rings.

Silence. Just when I think I need to give encouragement, the softly spoken answer reaches my ears. "Marc. You can call me Marc."

"Marc?" I huff a laugh.

"Yeah. It's the pet name my family gave me."

It's the first piece of real information that's been shared. And now knowing a name makes our call seem less formal.

"Take care, Marc." I lower my voice. "Don't take any risks. Stay away from the fuckin' Herreras."

But Marc makes no such promise, just ends the call with, "I'll keep in touch."

The Satan's Devils don't trust the police. Our only interaction is if any of us get arrested, and then we have the club lawyer to help us get out. We've been cleaning up the club, earning money from the legit businesses we own, staying clear of drugs and only running guns when we need to. Most arrests nowadays are on a trumped-up charge, simply because we're known as outlaws.

We have no involvement with law enforcement. I shouldn't be encouraging the cop, but something doesn't sit right. I don't know if Marc is right to suspect the sergeant and partner. As I stay seated on the bed, I go back over the conversation. Archer's dead, but for some reason he's still being protected. The cop's right. I don't like it.

Is it simply to cover up they had a dirty cop? Or does it go much deeper than that? All I do know is that I don't like the thought of Marc following it up alone. But what the heck? What do I care about a detective who means nothing to me, but who's willing to put their neck on the line? Fuck all. I've got far greater concerns than that—like how to survive today and tomorrow. I toy with the idea of contacting Drummer, but he made clear he wasn't my prez anymore. Without checking, I know he'll do everything to protect my daughter, even if I'm not there. Marc's identified no real risk, just a gut feeling, intuition.

The cop might be jumping at shadows and could be totally wrong. It might just be the department not wanting to investigate now that Archer's dead, a cleaner result than admitting he was corrupt. Nah, I don't think I should do anything, not unless something else turns up. If I had any real sense Amy was in danger, I'd be on the phone to Drum like a shot. But there's nothing concrete to go on, and I trust the club to have completed the job. I know more than Marc. I know Drum met with the Herreras. I know everything the cop doesn't.

No, there's no need to raise the alarm.

Finally, my mind winds down enough for me to sleep. Waking the next morning, I realise my time at the park is coming to the end when I once again learn via the television weather forecast that icy conditions are on their way. Not wanting to be caught in bad weather, I check out of the lodge and get back on my bike, leaving the scenic park behind me, and get back on the move.

Sorry to cut it short, babe, but it's time to get on.

With the familiar sensation of arms around me, I set off on my way, quickly realising the two weeks' stop-off has done me some good. Now stronger, I'm not fumbling so many gear changes. My muscles don't protest as the weather grows relatively warmer as I head for the coast, nor when it drops again as five hours later I arrive on a wet, foggy day with the temperature hovering in the mid-fifties at what was to be our next destination, San Francisco. Yeah, Crystal and I had planned to make this trip in summer, but in some ways it's fitting, as the cold and dismal grey suits my mood.

Unpacking my saddlebags in yet another anonymous room, I make a mental list of the things we'd planned to do while here. Taking a cable car is a must, as is a visit to Fisherman's Wharf, and then Alcatraz.

It's not until I venture out the next morning and make my visit to the first of the sights on my list that I realise the burning anger I previously couldn't escape has at last started to fade. In Yosemite I'd gotten into the habit of eating and sleeping—the fresh air and exercise helping banish my insomnia. Physically I'm recovering, and my body is healing. I miss my wife like fuck, yet when I try to conjure up Crystal's face in my mind it's fuzzy, her features indistinct. I remember them like a snapshot, a picture, but not in 3D.

But fuck, I'm not imagining the hand on my shoulder, and the soft touch around my waist as I ride. She's still with me. *She'll never leave me.*

I can't let her memory fade. As I ride back to the motel from Fisherman's Wharf, I'm struggling to recall exact details about her—her scent, the touch of her skin under my fingers. *I must keep her with me.* Suddenly feeling alone and afraid, I retreat to my room, bending double as I let out the sobs which wrack my body.

I've got to go on. I'm not sure I'm strong enough.

I stare at the phone, which doesn't ring, wishing for living human contact, someone to tell me there's a reason to go on. And if it's just reassurance from that cop, right now I'll take it. If I hadn't fucked up, I'd still have my brothers behind me. There's no one to speak to, not even my ex-Army buddy who I'd stayed with after I left the hospital. I'd pissed him off as well by return-ing, albeit briefly, to the club.

I'm a man. I can't remember ever crying before in my life, but now started, the tears won't stop falling. I miss Crystal so fucking much. *Why couldn't it have been me that had died and not her?* Amy wouldn't be missing both her parents, Crystal wouldn't have abandoned her.

Now I start hating myself for not spotting the truck that had been bearing down on us and evading it, for leaving my daugh-ter, and the way I forced my brothers to turn me out of the club.

Eventually, feeling more like a woman than a roughened male biker, exhausted, I cry myself to sleep.

With reddened eyes the next morning, I feel strangely refreshed, as though some of my grief was expelled alongside my tears. With even a little enthusiasm, I resume our itinerary, riding through the city and parking up for a moment to admire the Golden Gate Bridge, taking advantage of the brief moment when the sun is shining. After that I simply mooch around, riding the unfamiliar streets purely for the enjoyment of being out on the road, and relishing that my leg is now strong enough to cope with the gear changes necessary on these hilly streets. Eventually I spy a Harley dealer and, like any biker, can't resist pulling up outside and taking a smoke out of my pack as I eye up the glorious machines parked in a line.

Disposing of the cigarette butt and remembering Adam's bike isn't mine, I decide to see if there's a model that catches my eye, something to think about for the future. The thought pulls me up and I start. *Future?* Am I starting to see a way past this at last? Dismissing the thought which seems too difficult to think about, I stand frozen to the spot, my earlier interest in the latest additions to the Harley stable suddenly taking a back seat.

As I stand, battling with the thoughts in my head, a thun-derous roar reaches me, and ten or more Harleys come and park up. *Oh shit.* I'd forgotten San Francisco was where the Wretched

Soulz had started. How could a biker forget something like that? Unless he had a death wish, of course.

Even in the circumstance under which I became a lone biker, exiled from his home, I retain a strong loyalty to the Satan's Devils, and a desire to represent the club in the same ways that I would in Tucson. So far I've done nothing to draw attention to myself, or have come across trouble on the road, and had hoped it continues. Now, unless they ignore me, I'm to be faced with my first challenge.

I wait, a lonesome biker without his pack, wearing a leather vest with lines of holes demarking where patches once sat.

I don't turn and look at them, just stand as if I'm interested in the new bikes. I hear talking behind me, general chitchat, suggesting they're leaving me alone. The sun's come out again, the day warming up. Suddenly too hot, I slip out of my cut and reach behind me and pull my sweatshirt up…

"What have we here?"

Shit. I must have bared my back. Throwing my sweatshirt on my bike, I hastily pull my long-sleeved t-shirt down and, nonchalantly as I can, put my cut back on.

"Brother." As the man comes around in front of me, the words are said with a friendly enough nod. The stranger walks around my bike and examines my cut. His eyes fall on the one patch I do have. "Ronin?"

Careful to show I'm not reaching for anything else, I pull out my wallet and dig around, coming up with the business card-sized token, and wave it under his face. He takes it and reads it. Then going behind me, his hand grabs the back of my shirt and pulls it up. I know what he's seeing, my full back patch tattoo. "Long way from home."

I let a small smile play on my lips. "I'm a Ronin. My home's everywhere. The wide-open road."

"But you're from Tucson? Originally a Devil?" Once a Satan's Devil, always a Devil. I just nod.

"Out bad, but your ink's not blacked out?"

"Fuck, no," I throw in sharply. "I left in good standing, Brother."

As he comes to my fore again, I don't see anything in his face to suggest he doesn't believe me, but a look of suspicion has appeared. "Any reason you've come to San Francisco? Are you here on behalf of your club?"

He thinks I might be scouting for a new club location. Big disrespect if we haven't approached the dominant club first.

I shake my head rapidly. "No, I'm not Nomad nor representing my club. I'm here for personal reasons. Keeping my head down and trying not to attract attention."

"But you've caught ours." It's said conversationally, and he points at the pack of smokes I've untidily tucked into the pocket of my cut. Noting the enforcer patch on his, thinking some things never change, I take them out quickly and offer him one.

After I share my lighter, I try to explain. "You know how it is, man." I point to the new bikes. "Can't resist having a look when I come across a shop."

His eyes seem to look through me, then he starts to walk around my bike. "You've already got a nice ride," he compliments, but automatically. No one would insult another man's bike.

"It's not mine." The words come out without filtering.

"No?" And there's a brief accusation in case it's been stolen. No biker would steal a brother's sled. They'd be out bad, for good. Or dead.

Hastily I speak, knowing I need to offer some explanation. "Was run off the road, man. My bike was totalled. This belonged to one of my brothers who was killed last May. You know how it is, he might have no need for it anymore, but I don't feel like it's mine."

Again he examines my face. "Run off the road? It wasn't an accident?"

"No," I reply through gritted teeth.

"Sounds like there's a story there. Come back to our

compound. We'll share a beer or two and you can tell us what happened."

Or they might kill me and bury my body. Or give me a beatdown for being on their turf. It's impossible to tell. During our conversation, his brothers have sat, waiting impassively. As I take another drag on my cigarette, I feel that hand on my shoulder like it's reassuring me. What do I care what they want to do to me? I'm outnumbered and there's no way out. It wouldn't be suicide if I go with them and end up dead.

He hasn't given me a choice, instead he's issued an instruction. Losing my chance to look around at the new Harleys, I swing my leg over the saddle of Adam's bike. This time I'm riding, I don't bother taking in any of the scenery, as in the middle of a bunch of Wretched Soulz, I'm escorted back to their chapter's house.

Fuck. I may be getting my wish granted after all.

Taken inside, I find myself in a typical biker clubhouse. Bar, scantily dressed girls. It reminds me of home, and for a second I feel homesick for what I left back in Tucson. Then with a pang of regret realise it's lost its appeal as Crystal's not there, once again acknowledging I can never go back.

I'm morose as I follow the bikers through their clubroom, ready to accept any fate they decide. I can't say they don't make me welcome. A beer, a chair. Then the enforcer who'd insisted on me coming along with them leaves me with some of his brothers. We talk in our own language about bikes and the road, me at first reluctantly, then as I'm drawn into discussions that have nothing to do with my dead wife, a little more enthusiastically. Another beer, a couple of smokes, and then the enforcer appears once again.

He pulls up a chair and sits astride it, takes a pack out of his cut, and offers me one. Okay, so maybe things are different here and not all men holding that position are tight-fisted assholes. I offer a half-smile as he flicks his lighter then lights us both up.

After taking a drag and exhaling, he starts, "Talked to your prez."

Trying not to let my unease show, I act nonchalant. "Yeah?"

"Yeah." His pointed look seems to suggest he expects me to say something, but I don't know how much Drum has spilled, so keep my mouth shut.

"Heard about your wife. Sorry."

He seems sincere, so I accept his condolences with a nod.

A prospect comes up and replaces the empty beers on the table. My companion makes a sign and the bikers around us disappear. He leans forward. "You got a death wish?" he asks without preamble as he lights another smoke.

Shocked, not knowing how to reply, I keep my mouth closed.

Leaning back on his chair so it balances on the back legs, he brings his bottle to his lips. "Lost my wife to cancer some time ago. It was hard to keep going. Reckon I know just how you're feeling. Probably worse, at least I had some time to prepare when my ol' lady went."

I go to express sympathy of my own, but he hasn't finished talking.

"Reckon you're not up to doing a Jax Teller, seeing as you've lasted this long."

Now I frown, not quite understanding.

"Putting yourself in the path of a truck. Suicide's another word for it."

No, something's stopping me from doing just that.

He nods. "From what your prez said, I half expected to come out and find you being held down by my boys."

My face burns as I wonder just how much Drum had told him.

He nods. "Hot temper, he told me. Been through that myself. Times when your just itching for a fuckin' fight, not caring where it gets you."

If it's possible, my cheeks flare even redder.

"If someone takes you out, they'll be doing ya a favour. So we don't intend to give you what your looking for."

Now I open my mouth, but he holds up his hand.

He inhales again, then lets the smoke out. "What are your plans?"

"Finish up in San Francisco, then I'm heading off down the Pacific Coast Highway."

Putting his elbow on the arm on his chair, his fingers rub his forehead. "We ain't got no beef with the Devils. Drummer's always been straight. Given us support where we needed it."

That's good to know. The Wretched Soulz *are* the dom club in California, and Arizona as well. Clubs like ours give them respect, and they allow us to get on with what we're doing unless we step on their toes. It's a way of keeping all the smaller clubs in line, as long as no one upsets the dominant club.

"Figure you need some time to get your head right. Wretched Soulz won't be bothering you on your trip. We'll put the word out to watch out for you. Far as we're concerned, you're a biker in need."

My eyes go to his. If my desire is to keep living, that's all I can ask for. Clear passage on my journey.

"Reckon you've already come some way since you've left your home." Another gulp of beer and he continues, "Your pain will come and go until things get easier. But," he leans forward and the front legs of the chair smash down again, "Soulz ain't gonna help kill ya."

CHAPTER SIX

*M*arc…

I've avoided speaking to Heart for a couple of weeks now. I can't understand what made me offer up the nickname my brother had given me before I even was in my teens, and which had caught on with the rest of my family. The name I've not heard for eight years. I'd put down the phone, my cheeks burning.

I don't want to become his friend. I owe this man Heart nothing more than to get to the truth, the honest facts that I believe he needs to know. Justice. The reason I took up the career that I have. To put the bad people in jail so the good can walk free and unmolested. High ideals, and I'm just a very small cog in a huge organisation that at times seems to fail as often as it succeeds.

How many times has a guilty man been freed by a judge and jury? More times than I like to think on. Or worse, an innocent man committed.

Archer wasn't innocent, of that I'm convinced. But how to move on and prove it? Sergeant Reynolds has rewritten my report, almost all my words gone and replaced with his own, his story so fictional it would make me laugh if it wasn't so serious.

He's even recommending a posthumous commendation for the man I'm certain is responsible for murder.

Apart from my embarrassment, I've another reason not to contact the biker. Even my own investigation has stalled. I've failed to get a meeting with Leonardo Herrera. Well, to be honest, it's been impossible. Garza has his eyes on me the whole time, and if I'm right and he's in with the crime family, any mention of me visiting their business headquarters might get back to him. Until I know more, I don't want to step onto what might be very shaky ground.

I hate my new partner, really detest him. I'd thought the worst was that he was lazy, but it goes further than that. He's slimy. Every chance he gets, he's touching me. A hand over mine as I'm driving the car, or his touch on my knee. He hasn't yet crossed over that invisible boundary, but it's coming soon. I know there's a reason Reynolds partnered him with me, and it wasn't just expediency as Garza's partner is out of action. No, it's an outright attempt to intimidate me.

But Reynolds and Garza don't know who they're dealing with. I'm just waiting for that mistake which will inevitably come. Playing it, for now, as a dumb blond, lulling Garza into a false sense of security, hoping he'll let something drop accidentally.

If they're watching me, it means there's something to be found. Some knowledge or information that's within my reach to discover. I just have to be patient and watch until what it is becomes clear.

Another day passes, and I get back home, running a shower while wishing I had a tub I could soak in, using far too much water to wash the stench of the day, and my partner, away. Eating my dinner, then checking the television to find nothing I want to watch is on, my hand inches toward the phone. I pull it back, not understanding the strange compulsion I have to make the call only to say that I've got no news.

Pouring another glass of wine, I settle back on the couch,

putting my feet up on the recliner. Oh damn it! I pick up the phone again.

"Yo."

"Heart?" There's loud music in the background, and a lot of men's voices.

"Hi, Marc. Give me a sec and I'll take this outside."

"I can call back."

"Nah, you're alright." I hear a door opening and slamming shut, then the music is muffled. "What can I do for ya, darlin'?"

Darling? That's different. I smile to myself. Heart seems lighter than he was the last time we spoke. "Just wanting to catch up. How are you doing?"

"Not bad," he admits. "Got myself some company tonight."

"You've been drinking." I don't mean it to come out as an accusation. In fact, he sounds more relaxed than I've heard before.

"Yeah. You gonna come arrest me?" He laughs. His tone far more relaxed than I've heard before.

"Hmm. I don't think so. Where are you?"

"San Francisco. With the Wretched Soulz."

What? "You alright?" My cop sense makes me concerned.

"Yeah. Good bunch of brothers here, I tell ya." He pauses before continuing, "Just what I needed, you know?"

"You shouldn't be alone."

"Sort of goes with the territory, darlin'. Ronin, remember?"

"You going to be in town long?"

"Hard to say. Still got places to go. Tell you the truth, darlin', trying to keep off the road for the moment. Fuckin' trees and lights going up everywhere."

"You don't like Christmas?"

There's a pause, then, "Crystal loved it."

I bang the heel of my hand against my head. I didn't mean to bring his memories to the fore. "I'm sorry, Heart," I whisper.

"Ain't got nothing to be sorry for, darlin'."

But I have. Perhaps if I'd seen who my ex-partner was, I

could have prevented him going after the biker and his wife. There. I've admitted my guilt, and probably the real reason why I want to put this case to bed.

"Tell ya, darlin'. Think I'll ride on and find me a place to keep out the way until the festivities are over."

A new voice can be heard, female and probably drunk. "Heart, you coming back in, babe? Thought you and me could get together."

"Not now, pet." He waits for a moment. "Club whore," he explains. "But I ain't gonna go there."

I breathe in sharply. Heart can fuck who he wants. "You don't have to explain to me. Look, I'm sorry, I just rang to tell you I haven't gotten any further." It sounds lame, even to me.

"Good. I told you to leave it alone. I don't want you putting yourself in danger."

It's what I do. "Don't worry about me, it's my job."

"No, it's not," he speaks forcefully. "You don't know what you'll be going up against if it's the Herreras—"

"I'm a police officer. My job is to catch the bad guys."

I can hear him breathe in, then his breath huffs out. "Not this time, darlin'. Don't want another death on my conscience."

They wouldn't harm a cop, surely? No, it's my job here in Tucson that's at risk, not my life. I don't want to lose that. Putting criminals away is what I've always wanted to do. As far as I'm concerned, my sergeant and partner, at the very least, have some explaining to do, but I don't tell Heart that.

I settle for, "Well, I'm sorry I don't have more to report. I'll let you get back to your party. Give me a call sometime when you're free." *Why the hell did I say that?* This isn't some friend I'm casually chatting to. This is a victim of a crime, and I should be professional.

When he ends the call without adding more, I shake my head in disgust with myself, asking not for the first time why I can't let this go. What is my fascination with this man whose wife was so cruelly taken from him? My guilt that I hadn't seen how dirty

Archer was? Or something to do with the man himself? Something that drives me to find justice for Heart.

Whatever, I'm compelled to keep looking. Pulling the laptop toward me, I tap a pen against my mouth. I've gone over everything a hundred times before, but there must be something I'm missing. I've no doubt that Archer was responsible for Heart's crash, though I've nothing really more than intuition to go on. The explosion at the house where he was killed was not accidental, and the incendiary device was made by an expert. No clues as to the maker, as the intensity of the fire destroyed almost everything, and anything the investigators managed to piece together meant there was nothing to point to who could have planted the bomb.

There was nothing to suggest whether the house's occupants were dead or alive before the explosion. It burned so hot as to destroy all flesh. But reports of gun shots from neighbours suggest there was a shooting before the fire.

Now I look at the files on the other deaths that night, some of the most violent crimes that have been seen in Tucson. Five houses were targeted, and members of the Herrera family taken out. Each by a different method. Nothing to link all the murders together except for the timing. My pen taps more vigorously. Could it have been the Satan's Devils? Or was it someone else? *If the Satan's Devils had somehow discovered that Archer and the Herreras were behind Crystals death...* But then, why target the other houses? Yet again, I've reached a dead end.

I call up the information we have on the Satan's Devils members. There's one name that jumps out, a Jeffrey Andrews, who has the road name Slick. He was in munitions in the Army, and looking at his service record, building a bomb would be child's play to him.

The house Archer was killed in had been named as a place for child prostitution. A young victim had come forward after the event. Given Archer was trying to help Clyde get her hands on her grandchild, was it, as Sergeant Reynolds suggested, too much of a stretch to think he was involved in the child grooming ring? Or am I correct that the fact my sergeant doesn't even want to consider the possibility suggests a cover-up to protect the dead police officer?

I look over the reports again. Only very rudimentary investigations followed the murders that night. Cases closed on the little evidence that we had. But what's odd, there seems to have been no retaliation. If five members of the major crime family were killed all on one night, surely the Herreras would have jumped into action? I shake my head, unable to understand it.

If the Satan's Devils had taken revenge on the death of an old lady by killing the Herreras, surely Tucson would have become a blood bath? It doesn't make sense.

Why didn't the investigations go further? Why aren't our streets running red?

I call up the information on the Herreras. Their list of crimes is long. Extortion, drug distribution, gun running… But nothing to do with the sex trade. Could the Herreras have disposed of their own unsavoury element, and it was nothing to do with the Satan's Devils at all? My mind quickly runs through the options. As far as I know, none of the police in Tucson are in the motorcycle club's pocket—their members certainly don't get preferential treatment when they're arrested, and indeed, eager fingers are pointed in their direction when they've nothing to do with the crime. The Herreras though? Well, I can't remember a time we've brought any of them in.

If Reynolds and Garza are being paid, my gut feel is it's more likely to be the crime family. Hence, they don't want my report to surface as it links to Archer, who is a member of that family through his maternal line.

Could Archer simply have been caught up visiting family that night? There were other bodies discovered, but they were all men. No girls at all. Perhaps I'm wrong and it was innocent…

But he rented the fucking truck! Everything brings me back to that and my suspicions he was behind Heart being run off the road, even if he hadn't been driving it himself.

I'm still being kept away from certain files, which confirms my thoughts that something's being kept hidden from me. But what is it? Reynolds and Garza's past misdemeanours? Are they afraid I'd find some sort of thread? Something to link them to whoever's paying them? All I know is, I haven't an ounce of trust for either of them.

When Archer blocked the investigation into Heart's crash, did Reynolds support him? Did he know, or encourage him? And if it is rot I'm smelling, just how deep does it go, and how far does it extend?

Or am I seeing monsters where there are none at all?

Is it simply they don't want me to discover just who's paying them? Or am I on the trail of something more sinister? Did I tell the truth to Heart when I told him Amy was safe? What if the grooming ring is still active?

With a sinking feeling of dread, I go back over the notes I made when I visited Susie Clyde. I'm certain from her reaction that her debt to the Herreras has either been paid or written off. But by whom?

Quickly, I start going through all the reports to the police stations in and around Tucson. Although children being groomed are usually controlled by threats to keep them quiet, there's just the possibility that some eagle-eyed parent might have seen something was wrong. My eyes skim through the pages, not really knowing what I'm looking for, just wanting something to leap out at me and say, 'here's a clue'.

Then I go back up through the last few names read. *Jayden Greenway*. A fourteen-year-old listed as a missing person a few months ago. Why does that name ring a bell? Where have I seen it? I'm sure it was somewhere tonight. Hastily I review the documentation I've gone through so far, and then I see it. Jeffrey Andrews, Slick in the MC world, married an Ella Greenway in

Vegas in September. It's enough of a coincidence to make me view the details of the report once again.

Having done so, I lean back on the couch, wine in my hand, and let out a deep breath. Jayden wasn't reported as missing by her mother, but by Archer. I've read the report twice, there's no follow-up interview with the mother. No interview at all with Ella or anyone else. So why had Archer noted it down? What significance does it have? Could this, at last, be a clue that will help me unravel the tangled web? It's still active. The police are still supposed to be looking for Jayden. *Is she really missing? Or does someone want her to be found?*

Stifling a yawn, I glance at my phone, shocked to see it's two in the morning. I didn't realise I'd been researching so long. Time for bed. I cross the living room, switch out the light and have my hand on the bedroom door as I hear a car coming up the street fast. *Speeding*. Oh well, the traffic cops can deal with him, I'm off to get some sleep.

I hear a squeal of brakes, then a flash and a bang.

CHAPTER SEVEN

*H*eart...

The Wretched Soulz offered their hospitality to a lone biker on the road. Relaxed and surrounded by like-minded brothers, my tongue loosened by alcohol, I'd spilled everything about Crystal's death, which led to sympathy all around. Maybe it was because I was minding my manners, but this time it was slightly easier to accept their compassion with more grace than I have been doing. Then thankfully, the Soulz had taken my mind off the subject and stopped probing when they saw my pain.

I'd been invited back a few more times, enjoying the camaraderie of like-minded men I hadn't realised I'd been missing, being given a room to bunk down in when I'd had too much to drink. Before I knew it, another month had gone past, the dreaded Christmas season passing without note at the clubhouse except for a Christmas toy run they'd organised and a meal for all to enjoy.

Now it's January, and at last the decorations in the streets have come down, and I breathe easier as the season my wife had so enjoyed is now over and behind me. And so is my time in San Francisco. I need to move on and cross off the next item on Crystal's bucket list. Yeah, I've come to think of it that way, in part wondering whether it was also mine.

I've caused no trouble, and as quietly as I had arrived, leave the San Francisco Wretched Soulz, with an emphasised instruction to keep the dirty side down. Not too much of a journey, and I've come to San Jose to visit the Winchester Mystery House, purportedly the most haunted house in the world. *Crystal loved this mysterious crap.*

Whether its reputation is based on fact or not, it's an experience to see such wonders as the door to nowhere, stairs that led only to the ceiling, and other strange constructions built to confuse the spirits of the people killed by the rifle her husband invented, and who Mrs Winchester had been convinced were after her. One hundred and sixty-five rooms in all, a hundred or so of which are open to the public, causing guides to warn us not to stray from the tour party, as it would be easy to get lost. The atmosphere even affected me, a hardened biker. A shiver ran up my spine at the haunting tales.

Crystal, are you with me here? Although it makes me feel alone, here is the first place and time I'm pleased not to feel a ghost's touch to my shoulder.

Halfway through the tour, I start to get very uneasy. *The spirits are waiting.* The words of the coyote echo in my head. *Dead man walking.* Feeling cold air, a draught on my back, I shudder, then notice a man watching me almost accusingly, as though I'm the source of the spookiness around us. *Am I? Could I be the cause? Is there an aura surrounding me?* The palms of my hands grow sweaty as he turns away, and I try to laugh at myself. He sensed nothing about me, other than being taken aback seeing a biker on the tour.

The spirits are waiting.

I hadn't thought about the coyote for weeks, nor the owl that seemed to stare at me. Well, I did once, I correct myself, remembering them when I saw a mouse run under the Wretched Soulz' clubhouse, pausing to look back out at me through its beady black eyes. Now I feel a vibe in the air as though I've kept them waiting too long. The hair pricks at the back of my neck, and instead of soothing touches, I feel another cooling breeze on my face where there are no windows open and no fan. I've no trouble believing the rumours of haunting in this ghostly house. A noise has me spinning, but there's nothing there.

I want out of this place. But abiding by the warning not to try to find an exit by myself, follow the guide. I put myself in the middle of the group, as though seeking safety in numbers. My heart's thumping erratically, and I've a deep sense of dread.

As the tour guide helpfully tells us there are secret passages within the walls, I stare at the plasterwork, starting to hear whispering in the air, words I can't quite take hold of. When we're shown the séance room, the murmurings become clearer. I freeze. *Waiting. Waiting. Waiting.*

"Sir? Are you alright?"

It's not just one man's eyes on me now, but the whole group.

"You look pale. Do you need to sit down?"

Annoyed that I've brought attention to myself, I shake my head. *What I want is to get out of here.* This place feels like it's a conduit to the other side, and while all I've wanted to do for months is to go to Crystal, I don't want to join whatever I feel in this house. "I'm fine," I say tersely.

The guide examines me for a moment then, seeming satisfied, continues his spiel.

Fuck it. I try to concentrate on his words, while feeling more like I'm on a roller coaster ride, eyes closed, holding on tight, just wanting it to end.

When the tour group finally emerges into the sunlight, I don't even look back at the house, not ashamed to say I'm scared of what I might find looking out of one of the windows. *I'd promised to join Crystal.* But I went back on my promise. I'm still breathing.

I'd thought to have a look at the firearms museum, but all I want to do now is put distance between myself and that unearthly place. Going back to my bike, I hear a loud cawing above me, and the shadow from a bird flying overhead crosses my bike. Even free of the house, the bird's loud call makes my chest pound and my scalp tingle. Something niggles at the back of my mind. *Coyote, owl, mouse, and crow.* Omens or portents, predicting misadventure I believe, recalling a conversation I'd had with Mouse, sure he'd mentioned something like that.

Wanting nothing better than to get myself away from here, I get back on my bike and give myself a mental shake. Birds fly overhead all the time. I try to laugh, but it's not easy to rid myself of the weight of the house and the things I had seen. *There's no guarantee you'd be going to the same place as Crystal.* I don't want to join the entities of the house where I'd just been. For the first time since I left Tucson, I pull away from the kerb taking greater care. *Crystal, forgive me. But I don't want the likes of these spirits to take me.*

When I'd left San Francisco, I'd started on the Pacific Coast Highway, and now, after the brief detour that I wish I never made, I rejoin it, my dark thoughts slowly dissipating as I leave the haunted mansion behind. Resuming my journey, I continue down to Monterey, where I treat myself to a meal of snow crab at a restaurant on a pier watching pelicans dive from the sky and sea otters floating on their backs eating fish. Such a peaceful place, it eases my soul. *You seeing this, babe? Fuck me, you would have loved it.*

A few more miles under my belt, and I stop for the night.

"One room, sir?"

"Please." Christ, the simple word reminds me how I'd been forgetting basic pleasantries up to now. I even remember to thank the woman as she hands me the key and give her a wink as she blatantly studies me, her eyes gleaming with interest. I won't be going there, no insult to her, no woman would be able to arouse me, but there's no need to be rude.

She puts me in mind of another woman, a woman I haven't

spoken to in a while—the rat bike riding cop. One side of my mouth turns up as I think about the voice that's kept me company on the road, suddenly realising it's strange for her not to have been in touch for so long. *Maybe she hasn't any new information to give me?* Or perhaps she did what I told her not to do and went to visit the head of the Herrera family, and now her body's lying in a ditch.

I go cold, and this time it's got nothing to do with spirits. Maybe I'm overreacting. She's probably got a new case is all, and the lonesome biker is long gone from her mind. Why should that concern me? I know Crystal's murderer is dead and delving deeper could only expose the club. I should be pleased that the cop's finally leaving me alone. If there is anyone else involved, anything left to handle, I'll speak to Drummer when I get back in, what is it? Only a couple more months now? Fuck, where does the time go?

Well, I'll be fucked. My shoulders draw back as the direction of my mind's ramblings hit me. It's the first time I've even considered going back to Tucson. When I left, I'd had no intention of ever returning. Could I really stand to go to the place which holds such memories? Perhaps it's best to destroy my cut, get my ink blacked out and just keep going on the road. I never envisioned revisiting the place that holds so much pain for me. And Crystal, who's only a…

Goosebumps cover my skin. Shit, going to that house today must put spirits on my brain. I can't think of Crystal as a ghost.

Suddenly wanting to hear a friendly, living voice, before I can reconsider, I pull out my phone, scroll through the few incoming calls that I have, and get to the right number. Hoping that my fears for her are unfounded, I press to connect.

"Hello?"

That's not her. Have I selected the wrong number? "Who is this?"

"This is Marcia Hannah's phone."

Marcia. I smile. So much more appropriate, but somehow less fitting than Marc. "Can I talk to *Marcia*?"

"She's sleeping at the moment. I answered her phone so as not to disturb her. Can I tell her who called?"

A woman answering? Checking the time on my phone with a groan, I notice it's the middle of the night. *Is she a lesbian?* A grin comes to my face as I consider it, and suddenly I want to pry. "And you are?"

"I'm her nurse."

Her nurse? Fuck. All at once I'm sitting up straight. "A nurse? What's fuckin' happened? How's Marc, Marcia? Is she hurt? What the fuck's going on?"

"And who are you, sir?"

"I'm a…" *What the fuck am I?* A case? "I'm a friend." I soften my tone. "Please, tell me how she is and why she's in the hospital."

"I didn't tell you she was a patient."

I sigh with relief. *But then why is she sleeping? And why are you, a nurse, there?* What else can she be? "Please." I put a whole world of pleading into that one word.

There's silence as the nurse thinks. "She's not got many friends, has she? No visitors have come to see her." Another brief pause, then, "Look, I'm not telling you anything that's not been all over the news. There was a bomb thrown into her residence. She's lucky to be alive, escaped with minor burns and a concussion."

Fuck! Marc, what have you been doing? "How bad?" I ask through gritted teeth. "Is she gonna be okay?"

"I can't go into details, sir. But she got off fairly lightly… Oh, sorry, hon, I didn't mean to wake you." The last doesn't sound like it was addressed to me.

Then I hear a murmured conversation, and then to me, "Who is this, please?"

"Heart." She relays the information, and then a more familiar voice speaks into the phone.

"Heart? Hang on a moment." More muttering, and then more relaxed, I take it the nurse has been dismissed. "Heart. I was going to call you when they let me out of this place."

"What the fuck happened?" I need to know. Pleasantries can wait.

A sigh. "I really have no idea. I was up late one night—lucky, if I'd been in bed, well, we wouldn't be talking. I heard a car, there was a flash and a bang, and my bedroom exploded. The door blew open, knocked me across the room. I lost consciousness and… There was a fire. I didn't know it, but my neighbour's a firefighter. He kicked down the door and ran in, luckily pulling me out before I got too badly burned. I've got burns to my left arm and a freaking big lump on my head. If he hadn't come in…" Her voice trails off and I complete the sentence for myself.

Fuck it! Someone does want her dead. A fucking bomb? "When was this?"

"A couple of weeks ago."

"You've been in the hospital for two weeks?" *Why hadn't she let me know? Why the fuck should she?*

"Yeah. I played your trick, stayed in a coma for a while. They were worried about the fracture to my skull."

Sitting on the bed, I cross one leg over the other. I don't like the words that I'm hearing at all. "Fuck, woman. I told you not to go sticking your nose into things." If I sound angry, it's because I am. Another woman in danger because of me. That's what I'm certain is at the bottom of this. She wouldn't let things drop and got so far that someone tried to take her out. Permanently.

"I'm a police officer, Heart. It's what I do."

Suddenly I'm hyperventilating. "No, this has to stop. Whatever's going on, you need to pass it on to your superiors and then leave it the fuck alone."

She sighs. "Great idea, if I knew who to trust, Heart. Please, don't go on about this. I'll just be more careful in the future."

"You'll have to fuckin' be." I'm incensed, and I'm not sure why. I don't want to talk anymore right now. We'll only end up arguing, and with a head injury that's the last thing she'll need. "Look, I'll let you get some sleep. I'm sorry for ringing so late, I didn't realise the time."

"Please don't go, Heart. Please."

It's a heartfelt plea, she sounds so desolate. The words the nurse had said go through my mind, that she's had no visitors. When I'd been laid up, my brothers hadn't left me alone, not even for a minute, one always beside me. I wipe my hand over my face and can't fail to remember the debt that I owe her. Lowering my voice, I ask more gently, "What do you want from me, Marcia?"

"Marc. Please. You call me Marc." There's desperation in her voice, as if I'm her only friend in the world.

She sounds so lonely, but it shouldn't be me she's speaking to. "Have you got family to come visit?"

I don't understand the sob until she explains. "I've got no family."

"Friends?"

A pause, then, "No, not really. Only work colleagues. And in the circumstances, I'd rather not see any of them."

"Because you can't trust them." She's got no one on her side, that's why she's clinging to me, wanting to keep me on the other end of the line. I could do without this, but I do know only too well the loneliness in the middle of the night, and nightmares, of course. If she was any other woman, I'd get one of my brothers to check up on her, but they wouldn't go near her because of her job.

Partly to assuage the guilt that she got hurt investigating something I already have answers to, I summon up some of the humanity I thought I had lost. Changing the subject, I pick the first thing that occurs to me. "So, darlin', you never told me. How you get your handle?"

"Marc? I was a tomboy, and that's what my brother called

me." Past tense again. *She said she has no family.* It suddenly hits me how she might understand the process of grieving so well.

"You lose him, sweetheart?" One handed, I take out a pack and tap out a cigarette. Reaching for my Zippo, I light it.

"Yes." Her voice wobbles.

Shit, my aim was to get her talking to cheer her up. Not send her into worse depths of despair. But now I've opened that Pandora's box, I breathe in smoke. "You wanna talk about it?"

As she goes quiet, I give her the space to decide, slowly inhaling and exhaling my nicotine fix.

My cigarette's half burned down by the time she answers. "You're lucky, Heart. You have no memory other than Crystal happy and riding behind you on the bike. I remember everything. Every fucking thing."

I can't remember having heard her swear before, it takes me by surprise.

She starts speaking in a monotone. There's hardly any emotion in her voice at all as she relates, "I was eighteen, Heart. We'd gone out on a family outing. Rented a seven-seater, you must know the type. My older brother was driving, my father beside him. In the rear were my mom, my sister, and sister-in-law. I was in the back, my four-year-old nephew sitting next to me. We were making silly faces at each other. I was sticking my tongue out to keep him amused. All the inane things I remember.

"Suddenly, I heard my brother exclaim. We were on a two-lane highway just coming up to the brow of a hill, two Mack trucks were coming in the other direction, you know, one trying to overtake the other, only gaining inches at a time. They were neck to neck as they breached the top."

I don't speak, don't prompt, just fill in the gaps for myself and let her finish her sad story.

"I was the only survivor. Everyone but my younger sister was dead at the scene. My brother did what he could to evade the truck, but it slammed into us on the driver's side, we rolled and rolled… I was trapped for hours, hearing my sister's moans gradually becoming weaker. Trapped with my whole family, and me the only one alive."

All at once I realise how lucky I am not to have those kinds of memories. Fuck, if I'd seen Crystal injured and had been unable to help her, I'd never have survived. Marc's a strong fucking woman, there's no doubt about that.

"How did you do it? How could you come back from that?"

"Like I've been telling you, one day at a time, Heart. One day at a time."

"Are you… are you over it?" If she can recover from that kind of nightmare, perhaps there's hope for me.

"No. And I never will be. I'll never stop missing them, wishing I could speak to them, touch them. Wishing they were here with me. But I've stopped thinking about it every minute of the day. I've stopped longing to have them back, as it's not possible. I'll never forget them or the way that it happened, but I survived for a reason, Heart. I have to believe it."

Jesus. I pull at the strands of my hair. And while she's injured in the hospital, she'll be missing them more than ever. *How can she do it?* "You think there's a reason to all this? Some greater good to come from surviving? Fuck, woman, I feel your pain, but I can't comprehend what you're saying."

"The driver of the truck that hit us, he walked away without a scratch. The investigation was fucked up. He got off the manslaughter charge on a technicality." Her voice has gone cold. "It's what made me do what I do."

"So you joined the police…?"

"To put the bad guys away. To follow the law and do everything right. To give others the satisfaction that I never had."

I realise this woman on the end of the phone blows me away. That happened to me? I'd have had my brothers behind me and the truck driver would have died a painful death. But I don't tell her that. Instead, I tell her the truth. "I think you're a stronger person than I am."

"No, Heart. I think you're wrong. You just haven't found your strength yet. You've got to allow the grieving process to take its course."

Pinching the bridge of my nose, embarrassed to tell her, but wanting to share the desperation in my heart "I took a walk out into Death Valley. I wasn't going to come back."

"I know, Heart," she says gently. "And how I know is because I did the same thing. Oh, not like you in the desert, but I tried to slit my wrists. Cut the first one, and it damn hurt, and the blood scared me. Pretty stupid, huh? That was the point, wasn't it?" She laughs. "I called 911 and told them a knife slipped as I was chopping vegetables. I've still got the scar, I'll show it to…"

Her voice trails off at her offer to show it to me. It's not hard to see why. Here we are, chatting like old friends, but meaning nothing to each other. But the thought that I'd like to know more about her, and how she coped with her loss, slowly creeps up on me. "Another couple of months, when I get back to Tucson, you can show me your scar."

"Along with my new ones." She's reminded me I'm talking to her in the middle of the night in her hospital bed.

"For fuck's sake, Marc. Just leave things alone from here on in." When I get back, I'll find out what she knows and get the club to look into anything we haven't found out already. If there are any loose ends, a lone cop shouldn't be going it alone.

Someone blew up her house. Someone's seriously got it in for her.

We talk for a few minutes, me trying to lighten the conversation and telling her about Monterey, avoiding any mention of my visit to the Winchester Mystery House, until finally I hear her yawning. As we end the call, it dawns on me I may have been too quick to dismiss what she's been investigating. Whatever she's found out is enough for someone to want her dead.

Is she right? Is what started with Crystal's death not over?

The spirits are waiting. Fuck, let them wait. I need to get back and find out what's going on. *Two months.* Then I'll be welcomed back into my family. Unlike Marc, who'll never have the chance to see hers again.

CHAPTER EIGHT

*M*arc…

There wasn't much I could remember about the night a bomb was thrown through my bedroom window. I recall I'd been going through the case files and some of my conclusions, but the rest remains unclear, obscured by a fog in my mind. I know I'd decided it was time to go to bed, had turned out the lounge light, had heard a car, but after that everything was a blank until I woke up in the hospital with a machine breathing for me.

My survival was a case of luck. The explosion caused the door I must have been opening to fly off its hinges, knocking into me and propelling me across the room, leaving me with a severe concussion and a minor skull fracture, but mostly protecting me from worst of the fireball. My hair was singed, my arm, not shielded by the wood, had first-degree burns. I'd spent the first week in intensive care on a ventilator for a few days, as my brain had swollen. Constantly monitored at the beginning, but now I've been moved to a normal room. My head aches incessantly, but even that now seems to be improving. I'd have been well enough to go home if there had been someone to monitor and look after me, but since the loss of my family, as I've prevented letting people get close, there is no one I could call on and nobody to take me in.

Two weeks I've been here. Two weeks too long. I crave getting out and starting to look into the case again.

"You up for a visitor?"

I cock my head toward the nurse, not sure who could be coming to see me. "Depends who it is."

"Gave his name as Garza."

Shit. He's the last person I want to see, but there's no good reason why I can refuse. "Yeah, sure." I pull myself into a sitting position and mentally prepare to face my partner.

He strides through the door, and not for the first time I notice his suit doesn't look off the rack, but instead made to measure, and I wonder how he can afford it on his salary. It's just one more clue he must be getting other money from somewhere. His dark hair is shorn short, which does nothing to hide the pudginess of his face or his thin lips. As I examine him, his own small and too close eyes inspect me critically.

"Are you here in official capacity?" I want to know who threw that bomb into my house. *How far have they gotten with the investigation?*

He seems to ponder the question before replying, "I came to see how you are." From any other person, the words would sound cordial.

"I'm getting there," I reply. "The doctors seem pleased with my progress. I might have a lingering headache for a few months, but I'll survive. Have you found out anything—?"

Avoiding my question, he interrupts me. "When are you thinking of returning to work?"

I shrug. "I'm not too sure. But it will be a few weeks before I'm fully recovered." I raise my right arm, still covered with dressings. "I have to avoid getting infection on this."

"You should take all the time you need. There's no point rushing back to the job. Reynolds said he thinks you ought to have a couple of months off." He points to my head. "Injuries like you had need to be treated with respect." If I didn't know him better, I'd think he was being sympathetic. But I do, so know that he's not. Reading between the lines, as far as he's concerned, the longer I stay away the better.

Coming closer, he pulls up the visitor's chair. He sits, legs splayed and hands clasped between them. "Forensics have analysed the fragments of the explosive device."

At last. I narrow my eyes and wait.

"It looks the same as the one that was used in the house where Archer died. They think it was built by the same person." His lips thin even further as he delivers the news. "Reynolds wants you to go back over any cases you and Archer worked on together to see if you both made an enemy."

I'm surprised. Reynolds knows as well as I do that I was only working with Archer a month or so before his death. I was new to the area. "There's nothing I can immediately think of." I snap back the comment that Archer probably made enough enemies all on his own. I would ask if they'd spoken to his previous part-ner, but he'd been killed in a car accident shortly before I arrived, in fact, causing the vacancy for which I had applied.

"Well, give it some thought."

During the awkward silence that follows, he glances around my bare room then huffs a laugh. "I suppose I should have brought flowers or something. The guys at the precinct send their best wishes. Oh, and Sergeant Reynolds said he'd be by if you're not out in a few days."

I brush off his insincere pleasantries. "Apart from it being the same type of bomb, have you got anything else? Any leads on the car? Did any of the neighbours see anything?"

"It was two a.m., Hannah. Your neighbours were all sleep."

I suppose they haven't much to go on. I have to thank God that one of my neighbours is a light sleeper, and a firefighter and medic to boot. I wouldn't be here if he wasn't.

He's got nothing more to tell me, and he's not someone to

make small talk. I'm relieved when shortly after, he leaves with insincere hopes for my swift recovery.

As I relax once his presence is gone from my room, my head starts whirling, going back to what I'd been doing that night. Somehow his visit has allowed me to focus, has triggered something that starts to clear the mist from my head. *That's it.* I'd been trying to find a link between Reynolds, Garza, and the Herreras. And I was using my work computer. Had I been stupid? Was someone checking up on my searches?

I reach for my phone.

"Yo." I smile as the now familiar voice answers.

"Heart." I check the door's closed. "I need to talk to someone."

"I'm listening."

I swallow and then take a deep breath. "Have I crossed your club? The Satan's Devils?"

He immediately knows what I'm asking. "What the fuck? You think they blew up your house? Fuck it, woman. That's insane. We don't go after women or children, even if they've crossed us."

Ignoring his anger, I continue, "I'm a cop, Heart. They might make an exception."

He pauses but doesn't answer the question. Instead asks one of his own. "What the fuck makes you even ask?"

Biting my lip, I think of how much to tell him. It's sad to admit he's the only person I feel I can trust. The only person I can speak to, and boy, do I need someone to listen. While it might not be the best decision I've ever made, I elect to come clean and tell him the reason behind my call. "I've just had a visit from my partner, Garza. He told me the incendiary device used on the house that Archer was killed in was apparently similar to the one thrown into my bedroom. Very similar. They think it was made by the same person."

There's silence at the other end of the line, then a cautious,

"Don't know what you're suggesting here, darlin'." The endearment is clipped, his voice sounds cold.

"Look, I'm not expecting you to admit to anything, but one of your members, Jeffrey Andrews, or Slick as you call him, is an explosives expert—"

"Who had nothing at all to do with blowing up any house." The retort comes quickly.

"You would say that, and that part doesn't interest me. I'm not going to argue whether Archer deserved to go out the way he did. Huh, I'm pretty certain, from the support he's been given, no prosecution would ever have resulted unless it could have been proved beyond doubt that he ran you off the road that day." I pause to draw breath. "Unless there was indisputable evidence, such as a dashcam recording, he'd have gotten away scot-free." Before he can interrupt, I carry on, "My gut feel is that he either was directly responsible for killing your wife, or that he arranged for someone else to do it. He definitely rented the truck, and under a false name. If the law wasn't going to deal with him, he deserved what he got."

I hear him let out a deep breath. "Not arguing with that, honey. But I don't know where you're going with this."

"If the Satan's Devils knew he was responsible, they'd be the first to want to take him out. I know they'd have your back, Heart." I take a deep breath. What I'm going to say next is against everything I'd sworn to uphold. "But even if you confirmed it, I wouldn't take it further. Remember what I said about not letting the bad guys get away?"

He's silent and doesn't answer.

"What I want to know, Heart, is if your club was responsible, what the fuck does it mean if the bomb was made by the same man? That's why I asked you if they're coming after me? And if so, why? If they weren't responsible for killing Archer, that rules the Satan's Devils out, and it's someone else. Someone who wants both me and Archer dead. But who?" Tears come to my eyes. I've always tried to treat people fairly. The idea someone wants me permanently out of the way is frightening. I'd feel better if I knew who it was, then I'd know who to fight. Will they try again?

"Has anyone else made this incredible link between Archer and my club?" he asks tersely.

"Not that I know of. My partner asked me to think of any mutual enemies Archer and I could have had. But there were other gang-related killings that night. Someone took out a lot of Herreras."

"So why come to the conclusion it was Archer who was targeted?"

"I don't know, Heart." I almost wail. "It just occurred to me when I was looking through the cases. I'm not going to kid you, I'm scared here. If it was the Satan's Devils who tried to kill me, I thought perhaps you could persuade them I'm no threat."

I hear a sigh down the line, a silence while he gathers his thoughts. When he speaks it's with utter conviction. "I can assure you it wasn't my club. I've told you before, you've got to let this go. I think you've been delving into things you shouldn't have touched. You've had a warning, now leave it alone. Concentrate on getting well. When are you going back to work?"

"Not yet."

"Good. Take as much time off as possible. When you getting out of the hospital?"

"In the next couple of days."

A moment of quiet, then, "Your house got blown up, by the sound of it, I guess it's inhabitable now. And even if it isn't, it's not the wisest place for you to return to. Have you got somewhere to go?"

I shake my head in an automatic action, wincing when the pain tells me I shouldn't have. "No, but I'll figure something out."

Again he doesn't immediately speak, then when he does, it's something I don't expect. "I'm still paying rent on a house in Tucson. Stay there while you get back on your feet. It's got a top-of-the-line security system, so it will be much safer than where you were living. I'll give you the agent's details and he can give you a key. I'll contact him to let him know."

"I can't ask you to do that…"

"You didn't ask, darlin', I offered, okay? And it's not as though I ever want to live there again. I just couldn't be bothered to cancel the payments."

"I'll take them over…"

"We can discuss the details when I get back."

I don't take long to think about it. Trying to find a new place to live would just be one more thing on my long list of what I need to do once I'm discharged. I escaped the worst of the fire, but almost everything I owned was destroyed, as I would have been if my neighbour hadn't gotten me out. His offer means I can cross my largest hurdle off—well, leaving aside trying to find out who is out to kill me. I'd be a fool to turn down Heart's suggestion.

I suspect he'll be able to hear the relief in my voice. "I can't thank you enough, Heart."

A chuckle, then, "Hey, it's me that should thank you."

"I did nothing, Heart."

"Think you did, darlin'." It seems we both take a moment to remember that call in the desert.

Suddenly I have the urge to see the man I've been speaking to over these last months. Only to thank him for the generous offer of his house, of course. "When are you coming back?"

"I'm due in Tucson in under two months now. I'm going to go to Los Angeles next. Then I'll stop off in San Diego and see Dart—he's my best buddy in the club and he transferred to that chapter. Then I'll be making my way to Arizona." He pauses. "I've been doing a fuck of a lot of thinking, and I've made up my mind, Marc. Won't be separated from my daughter again. Doubt you understand, but I needed this space away. Know it's been hard on her, but once I'm back, there'll be nothing I won't do to make it up to her."

I'm so pleased for him, his words work to cheer me up. Knowing father and daughter will soon be reunited, I end the call feeling brighter.

I can't deny I'm looking forward to him coming back and meeting him in person, seeing him as he is now and not as he was, angry and hurting in a hospital bed. Despite the immense difficulties our different chosen ways of life put between us, over the last few months I feel a genuine friendship has started to grow.

And if he didn't feel the same way, why did he offer me his house?

CHAPTER NINE

$\mathcal{H}$eart...

Putting my phone away, I shake my head, not certain what the fuck made me put forward the proposal for Marc's accommodation. Our home. Mine and Crystal's. The house I've not been back to since the accident, and can't see myself returning to in the future. It's a shrine to my dead wife. Part of the reason I continued paying for it. Nothing's been touched, disturbed, or moved since the morning we set out for Tombstone.

But the police officer who's been my lifeline since very possibly saving my life in Death Valley has nowhere else to go, and there's already been one attempt on her life. Knowing she's been investigating the man who I know killed my wife, I realise guilt had driven my strange offer.

Though the rent for the house is taken out of my account, it's paid to the club. The house being rented under a myriad of aliases and not in my name, it's buried deeply enough there's no connection to me or the Satan's Devils. If she wants to hide out, she'll be safe enough there until she's fully recovered. Nobody needs to know where she's staying if she doesn't want to tell them and, as I told her, the security's top notch. Which reminds me. I send a quick text to Mouse before I forget. He monitors the security systems for any of us with houses off the compound, and if I don't warn him, Marc is likely to get a fuckload of visitors on bikes very soon after she takes a step through the front door.

Thinking about the last time I was there, I frown, remembering she'll be walking into a mess. The contents of the fridge will need to be dumped, there'll be laundry half done, and Amy's toys all over the floor. Fuck, what a mess. But remembering the cloud under which I left, I can't very well ask any of my brothers to sort it out first. Maybe it's not the best place to convalesce. At the very least I'll need to warn her what she'll be stepping into.

The image of the house as we'd left it almost brings me to my knees, my head immediately filled with visions of Crystal laughing as she slipped on her jeans, already excited about going to Tombstone. The gunfight at the OK Corral another thing to cross off her bucket list—at the time it had just been a joke, neither of us had had any inkling that might be as far as she got, that all the other places and activities would go unvisited or undone. I'd mocked her for doing such a touristy thing, but to be honest, I'd never been to Tombstone myself, and while I was gently mocking her, was happy enough to act like any other sightseer for a day.

We'd dropped Amy off with Drummer and Sam, entrusting her to their care, and had then come back for the bike.

Amy. Neither of us knew Crystal had said goodbye to her daughter for the final time. Memories of that morning come back to me. I recall how Amy had woken us early, a cockblock if ever there was one. She'd been so excited about spending the day at the club, when we'd told her goodbye, she'd hardly given us a second look before running off to take Sam's hand. They were going to bake cookies or some such shit.

Amy. My daughter. The spitting image of her mother. The anger inside so intense when I'd recovered from the coma, I'd thought only of myself and refused to see her. And even later, when I'd returned to the club, I wouldn't give her the time of day, trying to pretend she wasn't there. My rage at my loss flaring so brightly, I was in part protecting her from being caught up in the flames. How could I comfort my daughter when I could see no way forward for myself? It wasn't fair to the kid now she was already settled with the prez and his old lady. It was better for her to forget both her parents.

The hand on my shoulder reappears to give me a shake. Christ. I haven't been fair to the child who's lost her mom. She should have been able to rely on her dad. Placing my hand on the empty space on my cut, I tap it to show that now I understand. When I get back to Tucson, presuming I'm allowed back in the club, I'll be the best father any kid could ever know. Fuck knows how I'll do it, but I'll do what I can to be both mom and dad for her.

She'll probably have grown out of her clothes. But Drum will probably have that covered, he won't let her go short of anything. *Best get what's at the house boxed up and given away.* What about all Crystal's shit? She'll never need anything again. Maybe that's something Marc can do while she's there. Then I can end the rental and move on.

Move on? I almost stagger as I realise at last I'm coming to accept Crystal's not waiting for me at home.

Almost without knowing how, my phone reappears in my hand. With shaking fingers, I call up a number I haven't used for nearly five months, unable to predict what reception I'll get.

It rings, and rings again, and then, "Yeah."

"It's Heart."

"I can fuckin' see that, Brother. Says it on the display. You don't think I'd check who was calling?"

He's his usual abrupt self, but I feel a wave of relief. "Thought you might have deleted my number."

The voice growls. "Almost five months with no fuckin'

word? Thought about it, Brother. Thought about it. What can I do for you?"

I swallow a couple of times, then ask, "Amy. How is she, Drummer?"

"Missing her dad," he replies without missing a beat.

Shit. Way to make me feel better.

But he hasn't finished. "She's doing great." He pauses. "Kid's done nothing wrong. Sam made sure she had presents from Santa, and one from you. You ought to know you bought her a bike. Little one is tearing around the compound on it getting under everyone's feet. Still got training wheels on, but they'll come off soon enough. She was oohin' and ahhin' over the babies earlier. Getting like a damn nursery here now."

Fuck! I'd forgotten to ask. "Sophie and Sam?"

"Sophie had a girl, Wraith's face went fuckin' white. First words out of his mouth were that she's never dating." He barks a laugh. "But Sam's given me a bouncing baby boy. Already got a mouth on him, that's for sure."

The thought of the new lives there on the compound shows me life still goes on. Thinking it's a polite question, I ask, "What are their names?"

"Wraith's girl is Olivia, but we're already calling her Ollie, just as it gets a rise out of Sophie. And my boy's Elijah. Eli."

"Congratulations, Prez. That's a good, strong name."

"That it is. Now, any reason you're calling apart to check up, *belatedly*, on your girl?"

I take a breath. "I've been in a bad place, Drummer. But I'm getting there. Just want to confirm I can come back to Tucson in a month's time."

"You pulled yourself together? We'll all be glad to see you home."

It's more than I deserve, and more than I dared hope for. I breathe out a heartfelt thank you, and after a couple of pleasantries, sending Amy my love and the conscious omission not to say anything about my conversations with Marc—that shit's best done in person—I end the call.

Did you hear that, Crystal? They bought the little tyke a bike.

A smile comes to my face. I can't wait to see her pedalling around.

A week later and I'm riding into Los Angeles after a brief stop at Santa Barbara, not certain I'm going to be able to complete quite everything on Crystal's bucket list. It will be best to come back and bring Amy to Disneyland rather than going by myself. I'm not sure what they'd think of a lone biker meeting up with Mickey Mouse. But I do Universal Studios and the Hollywood Walk of Fame.

I take a ride out to Venice Beach and sit on my bike people watching for a while. Fuck, Crystal would have loved all this! Then I start to ride back to the motel on the outskirts of the city, already making plans to go to San Diego the next day.

I'm looking forward to seeing Dart, who's now the VP of the San Diego Satan's Devils—he's done well for himself. It will be good to catch up and see how he's getting on, though first I'll need to make him and Alex, his old lady, a grovelling apology. Last time I saw them both I didn't show myself in a good light. They got the worst of the dark side of my soul. I'll need to first rescue my friendship with my brother, but he'll cut me some slack. We go back a ways, to the long days we prospected together. Out of everyone in the club, he was the closest to me, more like an actual blood brother.

Deep in my heart, I know he'll forgive me. I grin, though knowing him, he might make me work for it.

My turn's coming up. I ease back on the throttle and flick on the indicator noticing in my rear view there are bikes zooming up fast and overtaking me in the outside lane, getting in front of me and taking the same turn off. There are bikes behind too, doing the same thing. I get a tingling sensation at the back of my neck. Now I'm surrounded and boxed in, and can do nothing but slow and pull up at their signal.

Their cuts show they're the Los Angeles chapter of the Demon Sons MC. I've never heard of them.

Slightly concerned at the way they've stopped me, I take a deep breath. Without any info on their background or reputation, I've fuck all idea what they want. But balancing that out, I know we've never crossed them either, and the dom club in LA is definitely another chapter of the Wretched Soulz. I should still be covered by the promise of protection they gave me. I calm my breathing and decide to be friendly. *Take it easy.* I slide out my smokes and light one up, drawing smoke into my lungs, partly to show I'm not worried but relaxed.

The man who was the lead rider dismounts, a couple of others with him. He walks up close and stares me in the face. As I return his gaze impassively, I note the flash on his cut denotes he's the VP, and the one underneath that says he's named Painter. I take another draw on my cigarette.

He looks at my bike, at my cut with the Ronin patch, and then at the sweatshirt I'm wearing. Lifting his chin toward his brothers, he turns back to me.

"Bit out of your territory." He points to the sweatshirt I'm wearing. It's a cool day in LA, so I'd put it on to keep me warm. Did they spot our discreet SDMC logo from a distance? Whatever, I've done nothing to upset them.

"No disrespect, man. I'm not flying any colours."

"Well, whether you meant it and whether we take it are two different things. I suggest you come with us back to our club and explain yourself to our prez. It's up to him how he'll want to play this. You're a member of a rival MC travelling through our town."

It's puzzling how they've jumped to that conclusion so quickly. My brow creases in confusion, but I can't deny or pretend I'm nothing but a weekend warrior. As far as I know, the Satan's Devils and Demon Sons have never crossed paths. I'm sure I can explain things, apologise for any imagined infraction, and then be off on my way. It's not as though I'm planning on sticking around, and the fact I'm not wearing any patches shows I'm not here on official business and won't be stepping on their toes.

I shrug. "Sure, lead the way." Once I'm at my destination, I'll tell their prez to check with the dom.

I'm escorted the rest of the journey, no chance to escape even if I was so inclined. My only concern is if I have to partake of their hospitality, I might not make it back in time to do the two-hour journey to San Diego tonight. I haven't told Dart that I'm coming. I wanted it to be a, hopefully, pleasant surprise. I'm eager to see him, have built our reunion up in my mind. I'm not thrilled at a possible delay.

We ride up to their clubhouse, an old factory building of some sort in a deserted industrial area, and wait for a prospect to roll the gate open and let us inside. I back into a space at the end of the row of Harleys, noticing the asphalt is old and pitted, its surface breaking away and turning into grit. Not the best place to park bikes. Carefully I put down the stand and make sure of my footing before I throw my leg over the seat and get off.

"Cut." Painter's in front of me now, holding out his hand.

"Nope." I shake my head. My cut might be bare of its patches, but it's not leaving my back.

He sneers. "We can get it if Prez wants it."

I feel a momentary doubt. They could. They could easily overpower me. I begin to get a bad feeling about this. Carefully I take my keys out of the ignition, palm them, then slide them into the pocket of my jeans.

"This way, then." He waves at me to proceed him. Behind me I can hear the gates sliding shut with a loud ominous clang.

Now that seed of doubt becomes to grow. *What exactly am I walking into here?* And more to the point, *how am I going to get out?*

The inside of the clubhouse is dark and dreary, a bar along one side, mismatched tables and chairs sprawling over the rest of the area. It looks like something hastily thrown together. I cast a glance at the other members milling around.

Now I'm only just the wrong side of thirty, but few of the men here look even close to my age. They're not kids, but none wear the worn look of seasoned bikers. Even tattoos seem sparse, and I swear one doesn't look old enough to shave.

"Prez!" Painter yells, taking hold of my arm. "Prez!" The second time he's louder, almost shattering my eardrum.

"Yeah, yeah. I'm here. Whatcha want, Paint?" A man wearing the president patch saunters across.

"Brought you a fuckin' present. A living, breathing Tucson Devil." He spins me around, roughly pulls up my sweatshirt and t-shirt, exposing the tattoo on my back. He'd moved fast, before I had a clue what he was doing. Just as quickly, I pull it down, but the damage has obviously been done.

The prez's eyes grow wide as he stares at me, and proving he's no stranger to multi-tasking, rubs at his balls at the same time. I read the name on his cut under the president tag and something pricks at the back of my mind. *Scratch*. Now why does that name ring a bell?

I wait for him to speak first. The expression on his face isn't welcoming, and I'm fast thinking how I'm supposed to play this when suddenly he smirks.

"A Devil to play with. Can this day get any fuckin' better?"

Oh fuck. Maybe I won't be getting out of here so quickly after all. Or in one piece.

CHAPTER TEN

$\mathcal{M}$arc…

I have no problems getting the key from the agents, but I think I'm in the wrong place as I ride up on my bike. I pause in the road and check the address. Yes, I'm here alright, but the clean and tidy suburban dwelling was not what I expected as home to a biker. It's a decent-sized single-storey adobe house, the front yard and exterior kept well maintained. I expected to find a neglected building, shrubs out of control having not been tended over the winter. If this is really Heart's house, the only answer is that someone from the club must have been looking after it for him. In his state of mind, making arrangements to keep his property tidy would have been the last thing on his mind. He'd already warned me I'd be walking into a mess.

I hadn't objected. After all he was doing for me, getting his house cleaned and his wife's stuff boxed up was the least I could do.

I ride up the short driveway and park my bike. There's a garage to the side, but I don't have the key for that. I do, however, have one for the front door. Still doubting this is going to be my residence until I get an alternative arranged, I ring the doorbell just in case someone is inside. When no one answers, I try the key in the lock. It turns, and I push the door open. A loud beep sounds.

Oh shit, there's an alarm. Quickly I look around to locate it and find a piece of paper with a code written on it as well as my name. *I'm expected.* I quickly key in the number combination and the system goes back to sleep. Also printed on the paper are instructions and a description of the security system, explaining the front and back doors and all the windows are fitted with alarms. Beside the note sits a remote for the garage. *Heart told me this place was secure.*

My heart, which had sped up as I dealt with the security, starts to slow down, and it's only now I take stock of my surroundings. I've entered into a comfortable living room where I see two big couches, one facing a massive television on the wall. The floor's polished wood with a couple of rugs, one in front of what looks like a working fireplace, and there are comfortable cushions scattered around. The strong odour of polish assails my nostrils.

It's been cleaned. Despite Heart cautioning me, it looks like all the work's already been done.

Continuing to examine what will be my residence for a while, I spy an empty toy box off to one side, reminding me that this was a child's home too. Quickly, I pull my eyes away from that evidence and cross the room, entering a kitchen fully equipped and with modern appliances. It smells fresh and clean, and my horrific imaginings that there'd be over eight months' worth of food rotting in the fridge start to dissipate. But just to make sure, I open the door and find no rotting items, but a fresh bottle of milk and some basic commodities, and a whole shelf taken up with beer.

A smile comes to my face. Heart's brothers must have arranged to have it prepared for me. Now far more optimistic and eager, I check out the rest of the house. The first door I open is to a den. It's got a second television and is decorated with motorcycle paraphernalia. On one of the walls is a framed picture of Heart when he was in the Marines. He's kneeling, grinning, at the front of the photo, his comrades around him. I stare at it for a moment. I'd almost forgotten what he looked like. Obviously his hair's grown out from the crew cut he'd worn at that time, but his eyes are sparkling, his full mouth curved up. I'd hardly have recognised him as the same man I'd only seen in a hospital bed.

Another photo is of him, Crystal, and Amy, and my heart breaks for the motherless child and the woman who's gone. I put out my hand and steady myself on the sofa. They looked so happy, so good together, and so much in love. It reminds me I'm in another woman's home. She might be gone, but I mentally make a promise to take good care of it, just as if she was going to come home.

A short walk down a hall and I come to the bedrooms. The first door I open has to belong to a child. There's pink everywhere, and a toy castle, and the bed cover is that of a Disney princess—Ariel I believe—but I could be wrong, not being up on such things.

The room opposite is the master, a large airy room which seems too feminine for a biker, and dominated by a huge bed. Off to the side can be seen an en suite. I close the door quickly, feeling like an intruder.

Going to the last room, I find the guestroom. There are crisp clean sheets on the bed, and a plain grey comforter. This room's more masculine and will suit me fine. I sit on the mattress, quickly assessing it's going to be comfortable. The closet is open, showing it's empty of clothes and has plenty of room for the few new things I've been able to purchase when I stopped off at Target on my way here—basic underwear, a few t-shirts, and a couple of pairs of cheap jeans. After the fire, I need to replace everything, a mammoth task as I think of all I've lost. I slip off my jacket and lie back on the bed, cataloguing, not for the first time, my burned possessions.

Every fucking thing. Oh, except that the neighbour who pulled me out had helpfully grabbed things nearest to the front door which was luckily my Kawasaki helmet and jacket that matches my bike. At least I had my bikes as modes of transportation, the quick response of the fire service had prevented the flames spreading to the garage. While I've got my main ride here, soon I'll have to get a taxi and go pick up my Suzuki.

When I'd considered the fire when I'd been in the hospital, it was almost as if it had happened to somebody else. Now I've got to cope with the practicalities. I'm overwhelmed that everything I owned is gone. I've got no hairdryer, straighteners, just a hair-brush a helpful nurse had brought in for me. Basic toiletries that had come from the hospital shop. I've lost my laptop—although it was a work one—but my own tablet and kindle went up in flames.

I can see a lot of online shopping at Amazon is in my future and hope that one of the televisions is smart.

Tears roll from my eyes, though I'm not normally so emotional. I feel lost and alone, cast adrift, almost like the time I had to recover from losing my family.

I sit up sharply, making my head protest. I've lost possessions, nothing like people. I've got to pull myself together and move on.

My bladder is signalling me I have to find the bathroom, so after my silent admonishment I get up and once again go to the hall. There it is, next door to my bedroom. Stepping inside, I do the necessary, and then look around. Suddenly overcome with amusement, chuckling, then bending over with laughter.

I should have suspected when I found all the beer, it just hadn't occurred to me at the time. But the range of men's toiletries which had been supplied, razor and shaving cream, as well as the black and grey towels, shows me I'm not who was expected.

Nope. Heart must have given my name as Marc.

For some inexplicable reason I find the situation funny, and I'm still giggling as I return to the bedroom.

After putting away my meagre collection of clothes, I find the makings of an omelette and get myself something to eat. Then, moving to the living room, take out my phone and call Heart. I have to thank him for allowing me to stay in this beautiful house and for getting it prepared, even if the preparations are quite masculine.

Opening a beer, appreciating the generosity, though I would have preferred wine, I settle back and place the call. It goes unanswered.

Later that evening, I try calling again. Once more the tone rings, then cuts out. This time I leave my thanks via a message.

After two days I've got myself sorted. Shopping's been done, the house full of food that I prefer, and the garage is now home to two bikes. I'm settling in, but I can't get comfortable. I'm too worried. Every other time I've rung Heart I've managed to get him, usually on the first or if not, the second try—or recently, he's taken to calling back. I tell myself there's no need to worry, there's a load of explanations. Maybe I'm just unlucky and finding him on the road each time. Maybe he's lost his phone.

After a week my concern builds, expecting him to have contacted me if only to check how I'm settling in. We've spoken so regularly over the past few months, the calls increasing in frequency as time went on, and especially while I was recovering in the hospital. Our growing friendship meaning he kept checking up on my recovery.

Has he been arrested? Well, that's one thing I can check. I place a call to the station mand get them to run his name, and nothing comes up. I pace the room, biting my nails. He's a lone biker in unfamiliar territory. Anything could have happened to him. I try to recall what I know of his itinerary. He should have been leaving Los Angeles by now and visiting his friend Dart in San Diego. Perhaps I can call there to see if he's arrived?

But I don't have the club's number.

Now I've started fretting, I can't stop. *Where is he?* Telling myself there must be a simple explanation, I can't help grabbing my keys and go out to get my Kawasaki from the garage. There's someone who might help me. I owe it to Heart to try.

The first hurdle is getting into the compound.

The prospect manning the gate won't let me in. I tell him who I am, unashamedly using my police credentials. It takes a bit of to-ing and fro-ing, but at last the gate is rolled back. Once inside the Satan's Devils' compound, I have to wait to be escorted up to the clubroom. I'm hurried through the communal area, with only a moment to take in the suspicious eyes landing on me, then, at last, I'm in an office and in front of the man I've come to see.

"Drummer." I nod my head, then turn to the other person in the room. From my previous dealings with the club, I remember he's the VP, but check his name flash to confirm my recollection is right. "Wraith."

The man behind the desk frowns. "Detective Hannah. I'd say it's a pleasure, but…" He doesn't need to spell out police aren't welcome at the compound.

Pointing to the free seat in front of the desk, I raise my eyebrow. He nods, and I slip off my green and black jacket and place my helmet at my feet. He's obviously waiting for me to speak, so I don't disappoint.

"First, I'm not here in any official capacity. I'm on a leave of absence from work."

Drummer cocks his head to one side. "You been up to things you shouldn't?"

They don't know? They must know and are playing it dumb. But if they want to hear it all over again, I'll give them the short version. "I was injured and burned when someone threw a bomb into my house. I've only been out of the hospital for just over a week."

They exchange looks. Well, perhaps there goes my idea that

the Satan's Devils had anything to do with it. Unless they're very good actors.

"I'm sorry to hear that." Drummer gives me an appraising look. "Has that anything to do with the reason for this visit? If so, we can cut this short. My club had nothing to do with what happened to you."

I shake my head too fast and pause, waiting for the pain to subside, and I automatically put my hand up to my temple. It reminds me I should be resting, not cavorting around the countryside and meeting bikers. Drummer doesn't miss much.

"If you're on sick leave, should you be here?"

"I had to come," I tell him simply.

"'Bout time you told us why. We're busy men, Detective," Wraith butts in.

I nod, slower this time. "Please, call me Marcia. As I said, I'm not working. I've come about Heart."

Again, both men exchange glances, eyebrows raised as if they didn't expect that. "Heart's not here."

I know. I lean forward and put my hands between my knees, studying them for a second before looking the president in the eye. "I'm aware Heart has been gone for five months or so. I know he was banned from the club. I know exactly where he's been and what he's been doing."

Drummer sits up sharply and locks both hands behind his head. He stares at Wraith for a moment, and it feels like the temperature in the room has dropped by a few degrees. "You seem to know an awful lot of club business for a detective. I'd like you to tell me why the police have been keeping fuckin' tabs on him?"

Shit. I've walked in here with my personal concerns about the man who's become my friend, not putting sufficient emphasis on the fact that OMGs—outlaw motorcycle gangs as they're known by law enforcement—and cops do not mix. I've got to tread very carefully here. My eyes meet Drummer's, and I make sure to keep them on him, trying to convey my sincerity. "I'm going to tell you the truth, Drummer. When I first made contact, it was to update him on how the investigation into his wife's death was going." I frown. "Or not going as the case might be..." I break off and try to pull the right words together and in the right order, knowing I've got to convince this suspicious man that for once I'm on his side.

"And how is it going?" Wraith asks sharply, before I can say anything else, his eyes flicking to meet those of his prez.

"Not well enough. But we need to park that for now. It's not what I'm here to talk about." Once more, both men look surprised, but neither interrupt when I continue, "I called him first in my official capacity. One thing to cross off my list. Just another working day." In my mind I'm remembering that call. "I knew immediately Heart was in a bad way, but I doubt that comes as news to you. Let's just say we've got losses in common, and I understood his state of mind only too well."

Their expressions give nothing away.

"He told me he was out on the road for six months, but it was clear he wasn't going to last that long without someone on his side." I feel brave enough to glare at Drummer. "He never shared club business with me, didn't tell me the reason he was out on the road or why he was staying clear of the club. I surmised you thought getting him away from where all his memories were would be the best thing. But you were totally wrong. He was out on a limb with no support." I pause, knowing I've got to lay everything on the line if I'm going to convince them. Taking a breath, I continue, "He was suicidal when I first spoke to him. I'd go so far as to say if I hadn't called him when I did, he wouldn't be breathing today. Survivor's guilt is a hard thing to deal with. I've been there, done that, so I decided to help."

Drummer looks at Wraith, who grimaces. Drummer's face is impassive, but his steely grey eyes say a lot. I know MCs are a brotherhood, the camaraderie unequalled. Suddenly I feel enraged on Heart's part. "You sent him away at the worst possible time, with no back up, and no one in his corner. If he wasn't still here, it would be on your head."

Drummer's taken aback at my attack. But it's Wraith who speaks. "Did he admit what he'd done before he left?"

I shake my head. I guessed something had happened, but I didn't know what. "I had no choice." Drummer waves Wraith down. "It's on me. I made the decision."

"Club vote," Wraith quickly reminds him. "He couldn't have stayed."

"Leaving that aside," I take back the conversation again. Whatever Heart had done, it was in the past. "Heart needed someone. Really, he needed, needs, therapy, but I did my best. We got into the habit of talking, at first every couple of weeks, and then more often. He'd tell me what he was doing and where he was going."

I glance at one then the other. "Do you even care what he was up to? Well, I'll tell you anyway. He was travelling on a road trip that he and Crystal had planned, seeing the things she wanted to see. He started off at Death Valley, and very nearly didn't make it out of there. That's when I first spoke to him. After that, he made his way to Yosemite, San Francisco, then down the Pacific Coast Highway. Last time we spoke, he was heading for Los Angeles. From there he planned to stop in San Diego and visit the club-house where his friend Dart now is, before heading back here when his six months were up.

"He wavered this way and that about coming back to the club, but when I spoke to him that final time, he was fully committed that he'd return, and at last felt strong enough to look after Amy."

"You know a lot about him." Drummer doesn't sound comfortable.

"We've become friends. He needed one."

Now the president leans forward and puts his hands flat on the desk. "Have you come here to accuse us of not supporting him? You've got a fuckin' nerve. We were here for him. Never left him alone for a moment from the time he went into the hospital until he came out. But he pushed us away, did things that hurt the club. I sent him away to give him space to get his head straight once and for all."

I match his ire. "You nearly lost him for good." Then I remember the reason why I'm here. "And perhaps you now have."

"What the fuck are you talking about?"

"It's why I've taken the unusual step of coming to you today." My voice drops, my concern for my friend coming out. "I knew the reception wouldn't be friendly, but I'm asking you to put my connection with law enforcement aside. I'm worried about Heart, Drummer. I haven't been able to contact him for more than a week. He's gone missing."

A further look between the two men and some silent exchange passes between them. It's the VP who speaks. "Maybe he's gotten sick of you bothering him all the time."

"If he was sick of me, he wouldn't be letting me stay in his house," I snap back.

Drummer's eyes open wide. "You're Mark? Well, fuck me. What the fuck you using a man's name for?"

"Marc. M. A. R. C. It's short for Marcia." I don't know why I have to explain.

"You're a fuckin' cop and you're staying in a club member's house?" Drummer's cheeks blaze red.

Knowing I have to talk him down to get him off the subject of the strange friendship between Heart and myself, I start speaking quickly. "That doesn't matter for now. It's Heart that I'm worried about. And you should be too."

Drummer's eyes bore into me, then at last he nods. "You're fuckin' right, I should be worried about him. Letting a cop stay in a club's house for one thing." He glares at me until I get the point. I return his stare, almost unblinking, hoping what I thought of him would be true, that his worries for one of his members would override his hatred for the law. It takes a few more moments, during which I refuse to back down, then he wipes his hand over his beard. "Okay, working on the assumption that you're still pals, what makes you worried about him? What do you mean he's missing?"

"I can't get in touch." Then I tell him what little I know. When I last spoke to him, and where he was at that time.

CHAPTER ELEVEN

*H*eart...

Why the name Scratch sounds familiar comes to me while I'm standing in front of him wondering what the fuck this club wants with me. But it couldn't be the same man, could it? The Scratch I'm thinking of was one of the last Rock Demons out of Phoenix. One of two men who hadn't been killed when the Satan's Devils blew up their club. Slick had already taken out one and has a massive hard-on for that last man left standing, being as he was one of those who'd raped his wife, Ella. I'd heard the name in the club before I left. At that time, Mouse was pulling out all the stops trying to find him.

But *that* Scratch had been a prospect, as far as we knew—a nephew of their president who we'd blown up, but otherwise only of lowly club rank. The man Slick was searching for and this man in front of me couldn't be one and the same? How the fuck could you go from a prospect to becoming the prez of a club in under a year?

Despite the oddity of that possible promotion, there are two more things which give me chills in my gut and make me believe my suspicions are right. One that the names of the two clubs are eerily similar, and the other is that it's far from the hand of welcome that's being extended to me.

"Brought him in, Prez. Thought you'd want to speak to him." Painter laughs. "Didn't have too much trouble finding him."

"Thanks, Paint."

"Here's his stuff."

Scratch stops fumbling with his balls to turn to the newcomer and give him a chin lift. "Thanks, Witcher."

"What the fuck?" I stare in disbelief as the man wearing the sergeant-at-arms patch hands something to Scratch. It's everything I had in my saddlebags. They must have broken the locks to get at it. "You don't mess with another man's ride."

Scratch steps up so when he speaks he spits into my face. "We do what we fuckin' want."

If I hadn't already, I'd be having serious doubts about this club now. There's a code we all follow, which they don't seem to abide by. Sure, we don't give a damn what we do to an enemy… Fuck, that's what they think I am. *Is it the same Scratch?* Those chills in my gut become icy cold.

Scratch is rummaging through my spare clothing and has picked out the tissue-wrapped Christmas ornament I'd bought all those months ago in Flagstaff, taking it out and dangling it from one finger and then looking at me. "Pretty fancy stuff for a biker. And Christmas has long gone. Doubt you'll be needing this anymore." He tosses it to Witcher, who throws it to the VP. It's a small thing, but one whose loss hits me hard. I feel violated and have to suppress the urge to scream at them to give it back. It would only let them see how important it is. *I bought it for Crystal. I bought it for Amy.*

My eyes narrow. His eyes land on my cut. "Take it off."

I shake my head to refuse, and then two men step up, and though I struggle, successfully strip it off me and hand it to their prez. He holds it gingerly as if he doesn't want to touch it, then turns it around. As it rotates, he looks at the worn leather and the lines of stitch holes showing something's missing. His eyes crease and his mouth curves. "Looks like you've been stripped of your patches."

What do I want him to believe? That I'm out bad, or still a trusted friend of the club, and in little more than a month will return and resume my place as a member? But the decision is taken out of my hands when he gives a signal and the two men who divested me of my cut grab my hands once again. Scratch walks around me and pulls up my shirt, once again revealing the full back tattoo of the Satan's Devils' patch.

"You're not out in bad standing, else this would have been inked out." He walks around in front of me again. "Unless you didn't want to do it. In which case you're showing disrespect to this life."

It's him showing disrespect, and to the dom club, but perhaps he doesn't know it. I decide to come clean. "I'm no longer a member of the club, I've taken a break to go on the road. I'm a Ronin. I've got my card, and the Wretched Soulz have given me clear passage through California."

I didn't know what I expected, but it wasn't that Scratch would grin widely, treating me to a mouthful of white teeth that don't look natural. "And we'll need to thank them. Hearing the word was out to keep an eye on a Satan's Devils' Ronin promised safe passage by the Wretched Soulz was just what we needed as a heads-up to know you were coming our way."

Shit. They were waiting. I'd run into a trap laid for me. Deciding to take the initiative, I ask, "Just who are you? What do you want with me? You've obviously got something against our club. Why? We're hundreds of miles away in Tucson…" But I've got a very nasty feeling I already know the answers. And if I'm right, this is not going to go well for me.

Again I get spittle on my face. "I'm asking the questions here." Then he turns to Painter and beckons over another of his men. "VP, you and Zip take him downstairs and string him up." He turns back. "Yeah, I got some fuckin' questions for you, and you're going to answer every single fuckin' one."

Being taken to the basement by the VP and enforcer can't bode well. But there are a dozen men in the room, and if I try and fight my way out of it, I'll only earn more bruises before I have to. I put up no protest as they lead me away, and earn myself a round of name calling, with "pussy" and "fuckin' pansy devil" coming over the loudest. I square my shoulders. Insults I can handle.

Descending the stairs, I wonder whether there's a blueprint for MC torture chambers—let's face it, where I'm headed can't be called anything else. Chains hanging from the rafters are wrapped around my hands, and plastic sheeting hastily spread under my feet. Am I afraid? Fuck yes. My hands are sweating, my heart's beating fast enough to leap out of my chest, but I try not to let my fear show. Any weakness will be leapt upon and mocked. All I can hope is that I won't be reduced to begging for my life, or more likely for death. Remaining as stoic as I can, taking everything they give to me is the least I can do for my brothers I left behind in Tucson. To depart this life with dignity, showing what a Satan's Devil stands for, his club.

The spirits are waiting. Well, they probably won't have to wait long. There was a reason I'd seen the coyote, the owl, the mouse, and the crow. The warning that I hadn't heeded. *Dead man walking.* Well, yeah. That could very well be coming.

Might be with you soon, Crystal. But for the first time, faced with my almost certain demise, I don't think they'd be doing me a favour. Crystal's been dead for almost eight months. Now I'm faced with the real possibility of death myself, and not by choice. I belatedly realise she's never coming back, isn't waiting somewhere for me, and that I want to hang onto this life. My thoughts are more with my living daughter, Amy, than with my dead wife. It's her I need to be with, not a ghost.

Having chained me up, they leave me alone and switch the light off, leaving me in total darkness. This, I know, is the first part of the torture. Soon my shoulders and arms will protest being strained in such an unnatural position for so long. If

Scratch knows what he's doing, he'll leave me here all night. Hungry, dehydrated, tired, and hurting will have softened me up by the time day comes. But if I'm reading him correctly, he's inexperienced and impatient. And one thing's for certain, I won't be giving him tips on torture techniques.

I don't have long to wait to find I'm right. Not even an hour has gone by when light filters through the door at the top of the stairs, and I don't have to turn my head, recognising by the thumping of feet that multiple people are coming down. I'd fancy my odds against two or even three, or at least put up a good fight, if only they'd let me down. But of course they're not going to free me from my restraints. When they come into sight I've underestimated. There are four. Witcher, Painter, Scratch and Zip. By the looks on their faces, they've not come to pass the time of day.

Scratch lights up a cigarette and blows smoke in my face. I breathe it in. If that's the last taste of nicotine I'm going to get, I'll take what I can.

He takes a long drag, then blows it out, this time toward my feet. I've no desire to prolong what I expect is going to be a whole world of pain, but I've no desire to get it started either. I leave him to begin, in his own time.

And wouldn't you know it? He's starts by bragging. "You wanna know how we knew to pick you up?"

I don't move a muscle, don't utter a word. Yes, I do. But I'm not giving him anything.

He continues without any prompting. "You were riding with Arizona plates."

"You stop everyone with Arizona plates?" I can't quite keep the sneer out of my voice.

It earns me a sharp look. "It makes us take a closer look. Especially when you're wearing a cut with a Ronin patch, and word on the street was to watch out for you."

I have a mental image of them riding around doing nothing

but stopping bikers with my home state's plates. Seems a waste of time to me.

"Zip here has a brother with the po-po. Traffic cop. We just had him run your license through on his scanner." He pauses. "Seems you're a Devil who goes by the name of Adam. Knew you'd come looking for me sometime or the other."

"Why?" Not bothering to admit I'm riding another man's bike, I can't hold back my curiosity any longer, even though I might end up like the proverbial cat. "Why would I be looking for you?" I ask the question, even though I'm pretty certain I already know the answer. In my head, there's no longer any doubt. The man Slick's been trying to find and this Scratch are one and the same. But I'm not going to tell him my real name. Or anything else. I'll try to find out what I can, while not giving anything away. Just in the unlikely event I'll get out of here.

No one knows where I am. The Wretched Soulz knew I was making my way to LA, and so did Marc, but no one knew when, or exactly where. And LA's a big fucking place.

The look he shoots me is entirely malevolent. He grinds the stub of his cigarette out with his boot, then spits in my face. "You know who I am, boy?"

I resent a man clearly younger than me calling me that, but suspecting I'll shortly have greater things to worry me, let it ride. "The president of the Demon Sons?" I suggest.

"I was a Rock Demon! Phoenix chapter," he spits in my face. "Your fuckin' club blew our clubhouse up. My uncle, the president, is dead because of you."

I'm not admitting to anything, or pointing out that he wasn't a full member, as a prospect he never wore their patch. I'm not letting on I know anything. It's obvious they were our enemies, trying to get Sophie, the woman who became Wraith's old lady. We were the likely suspects, but we left no proof. "Why do you think the Satan's Devils were involved?"

"I don't think, I fuckin' know! Saw your prez with my own eyes." It's true, he could have. Prez let him and another escape.

A bad mistake. One we should learn from. And the person it's come back to bite is me.

Still keeping to my bluff, I tilt my head to one side, partly to ease the ache in my neck. "I heard about that. Word was only one full member escaped. You him?"

"That was Fang, my brother."

I glance at the men accompanying him. "The only other man to get out was a prospect." Witcher and Painter stand impassively, as if it's not news to them, but I wonder how much they know about the man leading them. On the basis that anything's probably worth trying at this point, I throw at him, "So what you're saying is that you were the prospect who escaped. How the fuck did you go from prospect to prez in such a short time? I'm surprised to see you're even a member. What's the time for prospecting at this club?" My eyes query Painter, who doesn't look at all perturbed.

"Whatever I fuckin' say. It's my fuckin' club."

"Have any of your members prospected? Started off as hangarounds?" I'm curious. "Patched in from other chapters?" Though that's unlikely. Demon Sons have never come up on my radar before, and from the name, I presume it's meant to be an offshoot of the Rock Demons, though perhaps it should have been the Demon Nephew, seeing as it wasn't his father in the club. Realising my thoughts are rambling, I bring myself back to the present and pay attention to his response.

"Don't need no prospecting time when you've men you can trust." He exchanges chin lifts with the two other men.

There had been a prospect manning the gate, but I'm not going to get into semantics now. I don't like the man standing in front of me and begin to wonder how much he can trust these two who are with him. How does the club make its money? Is it enough to keep these men by his side? In an MC, it's more than the love of riding bikes which bind us together. It's knowing every man has your back and would lay down his life for any one of their brothers. Even me, while I was being an asshole. The trust I'm thinking about is probably different to his. Trust can only be earned during the prospect stage, when a man has to prove he will do *anything* without question or complaint. It might be interesting to try to explore just how far these men would go.

"How long you been up and running?" I doubt he'll reply.

But he surprises me. "Six months. Four since we moved into this clubhouse."

Not long then. Certainly not long enough in my opinion to inspire loyalty. Unless these were all childhood friends, of course. And that's the reason why they all appear so young, because they are. No seasoned biker would join a ramshackle club like this.

"What about your articles and regs? You got a proper setup here?"

Ignoring my question, he moves behind me. "Got a good place to hide a dead body, and that's all you need to know." As his fist makes contact with my kidney, I gasp to take in a breath. He hits hard, I'll give him that. I'll probably be pissing blood if I live long enough to find out.

When I'm able to breathe I look around at Painter and Witcher, neither of them seem disturbed or put out at either the statement Scratch made or the action he'd taken. But it gives me an idea. Ignoring the pain in my back, I explain as calmly as I can while I'm still swallowing down the pain, "The dom club in the area are looking out for me. Can't set up a support club without their agreement. They see you've given me disrespect, well, you've disrespected them too. Cut me down now, let me go, and I'll keep my mouth shut."

Showing he's really stupid, as must be the men with him, Scratch snarls, "Don't give a fuck about the Soulz. I do what I want in *my* club. We'll deal with them if they come calling."

Well, that didn't work. There's probably no point in making him see sense, he's as stupid as fuck. *Taking on the Wretched Soulz?* No wonder he didn't move on from prospect in his previous club. And now it's his desire for revenge that's the overriding factor, I'm the one he'll be taking it out on.

"Come on, boys. I told you what violent murdering motherfuckers the Satan's Devils are. Now we've got one to ourselves, we'll show him how upstanding bikers don't have no time for that shit. Let's soften him up a bit and then get him talking."

As they come in front of me, I see Witcher cracking his knuckles and Zip, God bless him, sliding on a knuckle duster. I brace myself for what's going to come.

Then I'm given an unexpected reprieve, as Scratch signals for them to wait up. "You can save yourself some pain if you give us some info."

What can I tell them? I've been out of the loop for many months now. And during the short time I was back before I went Ronin, I only attended a couple of church meetings, and one of those was where I'd been on trial and kicked out onto the road. I jerk my chin.

"How many more Devils in LA?"

"None that I know of," I reply, honestly.

He narrows his eyes. "You been hunting us?"

"Didn't know about you until you introduced yourself. So, no." I'm not going to tell him Slick's gunning for him. Or that one thing I'd picked up, the other person to escape the conflagration at their clubhouse, Fang, is dead.

"How many club members do you have?" And this is where I'll keep my mouth closed. If I'm reading him right, and from his erroneous description of my club to his brothers, I expect I am, they'll be crossing the border into Arizona once they get themselves organised to bring trouble to the Tucson club.

But I do offer him something. "I haven't been in Arizona for five months. Don't know who's left or who's joined, so I can't tell you."

He ignores my evasive answer. "How did you know I was in LA?"

"I didn't. You found me, not the other way around." I smirk as I point out the obvious.

"You've been searching for me all down the coast."

Christ, he's insane. I haven't been looking for him at all. But that wasn't a question. He goes on to ask details about our businesses, and I'm definitely not going to disclose anything of that type. When he realises he's got everything he's going to get out of me, he gives another signal to Witcher and Painter. This time there's nothing holding them back.

CHAPTER TWELVE

*M*arc…

I'd caught Drummer's interest. He takes his phone out of his cut and places it on the desk between us. He dials a number. *I'm going to look such a fool if Heart answers.* But I'm hoping he does, and that I'll then leave embarrassed but relieved. I'd happily accept anything that proves this bad feeling inside me to be wrong. *My friend's in trouble.*

It's on speaker, and it goes straight to voicemail.

Drummer stares at this cell. When he looks up, he meets my eye. "He could be on another call."

"Or the battery has run out," Wraith adds.

He dials again and gets the same result.

The prez jerks his chin toward Wraith. "Get Mouse in here."

The VP gets to his feet and opens the door. "Mouse!" he yells at the top of his voice. It sounds like he must only be in the office next door, as I hear a door opening and shutting, and then the inaptly named Mouse appears—tall, well built, and with enviably long, dark, shiny hair. He's part Navajo, I remember from his file.

As Wraith returns and takes his seat, Mouse pauses in the

doorway, his face pointed expectantly toward Drummer. "Yeah, Prez. What's up?"

"Heart's phone. Can you track it?"

Without asking why, Mouse simply asks, "What happens if you call it?"

Drummer tries to place the call again. It goes straight to voicemail. "Third time that's happened."

Mouse tuts. "Either he's on a long call or the device is dead. If the batteries have run out, there's not much I can do. When was he last in contact?"

"Ten days ago," I butt in. Mouse gives me a strange look and raises his eyebrow, then turns his attention back to his prez. "You think something's happened to him?"

"Can't rule it out."

"I should be able to pull up the last location where it was used."

"That would be something, Mouse. Do that, will you?"

Drummer picks up his phone and places another call. This time he takes it off speaker. "Yo, Dart. How you doing in San Diego? Alex and the kid okay?"

"Good. Good. Glad to hear the boy's doing well."

"Yeah? Does he?" He chortles, and putting his hand over the phone, speaks to Wraith. "Kid still goes to bed with his fuckin' cut on." Wraith laughs.

"Yeah, Eli's doing great. Good fuckin' set of lungs on him. Ollie? She's good too. Got Wraith here if you want to give him some fatherly advice."

I twist my hands together in my lap, wishing he'd get on with it.

At last he does. "Brother, you heard from Heart at all? Word is he was heading your way before coming here."

"Yeah, six months almost gone now. Seems he's doing better at last. But you haven't heard from him or seen him?"

It's a negative answer, I can tell by the way Drum sucks in his cheeks.

"Yeah, keep in touch. That would be great. Brothers here would love to see y'all. You do that. And soon."

He ends the call, shakes his head, and then lowers his face, cupping his cheeks between his hands. After a moment he looks up.

"I take it you can't be contacted via the precinct?" Then when I gesture a negative reply, he continues, "Leave me your number. If we find anything we can share, I'll be in contact. Only to put your mind at rest, mind you. Whatever this fuckin' thing is between you and Heart has to stop."

I sit back in the chair, cross my feet at the ankles, and fold my arms over my chest. "Nope. I want to know that Heart's okay, and if he's not, do what I can to help. You're not leaving me out of this, Drummer."

"You're not here in an official capacity. And whether you're on active duty or not, cops and the likes of us don't mix. Now I'll ask you politely to leave us." As I go to refuse, his face grows dark. "Or I can easily have you escorted out. You've no right to be here."

Still in my defensive posture, I lean my torso forward, bending at the waist. "If it wasn't for me, Drummer, you wouldn't even know something was wrong. I've contacted the LA police, and he hasn't been arrested. He's not turned up in a hospital or morgue. He's gone completely off the radar, and that's not like him."

When Drummer tries to interrupt me, I put up my hand to stop him. "For the last five months, every time I've contacted him, he's answered his phone. If not immediately, he's gotten in the habit of returning my calls. While I was in the hospital, he was ringing every couple of days to find out how I was. Last time I spoke to him, he was going out sightseeing. He was getting stronger in his head, even joking about the things Crystal was making him do." I realise that doesn't sound right. "The things she had on her list," I bite my lip to cover a small smile, "though he did balk at Disneyland. The point is, if there had been anything wrong, I would have known it." I place my hands flat on the table. "Heart started out suicidal. For the past month or so he's changed. His focus was on getting back to his daughter. Something's happened to him, whatever you think. Something he couldn't control."

"Still doesn't mean you shouldn't leave it in our hands, darlin'." Wraith backing up his prez is what I don't want. Especially when he gets to his feet, obviously preparing to walk me off the premises.

I have a brief reprieve, as at that moment Mouse returns. "Found his phone. Must have run out of battery or something, but I can tell you where it was six days ago."

Drum opens his mouth, but I get in before him. "Where?"

Mouse just glances at me, then back at his prez.

"Look, Drummer. I might be able to call on resources to help."

"No cops. Whatever's happened to Heart, we'll sort it ourselves."

I breathe in deeply and let air out on a sigh. "Of course you will."

"Women aren't involved in club business."

"I'm not a woman."

Wraith laughs. "Could have fooled me, darlin'."

"That's not what I meant," I snap. "I'm not someone who sits around waiting for men to look out for her. I've been trained in self-defence, in high-speed driving. I carry a gun and am not afraid to use it."

"Don't matter what sex you are. You're not a member. You're fuckin' law enforcement."

"Doesn't Heart matter to you?" I stand up and slam the palms of my hands down on the desk. "If it was someone I cared for, I'd take all the help I could fucking get." I'm so angry my cheeks feel warm. "Thanks for the tip, Mouse. I'll get someone checking his phone and go after him myself."

"Don't talk to me that way ever again!" Drummer's voice thunders over mine. "Sit the fuck down."

Assuming my point has been made, I do as he says and snap my mouth shut.

After focusing his glare on me as though making sure I'm satisfied I've had my say, he looks behind me. My threat to use police resources to find out the same info that Mouse has obviously worked. He wouldn't want Heart to be officially listed as a missing person and have the police trying to track him down. "What you got, Mouse?"

"I've checked the location on Google Maps and viewed it on satellite. Seems to be an old factory of some sort."

"Any vehicles, bikes?"

Mouse huffs a laugh, but it's not one of amusement. "You know how old those images can be? There's nothing at all at the factory, which just means it wasn't used once, but could have been taken over now. Or, it could still be abandoned."

"Did it look like a place Heart would have lost his phone?" Although it would be a sensible move to keep quiet, I simply can't. I throw a look of apology at Drum as I see his eyes tightening.

Mouse answers, "Can't see what he'd go there for. It was a bit out of the way, not much around it. Even at the time the picture was taken, other buildings were run-down."

"Anything show on Street View?"

Now there's a glint in Mouse's eye as if I'm speaking his language. "Similar to Google Earth, if it's not older."

"No sign? Identification of any sort?" I look at Drummer. "If we knew who owns, or even owned it, we might get a clue what it's being used for now."

Smothering his annoyance that I seem to be conducting an interrogation, his eyes flit to Mouse, who shakes his head. "Sorry, Prez. Nothing. And before you ask, nothing on the buildings around it. Some didn't even have roofs or walls intact."

Drummer picks up a pen and twists it between his hands,

then he points it directly at me. "I admit, I don't much like what I'm fuckin' hearing."

"What are you going to do, Drummer?"

"Club fuckin' business. And none of yours." I'm reminded that I'm sitting in front of the president of what my colleagues would consider a dangerous OMG. And this time, when he gives me the instruction to leave, I realise he's giving me no choice.

"Now get out of here, *Detective*. I can't fuckin' deny I'm grateful to you if Heart is in trouble, you've given us the heads-up. And," he points his finger toward me, "you better start making arrangements to get out of Heart's fuckin' house. I'm grateful to you for looking out for my brother, so I'll let you know what I find. But this... friendship between you stops now. Club rules are members don't talk to cops. Even off-duty ones. Ever. You're gonna promise me here and now that you won't try to make contact with Heart ever again. Unless it is fuckin' official business, and he's got a brother or lawyer by his side."

That is a promise I can't make.

"VP. Get her out of here and then get everyone together for church." His eyes at last gentle. "I know you're concerned about him, but leave this to us. I don't want any cops involved."

I can agree to that. "My position's already precarious, I realise that. I assure you, Drummer, I'd be faced with questions from my boss if I started an investigation about Heart going missing. Questions I wouldn't be able to answer. As you've said, law enforcement and OMGs don't mix. I'd probably lose my job."

He gives me a sharp nod.

I stand and let Wraith lead me into their clubroom, passing me over to one of their prospects to escort me out. Inside, my mind is whirling. Drummer wants me to stay out of this? No fucking chance.

Since the loss of my family, I've purposefully allowed no one to get close, but somehow, over the past winter, Heart's become a good friend. I won't be letting him down. Sitting back and waiting for news isn't how I work. No, I'm going after him myself, and I know exactly how to do it.

Getting back onto my Ninja, I speed through the streets back to Heart's house and get my toy out of my garage—my ratty, mean-looking Suzuki. Harleys might be the preferred bikes for the MC, but I favour the higher speed, tighter cornering, and the bad-boy looks of my brute of a machine. And the best thing? Only Heart knows this beast is mine.

Guessing they'll only be having a short church meeting, and not doubting that the outcome will find them undertaking the eight-hour ride to LA, aiming to get there in closer to six by lane splitting and breaking speed limits to locate their missing brother, I know I've got no time to waste. I grab my black helmet, black jacket, and get on my black ride, tucking my blond hair up out of sight, becoming another anonymous biker on the road.

There are two routes they could take to LA. As it would be stupid to try and follow them from the clubhouse, I instead zoom past and park up on the shoulder just before Casa Grande and the junction between the I-8 and I-10. Then I wait, just a biker checking his route on his phone.

As expected, I'm not there long. Half a dozen bikers zoom past me, taking the straight route up to Phoenix. I smile to myself, knowing it's them, even though they already removed their cuts, there's no disputing it's Drummer out in front. Getting back on my Suzuki, I start it up and move out onto the highway. Twisting the throttle, I pick up speed, and am soon flying past them. With a couple of stops to top off my tank, I arrive in San Bernardino and again settle to wait. Now it gets harder. From here on I'll have to try to follow them undetected, as I've no idea of where exactly they're heading. *I can't lose them now.* I'm too close.

They're quite a ways behind me, but I'm patient. At last they come into sight, now all wearing helmets to abide by the California laws. Once they're a little way ahead, I slip into the traffic behind. I've done the surveillance course too and now put all I've learned to good use.

I'm a few cars behind as we pass the Hollywood sign, and I'm overtaking a car to get a little closer when I see them turn off. As they start to take turns left and right, I need to narrow the gap between us, determined not to let them out of my sight. *I can't lose them, not when Heart might be close.*

A left then a right, then a right once again. *Where the hell are they going?* Suddenly the bikes in front of me slow, and two peel off. I reduce my speed and hang back. *Oh shit.* In my rear view I see two bikers coming up behind me. I hadn't been as clever as I'd thought.

Their speed reduced once again, I'm suddenly surrounded and forced to stop. Knowing I need to identify myself quickly, I pull off my helmet and dark glasses and shake out my hair.

"Fuck me," Drummer says, getting off his bike. "What the fuck are you doing here, Detective?"

"I'm coming to find Heart."

"You're a persistent bitch, ain'tcha?" Drummer's shaking his head. "Must have broken a few laws speeding to get here."

"Yes, I did. And I'm prepared to break more if I'm right and Heart's in trouble. Anything it takes, Drummer. You're not going to get rid of me. So I suggest we go to wherever his phone was last pinged and start tracking him down." I gaze at him steadily, hoping to convey nothing he can say will put me off.

Almost without seeing where it came from, a gun's pointed straight at me. "Oh, I can get rid of you, sweetheart." His tone is chilling.

There's already been one attempt on my life, as the throbbing in my head reminds me. I stare at the gun, then toss a look of challenge to Drummer. "Isn't this just wasting time?"

As an answer I hear a click as he gets ready to fire. Well, if this is it, so be it. I'll have died trying to find the man I've come to like.

A pin would be heard if it dropped. The distant sound of traffic seems to fade.

"If you're going to do it, I suggest you're quick. Heart needs to be found." I can't explain the feeling inside which tells me he needs help. My worry seems to be for him, not for myself. I know outlaw gangs can't be trusted and have a probably rational fear of the police. I made my bed when I decided to follow them.

Seconds pass slowly, time seems to extend.

Then, as suddenly as it appeared, the gun goes back into its holster and Drummer's still standing in front of me, again shaking his head. "You're a brave bitch," he tells me, admiringly. "You must really have a thing for Heart."

Now it's my head that moves side to side, but in truth I can't really explain it. "I just want to know that he's safe. I heard what you said, Drummer, and I agree. Once Heart's back home, I won't have anything to do with him. Cops and bikers don't mix."

"If you come with us, you might see things…"

"I'm not a cop today. I'm not even here, I'm recovering at home, remember?"

He stands back a pace and looks at my bike, shaking his head once again. "Is that thing even legal?"

"I don't fucking care," I toss his way.

Another sharp look, then, "Mount up, brothers. Let's go see what we can find. And you, Marcia, can tag along at the back."

Before I can sigh with relief, bikes are starting with a thunderous roar, and then we're off.

Soon we're heading into an industrial area that looks like it went out of business some time ago, a ghostly, eerie place. *Heart can't be here, can he?* If I had a bad feeling before, it's certainly not being allayed by this place. It's the kind of place a cop would expect to find a body.

Drummer calls us to a halt and waves a man forward. "Blade. Wanna go with Mouse and take a look?"

Mouse is studying a printout. "There's a way around the

back, along the tree line there. Reckon we can get close without being seen." He breaks off and looks around the deserted area. "If there's anyone to see us, of course."

Drum nods, and they move off without wasting time.

No one speaks while they're gone, expressions are sombre. I guess everyone's thinking like me. On the one hand, if Heart is with his phone, chances are he'll be found as a corpse. On the other, even if he was here once, he might not be now. His phone could have been stolen then dropped. Snippets of my conversations with him go around my head. He'd come back from the precipice. He wanted to be a good dad to his little girl. He can't be dead. Impatiently I wipe a tear from my eye, the action not going unnoticed by Drummer.

It's not long before Mouse and Blade return. Blade's looking particularly grim. "You're not going to believe this, Drum. There's a dozen bikes parked up—mostly Harleys. We've stumbled across an MC."

"Any idea who?"

"Demon Sons," Mouse interjects. "Sign out front."

"Never fuckin' heard of them." Drummer takes his phone from his cut and wanders a little distance away. It's impossible to hear his end of the call.

After a few minutes he comes back. "Right, I've spoken with the dom. They've not heard of them either, and aren't happy they've set up on their turf, or if they've disrespected the Ronin protection extended to Heart. Want us to give them any info we find, happy if we have to take them out." He glares at me when he says the last, but I just stare back.

All I'm interested in is the man I've come to find. Even if I know Drummer's call had been placed to the Wretched Soulz, the dominant MC in California, to which other one-percenter clubs give due respect. I'm not stupid, and I know a club which appears overnight unknown to the WSMC is asking for trouble. If Heart's here, I'll be right behind Drum helping to finish them off. *If Heart's here and hurt, or if they've killed him...* My vow to uphold the law disappears in a flash, overtaken by my desire to take out the bad guys.

"You stay here and wait."

"No. There are a dozen bikes there, that could be a dozen men. You've got seven, including me." I take a deep breath. "Biker clubs like women, yeah?" I shake out my long hair and fan it around my face. It's only a bit shorter than it had been once the singed ends were cut off. Taking off my riding jacket, I reach under my tight t-shirt and unclasp my bra, sliding the straps down my arms and removing it from underneath my top. My fairly generous breasts are now clearly outlined, the nipples pushing at the thin material. I step off my bike, showing my legs are encased in figure-hugging leather pants. The only thing letting me down is my scarred arm.

"Would I pass for a biker babe?"

"I'd fuck ya," an admiring voice says.

"Shut it, Rock," Drum growls, but he's giving me an appraising look. "You go in there, you're likely to be eaten alive."

"I can handle myself," I tell him. "I'll see the lay of the land and let you know what I find."

"You armed?"

I pull up the leg of my pants and show him my ankle holster.

"Give me your phone." When I do, he enters his number. "Have it in your pocket and keep the line open. I want to hear everything that's said. Try and get us some info."

I nod, dial his number, and put my phone into my pocket.

His hand comes out and rests on my shoulder, his fingers gently pressing in. "Good luck, sweetheart. Now go and let's see if we can find our brother."

CHAPTER THIRTEEN

*H*eart...

I've no idea how long I've been held here in this dark basement, unable to tell whether it's day or night. It seems like I've been here a lifetime. A living hell. There's not an inch of me that doesn't hurt, to the extent I barely register new pain anymore, though that doesn't stop them. Further torture is ineffectual, my body's ability to distinguish the additional hurt has gone.

They're coming again, heavy footsteps thumping down the stairs. Though they're almost too swollen to open, I squeeze my eyes firmly shut, unwilling to give them any indication I'm conscious. As soon as they realise their new toy's awake, it all starts again until I pass out.

I'm weak from dehydration and hunger, though they've given me just enough water to keep me alive. Once they'd broken my legs, they'd taken me down from the chains, knowing I couldn't move if I wanted to. As well as being immobilised, both shoulders are dislocated from being strung up for so long. I'm battered and beaten, and numerous stab wounds cover my now naked body.

"Take him upstairs," Scratch instructs. "It will be easier to play with him there."

No reprieve. Even a change of location won't afford me the opportunity to escape. I couldn't even crawl at this point.

They drag me, my naked, broken body thumping up the stairs, bringing unwanted groans from my lips, providing them with satisfaction. They laugh and make jokes as they dump me unceremoniously in a corner, a dying animal, offered no dignity.

All I can do is curl up in the fetal position and hope for death. My new setting makes it easier for them to see when I'm awake, and now it's not just Scratch and his three henchmen, as all members of the club appear to relish in taking turns in putting me back under again.

Last night they chopped the ring finger off my left hand, my body unable to process the additional physical pain. The loss of my digit barely making itself known over the other agonies inflicted, but I felt the anguish as I was forced to watch them take away my wedding ring, my last physical connection to Crystal.

They don't seem to have a plan what to do with me other than to inflict the most torture they can. I know they wanted to use me as bait for Drummer and the rest of the Devils, but we'd come to an impasse. I refuse to give them his contact details, and they're too stupid to know how to find out themselves. Until my phone died, they kept waving it in front of me, but I refused to give up the passcode and haven't, for this very reason, set up touch. They kept trying to use my fingers, but it didn't work.

Earlier today I heard them placing bets on how long I would last, and the way I'm feeling now, each breath a struggle to get air into my lungs, the person who opted for this evening will probably win. Each time one walks past they spit on me to show their disgust, leaving me to wonder if I might die of infection before anything else.

I'm conscious now, but woozy. Just able to hear them making

arrangements to transport my dead body to Tucson and drop it outside the Satan's Devils' compound, a message the same fate is awaiting the rest of my brothers at the hands of the Demon Sons. *At least I'll be home.*

I've given up the fight to live, the spirits won't have long to wait now. I've started praying the next kick or knife wound will kill me. *Crystal, I'm coming.* But she's forsaken me too. I haven't felt her gentle touch for days. Even in the depths of pain-induced hallucinations she's left me alone, which is a mercy. *I wouldn't want her to witness me in this state.*

Though I've hoped for the end so many times, there's a small part of me unwilling to give in to death. I try to remain conscious as much as I can, quiet, unmoving, eyes shut so as not to alert them, but being human I still hope for the impossible. For a rescue. *I didn't have a chance to hold my daughter, to tell her I love her.* The thought of Amy keeps me hanging on, even while I cry out to whatever deity might be listening to put an end to my suffering. It's too much for a man to bear.

My ears are still working, analysing every sound, on the alert for footsteps approaching, anticipating another steel-capped boot to my side.

Now I hear the clubhouse door opening, not an unusual sound, but the footsteps sound lighter, different to any I've heard before. I strain to listen, if only to relieve the monotony of my pain.

"Who the fuck are you?"

"Thought you tough biker boys might be looking for women."

Despite my desire to keep my eyes closed, they snap open as far as they can as I recognise the voice. I must be delirious, there's no way Marc can be here. Turning my head a little to the right, my neck muscles protesting, I struggle to peer through my swollen eyelids. I can just about make out a woman in the door-way, her body silhouetted by the daylight behind. Long hair flows over her shoulders, and her hip is cocked to one side. It's a whore's pose.

It's coincidence. There's no way she could find me. It can't be her. I'm just dreaming, imagining the female voice I've come to know so well. *Someone on my side. Someone who's come for me.*

"Who sent you? How did you know we were here?" It's Scratch, asking harshly, as though he's suspicious.

"Word gets around," she drawls. As she steps forward, I can see her better. Now I know I'm dreaming. The staid police officer I'd only met a couple of times eight months ago would never be here, dressed in tight leathers and tits clearly on view beneath a tight tank top.

As I watch, she places her palm flat on Scratch's chest, seeming to study his cut. "Oooh. You're the president! I like you. Why don't you and I go have some fun?"

Scratch barks a laugh, and his hand shoots out to rest on her shoulder, her flirtation seeming to banish any thought of her being a threat. "Well look what we've got here, boys. Guess we're gonna have some entertainment tonight."

Get out of here, Marc. Before you see me. You'll only get hurt. Why the fuck have you come? And even if my mind's fantasising, whoever she is, she doesn't deserve what she's likely to get. Scratch and his men won't be gentle.

"Gonna offer a girl a drink first?" She nods toward the bar, and again Scratch laughs, and I watch as he adjusts himself in his pants and then leaves his hand there, gently stroking. "Sure, why not? We'll let you wet your throat. We've got all night, babe."

Like vultures, the others are circling around her. "Hope you're going to share, boss," Witcher says, and even from here I can make out his eyes glowing with lust.

"'Course I fuckin' am. You ever pull a train, babe?"

The woman shrugs. "Just get me that drink first, and…" Her sexy voice falters. Her eyes have been scanning the room and have fallen on me. Quickly she looks away and completes her sentence. "I'll do whatever you want. I'm all yours."

All doubt swept away, *it really is her.* I hold the little breath I can breathe in, hoping no one else had noticed her pause. But they're too intent on eyeing her tits to listen to what she has to say. My broken gut clenches. She doesn't know what she's walked into, and, I have no idea how she's going to get out. That she's here for me is certain. If they discover who she is, she's going to die along with me for sure. Even in ignorance, I wouldn't be surprised if they killed her for their amusement. *Leave, Marc. Before it's too late.*

"Ours, babe. The twelve of us." She must be terrified, but she's smiling, and fuck me, licking her lips. She has no fucking idea what she's setting herself up for.

What's her plan? Has she even got one? To check I'm here then go for help? By the hungry glances being thrown her way, she's not going to get out before she's been utterly broken.

Having been out of the room, Zip walks past me, sees I'm awake, and gives me a kick to my side. Unable to suppress my groan, my body automatically tenses in an attempt to evade him even though I'm too broken to move.

All eyes come to me, and Scratch roars with laughter. My suffering and a pretty woman has put him in a good humour.

Her attention brought to me, she's unable to ignore the body on the floor. She asks, nonchalantly, sounding completely disinterested, "Who's that?"

"One of our enemies."

She huffs a laugh. "Well I hoped it wasn't one of your friends." Then giggles as though she's made a good joke. Her face otherwise impassive, as if the sight of a broken man doesn't affect her at all. In fact, she ignores me and focuses on the biker standing before her. "So…" I pull myself together enough to see her hand going again to his chest, this time tracing the patches on his chest. "Scratch. If you're the top man here, do you fuck the best?"

He preens and puffs himself up. "Sure do, babe. And drink that drink up." Grabbing her hand, he exchanges it for his on his dick. "I'm primed and ready to go."

"I can feel that," she breathes in a seductive voice. She bends over as if to fondle his denim-covered cock. "Are you shy?" she whispers, but loud enough for me to hear.

Another chuckle. "Have at it, babe."

I watch, with a feeling of dread, wondering how this is all going to end as she kneels on the floor and starts to undo his zip. But in a flash her hand changes direction, shooting down to her ankle. She stands fast, her arm around Scratch's neck, her gun pressed into his temple as she warns, her features now gone from seductive to brutal, "One move and your president's dead."

"He's mine!"

As six men burst in the front door, guns raised and ready for battle, I recognise the voice that had spoken. *Slick.* Christ! What are they doing here? How did they find me? I follow up with the thought, *Brother, you're going to get your final Rock Demon.* Either they'll all die with me—I'm too broken to save—but I can go easily, knowing my brothers have come for me.

As the sound of gunfire starts, I'm unable to keep my eyes open. I give up.

Seven months ago, I woke up to the sound of hospital instruments beeping, and now I'm back listening to the same damn sound again. I can't move and there's a tube down my throat. For a moment I wonder whether the last months have all been a bad dream, a delusion caused by my injuries when I came off my bike. I hear voices and try to distinguish them. Can I hear Crystal? *Is she alive? Has everything been a nightmare?*

"I told you to leave." That's the prez.

"Not until I know he's alright." Hell, that's Marc.

I feel crushing disappointment that I hadn't been imagining my trip around Arizona and California without Crystal behind me. Hearing Marc's voice shows it wasn't a dream. I lost my wife a long time ago. The brief moment when I thought my grief had been imagined crushes me when I realise everything was real. *Crystal's dead, and has been for eight months.*

"He's going to be fine. You heard what the doctor said."

As memories come rushing back, I don't know how I'm still breathing, believing I would have died in that clubhouse. While Crystal might still be gone, to my surprise, I'm glad to realise I am still in the land of the living. Trying to control my swiftly changing emotions, I make an effort and open my eyes.

I've heard her voice so many times on the phone, sometimes business like, often sympathetic and supporting, and then, that last night in the lair of the Demon Sons, seductive and alluring. But I've never before heard her squealing with joy like a child at Christmas.

"Heart! You're awake. Thank God."

Drummer leans over me. "I'll get the doctor in. Don't try to speak, you're on a ventilator for now."

For the next few moments there's a flurry of activity. At last the tube's removed from my throat and I'm given some ice cubes to suck while the doctor catalogues my injuries. My weakened left leg has been broken and set, the right femur's been fractured as well. All things considered, I've escaped life-threatening injuries. My dislocated shoulders have been put back into place, a total of four ribs are cracked, and numerous stab wounds which will leave interesting scars have been stitched up, including one on my face. Oh well, I always was too pretty.

My broken fingers have been set, but I'll always have one missing. I reckon I can get on without it, and it's not as though I'll ever want to put a ring on that finger again.

Once the pain relief pump's been explained, completely unnecessarily—I am well used to using that—the head of the bed has been raised at my request, and the medical staff leave us alone.

After swallowing a few times trying to get moisture into my dry mouth, I rasp out the words, "How long this time?"

"We found you yesterday evening." Prez sounds concerned.

At least I've not been out of things for a month, but it explains the level of pain I'm experiencing. "Everyone okay?"

"If you're talking about the Devils, everyone's fine. Blade took a bullet to his leg, but he'll recover, and Peg got a knife in his arm, but it's only a scratch. As for the Demons, they're all dead."

I manage a grin, though my face is swollen. "Did you make them hurt, Prez?"

"Did what we could, Brother. At first we were outnumbered, so had to take them out fast. Marc kept Scratch occupied until Slick could get at him."

"Painter and Witcher?"

"The VP and SAA?"

I notice Marc's looking away. "We took care of them the same way as Scratch. Down in the basement."

Marc glares at Drummer. "You kept me away from that."

"Plausible deniability." Prez glares, then his eyes soften. "Couldn't have saved Heart without your help. You did good."

"I killed one of them." I notice she's biting her lip. Fuck me, a cop going in on the Devils' side and taking out rival bikers? That's some serious shit.

"Self-defence, sweetheart. It was you or him."

She shrugs, but it looks like she's having difficulty handling it. Then her eyes land on me again. "Hate to see you in a hospital bed again, Heart, but I'm so happy to see you alive."

Not as happy as I am. "How the fuck did you find me?" My voice is becoming hoarser. Marc passes me another ice cube to suck.

"That was down to Marc, here. Seems you and she have gotten friendly." Drummer's eyebrows draw down, showing how little he thinks about that. "But thank fuck you did, it saved your life. She raised the alarm you were missing, and Mouse tracked your last location using your phone."

My narrowed eyes find Marc's. "You put yourself in danger by coming into the clubhouse."

"I put myself in danger every day on the job. Wasn't anything different. And Drum needed info as to who was inside."

"You…" My voice breaks as I remember. "You offered yourself."

"I knew Drummer and his boys were outside. The most important thing was getting to you. I needed to check what was going on, how many we were up against."

"We'd have still come in gun's blazing, even if they'd moved or…"

Killed you, I finish in my head. A corpse is what I expect they thought they would find. I still can't quite believe I'm out of that hellhole. I lie back closing my eyes, pain making me press the button, and immediately I start to feel woozy.

Sometime later I awake, and now both Wraith and Drummer are with me. My eyes flick around to find Marc, but she's not in the room. *She's probably gone for a coffee or something.* Something's niggling at me. While I feel some clarity, the drugs are still preventing me from thinking straight. Scratch's image, holding something…

"Where's my stuff?" I croak out.

"Got your cut right here." Wraith holds it up. And fuck me, I don't know how they've done it, but my rightful patches are all back in place. A warm glow goes through me as the VP continues, "Fucker's hung it up at the back of their bar. Oh, and this was with it. It yours? Didn't seem to be like anything they'd have."

Fuck me, he's holding the Christmas snow globe in his hands. I don't know why it causes me such relief, but it does. The sight brings a small smile to my face, and Wraith decides to lighten the mood.

"Haven't you had enough of hospitals, man?" The VPs

shaking his head, but there's a gleam in his eyes confirming he's pleased to see me.

"What can I say? I seem to have a fetish for having my legs in casts."

Drummer's pacing the room, but pauses to chuckle at my response. "Fuck it, Heart. You're gonna have to be more careful and keep away from men trying a kill you. Medical expenses are fuckin' adding up."

I hold out my least damaged hand and try to bump fists with Wraith. "So fuckin' glad to see you, VP, Prez. I really thought my number was up."

Pausing his steps, Drummer scrutinises me. "Heard there was a time you'd have preferred that."

Marc's been talking.

He reads my mind and interprets my scowl. "Cop walking into the club bold as fuckin' brass? Comes with some story about you? Had to find out why she knew where you were and that you were missing. Wouldn't let her get away with just half facts."

I turn my head to the side, embarrassed my brothers know how low I'd sunk, and so terribly sorry for the things I did that made Drummer banish me as he had.

"Sending you away wasn't the best thing, I recognise that." His hand sweeps down his head and settles on his beard, his mouth drawn down.

"You did what you had to do for the club." I swallow and ask the question that haunted me on the road. "What happened to Tinker?"

"You can thank Dart's woman, Alex, for sorting her out. She and her had a long conversation, said you were in a bad place. Tinker returned to work. But I tell ya, Heart—"

"It will never happen again, Prez. Nothing like that will ever happen again. I haven't been near a woman since."

He turns to examine me. "Except for Marc. You seem to have

been cosying up to her. And fuck me, that's a fuck of a handle for a bitch."

Wraith huffs a laugh. "Rides like a man, though. Handled that big rat bike no problem. Left us at the starting gate."

Drummer takes a second to focus his eyes on the VP before turning back to me. "Gonna need to have words about exactly what your conversations entailed. But I tell you this, it ends, now, Heart. Whatever it is between you. No one-percenter club can have law enforcement on the inside. You know this."

"Nothing between us but a few chats on the phone. She kept me sane, Prez." I understand what he's saying, but it doesn't mean I like it. There were times on the road I just kept going to hear her voice. Drummer's taking my lifeline away, but perhaps I don't need it anymore, now I've again got my brothers at my back. Nevertheless, it still hurts me in the gut. *I'll miss her.*

"She needs to get out of your house, Heart. I've told her to go. Don't want there to be any relationship between her and the club. None whatso-fuckin'-ever."

I sharpen my eyes. "My house is secure, Prez. She needs somewhere to go where she can be safe. Someone's already tried to kill her."

Drum pinches the bridge of his nose. "I get what you're saying and accept you owe her a debt. If it wasn't for her, we wouldn't have known you were missing, and from the state we found you in, not too far a stretch to think you'd already be dead. I'll get onto finding her somewhere else and help out with the security."

"That would ease my mind, Prez. I owe her my life." My eyebrows draw down in a frown as I realise how big a part she played in my rescue. "She's saved me twice."

I'm about to reach for the pain pump when something else occurs to me. "You need to talk to her, Drum." Christ, he's going to lose his shit when I tell him this. "She asked me if Slick had anything to do with blowing up Lucas Herrera's house and killing Archer."

"You fuckin' what?" His voice thunders, making my head pound, and he takes a step closer. "That right fuckin' there is why we don't talk to cops. She been doing some digging?"

Wraith's on his feet and running his hands through his hair. "How the fuck did she come up with that? What were you saying to her, Heart?"

Now both my VP and Prez are staring at me as if I've betrayed the club. I raise my bandaged hands as though to ward them off. "Look, listen to me. She was trying to get justice for Crystal. Turns out, the word is Archer died a hero, they want to give him a posthumous commendation for some trumped-up reason. Before someone threw a bomb through her window, she was looking through the files because she thinks her sergeant and partner are dirty."

Drum's shaking his head. "How the fuck did she come up with Slick's name? We did it clean, left nothing for them to fuckin' find."

"Fuck knows, but here's the strange thing. She's been told the bomb that killed Archer was the same one that was used at her house. The suggestion was that both she and Archer must have crossed the same people. And one of the suspects is the club."

"For fuck's sake, Heart. Why am I hearing this now?"

"Because I've been a bit tied up," I spit out in frustration. "I told her Slick had nothing to do with her house being bombed."

"Too fuckin' right. But how have they come up with a match between the two explosives?"

Fuck, I hurt. Still my hand hovers above the pain pump, but I refrain from pressing it. "I think she's in danger," I say as forcefully as I can. "She's been digging too deep and stepping on someone's toes. Cops would know how to make a bomb that's a match."

"*She's* a cop." Wraith lifts his chin toward Drummer. "Club needs to look after its own. If she's in danger from her own people, she'll have proper channels to go through."

Drummer leans his head back and stares at the ceiling. "VP's right. Sorry, Heart. I don't see what else I can do. Club and LEO have to stay separate. No question about it. We owe her, so I'll see she gets settled, but can't go much further than that."

I make one last plea before succumbing to the morphine. "I owe her," I repeat. "She's safe where she is, and the house can't be traced back to the club. I won't be going there ever again. Couldn't stand to place a foot in it." My eyes meet his, in return he just stares.

CHAPTER FOURTEEN

Marc…

I heard Drum loud and clear when he told me I have to leave Heart's lovely house. The place that's helped me feel safe and secure. The out-of-the-way home where no one could find me. Now I've got to rent somewhere myself and have my name and address listed on records.

Parking the Suzuki next to its stablemate, I leave the garage and enter the house via the door that connects to the kitchen. My head feels heavy, two days of hard riding having taken their toll. Sure, Drummer told me to me to find new accommodation, but that means I've got to pour over available and affordable places to rent, and that's not going to happen overnight. I'm not going to pack and move out when my only option is to live on the streets like someone who's homeless, even if that is what I am. Surely even he must realise it's going to take me some time to sort out somewhere new.

It's not that I don't understand or appreciate his reasoning, but for the past few months, Heart's been my friend, and I've not really thought of him as a member of an outlaw motorcycle gang. But now he's being accepted back into the fold, if I want to hold on to my job, I do need to keep my distance. If he let anything slip, it would be my duty to report it.

But I didn't do my duty in the Demon Sons' clubhouse.

I condoned, by default, what I suspected was going on in the basement. They had hardly taken the men down there for a friendly chat. Haven't I already crossed that line? How can I be a good cop if I let things like that slide? Or even be prepared to go into a situation with guns blazing. *I killed a man and watched others murdered in front of me.* The first time I've ever pointed and used a gun in earnest against a living breathing human being. *But it saved Heart.*

I dragged my feet as I reluctantly left the hospital, feeling I was leaving my only friend in the world, and without saying goodbye. I wanted to stay, to see Heart make a recovery with my own eyes. I'd had to plead for Drummer to allow me to wait around long enough to make sure he regained consciousness. Over the past few months, Heart seems to have become a big part of my life, and now, as quickly as a switch being thrown, I'm no longer allowed to have any contact with him.

My head warns me it might be for the best if I was letting him get too close. I wouldn't be feeling this loss so deeply if I hadn't begun to get feelings. Maybe it's all for the better.

Wearing my sensible hat, Drummer had done exactly the right thing. Law enforcement regards anyone in a one-percenter MC as criminals, whether or not they've been charged with criminal activity or have done time. Unless I was officially sanctioned to infiltrate the group, my association with any of them would be open to question. And, if I had continued my friendship with Heart, the club would always have treated me with suspicion, and I'd have been unable to convince them I wasn't a plant.

I'd have been the first one to get the blame if something went wrong. I've already seen how they treat enemies of the club.

I hadn't missed how the normally easy-going VP had looked at me. It wasn't with the air of someone who wanted to be my friend.

But I want to know how Heart's getting on. I want to hear about Amy. I want to be included in his life in some small way. I freeze. That's why I don't get involved with people. When they are no longer there, it leaves too big a hole.

I close my eyes and rest my head, and immediately see Heart's face in front of me. We've barely spoken face-to-face, and yet I'm going to miss him. It feels like part of my life has been taken away.

The heel of my hand slaps against my forehead. *Don't be so stupid, woman.* You were there when Heart needed you, now he's moved on. It's time to focus on getting back to full fitness and returning to normal, going back to work and doing your job. *But can I ever be the same now I've sided with criminals?*

Going back to work and dealing with the likes of Garza and Reynolds. Now isn't that an uplifting thought?

After drinking wine and popping a couple of painkillers, I go to bed in the room that had been prepared for a man. This is such a comfortable, homey house, I'll feel sad leaving it.

Forcing myself to put my injured friend out of my mind, the next couple of days I spend looking through ads and trawling the rental agencies. But I've been spoiled, and the likes of the house I'm in is way out of reach of what I can afford. Having once been attacked in my own home, I pay particular attention to security, nothing too close to the street so another car could pass by. And I need a garage, of course, so an apartment is out.

Three days after I returned from LA, I hear the sound of Harleys coming up the street. For a moment my heart leaps, but of course it's not Heart. When I left him, he was unable to get out of the hospital bed, let alone ride. No, neither one of the two riders pulling up outside is the person I want most to see. The opposite in fact, it's the least.

The only reason why Drummer, president of the Satan's Devils MC is riding up to the house, must be to forcibly evict me from the house. He's even brought a man with him to help. The thought makes me giggle. I must have impressed him if he can't handle me on his own.

He bangs on the door instead of using the bell.

Opening it, I hold up my hand, palm pointing toward him. "I know, Drummer. I'm sorry I've outstayed my welcome. I've been trying to find somewhere else—"

"Invite me in. We need to talk."

"Look, if you've come to kick me out, I'll just grab my things and go stay at a hotel or something."

He stares but says nothing, the steely cold grey of his eyes makes me shiver. This isn't my house, and he isn't my friend, so I don't think I've got any option. I step aside. He nods and beckons to the man on the other bike. *Safety in numbers.* Even the prez needs a witness when talking to the law.

I walk over to one of the couches and stand behind it, my hand on the back. "I can leave today."

"You're not going anywhere."

What?

As my eyebrow rises he adds, "Not yet, anyway. Been talking to Heart. He reckons you need protection, and he reminded me this house is rented under a shell name. So you can stay here as long as you like. Heart won't be coming back here, so for all intents and purposes, you're the new tenant."

That won't work. "I can't pay, Drummer. I don't know what the rent is, but it's certainly more than I can afford." I bite my lip, remembering the level of rent of the shabbier properties I've been looking at.

"Club owes you for what you did for our brother. He could have died twice over if it wasn't for you. We'll accept payment the same as what you were paying at your old place."

"That's too generous." My eyes have gone wide at the offer I'm having difficulty processing.

Unlike me, who remains standing, Drummer sits down. The other biker stands by the door, hands clasped behind his back.

For a moment I have the wild thought that he's there to stop me escaping.

Drummer stretches his arms out to either side, his hands resting on the top of the other couch, his legs bent at the knee and splayed wide. He gives me that look again, the one that means I work hard to suppress a shudder. I wonder if it's one I can perfect when interviewing suspects.

"Heart said a few things. Such as you looking into matters you might not have been supposed to. You want to explain that to me?"

Knowing this won't be a quick conversation, I move around to the front of the couch and sit down opposite him, appreciating the irony in a cop being questioned by a suspected felon. I run my hands over my face, ready to curb my tongue, but knowing he'll already know everything I spilled to Heart. I sigh. "Archer is guilty. But I can't prove it. I went looking for something to prove I'm right."

"Let it drop. Guilty or innocent, the man's dead. Won't make no difference to Crystal or Heart."

"I know it doesn't alter what happened, but it should still matter. We should be able to identify the man who ran them off the road." I frown. I may have slid a little, but I'm a good cop and hate loose ends.

"Your sergeant told you to leave it alone?"

I nod. "Sergeant Reynolds, yes. And my new partner," my face twists, showing what I think of him, "Garza. Before I was hurt, I got the impression Garza was watching me. Stopping me from looking into things too deeply."

"So you continued to do your research in your own time on your own."

I nod. "Yes, I was examining all the files."

"Using your work computer and your work database."

I look up, surprised. "I don't think I told Heart that."

"It's the only thing that makes sense. The only way someone could know what you were doing." Drum sits forward. "Must admit, Marcia, my initial reaction was for you to take this through the proper channels to the police."

"I don't know who to trust."

"I figured that." He taps his fingers on his thighs. "Then Heart told me you were asking about Satan's Devils involvement."

Again my face twists, and my cheeks redden. "Probably shouldn't have mentioned that," I admit. My eyes flit to the man guarding the door.

"Why?" Drummer brings my attention back to him.

"Why?"

"Why finger us?" He gazes at me intently, as if he'd be able to catch me out in a lie.

My head's fuzzy, I put my hands up to my face.

"Well?"

I lift my head. "I'm not being evasive, Drummer. I've got a skull fracture, remember? Some things from that night… The stuff I was looking through, it's fuzzy and I don't recall anything that makes much sense. But I've got the feeling I was making progress. I remember Slick's name." I stand up and start to pace. Drummer keeps quiet as I try and figure it out. *Why had I targeted the Satan's Devils? Why had I remembered the name Slick? What led me to him?*

Shaking my head, I stop and turn around. "I'm sorry, Drum, I can't remember. I… Hang on." Through the mist something's becoming clearer. "Yes. Archer." I swing around, now animated. "Archer had done something which made me suspicious. Archer had… Archer." Suddenly it hits me like a light bulb going off. "Archer had filed a report on a missing person, but the thing is, I don't think she's missing," I say triumphantly as it comes back to me.

"Who was missing, or not, as the case may be, darlin'?"

"Jayden," I breathe out. "Jayden Greenway."

Drummer goes deathly still. If I thought his eyes were cold

before, they are glacial now. I've said something that he really doesn't like.

I continue thinking out loud. "I was going to go and visit her mother to see what was going on—"

Suddenly he's on his feet, his hand wrapping almost painfully around the back of my neck as he turns my head up to face him, and I get that intense stare head-on. "You ain't gonna see anyone. You're gonna keep out of anything that's not your fuckin' business. And right now, you're on sick leave. So even police business isn't yours."

Would I find a Satan's Devils connection if I went looking? Not one to back down, I try to meet his gaze with a steely one of my own. "What are you hiding, Drummer?"

He huffs a mirthless laugh, then abruptly releases me. He starts to pace, shaking his head as his feet touch the ground. Suddenly he stops, and his face turns toward me. "For a cop, you can be pretty stupid, darlin'."

Of course I bristle. "I just want to do my job."

"It ain't your job at the moment." Another shake, and then he goes on, "You fingered Slick for the bomb maker. I'll tell you this now, if Slick built two bombs, one that destroyed a house and one that was thrown into yours, he'd make damn certain that he left no calling card. The explosives would have been different. Slick knows his trade."

He's admitting to nothing, but has given me food for thought.

"What you need to do is use that fuckin' head on your shoulders. If the explosive was the same, who, apart from the bomb maker, could know how to build it to the same specifications? And who would benefit?"

"Apart from the bomb maker? Who you're suggesting can't be Slick, as he's too clever."

Drum raises his eyes to the ceiling and then gives me a sad look as though I'm a child. Making me jump, he barks out,

"Think, woman! Fuckin' think! Who knew the same explosives were used, the same detonator and timer?"

"Garza? He was the one who told me."

He nods as he would to a child who'd gotten the answer to a math problem right. "And how would he know?"

"The forensic evidence." That's an obvious one. My teeth worry my lip. There's something I'm missing, and all this talking is making my head pound. Then it dawns on me what he's saying. "The police would have the information as how to make another bomb similar to the first."

"Fuckin' got it at last."

Now I'm the one shaking my head. "They'd go to all that trouble to get rid of me?"

"You've got on the wrong side of someone, darlin'."

"And they want to make it look like the same person who killed Archer had killed me." That they hadn't succeeded was down to luck, and that I'd been doing the research they tried to stop me doing. If I hadn't been so engrossed that night I'd have been in bed, and would now be dead. I breathe out the words as I say the unthinkable, "Garza and Reynolds?"

"They're the ones you've fingered." Now I get a look of sympathy. "If you won't leave things alone, you've got to be very clever from here on in, Marcia. I've told you to stop what you're doing, but I think you're too pig-headed to do that."

I plop down on a chair and put my head in my hands. I knew Garza had been watching me carefully, and Reynolds is protecting Archer's memory. But to cold-bloodedly plan to kill me? *Could I see them doing that?* But Drummer has a point, and looking at it his way makes one hell of a lot more sense than anything I've come up with. Unless he's just trying to put up a smokescreen to hide the Satan's Devils' involvement. I shiver. They hadn't killed me, but that didn't mean they wouldn't try again. Is Drummer setting out red herrings for me? Trying to get me to follow false trails?

I raise my eyes and find he's standing in front of me. "Or you're trying to redirect me away from your club."

I haven't angered him. The opposite. He lifts one corner of his mouth in the approximation of a smile.

"If I tell you I'm putting a prospect here to watch over you, you'll think I'm doing that to keep tabs on you, but it's for your protection, darlin'. Least I can do for you, seeing as all you did for Heart."

And with that parting shot which I'm still trying to interpret, he leaves.

CHAPTER FIFTEEN

*H*eart…

I've been back at the clubhouse a few days now. My body is slowly healing, but it will take a bit more time until I'm mobile again. Today's the first day I'm attending church, ignominiously using Wraith's old lady Sophie's wheelchair that she'd kept in case she ever needed it.

Last time I was injured I was consumed by anger at having my freedom of movement taken away, as well as the love of my life. This time I'm grateful for the support that's being given to me, and grateful that for all the hurt the Demon Sons inflicted, with the exception of my missing finger, everything else will eventually heal. Of course I'm frustrated, but I'm not taking it out on my brothers, appreciating that if they hadn't come to my rescue, or had gotten there later, I'd be dead.

My normal chair's been moved aside to allow me to sit at the table, but because my hands are still bandaged, Beef's continuing in the secretary role.

I'd been worried how my brothers would greet me, apologies for all on my lips. But before I could utter them, they'd dismissed my concerns. Despite my crimes, all have forgiven me. I'd done my penance and had now returned. Almost six months to the day that I left, I'm attending my first church. Despite my current physical limitations, it feels good to be back, to be part of the club once again.

After Prez bangs the gavel to get our attention, his eyes linger on me, crinkling as he gives one of his rare smiles. "Good to see you here, Brother. I know you've been back a while, but not to church. So let me say it officially. Welcome home."

I raise my chin. "Fuckin' good to be back." I let my eyes fall on each man at the table, returning their nods and grins. "Now we're all together, I want to say this publicly. Fuckin' sorry for everything I did, the way I treated y'all." I pause to emphasise the sincerity of my words. "I'll never fuckin' let you down again, brothers."

Wraith raises his hand. "I'll speak for us all, Brother. What happened to you was so fuckin' hard. Not surprising you went off the rails. There's nothing to forgive. It's fuckin' great to see you back where you belong."

Giving him a chin jerk, I convey my silent thanks for his words.

"Right. First order of the day."

As Drummer leads us through the usual business, I listen and contribute where I can, feeling at this moment I've really come home. When we've sorted out what's going on with all the businesses, Prez turns to me and waves toward the wheelchair.

"How are you doing, Heart? What's the prognosis?" He already knows, this is my chance to fill everyone else in.

"Those fuckin' wannabe bikers were inept in everything they did. My left leg, which was weakened had to be re-pinned, but the break in my right was pretty clean."

Peg swears. "Not how we do it. Fuckin' amateurs."

Everyone laughs. Christ, I'm fucking glad they couldn't even get a torture right. But they'd done enough to reduce me to the current broken state that I'm in.

"Doctors reckon everything will heal in another month or so. Will need physical therapy of course."

"I'll help with that," our sergeant-at-arms offers. He means working me in the gym we've got. I nod my thanks, remembering how he'd gotten Sophie up and out of this wheelchair. If anyone can do it, he'll be able to do the same for me. Oh, I doubt he'll go easy on me, but I'm determined to work with him. I want to be up walking, *riding*, as soon as I can.

"In the meantime, we can arrange you a new ride," Prez announces, seeming to read my mind.

"What happened to Adam's?" The last time I saw it, it was still parked at the Demon Sons' clubhouse.

"Prospects picked it up and brought it back here. Now what do you fancy, Heart? Had time to think?"

The club's being generous, returning to their original plan of the club paying to replace the bike totalled in the crash which killed Crystal. But I've got other ideas. Me and Adam's bike had worked well as a team. I wait for the various suggestions to die down. "Prez, if it's okay with my brothers, I'd like to keep riding Adam's. Sort of got used to it while I was on the road." Looking around, I see no signs of dissent. "It's only a single seater, might keep the bitches from getting ideas."

That makes everyone laugh.

"Good fuckin' idea, Brother. Might fit one to mine. Fuckin' hangarounds keep on about me taking them for a ride." Joker's looking as though he's only just thought of that solution.

Lady bumps fists with him. "Might do that myself."

Prez is staring at me, and I wait for his answer. After a moment he grins. "Reckon Adam would have liked the bike to go to a good home. If there's no disagreement, I'll take it, that's settled."

"Just try to keep it shiny side up," Blade says drily.

Slick takes out his smokes, and Blade snatches the pack, making me grin and remember another enforcer in another club. He offers one to me, but I shake my head. I'd only started smoking at the beginning of my journey, and with a couple of weeks off the poison, feel no need to go back. I notice Drummer looking at me approvingly.

The respect of my brothers was something I'd lost. It overwhelms me that I'm starting to regain it. But there's still a long way to go. I've caught them watching me carefully at times, as if wondering if anything is going to set me off. And I've rightly gained the reputation of being an impatient patient. Something I'm consciously trying to control.

Blade lights up and inhales. As he blows out smoke his eyes fix on me and narrow. "What's the story with the cop?"

I knew it was coming. I'd broken club rules by speaking to Marc one-on-one, and on more than one occasion. *What punishment are they going to give me?*

"What I want to know," Blade breaks off to take a drag then continues, "is in any of your cosy little chats, did you talk about club business?"

I can answer that easily. "No."

Blade looks over at Peg, then at the VP and Prez. He inclines his head, passing the floor to Drummer.

"We'll take your word for that, Brother." Drummer's eyes scan the room. "I'm comfortable from talking to both Heart and the cop that their conversations were kept on the personal side and out of our business to the greater extent. They didn't discuss the club, except for the puzzle about who threw explosives into her house." His stare is still making sure we're all paying attention. "I think I've convinced her we're well clear of that."

Blade nods at him, then takes over again. "Whatever it was between you ends now, Heart. No more communication. She's a fuckin' cop and we're bikers. Not taking a chance on any more friendly conversations."

I knew that was coming. "Already had this out with Drum, Blade. Crystal's the only woman that I ever wanted to be mine, and that ain't changing just because she's no longer around. Marc helped me get through a bad situation, but that's all there is to it." I'm telling them what I've always known, but the image of a blond woman in my hospital room, her eyes full of concern that comes to my mind so easily, remind me I'll miss her, even though she was just a friend.

Part of me feels guilty. She's as lost as I am. As good as she was for me, I reckon I'd started paying it back in kind. I'm sure there's more I could have done for her. I try to make them understand the solid she did me. "Marc saved my life. If it wasn't for her, I might not be here. She pulled me back from the brink." I'll never forget that day in Death Valley. While I'd been laid up, I'd checked it out and found there can indeed be odd pockets of reception dotted around the desert, but what a coincidence that I happened to be in one when I received that call. Someone must have been guiding me, there's no other explanation for it. *And the coyotes*. She saved me. I shiver, thinking how closely I'd skirted the edge between this world and the next, and how I'd nearly come to being pulled over. It's then I notice Mouse looking at me, as if he can read my mind.

Tongue shifts guiltily in his chair. "We should have been there for you, Brother."

"Don't go there, Tongue. You had no choice. You'd have been within your rights to send me out in bad standing, or fuck it, take my patch *and* my life. I disrespected the club and would have deserved any punishment. You went easy on me." As others still look uneasy, I sit as far forward as I can. "Look at me. I'm back. I might not be the Heart you remember, but I'm the man who's undertaken a journey, a man who's learned about himself on the way. You did the best that you could. I'm not accusing any brother of doing wrong or not doing enough to help me. All I'm saying is that when I needed it, Marc was there to pull me back up." Sometimes I wonder whether Crystal had a hand in that, somehow, from somewhere, making sure support was at hand.

"And for that, Brother, we're helping her," Prez announces, and my eyes shoot to him. "But there are strings attached. You're to have no contact with her, or if in the unlikely circumstance that you have to, it will be with the lawyer or another brother tagging along."

That's fine by me. There was nothing between us that anyone else shouldn't hear.

"You didn't want it anymore, and its security's the best. I've seen her and talked to her. The outcome is, she'll be staying in what was your house. It's in her name now. We'll help her out by letting her off half of the rent. And, for now, I'm keeping a prospect on her."

My eyes widen then my brow furrows. "You checking up on her?"

Prez smooths his hand over his beard. "No. Though it might be useful to know what she does. But no, Heart. I don't like that someone tried to kill her and failed. Chances are they might try again."

Blade doesn't look convinced. He frowns. "Don't like spending club resources on protecting a cop."

Drum pauses his hand and his eyes narrow. "Hear what you're saying, Blade, but leaving aside what she does as a job, playing her part in bringing our brother home is a fuckin' good favour she's done for the club. Now I'm prepared to vote on this if there's any dissention."

"I'd vote we do what we can." Wraith rests his forefinger against his nose. "She brought our brother home."

Slick lifts his chin. "I like her, Prez, if we ignore what she is. The way she rode that bike and caught up with us."

"Damn good-for-nothing Suzuki rat."

"Left you for dust, Peg."

Peg snarls.

Yup. Fucking good to be back. I can't hide my grin. "I'm sorry I missed that." That earns me a glare from the sergeant-at-arms. "You know my thoughts, I personally owe her. If she doesn't get club backing, I'll find some way to help her myself. Keeping well in the background," I add quickly, seeing the look on Drummer's face.

"I owe her my thanks, Prez," Slick continues as if he hadn't been interrupted. "Got me my last Demon. Felt fuckin' fantastic to go home to Ella and tell her all those fuckers were dead."

In my opinion, no one was more deserving of a painful demise than that sadistic Scratch. I can't resist, having heard all the stories. "You cut off his dick, Slick?"

As Slick stays dumb and simply winks, Mouse starts to speak. "I'm happy for us to help, Prez. Slick and I thought about going over there to discuss security. She'll be getting a new laptop, and I'll be checking to see whether any tracking software is on it," he grins, "and giving her some lessons about staying safe while she's browsing."

Drummer looks thoughtful. "Can't have her drawing more attention to herself." He looks at me. "I tried to dissuade her, but she seems intent she can't let this drop. Yeah, Mouse, you make sure she can hide her tracks."

That's something that worries me. "Prez, I don't think she'll be able to help herself. She wants to put criminals away. If she thinks her partner and her sergeant are dirty, she won't stop until she's proved what's going on."

"She got a death wish or something?" Peg growls.

I think deep down she might have, and I understand the reason for that very well. I close my eyes briefly, then reopen them.

Prez is tapping the desk with his fingers. "What's worrying me is that link back to the other killings the night Archer met Satan. Flipside of the coin of helping her is that we can keep an eye on what she's doing."

"If she gets too close, we could take her out." Blade speaks while using his knife to clean his nails.

If I could get to my feet, I would. I can only bang my injured hands down as hard as I can onto the table. "We ain't fuckin' doing that!"

"You gonna find some other way of stopping her, Heart? If what she finds can hurt the club?" Prez pulls me up short.

Glancing at his raised brow, I just return his stare. Whatever he's thinking, he must know I'm never going to agree to having her killed. After a moment he tunnels his hands through his hair. "She ain't got a reporting line that she knows will support her. If we're right and her sergeant's dirty, he won't want to know who questioned Archer, as it might get out exactly what he'd been doing there." To rape young kids he means. "They won't want to question the club."

"A couple of cops can't take out the Devils." Joker laughs.

Peg glances down the table. "No, but if they're in league with the Herreras…"

Now I'd been in a coma when the club came face-to-face with Tucson's crime family. From what I heard, it was a cordial arrangement. But I'm not so stupid as to think that couldn't change at any time.

Drummer's frowning, his brow tight. "Heart's Marc has brought some things to our attention. Without her curiosity we'd have remained in the dark. We can't afford not to take them seriously. Firstly, she mentioned Jayden, and that Archer reported her missing." I glance at Slick, but he's obviously already been prewarned. "That might be an issue that died with the man."

"Not taking any chances, Prez. I've got eyes on her all the time."

"No fuckin' change there, Paladin. She's barely ever out of your sight." Dollar grins, sparking chuckling and lewd comments around the table. Since I've been back I've seen them together, many times, always in some game of pool or whatever. But I'd been out of it and then away when everything had gone down and still don't know the extent of the relationship between Paladin and the young teenager.

"Still got three fuckin' years," Prez points at Paladin. I promise myself I'll ask a few questions and find out what they're talking about.

Slick glares and the chatter dies down. Then he coughs and takes charge of the situation. "As Paladin said, we've got her covered. Don't know if it's a worry or not now Archer's dead, but not taking any fuckin' chances with Ella's sister."

Road, who'd apparently been patched in a few months back, waves his hand. "Any extra help you need, I'm there."

Slick thanks him.

Drum raps his hand again. "Then there's the problem of the two dirty cops, or at least, two that we know of. Who's keeping them in their pocket, and why? Think you can look into that, Mouse?"

Mouse looks at him confidently. "I'll have a fuckin' good try." He glances at me. "Your woman might be right, Heart. There might be something if she keeps going through the records, linking cases which haven't been tied up. I'm gonna set up some software so she can keep digging without leaving her footprint behind."

I start to open my mouth to refute that the implication that she's mine, but don't get the chance.

"Sounds like a plan." Prez looks pleased for a moment, then frowns. "Need to know who's paying them, and to do what. Mouse, happy if you stay close and keep her onside. Encourage her to share what she finds with us."

"I've got ways, Prez. This time I'll be the one doing the tracking."

I clench my jaw. It should be me that's close to her, not my brother, but they're keeping her well out of my way. As I've already agreed, I can't protest now.

Blade spins his knife, then looks up. "As long as we're not the target, should we care what she's doing?"

Prez nods. "Yeah, Blade. I get your point, but for now, we can't rule out that we're not. And Heart, I hear what you said. But she's a cop, and if she gets a hint of something we're involved in, do you really think your relationship with her is gonna make her stop?"

I stay quiet, unable to reassure him.

"They're trying to link the explosion on Marc's house to the explosion at Lucas's, where Archer was killed." Slick is also looking concerned. And he would. He made the bomb that incinerated Lucas's house. "I don't much like the thought of fingers being pointed at me."

Marvel tosses me a look of apology. "If this detective of Heart's has already connected Slick to the bombing, isn't it more of a risk keeping her breathing?"

Again, I wish I could fuckin' stand. But I can do nothing, and a growl emanates out of my mouth. If I could use my legs, Marvel would feel my fists.

"Marvel's got a point." And now Shooter's joining in. "Got to think of the club, Prez."

Now Viper's opening his mouth, but Drummer bangs the gavel. "Shut the fuck up." All mouths snap closed.

He stares around the table. "Firstly, she doesn't *know* that Slick built the first bomb. She's only going through the list of possible suspects, and of course, we'd be near to the top." He pauses to let that sink in. "Secondly, the bitch came with us to LA. She witnessed what went down at the Demon Sons' club. Fuck it, she took one of them out herself. We couldn't have found Heart without her coming to us, and might not have gotten to him in time had she not helped us out. Bitch put her job on the line… *for the fuckin' club*." He pauses to let that sink in. When he's satisfied we've taken on board his meaning, he continues with a glance toward me. "*I* trust her. From LA alone, she's got evidence to pull this club under, but she hasn't used it."

"Yet," Viper grumbles.

"She wants to put the bad guys away." I remember what she told me.

"And we're not the fuckin' bad guys?" Rock's eyes widen.

"No. Not in her eyes."

"Fuck, Prez. We must be doing something wrong." Now everyone laughs.

Drummer's looking at me strangely, as if something I'd said had struck a chord. Then he focuses his steely eyes on the rest of my brothers. "Then let's help her put the bad guys away, cops or whoever they are." After a short pause he continues, "I hear what you all say, brothers. Club vote needed to continue to keep Detective Marcia Hannah out of harm's way. Peg?"

The sergeant-at-arms gives a thoughtful aye. It's not a quick vote, and one of two look like they're wavering, but in the end it's all ayes, and Beef records it.

Leaving my personal investment aside, I must admit it's a strange day when the club votes to extend their protection to a cop.

arc...

"Detective Hannah. Are you giving me your full attention?"

Guiltily, I bring my eyes back to Sergeant Reynolds. I haven't really been listening to all the excuses as to why after another two months' recuperation he still doesn't consider me fit enough to return to my job, despite a doctor's letter declaring me fit. Yeah, I still get the occasional headache which can be debilitating when they hit, but little more than anyone who suffers from migraines. Most days I visit the gym and am probably the most in shape that I've ever been.

"What about putting me on light duties if I can't do my full job?" Though, with Mouse's help, I've got a lot to occupy me. I am getting bored staring at the same four walls and having little to no interaction with other human beings.

"I want you to see another doctor—an occupational therapist."

Why doesn't he take the word of my own?

"It's only out of concern for you, Hannah. Please understand that. I don't want you back until you're ready."

What can I say? My hands are tied, so all I can do is agree to meet with the professionals he's suggested who, I suspect, will say what he wants to hear. It's obvious there's something other than concern in his desire to keep me away from active duty.

Strangely enough, I've had no support at all from the department, either investigating the incident that almost killed me or during the time I've been recuperating. It's only due to outlaw bikers that I can feel safe in my own home, and, having received instruction from Mouse, can safely delve into the police files without leaving a sign of what I've been doing. I was amused to discover the software he installed was developed by a sheikh's wife who's apparently an expert hacker.

What I'm working on could get me fired, but as my eyes fall on the seedy countenance of my sergeant who, I've become more and more convinced is as dirty as they come, I feel no remorse. As I've been rapidly learning, sometimes justice can't be served by playing by the rules.

"I'm sorry, Sergeant." I put my hand to my head.

As expected, he takes my gesture to mean I'm in pain, and a justification for the news he's given me today.

I'm dismissed shortly after with insincere wishes for my continued recovery, and as I pause outside his closed office door, I wonder whether he was behind the attempt to kill me. It seems unbelievable, but I can't think why he's still blocking my report about Archer. And as for my erstwhile ex-partner, while I've been on sick leave, the remains of Archer were buried with full honours. Now that was a ceremony that would have been interesting to attend, just to see who turned up.

I leave the building, go to the parking lot and get on my bike, picking up my shadow soon after. I know Drummer arranged for me to be followed for my protection, but damn it, it restricts what I can and can't do. Wherever I go, Drummer will get wind of it.

But he's forgotten what my rat bike is capable of.

A Harley's got good speed on the straight, but even so mine beats it hands down. As for the cornering? I can almost lay mine down. I take the prospect, Hyde, on a ride to remember, hoping he'll give up rather than come off his bike. Soon he's far back in my rear view, and only seconds later, nowhere in sight.

Now riding more carefully, constantly checking behind me, I drive down town to the business district, pulling up outside an eight-storey building which looks like any other office complex. But this isn't anything so innocuous, this is where the Herreras' legitimate side of their business is conducted. Tucson's major crime family with strong connections with Los Zetas, the cartel. Perhaps I'm being stupid coming here on my own, as Archer was related to the Herrera family, but Leonardo Herrera has a reputation for being, even in his decidedly crooked sidelines, a straight arrow.

Backing my bike into the kerb, I switch off the engine, pausing for a second to again question the wisdom of my choice coming here alone without the benefit of a trusted partner. But I've gotten frustrated, having gone as far as I can with my investigation. Now I need answers from the horse's mouth. Setting my features into a look of determination, I enter the innocuous looking reception area.

"Can I help you?"

As I'd been meeting my boss today, I've dressed as neatly as I could while having to accept limitations due to my mode of transportation. I'm wearing black slacks, teamed with a white blouse and black jacket. Over my arm I carry my leather jacket and helmet. I probably look a mixture of things. Putting my motorcycle attire at my feet, I stand tall and smooth back my hair, which is tied into a respectable bun.

"I'd like to see Mr Herrera, please. Leonardo Herrera." I add the last, not wanting to be fobbed off with anyone lower than the head of the family.

"Do you have an appointment?"

I shake my head, get out my police ID and hand it over. She examines it for a second, then turning away places a call.

When she turns back, she's got a look of triumph on her face.

"Mr Herrera has back-to-back meetings today. His PA suggests you make an appointment for another time."

A not unexpected setback, though my identification would normally get me seeing the person I want. Herrera probably considers himself way above the law. "When will he be available?"

She consults a screen. "Not for another couple of weeks. It appears he's going out of town."

I can't insist it's police business, and I can't make waves. The last thing I need is for my visit here today to be reported back to Sergeant Reynolds. Dismissed, I leave with as much dignity as I can muster, get back on my bike, and point it toward home.

I get only halfway before half a dozen motorcycles swarm up and surround me. The sight of the Satan's Devils cuts both reassures and worries me. *What are they doing here?*

Boxed in as I am, I've no option but to go with them, but they don't deviate from the route I was originally on, and soon it becomes obvious what they're doing. *They're escorting me home.*

I've absolutely no idea why they're here or how they knew where I'd be. Perplexed, I drive up to the garage, opening it with the remote. As some of the other bikes peel off, Drummer parks up beside me. "Get your bike inside," he snarls. He turns to beckon at his VP.

The garage is a double one, and there's room for both him and Wraith to park alongside my two bikes. As the door rolls down, all the bikes are out of sight except for that of the prospect waiting outside.

He pushes me into the house, and I'm still confused, particularly as I feel the waves of anger rolling off the MC president. Okay, so I intentionally lost his prospect, but would that amount to such a crime? His anger is palpable, his cheeks red, his mouth pursed, and his eyes... I suppress a shiver. I'm a police officer, he's an outlaw. He shouldn't be able to intimidate me.

As soon as we're in the kitchen, his hand grips my shoulder

and he swings me around so fast I have to put my hand on the counter to stop myself falling.

"What the fuck did you think you were doing?" He growls so fiercely I'm afraid of his bite. He grasps my other shoulder, and with both his hands shakes me. "You're a fuckin' idiot."

My eyes go wide, and I bite my lip, not understanding what I'm supposed to have done wrong. I glance at Wraith, but he's looking equally furious. Hyde, who's also come in, looks a combination of embarrassed and angry.

"You don't even know, do you?" He releases me sharply and runs his hands through his hair. "I've got two options now. Throw you to the fuckin' wolves or bring you in under our protection."

Finding my voice, I point to the front of the house. "I thought I already was. You've given me this prison with a prospect as a guard—"

"Fuckin' lot of use he was."

Flicking my eyes toward Hyde, who's looking down at his feet, I jump to his defence. "My bike's got better handling."

He waves his hand in dismissal. "You really don't have a clue, do you? Or have you a death wish?"

I still don't know where I've gone wrong. "Look, Drummer, I went to see if I could talk to Leonardo Herrera."

"And painted a huge great fuckin' target on your back!" He just stares for a moment. "You were supposed to just stick to looking at the files, not going out investigating yourself."

"I didn't get anywhere. I didn't speak to anyone. Herrera was too busy to talk to me."

"And thank fuck for that!" He looks around as if preferring to look any way but at me, before he turns back. "It's a volatile situation at the moment. You could have gotten yourself killed."

"I'm a police officer."

"You think carrying a badge protects you? Christ, woman."

It should. I'm one of the good guys.

I go into the living room, placing my jacket and helmet on

the table by the door. "Drummer, I'm grateful for what you've done and the help you're giving me. But I need to do my job—"

The sound of machine gun fire reaches me only an instant before Drummer grabs me and throws me on the floor, covering me with his body. I start to shake as the shots ring out. I should have been more careful after the first attempt on my life, but I really didn't believe I was still under threat.

It seems an age, but probably could be measured in seconds until the shooting stops, and there's the sound of a vehicle speeding away.

"Now will you fuckin' believe me, woman? Stay the fuck down."

But as Drummer gets to his feet, I follow, getting to mine. I can't cower on the floor, I'm a professional. Wraith and Hyde are brushing themselves off.

"Fuck, Heart will have his time cut out keeping you under control."

And while I don't understand his explanation, my eyes widen as I look around the room, and then at the glass in the windows, which are incredibly starred but still intact. "Drummer?" I indicate where I'm looking.

"Bulletproof glass," he explains, almost absentmindedly. "Heart wanted every protection for his wife and daughter."

And thank goodness for that. It's quite possibly the second time my life has been saved. Realising how close my call with death could have been, my legs start to shake and I drop down onto the couch. *Someone tried to kill me. Again.* It's only because Drummer allowed me to stay in this house that I'm alive and unharmed. If I'd had a normal house without such safety features, I could even now be dead or fatally wounded.

Drummer's talking fast on the phone. In my dazed state I pick up a few words. 'Crash truck', 'SUV', and 'as fast as you can'.

I've got to do something. But Drummer's quicker and

snatches my own phone out of my hand. "What the fuck are you doing?"

"Calling it in." I look up, confused. That's exactly what I should do, isn't it?

Drummer's face softens, and he sits down beside me. "You're in my world now, sweetheart. We have to rely on ourselves."

"But my colleagues—"

"You know any you can trust?"

He seems to be waiting as I quickly run through everyone in the department. I'm certain they're not all dirty—surely I'd know?—but eventually I shake my head. Due to my habit of not letting people in close, I don't go out for after-work drinks with the team, or make time to socialise with anyone. Could I really swear who to report the shooting to with any conviction they weren't behind it? A rogue tear comes to my eye.

He notices and wipes it away with his thumb. "It's not gonna be easy, not for you or for us. But things are changing and fast. We can't protect you here, that's for certain. Next time, and there will be a next time, however much you want to deny it, they'll come better prepared now they know what they're up against." He points to the windows, now looking like they're covered in spider webs, like a stone breaking against a windscreen. "They might stop a bullet, but not a bomb or a grenade. I can't risk my men to keep watch, so you're coming to the clubhouse, where we can make sure you're safe."

That's unexpected, but he gives me no further time to question his statement. "Go pack your stuff, darlin'. The boys will be here soon, and I don't want to waste time getting back. Need to get you clear of here before we find out how determined they are to take you out."

"I'm on the right track. With the link to the Herreras."

"There are things you don't know, but I'm not discussing it now. Go get packed." As I walk away to the bedroom I'm still using, having refused to move into the master, I pack up the clothes that I'd slowly been replacing.

"Drum? I can't get this all on the bike."

He appears in the doorway. "You won't be riding. We'll get the bikes back on the truck. You're a target now, remember?"

"You going to let my Kawasaki and Suzuki onto the compound?" It's the first thought I've had today that amuses me. I can't hide my grin.

He grimaces. "Can't be as bad as letting in a cop."

I might not have called it in, but surely someone must have reported the sound of gunshots? I wait to hear the comforting sirens and official help that must be on its way, but outside the road is silent. The lack of the noise of my comrades responding is what helps make up my mind. I'm not safe here anymore.

The crash truck arrives, and as I watch my two bikes being loaded, I feel that my life's spinning out of control.

I'd taken up my career as I wanted to work for justice for all. While I had personal experience how the system regularly failed people, I wanted to do my part to make it better. In my previous posting, I'd excelled and received recognition. I'm still not able to understand what's gone wrong for me in what was supposed to be a fresh start and new opportunity to shine in Tucson.

Now, rather than working to put these members of an OMG behind bars, I'm not only agreeing to their protection, but I'm going to be accepting their hospitality. It's getting harder than ever to think of them as criminals and in terms of what my police colleagues would call them, less of an outlaw gang, and as they prefer to be called, a motorcycle club.

My world's done a complete one-eighty.

CHAPTER SEVENTEEN

---

*H*eart...

I pull myself to my feet, putting my weight on the crutches. Seven weeks after Scratch tried his best to dispatch me from this world, I've had the cast removed, and Peg has been brilliant, coming to physiotherapy with me so he knows which muscles to concentrate on while he works me at home. Those parallel bars that were put in for him after he came back from Afghanistan minus half a leg paying dividends for yet another victim.

I'd just finished a punishing session when we got the news that Marc had been visiting Herrera. The fear that went through me was unexpected, and I longed to be with them as I saw my brothers mount up their rides and go to see whatever the fuck was going on.

I'm not much wiser when Peg returns.

"What's happening?"

Peg waves me back down onto the couch and pulls up a chair which he straddles. "We got her home. That's all I know."

Breathing a sigh of relief, I brush back my hair, now thankfully the shaven side has just about grown more or less equal with the other, or enough so it doesn't much show. "What the fuck was she thinking?"

"No idea, man. All we know from Hyde is that she visited her boss this morning, as expected, and then took off on the way back, riding that rat bike of hers like a pro, losing Hyde in the process. Prospect didn't have a fuckin' chance to keep up. Thank fuck Mouse was monitoring her phone and knew where to send us in case we needed to claim a body."

My gut clenches at the thought. "But she's alright?"

"Didn't speak to her, but she seemed unharmed."

"Daddy, Daddy!" a high-pitched voice screams out and then repeats, getting progressively louder. "Daddy!"

My thoughts are interrupted as my daughter runs up to me, being caught in Peg's arms before she knocks into me. "What did we say, Amy?"

She pouts as she looks up at him. "That Daddy's got poorly legs."

"My arms are okay." I reach out and she runs into them. Her smile of delight as I pull her onto my lap still triggers a pang of guilt inside me. I've been back over a month now, and she still seems surprised and delighted every time she comes into the clubhouse and sees me still here. Sam and Drummer have been great. Until I'm healed, I'm staying with them up at their house, helping with Amy as best I can, first from the wheelchair, and now the crutches.

"What you been up to, Trouble?"

She purses her lips, just like Crystal used to do when I annoyed her. More used to it now, the familiar expression makes me want to laugh rather than cry. "My name's not Trouble. It's Amy." I kiss the top of her head, wondering how it is I'm so lucky to have this miracle with me, a part of my wife that I'll protect with my life. I can no longer understand my reasoning when I pushed her away, but constantly vow I'll never leave her again. There's nothing more precious than this little girl.

She's holding out a piece of paper. Taking it, I turn it this way and that. Okay, she hasn't inherited her mother's artistic ability, or if she has, there's no current sign. A frown comes over her face as she turns it in what is apparently the right way up and tells me, "That's your bike."

"Of course it is." I'd been trying my best to do some work on it yesterday, getting help from Slick to give it a service, itching to be able to ride it again. My bike now, no longer Adam's.

Peg, who'd disappeared while I'd been admiring the masterpiece, comes back in. "Drummer's called." Whatever he's heard I can see by the way his brow's pulled down that it isn't welcome. "Your place just got shot up, Heart."

"Fuck!" I can almost hear Crystal's voice in my ear as I cover Amy's ears just a little too late. "Prez and Marc okay?"

"Yeah, thanks to your over-the-top security. Fuck knows what Prez is thinking, but he's bringing her back, along with her fuckin' plastic bikes. Wants me and some brothers to give them an escort and the prospects to take the crash truck for her rides."

I'm reeling from a raft of emotion. First fear that she would have been hurt were it not for my desire to keep my family safe, and second, a leap in my heart that I'll see her again. Having let my brothers down so badly, I'd done as asked and hadn't even picked up the phone to call her. But I'd missed talking to my friend, missed listening to her and hearing her tell me about her day and those fucking bikes. I missed her encouragement, never quite successful in putting her completely out of my mind. Now I'm eager to see her again, and if I could, I'd tan her hide for getting herself into such trouble that the Satan's Devils are having to rescue her.

What the fuck will this mean for the club?

Slick's old lady's sister, fifteen-year-old Jayden, comes over. When she holds out her arms, Amy wriggles to get down. I mouth thanks. Jayden's been fantastic, she's got a way with kids, and when she's not in school she's been helping out with the babies too. I'd found there'd been changes around the club. The room next to the gym that we hadn't done much with has been converted into a nursery.

"You going to help bake?" Jayden crouches down to Amy's level.

"Cookies?" The teenager laughs and takes Amy's hand. "You and your cookies."

I grin. Amy's happy to be taken away. For a second I have a pang that she'll never be baking with her mother, but have come to accept what's done can't be changed. This is my life now, and Amy's. Slowly I'm learning it is possible to move on.

"Head's up, Heart. Prez is ringing Sam to get a room prepared. She'll be staying in Dart's old suite."

That's next to mine. Well, if I'm not up at Drum's house. But it makes sense. Dart's the VP at San Diego now, so his room's unused.

"When we get back, Prez wants everyone in church. Can you send a group text? Should be back in an hour or so."

I can do that. I nod as he leaves, then take out my phone and draft a quick text to the group, then take a note of the replies. It's just under sixty minutes later when I hear the sound of engines cutting as my brothers park outside. Grabbing my crutches I ease myself to my feet, then stand in the middle of the room, anticipating her arrival. Then thinking I'm looking too eager, change my mind and make my way into church.

What would I say to her? How would I act? This woman who'd come to mean so much to me, and who saved my life—not once, but twice? Right now I'm so angry with her, I'm not sure I could control my temper. *She should have been safe.* If she'd just kept her nose to herself. *You can't get all the bad ones, Marc. Not by yourself.* But even without the facts, it's already perfectly clear that's what she's trying to do.

I'm also irate she's involved the club. Prez isn't, and neither are I nor my brothers, the type of men who'd knowingly leave a woman hung out to dry. If she was anyone else, it wouldn't matter, but she's a cop. Now she's going to be here on the inside of a one-percenter club.

I take my seat, drop into it wearily, and lean my crutches up against the desk. One by one my brothers walk in. When Prez appears, he gives me a hard look.

"Who's not here?"

I wave to the empty seats. "Joker and Lady are out on a run, everyone else said they're coming. Road had something to finish up at Angels." After I fucked up my chance and Road was patched in, he was given the job of running Satan's Angels, our strip club.

Drummer kicks his chair out, sits down and leans back, resting his foot on the table. His hands toy with his beard. "Rumour mill working?"

Some nod their heads, some only just arrived shake theirs instead.

Prez looks directly at me. "We all knew Heart cosying up to the po-po could come back and bite us, and Detective Marcia Hannah tugged the tail of the tiger today. After visiting her sergeant and hearing news that she still couldn't do her job officially, she tried to see Leonardo Herrera."

A round of 'what the fucks?' or other variations on the same theme echo through the room.

Drum kicks down his foot, pulls his chair in, and leans his elbows on the table. "Someone shot up the house we're letting her stay in immediately afterward. I was with her. We were saved by the bulletproof glass Heart installed."

"That's why you brought her back?" Blade's frowning. "Wondered what the fuck she was doing here and why you hid her toys."

A small smile plays at Drummer's lips. "Yeah, she wasn't impressed when we put her plastic two-wheeler shit behind the shop. I might have led her to believe we didn't want her contaminating our rides. But if anyone comes calling…"

"I'll get them tarped up and out of sight."

Prez nods his thanks to Blade.

"Where's she now?" Slick's lighting up, and this time it takes more of an effort to turn down the offered smoke.

"Got Sam and the other old ladies setting her up in Dart's suite. Hyde's with them, and with a warning if he lets her out of his sight again he'll never get patched in."

"Never did like the fucker," Slick growls.

"Not having a discussion on Hyde now, Slick. Know you had problems when he first arrived. Give him a few more months."

"Doubt any of us could have kept up with her. That Suzuki all but goes horizontal around corners." Marvel gives his support.

Drum raps on the table. "Friday we were discussing what the fuck's going on with the Herreras. Mouse, any more news?"

Mouse frowns. "Yeah, Prez. Heard chatter the takeover is going ahead. Leonardo will take retirement, and his son, Javier, is stepping up. Doesn't stop there, some of the older lieutenants will be ousted too."

"Out with the old, in with the new. How does this affect us, Prez?"

"No idea, Peg. No fuckin' idea. But my gut feel is, I don't like it. I respected Leonardo, know nothing about the son at all. I don't like being in the fuckin' dark."

"His son wasn't there when we met with them. When we were shutting down the child grooming ring."

"Noted that at the time, Slick. Either he was being sidelined, or he doesn't share the same views as his father."

A fucking bad time for Marc to try to get a meeting with the man at the top. She was lucky to walk out of the building alive. *But they almost got her pretty soon after.*

Wraith seems to be studying his hands, which are clasped in front of him on the table, his face fixed in a frown. Suddenly he looks up. "Should we ask for a meeting once the dust settles?"

The prez covers his face with his palms. After a moment, he draws them down, pulling at the skin under his eyes. "Not sure about that. Until Slick's issues, we never met face-to-face, never had to. We've managed to coexist without stepping on each other's feet."

Slick's scowling. "You don't reckon Javier was part of the child grooming stuff?"

Fuck me. I hope not. Amy and Jayden were targets.

"That's too much of a leap for right now, Slick. But we'll keep the possibility in mind."

Paladin looks like he wants to add something. Drum stays him with a raised hand. "What I do want to discuss is our immediate problem. The fact we've got an enemy in our camp, and how we're going to deal with it."

Beef and Rock murmur something to each other, then Rock looks at me. "He caused the problem, he deals with it."

Prez raises an eyebrow in my direction, but what he says next isn't what I expected. "What we have to acknowledge is, if Heart hadn't gotten involved with Marcia Hannah, both he and her would probably be dead."

"Complete the job. Problem solved." With an evil grin, Blade points his knife toward me.

"Asshole," I spit back.

"Shut up!" Prez waits. "Right, Heart." He's got my attention, those steely grey eyes looking straight into mine. Then he pronounces in all seriousness, "You're gonna take full responsibility for her. Just like her being your ol' lady."

Grabbing my crutches, I pull them toward me. In my shock and horror, I misjudge, and they go crashing to the ground. I manage to pull myself up by balancing my weight on the table. "No fuckin' way." I'm shouting. "Prez. No fuckin' way. Only ol' lady I ever had or want is gone." As he doesn't flinch at the strength in my voice, I lower it and speak in a more reasonable tone. "I can't do it, Prez. I can't disrespect Crystal."

"Hey, you get to fuck her, you lucky bugger." Tongue grabs his junk. "I could do that."

Before I can voice that I've no desire to fuck anybody, Prez glares that glare—the one that normally means you're about to be dead—and Tongue, thank fuck, shuts up. "If she's treated as an ol' lady she doesn't get to know club business." His voice rises and gets louder toward the end. "Is that fuckin' understood?" He lets that sink in before adding, "She's law enforcement, and no one here should forget that. We'll hold you accountable, Heart. You have to own that. You stick to her like glue, vet what she sees and what she does."

"Prez, I can't, I simply can't." He might not actually be telling me to take her as my old lady, but even using the words in the same sentence as her name makes me see red. *That's Crystal's title.*

"You can, and you will. You got involved with her, you brought this on the club. Now it's down to you to make sure it doesn't hurt us." His stare fixes me again, and I can't argue with what he's said. He nods when he realises I know I've no argument to offer. *Except that I don't want an old lady.* "We've put her in the suite next to yours. Whatever arrangement you want to make will be between the two of you. But you watch her, make sure she doesn't poke her nose anywhere it's not wanted. She'll be trying to find out whatever she can."

"Doesn't have to be a cop to do that, Prez. Being female is all that's required." Slick's glum look suggests Ella is inquisitive, but Viper, Bullet, and Wraith's sighs seem to agree.

How the fuck am I going to do this? Treat another woman as my old lady? How long does Drummer think this farce needs to continue?

"As normal, we need to vote in an old lady." His eyes stare at us one by one. "In this case, we're agreeing Heart takes responsibility for Marcia."

There's not much enthusiasm, and a few uncertain looks are thrown my way, but soon everyone agrees.

"I'm not giving her a property patch," I say glumly. As my brothers move on to other business, I stare at the fingers of my left hand. *At least I won't be wearing a ring. That's one thing I can be grateful to the Demon Sons for.*

CHAPTER EIGHTEEN

----

*M*arc…

I've been to the compound on a few prior occasions, but never to see more than the clubroom or Drummer's office. The one time I could have explored, when Archer had somehow fabricated a search warrant, I'd stayed with Drummer, too embarrassed to take part in what was really an excuse for cops to go to town, destroying the possessions of a 'gang' they despised. Half of me knew they were handpicked by Archer and not here because they wanted to uphold the law. No, in part it was getting their own back on men who lived a lifestyle they envied.

Oh, back at the station they'd expressed disgust at club whores on tap, the vast amounts of alcohol found and the drugs that they didn't. Truth didn't matter, rumours abounded that they'd gotten one up on the whoring, drunk, drugged-up to the eyebrows detested bikers. It had fuelled many a conversation for the following week.

I'd seen some of the damage they'd caused to the clubhouse and knew they'd done the same to the living quarters too. I remember Drummer clearly asking me who were the criminals that day? I'd had no answer for him, or none that my job would allow me to put into words.

Now this same compound seems to have become my temporary home.

As soon as we arrived, and I'd seen my bikes unloaded and wheeled away out of sight—heaven forbid anything should sully their Harleys—Drummer had whisked his men away off to a meeting.

As a cop I'd received basic education on bikers, and now I'm about to be thrown into their midst. On the way here, I'd been tempted to question the prospect who'd been driving the crash truck, knowing from my reading the training material what being patched into a one-percenter club usually involves. *Is this one of the clubs where at the initiation ceremony all members urinate on the prospect's cut? Or make prospective members kill someone as part of their induction?* I found myself unable to ask, already thinking it seemed unlikely. It wasn't just that I knew he wouldn't give me the answer, but their cuts looked so clean, I couldn't believe they'd stoop to the first. As for the latter, the clean-cut young biker driving didn't seem like someone who'd kill in cold blood.

Other excerpts come back to me. *They pass their women around. Old ladies earn money on their backs...* Maybe the Satan's Devils are different, or maybe the fear factor amped up during my training sessions was fuelled by the same envy as the cops who'd destroyed the compound that day. Misinformation, making them seem more like the enemy.

The police have problems with the cartels, slave trafficking rings. Organised crime and protection rackets litter our streets along with the day-to-day robberies and violence, yet we still seemed encouraged to focus on biker gangs as our biggest enemy. Nothing in my dealings with the Satan's Devils has to date given me answers to understand why. Oh, they killed the Demon Sons right in front of me, but as I'd also been holding a gun, and Heart had been lying there dying, it hadn't been diffi-cult to determine right and wrong sides.

As I stand just inside the clubroom pondering the rapid change in my circumstances, realising my colleagues couldn't have gotten me to a safe house so fast, I feel the rush of adren-aline fading and go weak at the knees as it starts to sink in the lengths someone is going to kill me. *They shot up the house where I was staying.*

"Hey, you must be Marcia. I'm Sam, Drummer's old lady." I recall meeting her before, but it must be getting on for a year ago now.

I glance up to see a woman carrying a baby in her arms. I'm not surprised to see him wearing a Harley t-shirt. It's definitely a boy, I can tell that from here. Suppressing the normal pang that goes through me, I focus on the woman rather than the child she's holding. "How old?" I ask politely.

"Five months," she replies, planting a loving kiss to his head. "Meet Eli, Drummer's son."

"Hi, Eli." I feel silly speaking to a child, and as he turns my way, there's no doubt to his parentage. Already steely grey eyes look knowingly into me, but then his face splits into a grin and he starts babbling.

"Drummer's asked me to get you settled in. There's a suite been prepared for you in the compound. No, leave your bags. Jekyll? Can you grab them and follow us?"

The prospect takes my bags out of my hand. "Where we going?"

"Dart's old room. Come on, Marcia, let's get you settled."

Taking it for granted that I'll be following, she moves toward the door. A bubble of fear and anticipation goes through me as I take my first real step into this biker world.

I've read up about the Satan's Devils and know this compound used to be a vacation resort. When a wildfire came too close and swept through it, the owners sold it. So badly damaged no one else wanted to buy it, the club bought it cheap.

As I go up past adjoining blocs, each looking like they contain a couple of suites, I can see what a good job they've made of it—and that they've still got room to expand. There are still some burned-out hulks I see off to one side. *If they filled those with bikers we'd have a massive club on our hands.*

Should I be thinking like a cop now? Somehow that feels insensitive. These men are protecting me from an unknown foe. *Drummer could have been killed alongside me this morning.* I pause my steps, knowing I've got to make a conscious decision. Either I do my job and soak up as much information as possible, or I suspend that part of my brain. For the moment it's not clear what direction I should be taking. Deciding to leave the choice to be made a little later, once I understand what I'm stepping into here, I start walking again.

Sam stops in front of a bloc and Jekyll puts down my bags, opens the door, then picks them up again and carries them in. There are two doors separated by a small hallway. The prospect repeats the process as he opens the one and then hands me the key that was hanging in the lock.

I turn to thank him. He accepts my words with a fast nod, eyeing me a little suspiciously. As he walks off, it brings home my position. Turning to Sam, I sigh. "I'm not welcome here, am I?"

As befits the president's woman, her eyes narrow. "You here to bring down the club?"

Her direct question makes me come to the resolution I thought would take longer. How could I betray the people who were trying to help me? I glance at the baby still held in her arms. "No. I'm not." Then I qualify it. "Unless I see something I can't turn a blind eye too."

"And what's your definition of that?"

I think quickly. "Mass murder?" *But haven't I already witnessed that in LA? And I didn't point the finger then.*

Her grin is fast and genuine. "I hope I can assure you, you won't see anything like that."

I like her, this woman who according to her cut is the property of Drummer.

I'm still thinking on the dynamics of that ownership as we enter the pleasantly furnished suite. From what I'd been told, bikers share their women around, prostituting them out. Or even when they commit to one can move on to another, leaving their ex old lady to service their brothers. Or they might keep her and just be unfaithful by going with the club whores. From what I've seen of this woman already, I don't think she'd be someone to put up with that type of behaviour, or allow herself to be passed around. Once again, my training manual appears to be wrong.

"Fresh linen is on the bed. Towels and toiletries in the bathroom. I think you've got everything you need. If not, just give me a shout. Or one of the other old ladies. You'll be meeting them soon."

As I lift my suitcase onto the bed, ready to start unpacking, I'm surprised when she comes in and sits herself down on the mattress, laying a now sleeping child next to her. After a fond look in his direction, she glances at me, impishly.

"So, your Suzuki 7/11. That can do nearly two hundred, can't it? And the cornering. Wow, just thinking about it makes me wet."

I start in surprise, and laughter bursts out of me. Setting aside the task of unpacking for now, I push the case over and sit down beside her, hoicking one leg onto the mattress so I can talk to her face. "Haven't had it long. Put the new engine in myself. And wow, yup. When I can let it go, it's fucking ace."

Her eyes sharpen when I tell her I worked on it myself. "I've got an old Vincent. Rebuilt it from scratch. Apart from my men, it's the love of my life."

Now this is someone I could be friends with. "Hey, a Vincent Black Shadow? Can't recall seeing one in the flesh. I'd love to try it. Gears are on the opposite side, right? How do you find it?"

"It's a devil to ride."

I've heard that, and my respect for her grows. We talk bikes for a while, and my offer for her to ride my rat sometime has her glowing. We're getting on like a house on fire, laughing so hard tears are falling from my eyes as she relates the story of the dirt track behind the compound, and how she showed up the men by beating them all, when there are female voices at the doorway.

I turn to see who the newcomers are while half of me is still trying to process how Sam's prowess with her riding skills didn't faze any of these hardened bikers, again something my education hadn't prepared me for. It takes me a second to process a woman entering carrying yet another baby. *My God, haven't they heard of birth control here? Have they all got kids?* It's another thing I hadn't expected to find at the compound.

"Marcia, this is Sophie. She's Wraith's, the VP's woman, and her baby's just a month older than Eli."

"Olivia." Sophie beams as she looks at the child in her arms.

"Ollie," Sam throws back at her. Sophie sticks her tongue out, and I gather it's an inside joke I can't yet understand.

"Oh, good." She spies Eli on the bed, sleeping, and without asking permission goes and puts her daughter down alongside him.

It's only then I notice the other women behind.

"Hi, I'm Ella. I'm with Slick." A woman with her hair in a short attractive bob gives a little wave as she introduces herself.

"I'm Sandy—Sam's mother-in-law and Viper's old lady."

"And I'm Carmen, Bullet's my old man."

"Watch Carmen, she's a hairdresser and always on the lookout for more victims."

Carmen throws a mock punch toward Sam.

"Hello!" a smaller, less confident voice says behind them, and I look up to see a young girl still in her teens. "I'm Jayden." *Jayden? The* Jayden? She looks so sweet and innocent. I immediately wonder why Archer had her in his sights, and whether there's still any danger to her. It's only then I notice she's holding the hand of the most adorable child I've seen in my life. She's got reddish-blond hair that I suspect will grow darker as she gets older. She's sucking her thumb, but when she turns her blue eyes toward me, I recognise them with a start, and realise I've seen her once before, many months ago when she was a bit younger. This is Heart's daughter.

Jayden sees me looking at her and glances down fondly. "Meet Amy," she says, pushing the shy child my way.

"Pretty." Amy comes over and touches my long blond hair, which has escaped from its bun with all the action today.

Carmen barks a laugh. "Think she's been watching me." Although I'm still out of the loop, their infectious laughter and giggles have me joining in.

Obviously not a shy child, Amy holds up her arms to be picked up, and it seems natural to scoop her onto my lap. She fits into my arms and turns her face to inspect me. "What's your name?"

"I'm Marcia."

Sam looks curious. "Is that what you prefer to be called? Heart told us you liked Marc."

"Marc's the name my brother gave to me. No one else ever used it but my family."

Damn, I've become too relaxed. Sam's picked up on it, I can see by the way her eyes sharpen. In recent years, Heart's the only one I've willingly allowed to call me by my childhood nickname. And to this day, I have no idea why. As her eyes query me I shake my head in a silent plea, but watching her face, I see her lips curve into a small, knowing smile.

As the women come and surround me, taking up what seats they can find, a male voice barks in an amused voice, "Christ, you lot are like vultures sensing fresh fuckin' meat. Now scat, I need to talk with Marc for a while."

Glancing up, I see Drummer leaning against the door, his face softening as he spies his woman and his son. Sam gets to her feet. Scooping up Eli, she grins, nods at me, and then goes to the door, pausing so Drummer can take a kiss from her lips, so hot it almost makes me swoon, before he places a more chaste one on his son's head. "She prefers to be called Marcia by the rest of us."

I'm slightly stunned she picked that up so quickly and thought to tell him.

One by one the others leave, Sophie collecting her daughter, and Jayden trying to pry Amy from my lap. Amy protests, and her little hands grip me.

While we're trying to gently extract her, another voice sounds, "Amy, sweetheart. You can visit with Marc later. Go with Jayden now, darlin'."

"Daddy!" The child squeals and wriggles away, running over to her father. Heart balances crutches on his arms, and while he obviously can't pick her up, pulls her in against his legs and hugs her to him. My stomach clenches as I get my first sight of father and daughter together. Memories come back to me of our conversations on his journey as he went through the myriad of emotions, first wanting nothing to do with her, feeling he wasn't good enough for her, and then his longing to come home and see her again. I feel pride in my small part at bringing them back together, and discretely I wipe water from my eye.

After a cuddle, a tickle and a promise to see her later, Amy at last takes the teenager's hand and allows herself to be led away.

The temperature in the room seems to drop by a few degrees now I'm left with the two bikers.

Drummer moves into the middle of the room and Heart steps just inside the door, heavily leaning on two crutches. He may still have some way to go, but he looks a darn sight better than when I last saw him in the hospital. It's his face, though, that I notice most as a myriad of expressions crosses it, moving through gentle while interacting with his daughter, now settling into a frown as he looks toward me.

For six weeks I've tried to put him out of my mind. Now the fact that I've been unsuccessful slams into me. Particularly as I'm seeing him as if in full technicolour, rather than my previous sightings, looking pale and laid up in a hospital bed. He's tall, taller than I expected, attractive long dirty-blond hair reaching just past his shoulders. His piercing blue eyes which look bright and clear, well-defined tanned cheeks, and a full mouth, make me want to lick my lips. *Girl, pull yourself together.*

"Marcia," Drummer says sharply to get my attention. As I turn to look at him, I immediately stand. It's like being dragged into the principal's office. His smile for Sam has completely cleared from his face.

CHAPTER NINETEEN

*H*eart...

Whether it's just dictated by circumstances, or whether Drummer's punishing me in some way, I'm to become Marc's jailer with the instruction to treat her as I would my old lady. That leaves me with the responsibility for ensuring she doesn't step one foot out of line. I'm to be her shadow, making certain she's no chance to go poking around, keeping her away from any of our business, which is none of hers. While the majority of what we do nowadays is above board, we still keep ourselves to ourselves, unwilling to let any outsider in. A representative of law enforcement is definitely a person who's kept on the perimeter.

Old lady. The term that I've only ever applied to one woman and had never thought to give to another again. But even if I refrain from using the term myself, others will be exploiting it at my expense. It's a joke to them, a worthy punishment for getting involved with a cop. But to me, it's not right, it's borrowed. It's not hers. Crystal's been dead for getting on for a year, but that's not enough. A whole lifetime wouldn't be long enough to grieve.

As the real old ladies sort themselves out and leave, I look around. Dart and I used to have the two suites in this bloc, being best friends and often partners in crime. But his is now empty, as he's made the permanent move to become VP of the San Diego chapter. And mine, well, that's not been used for more than ten months, and even before that, once I was married, it had only become somewhere for Crystal and me to crash when we stayed on the compound.

The only difference between the two suites is that mine has a single bed along with a king-sized, shrinking the area, but meaning Amy can stay there as well. Although for now we'll see how it goes. While I'm babysitting law enforcement, Drummer and Sam have offered to keep my daughter at their house at the top of the compound, where up to now I've been living as their guest. At least I'm lucky that Marc will have her own space, as I will have mine, and they haven't gone so far as to force us to share a room.

But this situation means I'm forced to pick up the strands of my old life again. I'm not looking forward to entering my old space and seeing the ghosts which will be there. Although the girls had thoughtfully cleared her stuff out, everything else will remain much the same. *Fuck it, I still miss you, Crystal, still expect you to walk in that door.*

Drummer's looking at Marc as though he could kill her with his bare hands, although it was his decision to bring her back for her safety. Looking at his face now, I'm wondering if he's rethinking that hasty move. Why should he care what happens to one of the enemy? *He's done it for me, for the debt owed her as I'm still breathing.* I lean against the doorframe for support, hoping my gut feeling is right, that we can trust her, and that she's not looking to bring us down. My friendship with her wasn't that of a biker, just a lonely man on the road trying to recover from the loss of his wife. Now I've resumed my role as a fully patched member, the dynamics of our relationship will have to change.

"Marcia," he repeats, the tone of his voice making her stand up. "We're extending our hospitality to you. This morning proved you're a risk to yourself, and that you're not safe. Being here, though, well that brings its own problems." He pauses and gives her the full force of his stare. "I don't know what you know about this club. We have two types of women here. Sweet butts—our club whores—and old ladies." I see a range of expressions crossing her face, one being indignation as if she expects to be asked to service the men, but Drummer doesn't give her long enough to protest, just carries on explaining.

"When a man takes an old lady, he's takes responsibility for her. It has to be a club vote before we let anyone in. You're not sweet butt material." I watch her bristle as though she's being insulted, but again he gives her no time to object. "Heart has agreed to take you as his ol' lady. You'll answer to him, and he'll be responsible for your behaviour in and toward the club. As any other ol' lady, you're welcome in the clubroom, the kitchen, and such communal areas. Everything else is out-of-bounds. Heart will show you around and where you can go."

Her eyes have come to mine and are open wide. Beautiful blue eyes which flare. "I've not agreed to be anyone's 'old lady.'" She even uses her fingers to put the term in quotes. "I'm not looking for a man, and if I were—"

"You might not have gone looking, but that's what you've ended up with."

I never realised she had a temper before, but suddenly her eyes are blazing and she's standing up to the prez. "I'm a cop, have you forgotten? It's one thing for me to hide out here for a few days, quite another to be given a label of possession."

"A few days?" Drummer's face goes dark at her challenge. "You think all this will blow over in such a short time?" He flicks his eyes toward me. "Heart, take her gun, and check for her ankle holster too."

Awkwardly, having been a very long time since I had my hands on any woman, I do as he says, and as he expected, come up with two guns. Turning, I go and lock them into the safe in my room.

When I return, Prez is still watching her. He moves fast,

taking her by surprise and grabbing her by both shoulders. "Put one toe over the line, Marcia. Go where you're not supposed to, speak one word of anything you see or hear..." He pauses for effect. "And no one will find your body."

I watch her shiver, as if the air's grown cold, and have a strange desire to comfort her and explain he doesn't mean it. The problem is, I know that he does.

She pulls back her shoulders and stands straight. "I think I'd rather take my chances on my own."

"Not gonna happen."

While I'm still reeling with having her stuck at my side, I realise it's time I stepped up. I see the way her little hands are fisting, and I don't want to see what happens if she tries to take the prez on. "Marc." I swing myself over to join them. "Marc," I say more softly. "Whatever's going on will be sorted faster if we both work together. We've got two enemies in common, the Herreras and the cops. Pool some of our information," *not all, of course,* "and we might reach answers quicker. Mouse can help with your research, and you can tell us why you're targeting the crime family."

"I can do that without becoming your property," she snarls at me.

I don't blame her. "I like it about as much as you do." But I admire her spirit. Crystal was energetic, loud at times, always excited and enjoying life. But she'd have backed down at the slightest opposition, always looking to me to take the lead. Marc, though. Marc would challenge me every single step of the fuckin' way. *If she really was my old lady.* Which she's not.

She's staring at me, as though only just seeing me. And as we can count the number of actual meetings on one hand, and until today, almost all of those I'd always been lying flat in a bed, this *is* the first time. I'm a proud man, so when her face twists in a sneer and she turns back to Drummer, I feel the stirrings of anger that I've been so easily dismissed. *What was my earlier desire? To take her over my knee and spank her for putting herself in danger?*

Well, she might just have ensured she's earned that. She is, for all intents and purposes, my old lady after all.

"It's impossible, Drummer. If you insist on keeping me here, I'll repay you by being blind, deaf, and dumb. If you're going to do something I'll find hard to ignore, please keep it out of my sight. I don't shit on my own doorstep, and for a while, at least, it seems this is going to be mine. But I won't be given to any man whose job is to control me."

Strangely, Drummer's mouth is turning up at the corner, and I get the feeling he's actually enjoying this shit. Two unwilling people being forced into line.

"Hate to remind you, Marcia, but you fought by our side in LA when we extracted Heart. You killed a man. Your hands aren't clean, darlin'. You best remember that."

"You threatening me, Drummer?"

"Just reminding you of the truth of it." Her quick look away shows she's aware of what she did. Then she glances my way, as if hating her desire to protect me has put her in this position.

Drummer runs his hands through his hair and looks at me, then back to her. "Can't say any of us like this situation, but we will make it work. Marcia, you might have to put up with some dirty looks, maybe insults. Some of the brothers have had run-ins with cops."

Actually, I suspect most of us have. The changes I'd noticed to the compound were as a direct result of Marc and her partner, Archer, coming here with a warrant and smashing the place up. A small smile plays at my lips. Actually, they'd done us a favour. The clubhouse I'd returned to was far better furnished than it had ever been before. I suspect the influx of old ladies had something to do with that too. In a way it's lucky Crystal hadn't been here, it would have ended up far more colourful rather than muted and tasteful.

I thought of Crystal without getting that pain in my heart. The realisation makes me feel guilty, as if I've been unfaithful.

"Dirty looks, snide comments I can deal with. It's nothing I haven't coped with before. A cop's got to have a thick skin, Drummer."

I'd zoned out of the conversation and now bring myself back.

"You're not a cop here, darlin'," I tell her.

Prez jerks his chin in my direction. "You're here as Heart's woman."

Oh no, she's fucking not.

"I'm not fucking him!" Her hand goes to her mouth.

Drummer's face creases. "Never suggested you would. That's something the two of you can work out."

Marc's eyes are looking at me, widening in horror, but other signs betray her. Her cheeks are flushing, and she seems to be taking in air fast. *Is she attracted to me?* Fuck it, I haven't been with a woman since I was last with my wife. But in that moment, the thought that I'll spend the rest of my life as a monk suddenly becomes challenged. Marc? Well, if I had to, the first stirring in my cock in ten months suggests that I could. If I had to that is, to keep her in line.

Up to now I've only thought about the weight that Prez has put around my neck. Now I take pity on her. Closing the gap between us, I rest my elbow on my crutch and reach out my hand to touch her under her chin. I turn her head to face me. "Stop overthinking it. We'll work it out. Being claimed as an old lady gives you protection in the club. No other asshole will bother you. Just remember, we're on the same side."

"For how long, Heart?"

I shake my head. "For as long as it takes. I owe you, darlin'. I'm not gonna let you risk your life when you saved mine." And then I realise how I might be able to get through to her. "Good guys, bad guys. Stay and let's sort it out." She'd had it all straight in her head, and now it's gotten all twisted up. A brief wave of sympathy for her comes over me, knowing the reason why she chose the career that she did. "Once everything's settled I'll cut you loose, and you can go back to your home—my old house, or a new one, whatever you want. And your job."

She's not one of us, and never will be.

Drummer's nodding, but his expression has returned to a frown. I realise I'm being ungrateful. The only reason he's keeping her out of danger is because of the debt that *I* need to repay. He'll pick up flack for bringing her here. A favour he did for me. I nod toward him. "We'll sort it out." I repeat the promise I made to her.

Drummer turns to leave, patting my shoulder as he walks past. *Now what was that?* A gesture of support, or of sympathy? Fuck knows with the prez.

"Well, this is awkward," Marc says once we're left alone. As I raise my eyebrow she continues, "Up to now, we've only spoken on the phone, except for the times I saw you in the hospital. And now I'm supposed to be yours."

Using my crutches, I limp to the chair and ease myself down. "You're only mine so someone has responsibility for you. Drummer's right, women are only one of two things in the club."

"It sounds Neanderthal."

"It's the way it is, and it works for us."

I'm glad she's relaxed enough to go sit on the bed. "I feel like Alice dropped down the rabbit hole."

I smile, liking the analogy.

"What do you expect from an old lady, Heart?"

Now's the chance to put her straight. "Had an old lady. Could never replace her." As my cock twitches again, reminding me it might come back to life, I realise what I'd thought was impossible could feasibly happen. So I'm completely honest. "Not saying you'd never end up in my bed, you're an attractive woman, Marc."

She's on her feet again, her arms waving in the air. "It doesn't work like that. *I* don't work like that. I don't mind a fuck buddy, but I never get close, Heart."

Fuck buddy sounds good to me, and I'll be fucked if my cock doesn't start to lengthen. "Who says we're gonna get close? Can't give you that." *Crystal's still got my heart.* "We're friends already, Marc. Being in this position, if we both want it, means we can be friends with benefits."

"We became friends over the phone."

"Face-to-face just changes the dynamic is all." And fuck me, now I'm considering it, the thought of her in my bed holds some attractions. If my cock's started working again, like any man, I'd need a release. I'd probably have started using the sweet butts. Now I've got a decent enough specimen with no one to blink an eye if I take that next step, and no emotion attached. Ten months is a fucking long time not to get your dick wet.

She glances at me, and just as quickly away, and once again her face flushes red.

"How's your head? Are you healed?"

She gasps then spits out, "I'm not going to have sex!"

I chuckle. "I'm not asking for that. Darlin', I don't expect you to spread your legs right now. Just putting the offer on the table if you want to pursue it." When I walked in the room it had been the last thing on my mind. Now I realise I really wouldn't object to sinking what is now my very alert and interested cock into her cunt. "I asked to find out if you're going to have any problems. If you need painkillers or the like."

After glancing my way as if to test I'm not lying, she touches her hand to her skull, maybe to indicate where the injury was. "The bones have fused and healed, but yes, I'm likely to get headaches for some time. They'll gradually fade, and already I'm getting them less often now. I brought painkillers with me."

"They incapacitate you?"

"Some do, like a bad migraine, you know?"

Crystal used to get those, so yeah, I do.

She looks around. "Am I staying in here, Heart?"

After all that I've said, probably too much, I can see she's worrying. I need to reassure her I'm not going to force her into my bed, and I'd like Amy to have the option to stay with me for a start. "You can make yourself comfortable in here. I'll be over the way." Nodding my head toward the suite opposite, I sigh.

"Until I know I can trust you, we'll keep the doors open, and I'll lock the outer door and keep the key."

"I'm more prisoner than your old lady."

"You're a cop. And much as it pains me to say, I don't really know you." I pull myself to my feet and get the crutches beneath me. "You know why we make the new members prospect for a year or more before they're patched in?" She doesn't, I can read it on her face. "It's a chance for all members to get to know them. And know they can trust them to do whatever's necessary." I pause. "Hyde may need to wait a little longer after pulling that stunt today, when he lost you."

She widens her eyes. "That's not fair. It wasn't his fault."

I shrug. "Doesn't matter. He failed to do the job he was assigned."

Her head tilts. "So it's pretty hard to gain that trust and become a member." She nibbles her lip, drawing my attention to her mouth. "Am I a sort of prospect then?"

Now that does make me laugh, the thought of her doing all the shit jobs we give the men trying to get patched in. Particularly the thought of her burying a body. "No, darlin'. But like them, you've got to earn mine and my brothers' trust. Just using them as an example that we don't trust easily. Ain't gonna just take your word for it."

She's right. It is different talking to her in person. On the phone I could hear the little nuances in her tone, but now she's in front of me, her changes of expression and her mannerisms are bringing her to life. The way she's biting her lip shows she's nervous about what she might be getting into, but the strangeness of the situation hasn't put out her spark. Her hands fluttering by her side show she doesn't seem to know what to do. It occurs to me as she glances my way, then around the room, that this is a woman who doesn't like time hanging on her hands.

My thoughts are confirmed as she opens her suitcase and starts taking out her clothes. While she's occupied putting them away, it gives me a moment to study her. She's tall for a woman, though shorter than me. She's still dressed as she'd probably been this morning for her meetings, dress trousers tailored to her long shapely legs, a white blouse tucked in giving a hint of curves underneath. She's not hugely endowed, but as she leans over, a hint of cleavage comes into view. Strangely, as she's keeping hidden what the sweet butts have on display every day, there's another twitch in that organ that's been dormant for some time.

Fuck me. Now's not the time to get my first full erection since the day I was knocked off my bike. But part of me is pleased she seems like she could be an acceptable alternative to Viagra.

I sit down again, watching the woman who inadvertently caused the reaction. Her long blond hair sways as she moves, her skin is fair, suggesting her hair colouring is natural, and that she hasn't been out much in the sun. I can see a smattering of freckles, and when she glances at me, cornflower-blue eyes peep out from under long eyelashes. Her face is oval and her neck slender. The way the whole package is put together suddenly makes me pleased Drummer suggested I treat her as my old lady. Otherwise, I'd be fighting my brothers off with a stick. If they can get past her occupation, I'm sure they'll see what I'm seeing. She's a very attractive woman.

At least being called her old man gives me a reason to protect her—not just from our enemies outside, but from horny fuckers within. It's something I hadn't previously factored in.

Her clothes put away, she's fiddling with the last item to put on a hanger. All those phone conversations, and now we're face-to-face, it's difficult to find something to say.

As I'm wondering how to break the silence, she fills it herself. "Who do *you* think is after me, Heart?"

Right now, I can be honest. "I don't know, darlin', but someone is for sure."

"What does the club think?"

Once again, I get to my feet and move over to her. Balancing one crutch under my arm, I reach out my hand and again turn her to face me. "Club business, darlin', and none of yours."

She rears back. "Isn't it mine when it's my life on the line? That's not how I work, Heart."

I close my eyes briefly and take a deep breath. This is going to be every bit as hard as I expected. "It is now, darlin'. We might not find out information by the same methods that you would. We might take actions that you won't want to know about. If there's anything you need to know to keep you safe, then we'll tell you. I promise you that."

She pulls back those shoulders again, completely oblivious her peaked nipples are poking at the flimsy material. "I can't be kept in the dark."

I harden my voice, the biker coming to the fore, which she hasn't heard before. "You'll know what you need to, but nothing more."

"There's that plausible deniability again."

If she understands what she's saying, then the penny has dropped. "Exactly," I confirm.

She puts the last shirt on the hanger away, but the stiffness of her posture shows while she's accepted my meaning, she doesn't like it. I don't want to leave it like that.

"Hey." I pull her attention back to me and spell it out. "When all this is over—and it will be over—you'll be able to go back to your life. You won't have to think of what you can and can't say, and as long as you stay out of our business, you won't have a clue how we work. That's for your benefit, as well as ours."

She bites her lip, and fuck me if my cock doesn't start to swell again, particularly when she looks at me with the full force of those beautiful blue eyes. They're so big, a man could drown in them. "I'm being an ungrateful bitch, aren't I? You needn't be helping me at all."

I smile at the name she's coined, but have to admit she's kinda right. "You're inquisitive by nature, darlin', and you have to be for your job. You don't get to be a detective if you don't try to seek out every detail."

She takes a sharp breath, shakes her head, then laughs at herself. "And that's what got me here in the first place, never knowing when to leave well enough alone."

"You always want to go after the bad guys yourself. But now, for once, trust us to go hunting."

CHAPTER TWENTY

*M*arc…

Trust them? I glare at Heart. He's asking me to do something he won't reciprocate. He's just taken the time to explain that it takes a year or more to become trusted by the club, and now he's glibly asking for mine straight away.

Well there's one thing we have in common. I don't trust easily. Since my family died, I haven't put my faith in anyone. Not even the person I was partnered with, even though it was expected I should. It's only ever been me. When I'd lost everyone, I never wanted to lean on anyone again or expect them to be there for me. Now he's expecting me to depend on others to do what I've always done for myself.

And look where it got me? Holed up in a biker compound. Living with the very Devils themselves. If the situation weren't so serious, it would be funny. *And* I'm apparently an old lady.

If I hadn't been shot at this morning, only saved by the overprotective measures Heart had installed to keep his family safe, I'd be reacting much differently. My head is spinning, unable to keep up with everything that's happened today. I turn away from Heart and stare at a blank wall instead. The Satan's Devils are criminals. I should be soaking up everything I can, finding evidence to put them behind bars.

The Satan's Devils saved my life and are doing all they can to keep me in the land of the living.

Someone knows I've been investigating things which they don't want me to. Only my colleagues at the precinct would know, and either they or someone they've passed the information to are trying to kill me.

Who's in the right, and who's in the wrong? I can't even identify the criminals who I should be after anymore.

My hand goes to the head. *This is all wrong.* As the pain starts pounding, I put my fist to my mouth, biting down on my hand. I'm a cop. The only people who should be a threat to me are perpetrators of a crime. But while I should feel at risk here, I don't.

I feel a hand on my shoulder. "It's gonna be okay, Marc."

Ashamed of my weakness, I stifle a sob. I'm lost and overwhelmed.

"Don't worry about things you can't control, okay?"

Easy for him to say, much harder to switch my whirling mind off. I need to try, otherwise the warning signs are there that my headache's going to turn into a full-blown migraine.

His hand starts massaging my neck, only one, as he needs the other to balance on his crutch. I roll back my head, relaxing into the soothing touch. Nobody's touched me like this, not since I lost my family. "That feels nice," I tell him, honestly.

"You're too tense. But all this has been a lot for you to handle, and so much thrown at you all at once. Hey, it's getting late. You must be hungry."

I frown, not having considered it, but the last meal I'd eaten was breakfast, and that was a long time back. "I am." Another truthful admission.

He applies gentle pressure and I turn around. "Come on then, let's see what's on offer in the clubhouse."

Leave this calm oasis? Mingle with people who will view me

with distrust? I'd rather stay here. But I can't hide out forever, and I might as well start facing the music now. Raising my hand, I pretend to take off an invisible hat. "There. Cop uniform discarded. I'm just one of your club women."

He gives me a very strange look and then says, seriously, "You're certainly not that."

I feel my cheeks flushing red, remembering what I've read about women as club property. *Shit.* I have to be careful until I learn all the terminology here. *What makes a woman give herself to all these men?* Heart's wide grin, which he is unsuccessful in hiding, makes me turn away. It reveals he knows exactly where my mind's going.

"Come on."

Waiting for Heart to get his crutches beneath him, I walk slowly beside him as he works himself over the slightly uneven ground, taking the opportunity afforded by the slow pace to look at my surroundings. Goodness, this place is a beautiful spot, views of the desert stretching for miles over to the Tucson mountains. Saguaro and other cacti dotted all around. I'm not surprised the club bought up this land. It's far enough from Tucson for them not to be bothered, but close enough to get into town and their businesses there.

The air smells sweet and carries the sound of cicadas, and while the summer sun beats mercilessly down, it's not such a harsh heat as in the midst of the city.

The clubhouse is much cooler, and Heart leads me straight to the bar. "Jekyll," he yells. As his head pops up, he already has a beer in his hand.

"What d'ya want?" the prospect asks me, but not in a friendly voice. I suspect I've been the topic of some conversation since I've been ensconced in my room.

"Er…" Mentally I run through my options, eyeing the shelf and wondering what they stock here. "White wine?" I ask, a little optimistically.

He goes to a fridge and pours a large glass, sliding it to me over the counter. I give him my thanks, which are all but ignored.

"Bring it with you, darlin'." Heart touches my arm and points to a room off to one side. Following him in, I find it's a kitchen. There's a woman sitting at the table eating a meal. Heart tells me to sit down and then goes to open the door of a large fridge. "Fried chicken okay?"

As I nod, he starts pulling stuff out and taking it to the microwave to heat it up.

I stand, seeing how awkward it is for him to manoeuvre his crutches. "I can do that."

"Nah, I can manage."

I sit down again, unashamedly watching his muscles flex as he goes about his task. Christ, that man has a great ass.

"You shouldn't be here. You're a cop."

My attention turns to my companion at the table, recognising immediately this must be one of their whores. I don't even need to be a detective to figure that out. She's not one of the old ladies who'd come up to the suite and is dressed much differently. Her top is little more than a tiny bikini, her breasts barely confined and pushing out of the top, affording me the hint of a nipple. Despite her sneering tone, I decide to be friendly. "I'm Marcia."

"Don't give a fuck about your name, *Cop*. You stay out of my fuckin' way and keep your hands off the brothers. You've no business here—"

"Shut the fuck up, Jill. And show some respect to my ol' lady." Heart's rounded on her, his face stern, his voice angry. "Now get lost and allow us to eat in peace."

I've heard the saying about eyes bulging out of someone's head, but haven't actually seen it before. With her mouth gaping open and without saying another word, she stands, allowing me to see her skimpy skirt and almost everything it barely conceals, takes her plate to the sink, then looks at Heart and then me. With a disbelieving shake of her head, she leaves the room.

Heart comes over and puts a plate in front of me, then gets

one of his own. Sitting down, he nods to the door of the kitchen. "Sweet butts get possessive over the brothers." He smirks. "It seems even one's they're not fuckin'."

"Am I going to have a cat fight on my hands?" I'm not worried, with my martial arts training they wouldn't have a chance.

Heart's mouth twists as if he's trying not to laugh. "Much as I'd pay good money to see that, sweetheart, the answer is no. Not as my ol' lady. They give you grief? You tell them where to go. Sweet butts are at the bottom of the pole, if you get what I mean."

I do.

We eat, I clear the plates—including the one left by Jill—rinse, then stack them in the dishwasher.

"How's your head?"

Again I automatically touch the place where there was a crack in my skull. "Better after something to eat."

He considers me for a moment, then pulls his crutches toward him and stands. "Come on then, now's as good a time as any."

Not quite sure what he means, I let him lead me back to the main room and over to a table.

As we approach, all conversation stops. Heart doesn't seem to notice, or ignores it, and points to the only empty chair. One of the men gets up and brings another over for him. I recognise some of the men I've met already, or got to know briefly in Los Angeles—Wraith, the VP, and alongside him, Peg, the sergeant-at-arms, then Blade, the enforcer, Rock, and Slick. Dollar and Tongue are introduced to me, the latter opening his mouth seemingly to give me a good view of his stud. When he waggles his tongue suggestively, Heart throws him a sharp look. The prospect runs over and brings us new drinks. I take a sip of my nicely chilled wine and realise I've got to be on my best behaviour.

Blade takes out a knife, puts it on the table top, and starts spinning it around. I hope that it's habit and not a threat or promise. From his other pocket, he takes out a pack of cigarettes and extracts one.

Wraith's mouth curves in amusement. "Reduced to buying your own now?"

The whole table laughs as Blade uses a Zippo to get it alight. I snap my mouth shut and refrain from mentioning you shouldn't smoke in public places, treating the situation as I would in someone's home. I suppose this is a private members club, and I'm just a visitor.

I also hide my distaste as smoke blows my way.

The situation is awkward, as if no one knows what to say. They're not going to continue their previous conversation, and I'm not confident to start a new one. I'm well aware I'm taking too many sips of my wine to give my hands something to do. Just before the silence becomes unbearable, Rock points to me.

"Impressed with your riding. Your bike sure can move."

"Yeah, but it ain't a real ride, Rock. It's a ride for the ladies. She probably couldn't handle a Harley." Wraith softens his words with a wink.

A subject on which I can hold my own, and at least it's safe ground. "Harleys have their place." I let that sink in, then add, "For riders who can't handle the speed."

A round of jeers greets me, a glance at Heart shows he's grinning. Suddenly a new voice greets me, and another man pulls up a chair. The others shift to give him some space.

"They can't handle the track either. I'm Roadrunner, Road." He holds out his hand and I take it. "I've got a competition bike which they like to yank my chain about."

So at least there's one other person who can have my back on this.

"Ever ride a real bike, sweetheart?"

I nod at Blade. "Sure have, but I prefer Jap bikes, sorry to say. Though I wouldn't mind a Ducati."

"Fuck that Italian shit. American built are the best."

I keep my mouth shut, knowing I'm never going to be able to convince them. I look around the room to give my eyes something to do and suddenly there's a roar from our table.

"Leave that the fuck alone!" Peg's got to his feet and is glaring full force at the man leaning over the bar. His brother—Joker, or something—steps clear holding his hands up in surrender. "I'll play it a fuckin' second time if anyone else interferes."

There's a mass shaking of heads. Heart leans forward and says in a stage whisper, "Musical choice is usually Peg's."

I tilt my head and listen more carefully. It's certainly not music I'd expect bikers to play, but isn't bad. I pick up my wine again and ask after I've taken a sip, "What is it?"

Peg's sharp eyes meet mine. "The Eagles. *Long Road Out of Eden*." He scowls at Blade. "Both albums."

"I like it," I tell him honestly.

"Trying to get into my good books, darlin'?"

I give him a shrewd look. "Is it working?"

"Nope."

As he pops the p, giving the word finality, I can't help but laugh.

The woman I remember is called Sophie comes over. Wraith pushes back from the table and she plonks down on his lap. His lips lovingly find hers in a panty-melting display. I'm no virgin, I've had a few boyfriends before, but never a relationship, as I wouldn't let things go that far. And I've never been kissed the way the VP's kissing his old lady.

But the kiss, however ravishing and over-personal it might seem, is nothing to what I see when I turn my head to give them some privacy. The woman, Jill, is on her knees, enthusiastically giving an unknown biker a blow job out in full view. He's leaning back on the sofa, his eyes closed, a look of ecstasy playing on his face. Thinking looking the other way might be safer, I see another sofa, and another club girl straddling another man's lap, her naked butt showing exactly what they're doing.

"Time to go." It's Wraith's voice, and he's obviously speaking to Sophie. As I look back around, I see the pair leaving the room.

Along with the cigarette smoke and the sour odour of beer, the scent of sex and sweat now invades the air.

I've never considered myself a prude, have seen my fair share of naked bodies, and have even once been on a raid to a porn film studio. But I've never been in the position of sitting, sipping my wine in the middle of a live sex show. My hands twirl my empty glass, and I feel my cheeks starting to glow.

"Do you want another, or to go?" Heart's looking at me, there's a twinkle in his eyes.

Peg tuts and leans toward me. "Ol' ladies usually leave when the sweet butts start working."

Meeting his eyes, seeing while they're still cold and full of suspicion, he's being helpful giving me a way out. I nod my thanks, then answer Heart. "Seeing as I'm supposed to be an old lady, I'll do the same." Then, realising I know nothing about this man, add, "I can make my own way back if you want to stay."

"You stick with your ol' man," Blade rasps out. "You're not wandering around on your own."

At that moment another scantily clad woman comes over to the table. Blade pulls her down on his lap and then throws a look of challenge my way.

"Come on, Marc. That's our cue to leave." Heart's already on his feet, his arms hooked over his crutches. "Let's get back to the suite."

CHAPTER TWENTY-ONE

*H*eart...

She's had an induction into our club, seen the way that we live. As I watched her taking in the club whores doing what they're here for, I tried to analyse her reaction. Shock, for certain. Disgust? Nah, it was more like intrigue. Too embarrassed to look for too long in any one direction, but no particular judgement that I could see.

We walk in silence up to the suite and then pause awkwardly in the short hallway between the two rooms. She seems hesitant to go into hers.

"You wanna talk about it?"

Her tongue licks her lips, making my cock come to life. "Your life is free, isn't it, Heart? The freedom of the open road which I can understand, and the freedom to take what you want."

"If you're talking about the sweet butts, we don't take, they give. Ain't no woman forced here, darlin'."

She considers that for a moment, then, fuck me, she grins. "What got me is how it's all so open."

"Not everyone fucks in the clubroom." Though I admit I've done it in the long distant past. Before Crystal. "There are back rooms where people can go if they want privacy. But yeah, you could say most of the brothers aren't shy."

She shivers, and I notice she's pressing her legs together hard, and through the material of her t-shirt I can see her nipples are hard. *Christ, she's turned on.* The idea that the sights she's just seen has made her horny make me grin, and my cock swells. Putting one crutch under my arm, I reach out and curl my hand around her neck. "Did you like being a voyeur, sweetheart? Did you like what you saw? Did all that testosterone get to you?"

Then it slams into me that watching my brothers was one thing, wanting to be the woman servicing them was another. "You ain't gonna be fuckin' my brothers. Wouldn't look good if you went with anyone else. You're my ol' lady, and if you want to fuck anyone, it's gonna be me."

Her eyes flick to mine, allowing me to see her pupils are dilated. My possessive grip tightens.

Fuck! I can't do this. My cock says I can.

We stand like that for what seems like ages. A blind man could feel the tension in the air. Both of us horny as fuck, and neither of us prepared to do anything about it. I want to send her away and take care of myself in the shower for the first time in months, while thinking of Crystal, using my memory to exorcise thoughts of this living, breathing, *sexy* woman in front of me from my brain.

Her tongue licks her lips again, and her hand comes out and touches my chest. I can feel the warmth like a burn to my skin. "I don't do relationships, Heart, but I do use men to get my rocks off. Perhaps not as indiscriminately as the whores, but I'm little better than them."

"You fuck without any involvement." If that really is the case, she doesn't know how she's tempting me.

"I can't afford to get attached."

Because everyone leaves her, like I will. This pairing has an end date.

The way she's looking at me, she's just issued an invitation. I need to be sure. "You wanna fuck?"

Again her eyes shoot to mine and there's a slight hesitation as if she fears rejection, then she says quietly, "If you do."

Notwithstanding the sweet butts, it's about the coldest arrangement that I've ever been offered, nothing more than getting my rocks off with a whore. No emotion, no ties, no strings. A way to relieve a mutual physical need.

My desire to remain celibate has flown out the window. My fears I'd never get it up for a woman again disappear. *Because of her.* She's got something that entices me. My cock's now so hard it's needing some kind of relief. And being a man, I'd prefer it not to be by my own hand.

Feeling a madness about me, reaching past her, I open the door to my room. "Coming in?"

A moment of indecision, and then a decisive quick up and down dip of her head. "This doesn't mean anything, Heart."

"Nothing at all," I confirm, putting my hand to the small of her back and gently pushing her inside.

How do I do this? If it had been uncomfortable between us out in the hallway, it's doubled as soon as we're faced with my king-sized bed. The item of furniture I last used with Crystal. I stare at it for a moment, trying to see the ghost of my wife there. But the churning in my balls pulls my mind in a different direction.

I was married for four years, and for all that time faithful to my wife. I knew what she liked, what she wanted, how to touch her and where. Crystal had been a good woman, but not particularly imaginative during sex. She'd satisfied me enough that I never wanted another.

Now I've a different woman who's gonna be with me tonight. The thought excites and arouses me more than I would have thought.

She's standing, unmoving, as if waiting for instruction. I have no fucking idea where to start. For years it was to come home to a warm body already naked.

Resting my crutches against the wall, I balance carefully on my healing legs, running both hands up and down her arms, feeling her tremble beneath my fingertips. "You're gonna have to help me here, sweetheart."

"Your legs?"

"Yeah." I can't put my weight on my knees, so there's only one way this can go. "You're gonna have to be on top."

"I can do that," she whispers, her voice low and husky.

She steps out of my reach and moves to the middle of the room. After only a second's vacillation, she unbuttons her pants and kicks off her shoes, and then she's pushing them down, and her bottom half is almost naked.

I'm leaning lazily against the door, taking a sharp breath as I see a firm heart-shaped ass covered only in flimsy lacy material. Underneath the straight-laced cop is a woman who invests in expensive underwear. I grin.

"Turn around," I instruct. "Take off your top."

She shakes her head. "I can't do that, Heart. I'm… scarred."

I remember she'd been in an accident, and I feel a wave of sadness for her. "I'm scarred too, darlin'. Not afraid for you to see that."

"I don't mind, Heart."

"Why would you think I do?" I ease out of my cut and place it neatly on a chair, then gingerly push away from the door and go to the bed, having to sit to take the weight off my legs. Leaning forward, I take off my shoes, then lean back to undo my pants.

"Let me help."

Without waiting for permission, she comes and takes hold of my waistband. I lift my ass so she can slide them off. As I told her, my legs are covered in scars from the operations I've had, and from stab wounds. And if she could see under the skin, she'd find metal holding my bones together.

"Touch here." I take her hand and let her feel the almost

invisible lump. "That's from my first op." She doesn't grimace or react as she touches the rod.

In one move, I've dispensed with my t-shirt, and now the wounds on my upper body come into view. The ones courtesy of the Demon Sons healed, but still raised and red. My body a memorial to pain. My skin puckered, my tattoos distorted.

But she's not cataloguing my injuries, her eyes seem fixed to that part of me that's now tenting my boxers, making them seem alive as it twitches under its cover. Grinning slyly, I instruct her, "Take them off."

Again, I lift myself up to help her, and now I'm naked and her gaze is transfixed to my cock. And fuck me, she's leaning forward, flicking out her tongue to lick the pre-cum off. I haven't felt anything like this in fucking years. Crystal wasn't fond of giving me a blow job, but I didn't miss it as much as Viper. But fuck me, as she wraps those lips around my length, trying to take as much of me inside as she can, I can't remember a time it ever felt so good. *She looks like she's enjoying it.*

I collapse back on the bed and give in to sensations I never thought I'd experience again.

It feels so good as she hollows her cheeks and sucks me in until I'm touching the back of her throat, then pulling back, then taking me in again. When she swallows around me, I've come close to shooting my load. "Sweetheart, stop. Come here." As she continues to mouth fuck me, I take hold of her hair and gently pull her away.

Her eyes are glassy, her mouth swollen, and her cheeks flushed with desire. "Didn't you like it?"

"Fuckin' fantastic, darlin'. Too fuckin' good. But I need to get you off first." Inching myself up the bed until I'm lying straight, I pat the pillow under my head. "Come here, darlin'. Straddle my face."

She wavers, uncertain. Then whispers in that sexy voice, "I've never done that before."

"Give it a try."

Slowly she grins, and then puts one leg over me, followed by the other. The material of the shirt I've yet to make her discard flopping down over my face. I push it away. As my hands start raising it, she stills, and her palms stop my progress. "Don't, Heart, please."

"You've seen mine, only fair I see yours."

I give her a moment, then when she doesn't protest further, I take off her top. As it catches on her head she helps me, then covers her chest for a second before coming to a decision and throwing it away. Then she makes short work of her bra, and I hear her indrawn breath. But my eyes don't focus on the scars beneath, fixing instead on the beautiful globes above. Pink-tinted nipples that cry out for my attention.

As my fingers lock onto those peaks, her head goes back and she gasps. When I pinch harder, I doubt she knows what she's doing as her body drops, and she starts grinding herself against my chest, leaving a trail of wetness behind.

I can smell her from here. I need a taste as much as a man needs water in the desert. "Move up, darlin'. Sit on my face."

Still unsure, she moves slowly, but then she's above me at last, and what a fucking beautiful sight. She's got short pubic hair, perfectly matching her hair, a natural blond. A landing strip points the way to her labia, and as she stretches her legs wide, it opens for me like a flower, her arousal glistening like the dew of early morning.

The perfume makes my nostrils flare, and her little exclamation as I pull her down and slide my tongue around her clit goes straight to my cock.

"Heart!"

It's been ten months since I've tasted a woman, and I've forgotten how it stimulates my taste buds, sending sensations straight to my cock. Her flavour's different to Crystal's, a little more salty, but intoxicating in its own way. As my tongue toys with her, her moisture's increasing, and I lap it up, like a man dying of thirst. My eyes watch her. She throws her head back again, her features contorting as she chases the peak I'm trying to get her to.

She's all I can hear, touch, taste, smell, and see. My mind, my brain, totally focused on her. I try circling her clit, then pressing harder, then I sweep my tongue in her channel again. Recording every nuance, every change, every sound of encouragement, learning this body so new to me.

I feel her muscles tense, her legs moving closer, becoming a vice around my head. Her movements are erratic, she's all but smothering me as she approaches her release.

Then she's there, and my name comes out of her mouth as a wail. I grin into her pussy as I lick slowly, helping to bring her down.

I see her face looking down at me with an expression almost like surprise. "Fuck, Heart. No wonder bikers have a reputation."

Helping her lift herself up, I grin. "Like that?"

She huffs a laugh. "Just a bit."

"A bit? Then I'll have to try harder. Move down me, darlin'. I told you you'd have to do all the work."

"I think you just proved yourself wrong." She gives a deep throaty chuckle that makes my cock jump. Then she's sliding down my body, her hands tracing the scars on my chest, but she doesn't linger or take her time.

Soon her knees are either side of my hips, hovering over my dick, her teeth biting her lips in concentration as she positions me beneath what my tongue has already told me is a very tight pussy.

I recover my wits. "Condom."

"I can't get pregnant, and I'm clean, Heart. I was tested as part of my medical and haven't been with anyone since I left South Carolina."

"I'm clean," I manage to stammer out. My cock, growing even harder, seems to think her being on the pill or whatever is exciting. Raising my head, I reach out my arms and place my hands either side of her hips, applying slight downward pressure. She positions me right and starts to lower herself.

The head of my dick disappears, and the whole thing seems to thicken as I take in the sight. *Fuck, I can't wait.* Gripping her tighter, using the strength I've built up in my arm muscles from using those darn crutches, I take charge, pulling her body down hard.

She's tight, but wet, and I slide in easily.

"Heart!" she cries out as her face twists with shock.

"You okay?" It's hard for me to form words.

"Just a bit more than I'm used to." She's struggling to breathe.

I give her a second to adjust, while feeling a blast of typical male pride. Then she starts moving, easing herself up and down on my cock.

I'm already primed by her blowing me, aroused to fever pitch by her taste in my mouth. Her speed is too slow, too torturous, keeping me hanging.

My fingernails leave marks in her skin as I struggle to hold back. I lift her up a little, then tug her down, thrusting up at the same time. I quicken the pace, and she's right with me. Her eyes open and fix on mine.

After the months of abstinence, I'm not going to last long. "Get yourself off, darlin'. Play with that pretty clit."

Her hand snakes round and starts rubbing, her rhythm keeping time with my up and down strokes. A familiar tingling starts in my spine, and my balls grow heavy, the delicious reactions of my body that I'd almost forgotten.

"Are you close?" I gasp, but I needn't have asked. Her muscles contract, squeezing my cock.

As the first cry comes out of her mouth, I wouldn't be able to stop even if I wanted to. Ten months' worth of cum shoots up my dick, and keeps coming and coming, in the longest orgasm I've ever had.

We take a moment without speaking, both our chests heaving

as we take air into our lungs. When the flush on her skin begins to lighten, she lifts herself up, my release flooding from her pussy and soaking my pubic hair.

"Had a lot stored up there," she observes. Her hand comes up to cup my face for a second, then she moves off the bed and goes into the bathroom to clean herself up. I hear the toilet flush while I lie here, totally drained with no energy to move.

She returns, carrying a washcloth she's found, and fuck me if she's not cleaning me up.

"Hey, that should be my job," I tell her with a smile.

"You can return the favour next time."

We both freeze.

When Drummer told me I had to take her as my old lady, getting fucked was the very last thing on my mind. I've no fucking idea what came over me, or how the hell we ended up having sex. From the bewildered expression on her face, neither does she.

"Marc," I begin, but she shakes her head to stop me.

"It's alright, Heart, I understand." She nods as though to impress that she really does get it. Then quickly finding her clothes, only stopping to put on the top which covers her scars, she carries the rest out of the door. She closes it behind her, then after a second she opens it again.

She glances at me, gives a half-smile followed by a wink, then disappears into her room.

She's remembered my instruction to leave both doors open.

I listen to the sounds of her getting ready for bed, and then the lights go out. I turn my own bedside lamp off and am enveloped in darkness.

I should be lying awake. I should be wallowing in misery, regretting what I've allowed to happen, worrying about the ramifications and the effect that my betrayal will have on me.

But instead, my body so weary, I go straight to sleep.

CHAPTER TWENTY-TWO

*M*arc…

Almost before I turn out my light, I hear gentle snoring coming from the other room. I smile to myself, typical man falling asleep after sex.

I thump the strange pillow, trying to get comfortable, and start regretting what I've just done. *What the hell made me go with him tonight? Was I so desperate any male could have serviced me?* Whatever the reason, and however good he made me feel, it can't happen again. I can't get in any deeper than I already am with these men. I'd be risking my job, my career, and my future.

And my heart. While Les had been my fuck buddy, I felt nothing other than friendship. We didn't date, just hooked up when we were both in the mood. It's different with Heart, I already like him. That I missed him so much while we were apart illustrated that. What I should be doing is building up my walls to keep him out, not to allow him closer inside.

When he'd gone missing in Los Angeles, I should have recognised the first warnings. My frantic worry made me throw caution to the wind and brought me to Drummer. I should have seen the signs and made a conscious effort to stop caring. *But if I had, Heart would be dead.*

I turn over the other way, but while the bed's soft it doesn't seem conducive to sleep. Okay, I admit, I like him more than I should. But for the sake of my sanity, this can't go any further. From now on, I'll keep my distance.

Then I scoff at myself. That won't be hard. We're two adults who had sex when they both needed the edge taken off. There was no emotional involvement or connection. We didn't even kiss, and no after-sex cuddles. I'd behaved just like one of their club whores, and being still hung up on his dead wife, that's all he wanted.

And all I wanted from him. Isn't it?

At long last, my thoughts stop circling and my brain eventually shuts down. When I wake, I'm annoyed that I spent so long worrying about a man who's got nothing to give, and didn't spend the time in more profitable ways, thinking about how best to minimise my stay at the Satan's Devils' compound.

Pulling the door closed for some privacy, I get showered and dressed for the day, appreciating the accommodation, which is far more luxurious than I had expected. I could almost be staying in a vacation resort, certainly nothing like my training and research had led me to believe. I open the door and step out onto the balcony, leaning over for a second, enjoying the view and the warmth of the sun and breathing in fresh, untainted air. The desert is laid out before me, stark in its beauty, and the glorious cloudless blue sky seems to have endless promise for the day. It resembles the calm before the storm.

I've dressed in skinny jeans and have chosen a t-shirt with a Kawasaki logo on it. I'd pulled it on over my head with a grin.

I'm just about ready when there's a knock at my door. Going to open it, I'm not surprised to see Heart.

For a moment, he looks at me searchingly. "Breakfast?"

"I'm starving." I could add that it was the late-night activity that's made me that way, but I don't. He doesn't allude to it either.

"I've got to work out with Peg in the gym this morning." He swings along on his crutches.

"Got a punching bag? Weights?"

"Got the fuckin' lot."

"Mind if I tag along?"

He looks a little surprised, but then grins. "Saves me getting someone else to watch you."

The clubhouse is different to how I'd seen it last night. Quiet conversations are being exchanged between more subdued bikers, and there's no music playing. Jekyll and another prospect I haven't yet met, but who Heart tells me is called Fergus—though apparently just shouting Prospect will do as well as a name—are wandering around with black garbage sacks, emptying ashtrays and picking up empties. Once again, we head for the kitchen.

I've met the other old ladies before, so give a nod and a smile as a greeting, which I'm pleased to see is returned—at least there seem to be some people prepared to be friendly—then Heart directs me to a seat at the table, and sits alongside. Sophie puts a couple of heaped plates in front of us and then follows it up with steaming cups of coffee. I express my heart-felt thanks.

There are sounds of a child laughing and a baby crying. I turn around to see Sam and Drummer walking in. Amy drops Sam's hand and makes a beeline for Heart, clambering up onto his lap. Her fingers sneak out and snag a piece of bacon.

"Little monkey." Heart laughs fondly as she stuffs the food into her mouth.

"Here, give this to her." Sophie puts down a smaller plate of scrambled eggs. Amy picks up a fork and starts digging in, and Heart doesn't blink an eye when some lands in his lap, nor when little greasy fingers tangle in his hair.

Sam's rocking the crying baby. Drummer pulls out a seat and hands her a blanket. She covers herself and discreetly puts the baby to her breast. No one takes any notice. When she's got him settled, she looks across to Sophie, who's leaning against the counter with a coffee in her hand. "Where's Ollie?"

"*Olivia* is with Wraith. Having some daddy and daughter bonding time."

Sam laughs. "You mean she's screaming her head off and you wanted some peace."

Sophie frowns as if she's going to disagree, then grins. "Something like that."

The whole scene around me seems totally incongruous. This is a biker compound, the criminal element my police colleagues want to see put in the ground. But what I'm seeing is a loving family, chores shared, babies fed in plain sight. Something I never would have expected. I'm taking a lot from my stay here, but if Drummer's worried I'm storing up tips as to how to take him down, he's completely wrong. I'd never want to do anything to destroy this seemingly idyllic life.

I feel like an outsider. It's been so long since I was part of anything. As Heart pulls my finished but not empty plate toward him and starts eating my leftovers as if it's the most natural thing in the world, I feel my eyes becoming wet. It's just what my older brother would have done.

I stand and walk to Sophie. "What can I do to help?" I point to the finished plates stacked up.

Within moments she's got me working, and busying my hands stops the threatening tears.

Other bikers wander in and I help Sophie serve them, getting strange looks, and a huff from Peg as he notices my shirt.

"Peg. Keep your eyes off my old lady's tits," Heart tells him firmly.

Peg's eyes widen, then points at the logo. "Prez, can't we ban stuff like that?"

Another biker who's name I don't yet know, laughs. "Bring it up in church, Peg."

Church. That's a common term for bikers to call their meetings.

Breakfast eaten, men get up with comments such as 'got to get to the shop', or 'bar needs stocking at Angels, I'll be there all day' and 'got to go help Marsha at the restaurant'. Just like any other family getting ready to do an honest day's work. *Where are the comments about weapons deals? Or about burying bodies? Why's nobody taking or mentioning drugs? Is it just because I'm here?* But the remarks flowed so naturally, nothing seemed to be put on for my benefit.

"An hour, then meet you in the gym?"

"Sure thing, Peg."

"Daddy, bike!" Amy's eyes light up, and she tries to drag Heart out of his seat. He laughs and tells her to be careful, then follows her outside.

She's got a kid's bicycle, one with training wheels, and she mounts up then starts zooming around. Heart's looking at her with a look of love on his face. He turns to me. "Reckon she could have the training wheels off now, but I can't run alongside her."

I watch her, seeing what he means. "Want me to help?"

He turns, his eyes assessing me. "Yeah. If you don't mind." At my nod, he summons the child who claps her hands excitedly as he starts to take the small stabilising wheels away.

We take her to a piece of land with flattish grass, their barbeque area by the look of all the grills and firepits scattered around, and for the next hour I'm running alongside the bike, at first using my hand to balance her, and then when I think she's ready, stepping back and letting her do it alone. *I remember my father doing this with me.*

When she realises she's riding all by herself, Amy can't stop, so pleased with herself. After a few minutes she throws the bike down, runs back inside, then comes back out, followed by several bikers she's managed to round up, and demonstrates her new found ability to them. Sam and Sophie come out, babies in arms, laughing and cheering her on.

"Hey, Heart!" It's Peg yelling.

"Go on, I'll watch her," Sam offers.

With one last fond look at the little girl I helped teach to ride, I follow Heart into a well-equipped gym.

I'm unprepared and not dressed for it, but hey, if I ever need to defend myself I won't be able to stop and put on sweats, so I tackle that punching bag as I normally would. At first, I watch Heart out of the corner of my eye as he's put through his paces by the unrelenting sergeant-at-arms. Then I become focused on what I'm doing, pausing only when strong hands grip and stop the bag.

"Go on. Give it another shot. You're weak on your left side."

Thanking Peg, I start again, listening to his instructions, altering my stance and perfecting my punches.

When I'm exhausted, I bend double to breathe. Peg goes back to Heart, patting me on the shoulder as he passes. "You did good, girl." I take it that's great praise from the taciturn man.

He slings a towel at me, and as I stand wiping sweat off my brow, my eyes again find Heart, realising how much effort he's putting into getting strength back into his legs.

At last Peg thinks he's done enough, and even I can see the exhaustion on Heart's face.

"Drummer wants us in church. To discuss..." Peg jerks his head back over his shoulders and toward me, making it clear what the subject of their discussion will be.

I seethe, knowing I'm not going to be invited. But with a sigh, I realise it's not unlike when the higher ranked officers at the precinct would have a closed meeting, only feeding information down the ranks on a need-to-know basis. Even so, I'm not happy that others are making decisions for me.

Jekyll's given strict instructions not to let me out of his sight, and I'm left in the clubroom, along with the Sophie and Sam, their babies, and Amy. Carmen and Sandy have apparently gone to work, one a hairdresser and one manages a restaurant, and Ella has gone shopping in town. Such normal activities and, again, unexpected.

The babies are on playmats, kicking their toys. Sophie's encouraging Olivia, who's apparently eight months old, to crawl. We all clap as she rolls onto her stomach. Amy is playing with a toy motorbike and some dolls. I get down on the floor and start dressing them with her, soon making them talk and have conversations, which makes her giggle.

After a while Sophie looks up. "It's a warm day outside. Who fancies a swim?"

Sam's eyes light up. "That would be fun."

At the same time, Amy leaps up and starts jumping up and down. "Swim!"

Sophie looks at me. "I can lend you a suit if you don't have one."

"Swim?" My eyes narrow. "Where?"

"Surely you've seen the pool?" I did, when I was outside with Amy, a glimpse of blue behind some hedging.

"Is it clean?" I'm dubious.

They both burst out laughing, and Jekyll seems to make a strangled cough from behind.

"If it's not, the prospects won't get patched in. Right, Jekyll?"

I turn to look at the man, who's looking disgusted, but nods to agree. He then speaks, "Hyde tested the water last night. It's all good."

Sophie gets to her feet. "Well, come on then."

The bathing suit she provides is a tiny bikini which I view doubtfully, before deciding I can keep my t-shirt on.

The pool's lovely, the October day not too hot or too chilly, just right for lounging around. Amy's latched onto me, and I play with her in the water, realising I'm becoming attached to the little girl. She wants to learn to swim, so I take her into the shallow end where she can just stand. Soon she's got her water wings off and I'm encouraging her to try taking a few strokes toward me, proud as punch when she manages a couple of seconds keeping afloat on her own.

When we've all had our fill of the water, we go back inside.

Sandy, back from the restaurant, is already in the kitchen, and I help her as Sophie and Sam make sandwiches for lunch. The water's tired the kids out, so we take them to the nursery they've got set up, and even Amy lies down for a nap on the cot there. Obviously used to this, both women switch on monitors, making sure they've got the relevant parts with them, and we return to the kitchen again.

Halfway through her sandwich, Sophie looks across at me. "You're a natural with Amy. You should have a kid of your own."

And just like that, my enjoyment of the day disappears. My face must drop.

Sam spots it immediately. "What's up, Marcia?" I shake my head, but she's not going to give up. A friendly hand touches my arm. "Come on, spill. You're among family here."

I might be accepted by these old ladies, but know I'm not by the men. This is a family, just not mine. I lost my family eight years ago. Angrily, I swipe the tears from my eyes.

"Oh, come on, love." Sophie's arms come around me. "What's up, hon? Didn't mean to upset you."

I look from one to the other, and then fuck knows why, but I let it all out. I take a deep breath and let the words tumble out. "I was in an accident," I explain. "I lost my family and was badly injured. The doctor's told me I'd never be able to have a baby."

The women exchange looks of horror. "Oh, hon. When was this?"

"When I was eighteen." I try to shrug it off, summoning up what I hope passes for a smile. "I've had plenty of time to get used to the idea."

That's a lie. I never have, and never will.

CHAPTER TWENTY-THREE

*H*eart...

"You get fucked or something, Heart?" Tongue throws at me as I take my seat at the table, my legs protesting at the workout they'd just gotten under the careful scrutiny of Peg.

Tongue's caught me unawares, and I stutter my answer. "No, what? What the fuck? Why the fuck you think that?"

Marvel's watching me carefully, his face splitting into a grin. "You look more relaxed. You've gotten rid of your pent-up tension some way or the other."

"And," Blade sitting opposite points his knife my way, "you have picked up an ol' lady."

"For fuck's sake." I round on them. "I've been working out. Fuck, you're worse than kids in a playground."

Drummer enters and takes his seat at the top of the table. *Thank fuck for that. He'll shut it down now.* But he too is given me an intense scrutiny. "Everything working out with your ol' lady?"

Inhaling sharply, I toss a glare at them all, but for once I can't respond I haven't got an old lady. I actually have. Just not the one I want. And what Marc and I did last night? I'd woken in the small hours and spent the rest of the night convincing myself there wasn't any betrayal involved. We were two people coming together just for one night. Two horny fuckers who both had the same need. It wasn't like anything I shared with Crystal, no loving touches, no kisses, no closeness involved. But it was fun, I can't deny that. I hate that a smile's come to my lips.

Quickly I force the corners back down and respond to the prez with a gruff, "She's behaving herself."

As suggestions come my way about exactly what form her good behaviour might have taken, I swear under my breath and straighten my shoulders. They might mock all they want, but I know the truth.

"Hope you gloved up. Don't want no cop-biker spawn." Joker's comment is louder than the rest.

Now wouldn't that be a fuck up. And I didn't, of course. She'd told me she was covered so she couldn't get caught. *I trusted her.* And only shortly after I finished explaining why it would take a long time before she earned my trust. She wouldn't have lied, would she? Nah, she's got as much to lose as me.

A loud bang of the gavel gets my attention.

"Right, everyone shut up. Heart's got his work cut out watching his ol' lady. If we want the cop out of our hair, we need to sort a few things out."

"Like who's after her, and whether it's got anything to do with us." Wraith nods at the prez.

"Exactly." Prez raises his chin at the VP. "Right now we've got a whole lot of coincidences and nothing to connect them. Heart, you up for recording this shit?"

"Sure am, Prez." I flex my fingers, well, nine of them anyway, demonstrating they're all healed up. It feels good to step into my secretary role again.

Drummer tugs at his beard. "Right, put the Herreras at the top of that list."

"My name should go there, Prez. Someone copied my explosives to blow up the cop's house."

"Yeah, Slick. And add Jayden's. That might be a dead end,

and I fuckin' hope it's just that, but we need to be careful and not dismiss it."

"Should I note down the change at the top of the Herreras?"

"Yeah, Heart. Right now we don't have a fuckin' clue how that will affect us."

Lady taps the table. "What about the names of those cops Marcia's knocked heads with? Her sergeant and partner."

Drummer scrunches up his face. "Reynolds, wasn't it?"

"Yeah," I drop in, "and Garza."

"Found anything on them, Mouse?"

"Interestingly, both are squeaky clean. Nothing to find in their records." He looks from his laptop to the prez. "If they've got someone on their side who can trace Heart's ol' lady's activities, it's more than possible anything they don't want found has been removed."

So that's a red herring.

"We ever come across them? Any of you assholes been picked up or questioned by them?"

Joker raises his hand. "I was pulled over when I first patched over, for having Nevada plates. I think it was Garza who questioned me. If it was, he's got a hard-on for bikers, I can tell you that. All but took me to the border and pointed me back home."

"Why did he pull you over?"

"He didn't, but he talked to me once they'd taken me in. I had a Tucson patch and a bike from out of the area. They tried to pin a theft charge on me. Course my documents sorted it out, but they held onto me as long as they could. Fuckin' pigs."

A murmured grumbling around the table shows that everyone here agrees with his views.

"Let's get back to the Herreras. I didn't like that we had to come up against them a few months back, it put us on their radar. Before Slick's ol' lady's problem, we kept to our side of the street and they kept to theirs."

Slick looks down. He'll be feeling sorry he was the reason we got put in their sights, but none of us care. All of us are prepared to lay our lives down for our brothers. And his woman's sister was saved, but not before she'd been groomed and molested—or so I'd been told. From what I've seen of her, she's on her way back. My eyes go to Paladin, and I see him clenching his fists. He's certainly got a soft spot for young Jayden. Any mention of the girl and he's ready to leap to her defence.

"What happened that night when you met them, Prez?" I'd been in a coma at the time. Oh, I've heard the story about the Satan's Devils being set up as hit men to take the rogue elements of the family out—the men who'd been leading a child grooming ring, the same one that Jayden had been caught up in. Archer's death had been swept up in that. But I can't remember hearing the full version, or what happened when Prez, Peg, and Slick met Leonardo Herrera and his lieutenants.

"Not much to tell, Heart. We met with them, they backed us into a corner and offered us a deal."

"Didn't trust them," Peg adds. "That's why we got the women out of here and sent them to Vegas, just in case it all came back down on the club."

"Herrera gave me no sign they'd come after us. In fact, what we'd done had gotten the family out of the sights of the cartel. In his view we did them a favour."

Slick raises his head and lifts his chin toward me. "Cartel deals in skin, Herrera's arrangement with them is that they don't."

"But that was Leonardo and his lieutenants. Now there's a change at the top, things might be different," Prez takes over again.

Wraith taps his hand against his mouth. "What if the new head wants to start up the trade for themselves? Fuckton of money riding on that."

"They'd be putting themselves up against the cartel." Peg's brow creases. "And we need to steer well clear. We don't have the manpower to put us in the middle."

We throw ideas around for a while. Hyde's been called in

twice to refresh our beers. After a while, Road says he's got to get back to the strip club and get it ready for opening, so Drummer sums up.

"We keep coming back to the Herreras. Archer was family to them. If it's simply that they're putting pressure on the cops to keep his record clean, I think you should persuade your ol' lady, Heart, to leave it at that. The man's dead. We know what happened to him." He nods at Slick who grins, having shot off the man's dick. "Don't much care whether they think he's a hero or not. He's not in our sights anymore."

"What about my sweet mother-in-law?"

There are sneers around the table. "Wouldn't use that description for the bitch."

I give an evil grin. "Neither would I."

"We were waiting to see what you wanted to do with her, Heart. Seems that time might have come."

I'm thinking aloud. "As long as I'm living she ain't got no rights to custody. And now Archer's gone, no one to help her."

"She's still got to clear her debts." Prez's hands link behind the back of his head. "If you die, Heart, or she can prove you unsuitable, she's next in line to look after the kid if she can clean herself up and convince a judge. That's what your woman was worried about when we were still wondering whether you'd make it. Marcia wanted to get the kid into foster care to protect her, but obviously we weren't going to allow that."

"Yeah, she seemed to think bikers weren't good enough family. She tried to take her away, didn't she, Prez?" Wraith's eyes crease as he remembers.

The words register, but for now wash over me. I'm still thinking how to ensure the best provision is made for my daughter.

Mouse nudges me. "If the cops are involved, you could be picked up and jailed on a trumped-up charge. That would allow Clyde to step straight in."

Having survived two attempts to kill me, I'd really rather not think there would be a third. But with my luck, it's a possibility, as well as a very valid observation by Mouse. I lift my chin at the prez. "I'll see the lawyer, make a new will. Anything happens to me, I'll see you and Sam get custody."

"Sam," Drummer corrects. "Put it in Sam's name. She's an upstanding citizen." There are a few smiles. Yeah, when she's not being the old lady of the president of an outlaw motorcycle club.

"Hate to say this, Heart, but might be time to go visit with Susie Clyde."

My mouth drops open. "Prez, the hatred between us is mutual. Fuck, she even hated her own daughter."

"If you're that afraid of the bitch, take someone with you." Now people laugh, but it's no joke. She's a foul woman.

Shooter raises his hand. "I'll come with. Reckon I can hold my own with a drugged-up bitch."

All emotion is suddenly wiped off Drummer's face. "If you get one whiff that she's not keeping straight, get an inkling she's still got the hots for your kid, we'll take her out. I don't think the world will be a worse place for it."

I jerk my head. He's completely right.

"Okay. Let's wrap this up. Mouse. Can you get the contact information for the son who's taken over from Leonardo Herrera? Not committing right now, but I may need to go have a chat. And everyone, keep thinking. And you, Heart. Talk to Marcia and see if you can find out what else she knows, any little thing that doesn't add up. We'll meet again when we've got something to discuss."

When I stand, I do so carefully, my legs having become stiff after sitting for so long. I exit the room and see Jekyll standing in the entrance to the kitchen, looking bored out of his head. That must mean Marc's in there along with the other women, and I hope they're not giving her a hard time. I hadn't realised I'd be leaving her to have such a long meeting. But as I limp across to find her, laughter soon reaches my ears.

"So I said to him, if I wasn't so blimming knackered I'd have dropped my knickers there and then. The pillock just looked at me as if I'd lost the plot. I'd just have soon settled for a cup of char. And that's how it all went pear shaped."

As I enter, I see Marc with her mouth open, and the rest of them doubled up.

"Would someone please translate?"

Sandy slaps her on the back. "Stay around and you'll start to pick up how to speak her language. Then you won't look so gobsmacked."

"Sandy!" Sophie yells in delight. "You're learning."

Fuck me, these women. I get a strange feeling when I see Marc's settling right in. And then a deeper emotion as Amy, who hasn't noticed me yet, is running over to her, and Marc sweeping her up into her arms. "Can we go swimming tomorrow?"

As Marc goes to answer, she catches my eye. "If it's okay with your dad."

"Daddddy!" And now I'm subjected to the full-on force of my daughter.

I lean down to cuddle her close. "Swimming, eh?"

"Marcia's teaching me how to swim."

"Is she now?"

Marc looks slightly sheepish, and I'm not too certain what I think about her getting so close to my kid. She's only got a temporary position in my life. I think back on what I hadn't paid much attention to at the meeting. Marc had wanted Amy out of the club and out of the biker life. Well that's not going to happen, not even over my dead body.

But she can't want to do me wrong, can she?

As my head's spinning with so many problems we need to sort out, I park that extra one for now.

CHAPTER TWENTY-FOUR

Marc…

I've thoroughly enjoyed the day interacting with the old ladies and their children. Although, as always, it hurts being around mothers with babies and young children while knowing I'll never have one of my own, somehow I haven't felt lonely enough for that to prey on my mind. Amy's kept me busy, and I've been included in all the conversation and gossip.

Having no family, I haven't been forced into such close proximity with youngsters before today, and despite my personal circumstances, found I've actually loved being around the little ones. As long as I've kept my hurt and sadness locked tightly away, it's true to say I've had, on many levels, a surprisingly good time.

Sandy had helped to put things into perspective. She and her old man, Viper, couldn't have kids, so made the best of it, ending up delighted when Sam had turned up as Viper's fully grown daughter he never knew he had. Now they've got a grandchild, little Eli. And, my, hasn't Sam's got her hands full with that kid? A couple of times today I've noticed he's definitely Drummer's son, if that can be measured by the way everyone jumps when he demands attention. He's only just over half a year old.

Now Olivia, she takes after Sophie, happy and content and seeming to get pleasure in making people smile and laugh.

And Amy. Well, I was taken by the sweet little girl when I first met her, wanting to make sure she stayed out of the clutches of her grandmother. Relieved when I knew how well Drummer and Sam were looking after her, but still wishing that Heart would end his travels and come back and be her dad. I'm over the moon and delighted to see them together, and no one could miss the love that he shows for his little girl.

She's easy to love. Even I've fallen for her. Helping her learn how to ride her bike without training wheels and swimming with her in the pool was fun, and I'm glad to be allowed, if only in a small way, to be part of her life.

Heart's cuddling his daughter, but giving me an assessing look, his face blank so I can't read what's on his mind. Something seems to be different about him, making me speculate just how their conversation went in church. Or is it that he's regretting what we did last night? Mingling with the women and children had made me forget the problems at my door for a while, but the good mood brought on by my unusually relaxing day starts to dissipate.

The easy relationship we've developed is still strained when we join the others for the buffet-style dinner I'd help to prepare, and then Heart moves away and seems to be in deep conversation with Sam. Their gesticulations make me think they're formulating some sort of arrangement about his daughter. The discussion ends when Sam takes Amy's hand and leads her away.

It's only then that Heart gives me his full attention, but his eyes are narrowed and his face drawn. I don't know what to expect as he approaches.

His hand touches my shoulder and gives a gentle push out into the main room. He points to a table and holds up his hand to Fergus. Almost before we're seated, there's a beer and a white wine in front of me.

"Spit it out, Heart. What's happened?" He barely resembles the man who I was in bed with last night. "Or are you having regrets about what we did?" Get things out in the open, clear the air.

"Last night shouldn't have happened." He confirms that I'm right. "There can be nothing between us, you know that as well as me."

"Didn't mean anything—" I start to say.

"No, it didn't," he interrupts. "Look, Marc. Even if you weren't a cop, I'm not in the right place to start anything. I took what you offered, and I'm ashamed that I used you. You're not a club whore."

I'm certainly not, but I treated him the same way. "Don't let it worry you, Heart. Let's mark it up to experience and put it behind us."

He stares down at his beer. "Thing is, Drum's got my head all screwed up. Giving you the ol' lady label was a step too far. Brothers have started thinking that way, and that's gonna cause trouble in the club."

"Because of what I do."

"Yeah." He picks up the bottle, downing half of it in one. "But you're here for the duration until we get to the bottom of whatever's going on." His eyes meet mine for perhaps the first time. "I want to know what you know. See if we can't kick-start this thing. At the moment we're going around in circles trying to understand."

"What do you want to ask?" I take a sip of my wine, working on stopping my hand shaking. Reading between the lines he's not going to let what I thought was our friendship come between him and his club. Not that I really expected it, but he'll be giving me my cue to leave as soon as he can. After today, having seen such a different side to a biker club, I'm no longer sure that's what I want.

His hands play with the bottle, picking at the label. "Leonardo Herrera is no longer head of the clan. His son, Javier, has taken over. You aware of that?"

I shake my head. "If it's happened recently, I've not been in the loop."

"Why do you think your sergeant was so adamant about protecting Archer's reputation?"

Now that I have thought about it. "Archer's dead, so it makes no difference to him. The Herrera family might want to protect their name." I grimace quickly, not knowing how much I should tell him. What I know comes from police reports. "We all know the cartel's at the top of the chain, everyone below picks up scraps or works for them. It's they who deal in the skin trade. If Archer stepped into that territory, the Herreras might want to keep that quiet."

That doesn't come as news to him. Suddenly he slams his now empty bottle down on the table. "For fuck's sake, Marc. You must know who would want to take you out?"

I reel back, his force startling me. "Heart, I don't know. The only thing I've done is present my suspicions and my evidence against Archer. I haven't been here long enough to work on many other cases, and there's nothing else I can think of."

"If you're right, and the Herrera's are behind the efforts to shut you down permanently, then you're putting the club up against that family. Fuck knows where the cartel stands in this."

"Cartel would have shut them down themselves if they found they were dipping into their trade." Again, I get the feeling there's something he's not telling me.

Before either of us can say anything more, Sam comes over, her eyes flicking to me then to him. Then her hand rests on his shoulder. "Ten minutes?" she asks.

"Yeah, I'll be there." As the prez's woman gives me a friendly smile and walks away, he turns to me. "I'm going up to the suite."

"I'll come with you. I could do with an early night."

A quick glance my way, and I realise I've alluded to last night being a late one, and raised the spectre of our indiscretion in both our head's once again.

While I've no real reason to go to bed this early, I don't much fancy the idea of staying in the clubhouse as the old ladies go home and the sweet butts come in to service the men. Add to that, none of these men are particularly friendly and won't want to talk with a cop in the room. When Heart stands, I get to my feet as well. At least it will save him assigning another babysitter to me.

But before we can reach the door Drummer gets his attention. "Heart, need to speak to you."

"I'll go on up." I start walking again, but get a hand forcefully holding my arm.

"Prospect? See Marc up to her room, will ya?"

And there, I've picked up a minder again. I bristle. I had no intention of going anywhere else, particularly after this afternoon and my good time with the ol' ladies. I'm not here as a spy, and it hurts that Heart believes I might take the opportunity to poke around and try to find evidence on the club. It's another confirmation that we can never mix.

I enter the suite, knowing Hyde is waiting outside—my jailor until Heart returns. I've left my bedroom door open, as instructed.

I've only time to visit the bathroom and freshen up before the outer door opens, but it's not the man I expected, it's Sam and Amy.

"Hi. Heart wanted Amy to sleep in his room tonight. Is he around?"

"Still speaking to your old man, I think." So that's Heart's plan, to put a buffer between us. That would work.

"Oh, well, I doubt he'll be long. I'll get her settled, shall I?" She appears a little flustered.

Knowing she's got a young baby of her own to look after, I

cross the room and go to the hallway. "Why don't you leave her with me for a bit? We'll be fine, won't we, Amy?"

Remembering me as the woman who was playing with her most of the day, Amy grins, showing she's got no problem with my suggestion.

Sam looks relieved. "Thanks Marcia. Jayden wanted to get away, so I'd love to get back to Eli." Then as she turns her attention to the child, her face becomes stern. "Marcia's going to get you ready for bed, Amy. You be a good girl now, you hear? And don't play up." She hands me a book. "It's her bedtime story. She likes this one. She'll be tired after the day, and so should soon be asleep. Just don't get her hyped up or she'll never go down."

I'm grateful for the tip, not having been around children. *No boisterous games if I want her to sleep. Got it.*

"We'll be fine," I repeat, holding out my hand for the girl.

"She just needs a quick bath, then here are her night clothes." Sam turns her tired eyes to me. "Are you sure this is okay?"

Bending, I lift Amy into my arms. "You go get some rest, Sam. You look like you need it. I'll sort this one out."

Sam's hand touches mine and gives it a squeeze. "You're a lifesaver."

As she walks out the door, I'm not sure about that, but following instructions I put Amy in the tub, then get her out and dry her. Once she's in her Disney nightie, I put her to bed. It's a single, but there's room enough for me to lie on top while she's snuggling under the covers. I open the book and start to read.

There's some pop-out shit, and Amy loves seeing the pictures of animals snap out as I turn the pages, so it's natural to start making sounds. Soon she's in fits of giggles and laughter, especially when I make a cow bark.

"Cows don't bark."

"Don't they?" I act surprised, then neigh like a horse.

"Nope. They don't do that." She's shaking her head so seriously, I bite back another laugh.

"What sound do they make then?"

She jumps up and sits astride me, her little face beaming. "They go *mooo*, silly."

"Oh, I'm silly now, am I?"

Forgetting Sam's instruction to keep her quiet, I tickle her. Soon she's crying and begging me to stop, so I halt my torture.

With a child's innocence she throws herself into my arms, kisses my cheek and cries out, "Love you, Marcia."

"What the *fuck*?"

The loudly barked exclamation has my head turning to find a furious-looking Heart standing by the door. After a second he throws down one of his crutches, and balancing on the other, swings himself over to me. His hand bites into my arm.

"Amy, get yourself back into bed. I'll come and see you in a minute." His barely controlled anger makes his voice harsh, and I can see Amy's lip trembling as she hurries to obey.

"It's alright, sweetheart. Daddy's not upset with you. He just wants to speak to me." Leaning down I plant a kiss on her forehead and then am ripped away by that grip on my arm.

"Get in your room, now," he growls.

Not wanting Amy to get distressed, I give her a confident smile, then do as instructed. Behind me I hear quiet murmuring, and can only hope he's settling her down.

It's not only the child that doesn't understand his sudden burst of temper. I have absolutely no idea what I seem to have done wrong. I'm pacing my room when he comes in, shutting the door behind him.

He hisses, "You keep away from Amy, you hear? She's my fuckin' daughter, not yours."

I don't have a clue what he's talking about. "Heart, I was just looking after her. You were delayed, and Sam had to get back to Eli. I was helping out is all."

"It was more than that. You've been getting in tight with her all day! Teaching her to ride a bike, swim. All the things that I can't fuckin' do." He comes in and looms over me, reaching out his hand and grasping my hair, pulling my head back. "You've been doing it on purpose, and it fuckin' worked, didn't it? I heard what she said to you."

"Kids love everyone! Even I know that. She meant nothing by it, Heart. She'd probably tell any of the women, fuck, any of your brothers who put her to bed that she loved them."

He lets me go so fast I almost lose my balance, but manage to recover it. Placing my hands on my hips, I glare at him.

"She said it to you. Bet you thought everything was going to plan."

"Plan?" I shake my head, completely at a loss here. *What am I supposed to be planning?*

"Yeah, your plan." He advances again. "You never told me, did you? That crucial fact that you can't have kids."

My eyes widen. It's true, I never did. It didn't come up, and it's not something you casually drop into conversation with a *friend*. I'd only told the old ladies this afternoon, as the subject occurred naturally. That's how he knows. "Heart, it's not something you needed to know. I only told the old ladies—"

"And luckily they told me. And with all the other things I've heard, it's all fallen into fuckin' place."

Bemused, I can only stare at him.

"You tried to get your hands on Amy while I was still in a fuckin' coma. Wanted her off the compound. Now I reckon you want her for yourself. To make up for kids you can't fuckin' have."

I gasp. He couldn't be further from the truth. "You're wrong—"

"I'm right. All the time you've befriended me it was because you had the hots for her. You never wanted to leave her in an *Outlaw Motorcycle Gang*, did you?" That he's so angry is indicated by the way his voice, dripping with sarcasm, gives his club the name law enforcement use for it. "All those times you were getting close to me over the past months was to get to her."

"Heart. What you're saying is ridiculous. Next you'll be

saying I planted the bomb myself. Arranged for a drive by shooting."

His eyebrows go up. "Well, did you?"

I throw my hands in the air. "Just listen to yourself, Heart. Yeah, of course I can make an explosive. Though obviously I'm not good enough as I cracked my skull and got burned in the process."

"Just shows how fuckin' incompetent you are." If he was shouting at the top of his voice I'd understand it, but his tone is icy cold, which is worse. "Just like you're only half a woman and unable to have a baby yourself."

I slap his face. Hard.

He grins, but it's not from amusement. "Caught you out, didn't I, *darlin'*. Fucked up your plan now I know. I'll make sure you're not given a chance to get close to Amy or any of the babies while you're here."

"I'm not staying."

"Oh yes you are. You'll be staying until we get to the bottom of what you really want. If I was suspicious before about you wanting to bring down the club, I'm even more so now." His face twists as if he can't stand looking at me anymore, and then just as quickly as he arrived, he's gone.

Forgetting his own instructions, he bangs my door closed, and then I hear a sound like an echo as he shuts his.

My hand covers my mouth to stifle a cry. *He's wrong. Totally wrong.* How has he come up with a twisted story like this?

You're only half a woman. His cruel words cause a sob to burst from my throat. It wasn't just my whole family the accident had taken from me, but the chance to give birth to a new life, to start a family of my own. *Half a woman.* As though a dam bursts inside me, huge cries wrack my body, tears flooding down my cheeks and swelling my eyes. I fall to the floor and curl up into a ball, my body shuddering and shaking with grief. Letting it out worse than when the doctors had first pronounced my fate, mourning that I can't, yearning for a chance that somehow I could be a whole woman.

Heart's voiced my worst fears, that a man would see me for less than I am because of my inability to bear him a child. But to consider for one second that I'd wanted to remove a kid from a good home? It's unbelievable. But obviously doesn't seem so to the man in the next room.

It's true all those months ago, when I first came onto the compound I was worried about Heart's daughter, but only because I knew her unfit grandmother was trying to get custody, and I knew nothing about these bikers. But once I'd seen the love they had for the child, and had met Sam, her main caregiver, all my doubts disappeared. I would have reported a child being neglected, but that wasn't the case with Amy.

During my conversations with Heart while he was on the road, I said everything I could to reunite father and daughter. How could he have forgotten? How the fuck did he come up with the thought that I had all of this planned?

By the time I stop crying, it's dark and silent around. I pace my room, knowing the last thing I want to do is stay on the compound one moment longer. It would kill me to be kept isolated, with the women I grew friendly with today eyeing me suspiciously and keeping their children out of my way. *Would anyone else think the same as him?* Even if they didn't, this is such a close band of men and women, they'd side with him and listen to whatever he had to say.

My fingers touch the side of my face which Amy had kissed, a spur-of-the-moment action along with those sweet words. I can't see I've done anything wrong. *I'm going to miss that kid.*

I bundle together the amount of clothes I'll be able to carry, constructing a makeshift bag from one of my sweatshirts. Making sure my phone's charged, I slip that, my charger and my wallet into my pockets, and then sit to wait.

Bikers party until late. If I want to sneak out undetected, I need to wait until the early hours of the morning. At least with Heart's door closed he won't hear me go.

At four in the morning I tiptoe out of my suite, out of the main door to the bloc, and dressed in black, quietly walk down the road. Nothing stirs, all is silent.

A decision, the rat bike or the Kawasaki. I may forfeit the one I leave here. Deciding on speed, I take the tarpaulin off my 7/11, regretting I've not even a helmet with me. I won't be breaking the law in Arizona, but it's my personal preference to wear a lid to stay safe.

Knowing it's the least of my worries, I wheel it to the gate.

"Where d'ya think you're going?"

I didn't expect anyone to be on guard. Turning, I notice a yawning prospect, the one called Hyde, who's already gotten in trouble because of me.

What do I care about these bikers? The ones I now feel are keeping me prisoner rather than giving me protection.

I move closer, swaying my hips suggestively, his eyes focusing on my assets rather than my face. I hold out one hand and touch him on the chest. He's taken unawares, not sure how to take my seductive routine. My other hand comes up the side of it and slices hard against the brachial nerve in his neck.

He falls unconscious at my feet.

Hoping I haven't done him any permanent damage, I press the button that opens the gates, jump onto my bike and fly down that track as though the Satan's Devils are behind me. Which they will be. That gate was alarmed.

CHAPTER TWENTY-FIVE

*H*eart…

At some point in the night, the little minx must have crawled out of her bed and into mine. I wake to a small, warm body curled up against me, and a commotion going on outside. Easing away from her, I pick up the jeans laying discarded on the floor and slide my legs into them, then grabbing a crutch with one hand, I take my gun from my drawer with the other and leave the suite. The door to Marc's is still closed.

Grimacing, I remember the words I'd spat at her last night, glad she seems to be sleeping, unlike me, who'd lain awake with our last conversation going around my head. *Had I been right, or had my reaction been misplaced and over-the-top?*

Shaking my head to clear it and focus on what the fuck's going on, I go out the door. Brothers are running down from their suites, seemingly in confusion. Knowing I need to know what's happened, but unwilling to leave my daughter, I wonder how the fuck I'm going to be able to find out while keeping her safe.

Before yesterday I'd have asked Marc…

"Heart! Is Amy in there?" Sam's running down from the

direction of Drummer's house. At my nod, she continues after pausing to draw breath. "I'll get her and take her up with Eli. You get to the clubhouse. Drummer wants you there."

That solves my dilemma. With only a chin jerk to say thanks, I follow the direction my brothers have taken, arriving to find the clubhouse in an uproar. People all shouting at once, and a sheepish looking prospect sitting down rubbing his neck.

"Church! Now!"

I can't remember ever having held church at this ungodly hour of the morning, but various words and phrases come to me as we obediently follow Drummer into the meeting room. I hear Marc's name mentioned, along with various versions of 'fuckin' cop' and promises that 'Hyde's done for this time'.

Marc. *Isn't she asleep in her room?*

Chairs are pulled out noisily, asses drop into seats. Drummer's banging the gavel, but it takes a moment for the exclamations to stop. When everyone quiets, I notice all eyes, including the prez's death stare, are focused on me. *Fuck.*

"What in the name of God's going on, Heart? What the fuck have you done?"

Me? What the fuck?

"Prez, I don't know—"

"Your cop's fuckin' gone. Just left the compound. The gate opening set off the alarm."

She's gone?

"What I want to know is why," Peg growls. "She learn something she's gonna report?"

"She hasn't been anywhere to learn fuck all." Wraith's rubbing his hands over his eyes. Finished, he directs them to me. "Unless you've said anything you shouldn't."

I shake my head. No, I didn't tell her anything about our business. All I did was… Fuck. I lower my head into my hands. Everyone's waiting for me to start speaking. "We had words last night. I went back, found her snuggled up with Amy. The kid told her she loved her. I lost it."

"What the ever-lovin'-fuck? Kids say things like that all the time."

"Jayden told me she loved me the other day," Tongue chimes in.

"She better fuckin' not," Slick and Paladin say together.

Prez ignores them all. "How exactly did you lose it, Heart? What made her run? And what direction might you have pointed her in?"

Pushing back my hands with my hair, I gaze down at the table. Looking back up at him, I realise only the truth will do. I take a breath. "After our chat, Drum, I overheard Sandy and Carmen talking about Marc. They said it was a shame she couldn't have kids of her own, and what a natural she was with them. Particularly Amy."

Blade takes out his smokes. As he looks at me I see his brow creasing. "And that sent you off the fuckin' deep end? Why?"

I look at Drummer. "Because you told me she'd already tried to get Amy off the compound. In church that's what you said."

If I'd thought I'd seen Drummer's face looking thunderous before, it's nothing compared to the expression there now. His hands hammer down on the table. "She was looking out for the kid. Trying to protect her from that bitch of a mother-in-law of yours. If I remember rightly, she was the one who said *we* should get her out of Tucson. Which we did, by taking her to Vegas. Fuck Heart, she didn't want Amy for herself. She was trying to protect her!"

Yet in my fucked-up brain, at the time, my assumptions made sense. I stare back at him, realising I've got everything wrong. What's at the root of it is that I overreacted because my daughter had told a woman who wasn't Crystal that she loved her. Knowing how badly I fucked up, I admit the rest. "I told her she was only half a woman. That if she stayed I'd make sure all the kids were kept out of her way."

"That's fucked up man." Unusually, Viper chimes in. "I've watched my ol' lady, *my wife*, take years to come to terms with the fact she couldn't have children. That's a hard weight to carry, *Brother*. I'd have killed any fucker who suggested she wasn't whole just for that. And in my case, it wasn't even her fuckin' fault."

"Ella's been worrying. She's getting herself twisted in knots stressing about not falling pregnant." Slick's shaking his head. Suddenly he's on his feet leaning over the table. "You know what, Heart? She can't have kids? I'll make her feel like the most loved and wanted woman in this fuckin' world! Not half-a-fuckin' woman."

"Sit down, Slick," Drummer roars. "And everyone else shut up. Heart's fucked up and fucked up good. Now there's a woman in the wind who we should be protecting."

Slick's still giving me a death stare of his own.

"I'll go out looking for her."

"You've fuckin' done enough already, Heart." The prez is looking at me and shaking his head as if he can't believe how badly I'd behaved. "I let you bring her here because I thought the two of you were friends. We agreed to treat her as your ol' lady to put her out-of-bounds of anyone else. Now she's out there alone and possibly in danger."

"I say we have to concentrate on the club, Prez. Can't go running after her and leave ourselves wide open."

"I hear you, VP, and that's what I'm thinking."

She's gone, she's hurting. She is probably in danger. And I ran her off.

"Yeah, Mouse?" Drummer's eyes look sharp, despite his lack of sleep.

"I know where she is." As all eyes flick to him, he continues, "I put a tracker in her phone. She's at the precinct."

"Knew it," Lady starts, "you can't trust a cop."

Surprisingly, it's Shooter who speaks up. "She's gone to the only other place she can go for protection. Same as us. We'd run to our own."

But it's her own who may be the ones trying to kill her.

"What we gonna do about the fucker Hyde?" Peg seems to be changing the subject.

"If I have my way, he'd be out."

"Slick. Put bygones behind ya, why don't cha?" He gets a glare from the prez.

"Marcia's a martial arts expert," Peg drops in. "I had a chat with her in the gym. Hyde didn't have a chance with that move she pulled. Especially as she took him unawares. She's one smart cookie."

"He still shouldn't have let her get the drop on him," Slick grumbles.

Prez is nodding. "You may well be right. So this is his last chance." *What?* I'm not following. Looking around, others seem lost as well. "We know where she is, we put him on her. He sticks to her like fuckin' glue."

"Rather do it myself, Prez."

"I told you, Heart. Apart from the fact you can't fuckin' walk, I'm not letting you near her. Right now, I suspect you'd do more damage than good."

Fuck knows what I was thinking last night. Would I have been of the same mind today if she were still here? But understanding now how I'd touched on such a tender nerve, hit her albeit only with words in such a raw place, even if I'd wanted to, I'm not sure how I could make it up to her.

Beef yawns loudly, Prez notices. He picks up the gavel. "Right, you assholes, go catch up on your sleep, drag a sweet butt out of bed, or do what the fuck you want. Heart, you stay back for a moment. The rest of you, we'll reconvene in the morning."

Like a kid kept behind after class, wishing he could leave with the others, I enviously watch my brothers leaving the room.

Pushing back his chair, Drummer slides open a drawer under the table where I know a gun is kept. I hold my breath until his hand reappears with two shot glasses, then delving back inside, comes out again with a bottle of scotch. He pours two drinks and slides one over.

His intense gaze fixes on me. "I thought we'd finished with this, Heart. Thought these impulsive rages had left you. Thought you were getting better."

My anger had taken me by surprise if I'm honest. I thought I'd stopped lashing out. "I don't know what the fuck happened, Prez. I was jealous she'd spent time with Amy, doing things I can't do because of this fuckin' broken body. I've already lost Crystal. When…" I break off, trying to gather my thoughts. "After what you said…" As he growls at the suggestion of any blame attaching to him, I correct myself. "When I saw her getting so close to Amy, my brain misinterpreted what you said. That with the fact she can't have kids of her own, well, somehow it seemed to fit that she wanted to take Amy away. I can't lose my daughter now. I'm only just getting my relationship sorted with her." I look down at my legs, fucking useless things that they are, stopping me doing half of what I want to do with my kid.

"It won't be long until you're fit again, Heart."

No, it won't. But I seemed to have lost my patience when I lost my wife.

Drummer drinks from his glass and then stares down at the amber liquid. "Did I make a mistake, Heart? Telling you to treat her like an ol' lady?"

One side of my mouth turns up. "Can't say whether you did or didn't, Prez. But it might have been better if you hadn't have put her so close to me. We fucked."

He doesn't seem surprised. "What's wrong with that?"

My eyes go to his face. "I shouldn't have done it."

"Did you force her? Hurt her?"

"Of course not," I reply indignantly. "It was what we both wanted. It was sex, pure and simple. We didn't even kiss. But it still shouldn't have happened."

"Why the fuck not? You're both adults."

I put my glass down a bit too heavily. "Because of Crystal."

He rolls back his head, then brings it back down and moves it side to side. "Can't say I've ever been where you are, Heart. Never lost someone that close. But would Crystal really expect you to stay faithful to a memory? Expect you to feel guilty if you look at another woman? I knew Crystal from the time you first met her and brought her to the club. For the four years or so you were married, I saw that girl almost every fuckin' day. And from what I had seen, she wouldn't have wanted to stop you moving on. Honour her memory, yes, but cut yourself off from ever enjoying life again? The woman I knew would have been cheering you on all the way."

"She's never coming back, is she?" For a second I wonder whether Drum will think I'm talking about Marc, but he's on the same wavelength as me.

"No, Brother, she's not. I saw her put into the ground with my own eyes." A funeral I didn't get to go to. The identification of her body done by Drum and Slick. "And there ain't no way you can go to her."

I'd come to that conclusion myself. It was why I'd stopped thinking of ways to die. Oh, there might be a slim chance that the Christians have got it right, but even if they have, she's probably up there overhead, and I'll be going the opposite way.

"Marc's a cop. Thinks like a cop. Acts like a cop."

Again, my out of the blue comment doesn't faze him, catching on to exactly what I mean. "You won't stop being a biker, Heart. You proved that by coming back to us. We're your family and your way of life. And no, she won't stop being a member of law enforcement. It's in her psyche. What was it you said? She wants to put the bad guys away."

"Because of the time one of them walked. The man responsible for killing her family. Yeah, Prez. Her shit runs deep too."

"Then, Brother, there's nothing more to say. I regret that she's gone. I liked her myself. Any other occupation and she'd have made a great ol' lady, but oil and water don't mix. I don't like how it happened, and maybe I was wrong bringing her here. Perhaps it's all for the best."

Maybe he's right. But it was me who ran her off, and in the worst possible way, forcing her to go and face the threats on her life. In my mind's eye I see her running with Amy, teaching her how to ride that bike, cooking dinner with the old ladies, and looking like she could settle in with our way of life. In doing so, I realise, I might have taken the promise of a family, mismatched and screwed up as we might be at times, away.

She's on her own now.

And there's not a damn thing I can do about it.

CHAPTER TWENTY-SIX

*M*arc…

It's early in the morning, and the only place that I can think of to run to is the precinct that I work out of. Something ingrained in my gut tells me this is a place of safety, even though my head warns me otherwise, reminding me I need to be careful who to count on.

I couldn't stay with the Satan's Devils any longer, so now I'm about to hand over my safety into the hands of the people who may be in the pocket of those trying to kill me. Everything's happened so fast, I've got no strategy in place. But the building in front of me lures me with its sense of righteousness. There are good people inside, men and women who should have my back. Out here I'm a sitting target.

I leave my bike in the parking lot and let my feet be drawn forward. A couple of police officers come striding out—*state troopers, I must remember their still relatively new designation*—obviously sharing a joke before they go out on patrol. They pass me without a hint of recognition, which isn't surprising. Unless we cross paths on a case, I don't know too many of the uniformed officers, working as I do out of the Investigations Bureau of the Criminal Investigations Division.

But sitting behind the desk is a familiar face.

"Detective Hannah. I didn't realise you'd returned to duty." His face frowns. "And you're a bit early for your shift, aren't you?"

The clock above him says five a.m., and unless I'm on a case when I can work all hours, I normally would clock in at eight. "I'm not officially back, yet…" I struggle to remember his name. "Johnson. But hopefully I will be after today. I've come in early to prepare for a meeting."

He nods, looking bored. He wouldn't give a damn why I'm here, so I'm not certain why I'm trying to justify myself.

Taking my card out of my wallet, I swipe it through the reader that lets me into the heart of the building and ride the elevator up to the third floor where my office is situated. Walking into the open-plan area, nodding to a couple of tired looking detectives working, I step up to my desk only to find it covered with paperwork from a case I've not been dealing with, and beside the computer a photo of a family which isn't mine. I pull open a drawer, seeing an unfamiliar cup and other personal things there.

Motherfucker! Someone else has been assigned my space. In my absence, I've been wiped out of existence.

Not sure what message this is, I go over to the low table in the corner and grab myself a coffee from the machine, knowing it will taste as awful as ever, but at least strong enough to wake me up and give my hands something to do.

A man comes over and sits down opposite. "We thought you'd left."

"No, Reed. Just on extended sick leave. I see I've lost my desk."

"Garza boxed up your stuff. It will be around somewhere." He glances around the room. "Think it might be over there in the corner." He turns back and his eyes sharpen as he examines me. "How are you?"

"Much better."

"Do you mind if I tell you, you look like shit?"

A strangled laugh escapes me. I expect I do. Crying all night and no sleep will do that to you. I only hope that is my box over there, as I keep spare makeup here to freshen up. From what Reed has said, I've got one hell of a job on my hands to make myself look anywhere close to normal.

I take a sip of my coffee and grimace.

"That bang on your head affect your memory? You seem to have forgotten how that tastes like shit."

A more genuine smile now. "Always thought we should use it in interrogations. Force suspects to drink it until they spill the truth."

He grins. "Great idea, Hannah. Might use that myself. *If you don't start talking, I'll get you another cup.*"

My smile widens. It's good to be back amongst like-minded colleagues and not feel out of my depth in the midst of people living a lifestyle I know nothing about.

"So, is this a formal return to the job? If so, you're a bit overeager." He sits back, arms folded, stretching out his long legs and crossing them at his ankles. His relaxed posture doesn't fool me. He's after information. I've seen how he works before.

"I'm here to try to convince Reynolds I'm fit to return to work."

His eyebrow rises. "Really? You've got paid sick leave, yet you willingly want to go out with Garza again?"

I'm not the only one who doesn't like him. "Unless his own partner has returned?" It's a hopeful question on my part.

"Nah. Terry's milking the sick card for all he can get."

I already suspect it won't be the day for good news.

"What's your plan?"

I haven't really thought it through, everything's happened so fast. "I might try and see Lieutenant Diaz." He's Reynolds' boss.

Now Reed's eyes narrow. "You're going over Reynolds' head?"

I sit forward. "Tell me what you know about the investigation into the explosion at my house, Reed. Surely people have been talking about it? There was an attempt on a detective's life. Isn't that being taken seriously?"

"You think your case isn't being thoroughly investigated?" Reed pauses. "It's reached a dead end, that's for certain. In the briefings all that's said is the explosive device used was built by the same person who blew up Lucas Herrera's house and killed Archer. The suggestion is someone was out to get your ex-partner, and whatever he knew, they think you do to." He frowns. "Obviously Archer's investigation is ongoing, but no progress has been made."

No progress in almost a year. It's not going to go anywhere.

"Where you living now? You got a new place."

"I've been away from the area." It's only a white lie, and I didn't go very far, just a few miles outside Tucson. Before that, when I stayed in Heart's house, I hadn't given anyone my new address. I don't have any inclination to return there now, other than to collect the rest of my things. "I need to find a new house to rent."

"You got somewhere to stay?"

I hadn't thought that far. "I'll check into a motel for now. Shouldn't take me long to find a place."

I want to get him off the subject of me. Looking around, I see the familiar whiteboard strewn with pictures and scrawled writing. "So, anything interesting going on?"

For the next few minutes he runs me through some of the cases the bureau has on its plate. My interest perked when he mentions some children have gone missing. Hopefully without giving myself away, I question him as though out of idle curiosity.

"How many, Reed?"

He's happy to talk. "At first we just thought we were dealing with runaways. A couple went missing from foster homes, and you know how unsettled kids of their like can be. Never too certain about the motives of the fosterers, you know?" I do.

Some do it purely for the money, but there are good ones around.

"But when we started getting reports from upstanding families, a pattern began to emerge." He unfolds his arms and points to the whiteboard. "Kids who do well in school, popular, and happy by all accounts. Nothing that on the surface would cause them to voluntarily leave home."

"Ages and sex?"

This time he uses his head to indicate the information on the wall. "It's all on there."

I get up and go over. Eight kids are missing, their ages ranging from nine to fifteen. *Fifteen, the same age as Jayden if I'm not mistaken.* Mostly girls, but a couple of the younger ones are boys. But these kids are actually missing. It's not the same as the child grooming ring. Those poor children were seduced then threatened into providing their services and keeping quiet, still living at home but becoming a shadow of their former selves. As I think of the pretty, happy young girl I met at the compound, I hope nothing like that ever happens to her.

Jayden was reported as missing. And by Archer. No, there can't be a link. Archer is dead, and any mystery to that must have died with him. But something's going on in Tucson. Something I don't like.

"I'd like to work this case," I say offhandedly, trying not to show my interest is anything more than professional inquisitiveness. A detective wanting a puzzle to solve.

"If you come back to work, you might well be. Garza's got it on his pile."

That's interesting.

"Anyway, I've got to be getting on. And yeah, I'm pretty certain now I think of it, your stuff is in that box."

"Thank you." As he gets up and goes back to his desk, I stare at the board for a moment longer and then go and find he's right. All my personal belongings are there, including my makeup bag. Taking it out, I go to the restroom, splash water on my face, then carefully apply foundation, mascara, and eyeliner, followed by face powder and a dash of lipstick. After I've pulled back my hair into a bun, I'm looking almost normal. Certainly it's put some colour back into my skin.

I pull back my shoulders and study my reflection. Yeah, I think I'll pass.

Returning to the table, I risk another cup of coffee then, grabbing some paper and a pen, start to make notes—all the reasons why I should return to the job. Although I hate the thought of working with Garza, what he's working on is what interests me. What's he been doing to find the lost children?

If he's been doing anything, that is.

My phone vibrates with a text message. I take it out. When I see it's from Heart, I almost don't open it, but when I do, there's just one simple word.

Sorry.

I delete the message, and the contact details. He hurt me too badly. The things that he said will haunt me forever. There's no going back. Next time I see a biker it will be across the table in an interrogation room. Cops and bikers can't associate with each other. I should have remembered that from the start.

Just before eight, I go down to the first floor.

"I'd like to see Lieutenant Diaz when he comes in, please."

The woman consults her screen. "He's got back-to-back appointments all morning, I'm afraid."

Hmm. Has he, or is she just putting me off? "Just a few minutes before he gets started?"

"I'm sorry," her smile seems genuine, "but the meetings are off-site. He won't be here all day."

Damn. Thanking her, I go back to my office again. Now I've got no other option, I've got to confront Reynolds. That's a conversation I'm really looking forward to. Not.

The sergeant's come in while I've been gone. His door is ajar, and he's got a cup of steaming coffee in front of him which obviously has not come from a machine. I knock, and his eyes come up to meet mine. He looks startled for a moment, as if he didn't expect to see me. *I've been missing. Does he think someone succeeded in killing me and burying my body?*

"Detective Marcia Hannah." He nods. "I'm surprised to see you."

"Sergeant." I give a polite jerk of my head in return and then dive straight in. "I'm more than ready to come back to work."

"Hmm." He taps his fingers on the desk. "You're sure your fit?"

"I certainly am."

He doesn't say anything about my employment, but goes down a different track. "We still don't know who threw that bomb into your house."

I take the seat across from him. "I hear you're linking it to the explosion that killed Archer."

"It makes sense, it was a case you were both working on."

This time I don't argue that Archer was as dirty as sin, simply shrug, letting him know I've doubts about his reasoning. "Not unless they weren't watching closely and assumed I was his partner at the time. We'd only worked together a couple of months." I think for a moment. "Was his old partner's death really an accident?"

His eyebrows draw down, meeting in the middle. "Absolutely. Don't you think we can do our jobs in Tucson? Cop dies, it gets investigated."

I didn't mean to annoy him. I keep calm and once again press my case. "I'm going stir crazy with nothing to do."

He stares, then sighs and pulls a folder toward him. "As long as you're not going to black out on the job, you can start today. With this."

As he pushes it over to me, I pick the folder up. It's the missing children's file.

"You'll be working with Garza."

From my talk with Reed I expected that, but it's still hard to keep the disappointment from my face.

"I know you have issues with him, but remember, you've not been at detective grade for anything like as long as he has. You can learn a lot watching how he does things. He's the senior detective on this one. I'll be asking him to report to me on your progress." He leans back in his chair, picks up a pen, and taps it against his mouth. "Before you were targeted, we had words, remember? About that report you drafted on Archer. I want no more of that. As far as I'm concerned, you're on probation, and I will be checking with Garza as how you're doing. I'm still not convinced you're making the grade."

That's so unfair, but I'm in no position to argue.

"Dismissed, Hannah. And I'm expecting to see some improvement in the way you work."

The relief I feel at being allowed back in my familiar environment is tinged with doubt on how Garza and I will get on together. But somehow I have to make this work. Particularly having been around the club's children, I don't want to see another happy kid picked up off the street. Yes, this case is at least something I can get my teeth into.

The day passes quickly, mostly taking up with finding a new desk, liaising with the IT department to get a computer set up, and subsequently going through hundreds of emails that have backed up since I've been absent. Garza's crooked grin when he comes up to see me doesn't put me at ease, but after transferring a file to me and telling me to get myself up to speed, he leaves me alone.

When I clock off, I'm beyond weary. My eyes, already sore at the start of the day, are now stinging and bleary. Now I've got to find somewhere to stay.

I go to my bike.

Now a normal person might have missed him, but I'm a detective trained to check for a tail. Over in the shadows is a man watching me. With one hand on my newly assigned weapon, I go to confront him, moving quicker than he does as he goes to get away. When I get close enough to recognise him, I call him by name.

"Hyde."

"Fuckin' hell," he mumbles, sounding disgusted.

"I'm sorry."

His eyes come to meet mine and he shakes his head. "Never gonna get patched in at this rate. Don't know what you've got against me, but this will be my third strike."

One of the others was down to me too. "It's okay, Hyde. You tell me why you're here and I won't say a thing. How long you been waiting?"

"Been here all day."

"Hanging around just for me to come out?"

He shrugs. I'm obviously on the right track. Putting my hand in my pocket, I take out my phone and show it to him. "Start speaking, Hyde, or I ring Drummer."

He raises his eyes to the heavens, then looks back down. "Club wants a tail on you. For your protection," he adds hurriedly. "Not gonna interfere with your job."

Tears prick in my eyes. No one in the bureau mentioned anything about the fact someone might still be trying to kill me. Yet although I've left the compound, the Satan's Devils are still watching out for me. I've already dismissed the idea that they're keeping tabs on me for their own benefit, though it might have concerned me if I was working on anything to do with them. Satan's Devils would be the last people to resort to kidnapping children.

The idea that someone's watching my back is warming. "Drew the short straw, did you?"

A quick grin comes to the young man's face. "Would you be offended if I said yes? That it's the price I'm paying for letting you go."

I frown, as I recall it, I didn't actually give him much choice. Then I begin to smile having thought about the way this could work. "Let me make this easier. Though I don't want to, I've got to go back to Heart's to pick up some clothes. Then I'm going to find a motel."

"Motel 6 won't cost you a fortune."

It's a fair suggestion. Somewhere clean, not a dump, but not too expensive. "Good idea. I just want to crash, Hyde."

The poor man looks like he does too.

"When do you clock off?"

Now his face twists and he looks miserable. "I don't."

"Twenty-four-hour protection?" I think for a moment. "As long as you don't snore you can share my room." As soon as my head hits the pillow, I'll be out like a light. And if Hyde made one wrong move toward me, knowing Drummer, he'd be out of the Devils before he even got in.

His eyes lighten. "You know, for a cop, you're alright. Didn't have much inclination to try to sleep on my bike."

I laugh, taking it as a compliment. "Well, let me get my bike and we'll head off."

CHAPTER TWENTY-SEVEN

*H*eart...

"How long we keeping Hyde on Detective Hannah." Blade looks up from spinning his knife. "Been a month now. Nothing's happened to her, and we're down a prospect in the meantime."

Slick perks up. "Does anyone miss 'im? I sure fuckin' don't." Blade just points the sharp end of his knife toward Slick and he shuts up.

Wraith shakes his head. "Fucker's moved in with her."

I bristle, but can't protest. I sent her away, she's a free woman. We've had regular updates from the prospect. She's rented a small house, and as the VP had said, Hyde's staying with her. Wanting to ensure there was full disclosure to the club, he'd admitted she'd picked up that she had a tail early on. The good thing to come out of that is she seems to appreciate her protection and didn't run him off. If it wasn't for the fact that there's another man in her house, I'd be happy to know she wasn't alone. *Are they sleeping together? What if she feels horny and wants some cock? She was casual enough about sex with me. Is he keeping his hands off?*

"Heart. You with us, man?" Blade throws an empty cigarette pack at me. "You zoned out there."

"You got something we need to discuss?" Drummer asks.

"Nah, Prez. It's all okay." *But I'm gonna have words with the prospect.*

"They've gotten into a routine." Peg starts his update. "She lets him know where she's likely to be going. Planned meetings are easy, off-the-cuff visits not so much. But she sends him a text. He follows at a distance. Fucker's actually quite good, not been spotted yet, even when her partner's with her."

"She still worried about Garza?"

"Hasn't given Hyde any details, but yes. That's why she's happy keeping Hyde around. There's a rumour where she works that she's living with a boy toy. Her idea, actually, smart bitch. If anyone visits, it gives him a reason to be there and puts off anyone trying to get in her house."

"Unless it's another bomb like last time."

Peg concedes the point, then continues bringing us up to date. "The case she's working on, Hyde managed to see some paperwork she brought home. Fuckin' missing kids in Tucson."

We've discussed that before. Both Slick and I exchange glances. The Herreras have come after both Jayden and Amy before. It was down to the prez they didn't get their hands on my daughter, but Slick's sister-in-law? She hadn't been so lucky.

Prez raps the table. "I feel we're living with a fuckin' cloud hanging over our heads. Can't rightly explain it, just a gut feel I've got. I think it's time I set up a meeting with Javier Herrera."

"You think he'll tell you anything?" Beef sounds concerned. "Don't know that we should be facing them head-on."

Drummer's fingers start strumming a beat. "Know what you mean, Brother. But Leonardo was straight. If Javier gives off the same vibes, then maybe we can breathe easy again. Reckon it won't be too hard to read him."

"You don't go alone." Peg's adamant on that.

"Wraith, you come with."

"Prez, I ain't been giving much around here lately. I'm willing to go too."

"You fit to ride, Brother."

I grin. "Took my ride out yesterday, and I'm fine."

He considers me for a moment. "And your head's in the right place?"

It's a fair question considering my behaviour recently, and that of last year. "Yeah, Prez. I can keep a rein on my temper." *Unless I think of Hyde living with Marc.* Why that thought starts the anger burning inside me, I have no fucking idea. One night in my bed, no, not even that, just an hour if I'm honest, gives me no rights.

But she'd been my old lady.

That was just a ruse, a way to keep her to my side and away from my brothers.

But I miss that friendly voice on the end of the line.

"Heart, man. Keep with it." Dollar nudges me in the ribs.

"I said you're in, Brother. I'll set something up and let you and Wraith know the details."

Getting a meeting with Javier Herrera proves to be more of a problem than we thought. Life goes on as normal in the compound while Drummer gets put off time and time again.

After another two weeks have gone past, I corner him in the bar. "Reckon we'll ever get into see Herrera?"

"No fuckin' idea, Heart. But you see the news tonight? It's been made public. Another kid's gone missing. Bright girl, twelve years old. Parents swear she was happy. They're appealing for her to come home, but say they've no idea why she would have run away."

My eyes go to Jayden, who's playing with Amy. The shit that girl went through? Wouldn't want to see it happen to anyone else. You wouldn't know she'd suffered such an ordeal, been groomed, given drugs, and raped by strangers, kept under control by threats. At least she got to go home each night. No, you wouldn't know, except when you catch her off guard and see that haunted look in her eye. And when it appears, Paladin's right there beside her, and quickly she's smiling again.

"You think the Herreras are involved?"

"Fuckin' stupid if they are, but this is organised crime. Unless all these kids upped and left on their own, which seems doubtful, someone has to be doing the organising. But if they are dealing in skin, the cartel won't like it."

"Unless they're working for the cartel. Or the cartel's doing it themselves."

Drummer points to the massive television up on the wall, now showing a game. "It's eleven kids now. Eleven kids disappeared into the blue. Kids who have no reason to go missing. And not one of them found. All from Tucson. Whoever is doing it has to stop soon, or they'll make a fuckin' mistake and get caught."

"I hope they do." My eyes find Amy. Although she's not yet in the age range of the kids who've gone missing, the Herreras had their eyes on her once.

Drummer raises his finger, and Fergus is right there. "Two whiskeys. From my bottle."

My eyebrows rise. If one's for me, that's an unusual step. Prez grabs the glasses and jerks his chin to show I should follow him. We end up in his office.

"Been meaning to talk to ya, Heart." He sips his drink with his eyes focused on me. *Has something happened to Marc?* But when he continues, it's to tell me I'm wide of the mark. "Club lawyer's been in touch."

Not sure where this is leading, my head tilts to one side.

"What do you know about grandparents' visitation rights?"

I don't know anything. In my lap, my hands curl into fists. "Susie Clyde is not seeing my daughter," I spit out. "She never had rights when Crystal was alive. Oh, she got to see her a couple of times as Crystal thought it might help her get clean, but she was never allowed to spend time with her."

"And while Crystal was alive, that wasn't a problem. In

Arizona, if both parents are together, grandparents have no rights at all." He pauses, and by the look on his face as he takes another sip, I'm not going to like what I'm going to hear at all. "If there aren't two parents together, grandparents can apply for visitation rights."

"Crystal's mother is not going anywhere near Amy," I repeat. My fingernails bite into the skin of my palms.

"Lawyer's told me she's petitioned for visitation."

I stand, my chair crashing to the ground behind me. "What's that fuckin' bitch up to? She never showed the slightest interest in the kid. I can't see she's had a change of heart."

Drummer shrugs. "Her daughter's dead, she might be missing having a family."

My eyes open wide. "Do you think there's the slightest chance of that?"

He laughs, but it's without any mirth. "No, I fuckin' don't. What I think is that we need to go see her. I don't like fuckin' loose ends, particularly not when it looks like they're trying to tie themselves together."

"She was responsible for crippling me and killing my wife, Drum. She tried to sell my daughter into a life I can't bring myself to imagine. I don't like the fact she's still breathing."

He slaps me on the back. "Been waiting for you to say that, Heart. Been waiting a fuckin' long time."

This has turned into a serious conversation. The last time we dispatched a woman to meet Satan it was a club whore who'd opened her mouth to the wrong people and nearly got Wraith and his woman killed in the process.

"We're talking about taking Clyde out. That's some serious shit, Prez. Need the club to vote on it? Specially now if she's started something in the courts. Fingers might get pointed our way."

"Already did, Brother. While you were gone. Unanimous vote. Every brother wanted to dispatch her to meet Satan, but as she's related by marriage to you, were waiting for you to have the final say."

I'm making a grim decision here. On one hand, with the risk to Amy it's an easy one to make. On the other, Susie Clyde is Crystal's mother. With no idea of who her father was, she's the only living relative to my dead wife. My wife she had killed. It doesn't take more than a minute for me to make up my mind. Clyde's days are numbered, but I am concerned about my club.

"I'll do this alone, Prez. Don't want nobody else involved. If the police come knocking, I'll stand up and take the rap. I know Shooter said he'd come with me, but ain't taking him along for this."

"Haven't just got you back to lose you to prison, Brother. You're not doing this alone. She's an addict, we do this smart. But it won't be Shooter going with you."

To my surprise, Drummer swivels his chair and opens the safe behind him. He takes out a packet and throws it on the desk. White powder is inside. My eyes rise to meet his.

"Heroin cut with a lethal dose of Fentanyl. Got hold of it after the club voted. No trace back to the club if we do it right."

With the packet in my hand it feels real. But Prez is right. It's time. There's only one thing left to ask. "When?"

"No time like the present. And *I'm* riding along. So, if you're ready, Brother?"

I'm more than ready. Leaving our cuts behind, we take a cage. It's almost eleven by the time we arrive, full darkness. Half the street lights are out on Susie Clyde's street, so we park discreetly up the road and then make our way to her house, keeping to the shadows.

There's a light on inside.

As she makes a living whoring herself out, we listen for sounds that would tell us she's got company, but she seems to be alone, the only light coming from the living room.

Prez raps on the door. A short pause, then we hear the latch turning.

Susie's eyes widen when she sees me standing there. I haven't seen her often, and never without my wife by my side. She's skinny, track marks up her arms. She smells like something rotten, and her eyes are sunken in her face.

"You heard about me wanting visitation, I take it." She's blocking the doorway, but it's no effort at all to push past. "Hey, I haven't invited ya in."

"Need a chat, Susie," Drummer says in a reasonable sounding voice.

"You gonna offer me money to stay away from the kid?" she asks, sounding hopeful.

"How much money do you owe now?"

She shrugs, but I expect it's a lot. She's got an expensive habit.

Drummer surveys the room and looks at the grubby chairs and makes no move to sit down. Instead, he reaches his gloved hands into his jacket and pulls out the plastic bag full of powder. Susie's eyes gleam, and her hands start to reach for it.

"Not so fast," he begins, slapping her hands away. "I've got some questions I want answers to. Then you can have it."

"What d'ya want to know?"

She's trembling as though desperate for her next fix. Guess we came at a good time, when she was out of her stuff or at least getting low.

"Archer. What was your relationship to him?"

We might prefer to remain standing, but she sits down, puts her head in her hands, and then looks up. "I owed money to the Herreras. A lot. Two men came to the door and dragged me out to their car. I thought that was the end, that they were going to kill me." Her eyes half close and she shudders as she remembers. "I had nothing to pay with until I remembered the kid. Once I mentioned her, I didn't know what they would say. The Herreras don't have a reputation taking children, but I was desperate. I didn't have a choice, there was nothing else I could offer up."

And that makes it all right? I don't speak, just fume in silence.

"They left me locked in a room, and then that man, Archer, turned up. Talked to me about Amy. When he heard her dad was a biker, he got really excited. Hyped up. Said it would be no bother taking biker scum out. And I agreed. Never did like you, Dale."

No, she didn't. I don't bother telling her the feeling's quite mutual.

"But Crystal?"

"Fucking waste of space. Never did anything for me."

But you did nothing for her. Just gave her a shit life.

Drummer growls, "Go on."

"Well, he got it all sorted, but it didn't work. You, Dale, you were still fucking breathing, and too well protected at the hospital. So he was gonna help me go through the courts." She pauses and picks at a scab on her arm. "They wiped my debt in the expectation I'd get Amy and give her to them. Was going to pay me more on delivery. Got a buyer lined up."

"Who?" I snarl.

"Didn't know, didn't care. They'd pay me the rest once I had her. But it didn't work out. Archer got himself killed, and I didn't hear from them again. All that money I could have had." Her tear is for the money she missed out on, not the death of her daughter, or whatever hell she was prepared to send her granddaughter into.

If I hadn't already decided to kill her, I would have done so now. My hands itch to strangle her, but Prez's steely gaze pins me to the spot.

"You've applied for visitation rights. You still in contact?" As he speaks, Drummer's tossing the plastic bag from one hand to the other.

Watching him, she licks her lips, and a crafty look sweeps across her face. "Let me have some now and I'll tell you the rest."

Like a magician, Prez magics the packet away in his jacket

again and shows her his empty hands. "Stop talking and you'll get nothing."

She huffs. "So Archer was dead, and I had no more contact. That stuff," she points to Drummer's jacket, "well, I've got a big habit, and it costs more than what I can earn. Debts started to mount up again. Got another visit, and they told me to get hold of the kid or I was dead. Told me how as well, that I could apply to see her, and you couldn't stop me."

"Got a name?" Drummer asks casually, though by the tension in his body he's far from relaxed.

"It was one of them Herreras." She taps her fingers on her knees, then looks up. "Alonso. That's it." She looks triumphant. "Now can I have my stuff?"

"Alonso Herrera? Are you sure?"

She nods eagerly. "Yeah. That's right."

Drummer looks at me. I give a nod, and he takes out the packet again. When he throws it to her, she catches it in both hands and wastes no time busying herself preparing the stuff. A fatal dose, though she doesn't know it. One that will stop her heart. Not that I think she's got one.

As if we're not there, she carries on. Preparing a syringe, she puts a sleeve around her arm, pulling it tight. A look of bliss comes over her face as she puts the plunger down. Then she leans back as though resting her head. She draws in a breath and lets it out. I watch her chest fall and rise.

Then it doesn't move anymore, the lethal combination working fast.

Both of us stand in silence, watching the woman who is never going to get her hands on my daughter.

As we go back to the cage, Drummer takes his gloves off. He pauses before starting the engine. "You okay, Heart?"

"That shit she spilled, Prez. Woman was pure evil."

"You don't need to worry about her anymore. And Amy's safe. That's all you need to think about."

CHAPTER TWENTY-EIGHT

*M*arc…

"I can't believe you've never watched this shit before."

I bump Hyde's arm with my fist. "Well I haven't. But it's great, isn't it? That Jax Teller? Mmm mmm."

"That's all you're watching it for." He scoffs.

"Well you've got a hard-on for the bikes, and for Tara."

I laugh as he casts a sneaky look down at his groin to make sure he hasn't.

As the titles roll he asks, "Another?"

"I think I'm all Son'd out. We've watched four tonight." As he goes to change the channel, I sit back with my glass of wine in my hand. "Is it really like that in an MC?"

Hyde laughs. "Not at the Satan's Devils. Though, like Jax wanted the Sons to do, we make our money straight, running the businesses. It brings the money in and keeps the heat away."

Hmm. While I know they're mostly clean, I reckon there are some things I'm better off not knowing. It's been a month now, and while there's no need for them to care whether I'm alive or dead, they still have this prospect looking out for me. Not all the time anymore, he gets breaks while I'm working. He follows me home from work, stays the night, and leaves when I'm back at the station the next morning.

Whether whoever was after me has lost interest or whether Hyde's company is enough to keep them away, I can't be sure. No one's come after me since he's been here. When I've suggested his presence is probably no longer necessary, he tells me I've got no choice in the matter, what his prez says is what he'll do. Sometimes I wonder whether Drummer knows more than me. If there wasn't a risk, why is he still keeping a man at my side?

It's good that Hyde's an easy companion, making himself almost invisible at times so I forget he's here. He's also useful. Like when I come home with a thumping headache, ordering in food so I don't need to cook. And when we're watching the Sons, he's quite a laugh and a mine of information. He must have watched this show a hundred times and gives a running commentary on things I might have missed, or what I should look out for.

I'm treating him like a younger brother, and he sees me in a similar way, never attempting to make a move on me, which may be because to him, I'm an older woman. The thought makes me giggle.

"What's got into you? Christ, women are unbelievable." He's shaking his head with a grin. "Thinking about Jax again."

"On that note, I'm going to bed."

"You might need new batteries in your vibrator," he calls as I'm heading out the door.

"Why? You been using it?" A cushion hits me on the back, and I go to bed laughing, realising I'll actually be sorry when Drummer summons his prospect back.

I might enjoy my evenings, but I absolutely hate my days. We've come no closer to finding the missing children. *Two more now*, I remind myself. Garza and I have interviewed and re-interviewed the families, but there's no pattern, nothing we can pick up on. After leaving the genuinely grief-stricken parents, it guts me that I can do nothing to help. Time's getting away from us. Every day that passes is an extra day those kids will be suffering whatever fate they've stepped into.

We've been following up leads, particularly suspected sightings. The faces of the kids are regularly on the news, but there's nothing to go on. Well, almost nothing.

"What you doing?"

"I might have found a pattern to the times they were taken." I nod up at Garza, who's stopped by my desk.

"There isn't a pattern. We've already established that."

"Yeah, but look. Two of them were taken before school, on the school bus one minute, disappeared the next. Two after school, one of whom walked home alone."

"And two at lunchtime, and one during a trip." He shakes his head. "No pattern. Nothing. And don't forget, the others from their homes in the evening."

"Phone records."

"Fuck, woman, don't you think we didn't go there first off? Checked their records, nothing came up with the last number that called them, and no unusual texts if that's what you're thinking. All the phones have been destroyed."

And found near the locations where they went missing. No chance to track them. But something got those kids walking off. No sightings of strangers approaching or talking to them.

I'm sure I'm onto something, but Garza's right. The phone records showed nothing. Everything we think of, we come up against a block.

Another unsuccessful day, like so many others. Hopes of finding the children at all, or at least alive, are fading.

Another two weeks and still no further progress, and another child gone. Warnings are being broadcasted, but still children go missing. We can't even give a heads-up to parents as to what to watch out for.

When I get home, Hyde looks at me carefully. "Nothing new?"

I throw down my purse and collapse on the couch. "Nothing. These poor kids, Hyde."

He nods, understanding my frustration. "You look exhausted. Want me to cook tonight?"

I roll my eyes. "Appreciate the offer, but no. You tried to poison me last time. If you want rid of me, just shoot me, alright?"

He'd told me he had no skills in the kitchen and then had gone on to prove it. Laughing good naturedly, he disappears, reappearing with the takeout menus. "What are you in the mood for? Not having you waiting on me tonight."

He's right, I'm too tired, the mental toll sapping me physically. We settle on pizza. He orders it and I go have a long soak in the tub. Then we're back to a couple more episodes of *Sons of Anarchy*. I'll be upset when we finish the last season. It's totally addictive.

The next morning, I wake feeling nauseous. Remembering how tired I was the night before, I think I'm coming down with something. If Hyde had cooked as he'd suggested, I might have blamed him. I'd like nothing more than to stay in bed, but today might be the day we get a clue that breaks the case open. For the sake of the missing kids, I can't afford not to go into work. I drag myself out of bed, soon finding it was the right decision. As soon as I'm dressed, I'm feeling more like my normal self again.

Life continues in the same vein for a couple of weeks, and the stress of the job is taking its toll. At nights I come home so tired I've barely got the energy to eat. If it wasn't for Hyde persuading me, most nights I probably wouldn't even have bothered about food. In the mornings my dread of the day ahead exhibits itself by an upset stomach, and the past couple of days, I've actually been sick.

Reed shakes his head as I walk into the office. "Look what the cat dragged in. Well, you look like what a cat would drag in, anyway." After making his joke, his mouth purses. "This case and Garza getting to you?"

"Yeah." I nod, putting one hand on his desk as if I need to hold myself up. "Hate that we're not getting anywhere."

Reed frowns. "Partners should support each other." He nods toward Garza sharing a joke at the top of the room, his sycophants surrounding him. "Can't be much fun working alongside him."

It's not, but I'm loyal enough not to discuss the man I'm coming to hate with another detective.

"Hey, shall I get you a cup of coffee? The real stuff, not from public enemy number one over there. Or should I say, our new interrogation tool?" He grins.

I summon a smile, remembering our early morning conversation almost two months ago now. Christ, it seems more than that. I consider his offer, but my stomach's still feeling queasy today. It's probably the thought of working with Garza is literally sickening. "No to the coffee. Thanks, Reed. Maybe later."

Going to my desk, I log on to the system. A smell of expensive but heavy smelling aftershave wafts to me, making my stomach roll. Garza pulls up a chair and straddles it without waiting for permission or invitation. He's far too close, right up in my personal space.

I swallow a couple of times until my stomach settles enough for me to speak. "Got anything new?"

"Sure have." He puts a report down in front of me. "Got a sighting. Man lingering outside a school. Plaid jacket, white shirt, grey trousers and loafers. The facial description's there." He nods at the paper. "Oh, and he had a bottle of some kind of spirit in his hand, taking a drink. He wasn't exactly in plain view, he was hiding behind a wall."

My sickness is banished by my excitement. The first possible lead we have. Of course, it could be a red herring, but even so, something to work on.

"Oh, and if you don't mind, can you brief the press this morning? Not that we've got much to tell them, but they'll still want an update. Reynolds has gone out, and I've got to be some-where else."

I don't mind at all. It means I'm not going to be stuck in the car with him and that repulsive smell all morning. Maybe by afternoon it will have worn off. "Sure." I tap the new report. "Want to release this?" It might get people calling to give us tips on who the potential suspect is.

"Sure. You do that, Hannah. I'll see you later, okay?"

The press eagerly eats up the one new lead we have, and by afternoon it's all over the news. It's even coming up on the news feed on my phone.

I go home feeling slightly more optimistic, and for once cook something for Hyde and myself rather than ordering in. But I still go to bed early, unable to keep my eyes open any longer.

The next morning starts just as normal. Hyde follows me to work and then peels off to do whatever errands he runs in the daylight hours. I go up to the office and pull out my chair, but immediately a shout reaches me.

"Detective Hannah!"

I sigh. Reynolds. What a way to start my day. Wearily, I walk to his office and see Garza already in there.

Reynolds' mouth is pursed, and his nose is pinched. He's breathing heavily, and his cheeks are red. He waits for me to enter but doesn't invite me to sit. Garza is leaning back in his chair, his hands clasped behind his neck. He pops his gum, and a small smile plays at his lips.

I don't like this at all.

"Well you've gone and fucked up now. Only knew it was a matter of time. Most useless detective I've ever had in this department." Reynolds is spitting the words at me like bullets from a machine gun. I turn to look at Garza, surely he should be worried as we've worked this case together, and he's taken lead. His smile has only widened.

"I don't understand—"

"You don't understand? I don't understand why you fucked up and now the bureau's going to have a lawsuit against it."

"What? Why?"

"You were specifically told not to release information on the sighting of a man near a school yesterday until it had been checked out."

That's plain wrong. "No, Garza told me to tell the press."

"Garza told you to leave that bit out." As I'm opening my mouth to contradict, Reynolds' hand goes to his forehead and doesn't give me a chance. "Turns out it was the fucking vice principal. He's been suspended from his job because of his drinking. He's suing us."

"He shouldn't have been drinking," I say automatically.

Reynolds throws me a look of exasperation. "The point is, your partner here followed down the lead and identified who it was and eliminated him from the investigation before your little titbit hit the news."

My eyes meet those of my partner. "Why didn't you tell me that?"

"Didn't see I had a need to. Had already told you not to release it to the press."

No, he hadn't. Had he? For a second doubting myself, I run over yesterday's conversation in my mind. He had definitely told me to release it, I remember it clearly. But when I look at him again, I see there's no point in arguing. *He's set me up.*

"An apology isn't going to hack it this time, Detective Hannah. Go to your desk and clear out your things."

"You're suspending me?"

"I'm firing you. Garza's been keeping me updated, and to be honest, you just don't come up to the mark."

I can't believe this is happening. "I'm going to fight you on this," I tell him. "I've done nothing wrong." I'll go to the union.

"It will all be in my formal report, and I think even you'll agree your performance has been quite lacking."

And a report, written by him, quite damning.

Stunned, knowing there's nothing I can say until I can get someone in my corner, understanding it's better to keep my mouth shut for now, I leave the office.

Garza follows me, that smile I want to knock off his face still taunting me as he stands and watches me get my things together. As he escorts me out of the office, Reed's eyes widen when I pass him, but I can't explain. It's hard to see through my frustrated tears.

At reception, I hand over my warrant card and police-issue gun and holster.

And that's it. Done. This job I so wanted to do some good in the world with has spat me out. The bad guys I wanted to put away? Well, they've won.

For the moment.

CHAPTER TWENTY-NINE

---

*H*eart...

A couple of mornings after Susie Clyde met her demise, I watch that little prick Hyde sauntering into the clubroom like he owns the place. I never had a problem with him before, but now I'll be inclined to side with Slick when it comes time to voting him in. *He's* the reason Marc was able to leave the compound in the first place, and what does he get for his punishment? Being invited to live with her in her fucking house for the last two months, that's what.

Fucker looks far too happy and comfortable. And so he would be, he's probably getting his cock in her every night. A brief memory of how it felt when mine was in her tight cunt has my dick swelling, and I change the direction of my thoughts fast. While I've been resisting the club girls, she's probably been getting it on with the fucking prospect.

No. No way is he ever getting my vote. He should count himself lucky if I don't put him in the ground.

He's chatting with Jekyll, they're sharing a joke together. Do the other prospects know how cushy Hyde's life must be? Fuck it, he's probably getting home-cooked dinners every night too.

"Prospect!" I yell and wave my empty beer bottle. Just the sight of him makes me want to drink.

"What's got you riled?" Peg walks over and pulls up a chair, turning to lift two fingers at Jekyll before he sits down.

"Fucking prospect." I nod toward the man walking over to join us carrying a beer in each hand.

"Whatcha done now, Hyde?" Peg asks wearily.

"What? Me?" He points to himself, looking confused. "Nothing."

"And that's the fuckin' point." Taking my beer, I point the bottle at him. "You got an easy life staying with the bitch of a cop."

"Bitch?" He seems taken aback. "She's nice."

She's fucking nice? My assumptions seem to be confirmed if he's sticking up for her. "'Bout time you got back here and did some real work."

Hyde's eyes widen. "I'll do whatever the club wants me to do."

Peg's watching me closely, but his words are for Hyde. "And at the moment we want you to watch out for Marcia Hannah." His good leg kicks out a chair. "Here, sit down. Have you seen anything going on that makes you think someone's still after her?"

Hyde takes the chair and plants his backside in it. With a wary glance my way, he addresses himself to the sergeant-at-arms. "Nothing at all. But she's not having it easy. Comes home dead tired each night. She's working too hard, and that partner of hers is putting it all on her. She's taking it to heart, too. Worried as fuck about finding those missing children."

My eyes flick to Peg's. We've been doing some digging of our own.

"And on top of it all, I think she's got something cooking in that oven of hers." Hyde sighs and rubs his hand over his face. "I'm worried about her."

"What d'ya mean she's got something cooking? Don't like the food she serves up?"

Hyde huffs a laugh. "Nah, I don't mean like that. I saw the signs when I lived with my sister. Sick in the mornings, exhausted at night. Going to bed early. She's lost weight too. My sister did at first. Hates the smell of coffee."

"She's pregnant?" My heart misses a beat.

Hyde shrugs. "Got all the signs. Don't think she's figured it out yet."

While thinking it's impossible—she *can't* get pregnant—I'm out of my seat and have knocked Hyde out of his and onto the floor. I get one shot at his face before Peg grabs hold of my arm.

"What the fuck, Heart?"

Hyde's rubbing his jaw, his eyes flaring with panic.

"He got her fuckin' pregnant! That's what!"

"What? Me? Heart, man, it's not mine. I've never touched her."

I can only see red and I don't believe him. "You're the one who's been fuckin' her." I wrench my arm out of Peg's hold just as Hyde gets to his feet.

He blocks my punch while screaming, "I've never fucked her!"

Now Peg's got his strong arms around me. "Get out of here, Hyde."

I struggle, but his arms are like a vice, and he only releases me when the prospect's out of sight.

"Now are you going to calm the fuck down, Brother? What do you fuckin' care if she's pregnant or not? If you want my two cents' worth, and your getting it anyway, Hyde's got far too much respect for her to go there. You can see it. He doesn't talk about her the way he would if he'd gotten up close and personal."

Slowly my heart rate slows, but not back down to normal. Peg might be right. Hyde might not be in her bed every night. Or any night. Which means he can't be the one who got her pregnant. Not unless there's been someone else, someone who snuck in the house without Hyde noticing, which is extremely unlikely. She'd told me she hadn't been with anyone since she'd come to Tucson, and she's been here a year or so. However I try to avoid it, there's only one answer I can come up with. The most likely person to have put a baby inside her… is me.

She told me she couldn't get pregnant. She took my cum into her body unprotected. I feel my cheeks start to burn once again as I realise she must have fuckin' lied.

I don't turn to look at him, just straighten my shoulders and say, "I'm out of here, Peg."

The autumn rain in my face goes unnoticed as I ride into Tucson, but it does some to cool my temper and to start me thinking rationally. Hyde might be wrong. She might simply be stressed out and tired. Even if he'd described the symptoms I remember Crystal having. She might not have lied, there could be something else wrong. First thing to do is check if Hyde's on the money or not.

I stop off at a pharmacy and purchase a couple of pregnancy tests. It's mid-afternoon, she'll be at work. I'll ring and tell Hyde I'll be escorting her home today. I'll tell him when I'm done, and he can go back to pick up the pieces. If she lied, there won't be very much of her left. The stress of her job will be nothing to the trauma I'll be leaving her with. Yeah, that's what I'll do.

Hyde rung, I go to the precinct. Fuck, if I'd been sensible, I'd have checked the time she clocks out, but I'll hover here in case. It will be easy enough to keep that rat bike of hers in sight.

Well, it would have been easy if it was in the parking lot.

Another call to Hyde. "She tell you if she was going out today? Ok, yeah."

Has she gone home early? If she's been sick, she might. It's a shorter ride to the new house she rented. I've not been here before, and immediately my practised eye is looking over the security arrangements. It doesn't take long, there aren't any. But there's a closed garage, so maybe her bikes are in there.

Without being particularly hopeful, I knock on the door.

The eyes of the woman greeting me are already rimmed red, but that's all I notice before pushing inside.

"Heart? Why are you here? Um, what are you doing?"

I take the tests out of my pocket and throw them at her. "Go do what you have to with these."

Bending down, she picks them up and holds them as though I've asked her to handle a poisonous snake. "What the fuck are these?" She looks up at me as if I've drowned her cat.

"Hyde reckons your pregnant. Take the test and find out."

She shakes her head and looks down at what she's holding in her hands, then drops them on a side table like a hot grenade and backs away. Her eyes flit to the packages again and then back to meet mine.

With an almost imperceptible straightening of her shoulders, she says coldly, "I clearly remembering telling you…" Her hand goes to her head. "Actually, no. I didn't tell you. I told someone else, and they shared my story. But you know, you fucking know, I can't have kids." Her voice, which had been quiet, gets louder. "I *can't fucking have kids,*" she ends with a screech.

Then she's moved toward me, her hands beating at my chest. "I can't have children, Heart. How dare you come here and be so fucking cruel." The unexpected force of her blows makes me take a step back. "I trusted you, Heart. All those months we were talking to each other, I let you in. Then you showed me who you really were that night before I left the compound." Her eyes meet mine again, and I almost see sparks flying. "I never understood what you could have done to get you thrown out of the club, but now I understand. You're a hateful excuse for a man. You're a fucking bastard. I hate you. I hate you."

I grab her hands and hold her captive. Her outburst, while surprising, hasn't weakened my resolve. "Go take a test," I say.

I'm holding onto her tight. She's shaking her head, then huffs a strangled laugh. "And what will you do when you see it's negative?"

"Leave," I promise her.

"And," she hiccups, "if it's… if it's positive?" I've never seen a woman have such difficulty getting words out. For a second I don't know what I'm doing here or what I hope to get from today. I shouldn't have taken any notice of what that fucker Hyde had to say. How does he know what he's talking about? Why am I putting her through this pain?

I still haven't answered her question, but I've only one thing I can say. "If it's positive, I leave."

"Well the sooner I do this the sooner I get you out of my hair."

She picks up one of the packets and spends a moment reading it, her hand fisting and going to her mouth. Then, with her shoulders hunched as though I've physically beaten her, she walks away.

"Marcia," I call. The time for nicknames has passed.

"What?"

"Make sure you pee on the stick."

She pauses, there's no fight left in her. "Wanna come watch?"

I trust her that far. "No."

She's back in a couple of minutes, leaving the wand on the side. She goes over and stands, looking out of the window, her hands wrapped around herself. When she starts talking, it takes me by surprise.

"You can't know the times I've avoided going down the pregnancy aisle, knowing it will never be me taking those tests. You can't know how I even avoid looking at contraception. Oh, I know well enough to use condoms for health reasons, well," she half turns her head, but doesn't actually look at me, "most of the time, anyway. But I knew I'd never have a pregnancy to prevent.

"It was hard being around the babies in the clubhouse, knowing I'd never be holding my own. But the old ladies, they were so friendly, and Sandy, Sandy helped. It helped to talk to someone who knew how I felt.

"But to be so cruel as to actually make me take the test where there can never be any hope inside. I'm never going to forgive you for that, Heart. Never."

She's talking from the depths of her soul. Every word she says, she believes. The truth as she knows it. The tone convincing me more than the words could ever do by themselves. Like a dagger piercing my side, a pain runs through me, recognising the damage and hurt I've caused her. A little action, peeing on a stick… means nothing to me. But it's devastating for a woman who knows she can never have a child.

She's right to hate me. I know there won't be any way back, but suddenly I wish there were. My hatred and loathing for Hyde, suddenly dawning on me, is not because I've got anything against him, but it's because he's been here, where I want to be, with my old lady.

I pick up the unused tests and hide them in my pocket and then go to remove the evidence of the one she'd taken. I'll leave nothing behind to cause her more pain. She's got enough without the sight of the packaging making her feel worse. I pick up the stick with every intention of throwing it away but for some unknown reason my eyes fall on it. I freeze. I get out the box it came from and read the instructions myself.

"Marc," I say, casually.

"What?"

"Hate to say this, darlin', but I think you're going to have to take another test."

"Why?" She's still gazing out the window at nothing.

Thinking quickly, I explain, "This one's not showing anything. It couldn't have worked." I open up the second box and take out a different test. Walking over to her, I put it into her hand. "Take this one instead."

The look she gives me would have destroyed me if I hadn't been holding something in my other hand. Keeping emotion from my face, I curl her fingers around the new test. "Must have been a bad batch."

"You just want to torment me." But after one last pleading look, she disappears once again. This time for a little longer.

When she comes back, she puts the stick down once again. "You have no idea how hard it is to pee twice in quick succession." Her indignant words almost make me laugh. I bite the side of my mouth to stop myself.

This time we wait in silence. While she was gone, I'd checked both the time and the instructions.

I pick it up and stand, looking at the result in silence. Her impassioned cries had gotten to me. *Whatever this shows, she truly doesn't believe she can get pregnant.*

Which means what I'm looking at is a fucking miracle.

I go over to her and pass her the results, putting my arm around her waist. She stiffens and avoids looking at me. "Just leave, Heart. I've done what you wanted. Proved I'm not a liar."

"But you are, babe." I raise her hand, holding both the wands up. She turns away. "Look."

At last, with a sigh that she'll soon be rid of me, she does what I've asked. Her eyes look at one, and then at the other.

Thank fuck I've still got my arm around her, as she collapses in a dead faint.

CHAPTER THIRTY

*H*eart…

"Doc, Marc's just found out she's pregnant and she's fainted. She didn't even know she *could* get pregnant. She fuckin' freaked out. Could you come see her?"

"Yes," I answer him, with my fingers pinching the bridge of my nose. "I know you're only an Army medic. But you've got medical knowledge."

"Yeah, yeah. I know you can dig out a bullet and stitch a wound. But my ol' lady's fainted." *I need help.*

"The emergency room?" My hands brush back my hair. "Yeah, I should have thought of that." Fucking stupid not to take her to the obvious place. I'm just so used to calling Doc for any and all medical treatment.

"Yeah, if there's anything you can do I'll let you know. Thanks, Doc."

I ring another number. "Hyde, need you here, man. Bring a cage. Marc needs to go to the hospital."

Pulling the phone away from my ear, I look at it in amazement. *Fucking prospect's swearing at me?* "What the fuck? No. I did nothing to her. No, she's not fuckin' hurt. She fainted."

"You threatening me, Prospect? Just get your ass here and I might forget you said that."

Fucking prospect. Accusing me of beating her up. I didn't, and never would, lay a hand on her.

She went out like a fucking light when she saw the results of the tests, scaring the shit out of me. She's so still and unmoving. If it wasn't that I can see her breathing, I'd be worried the shock had killed her. Such an adverse reaction, another pointer she was telling the truth. And there, in that flat stomach of hers, she's incubating my baby and has been for two months.

Thank fuck, she's starting to stir. I'm at her side in a flash. "Just lie still, sweetheart. Do you want some water or something?"

Her eyes are flitting one way then the other. "What happened?"

"You've fainted, darlin'. Didn't fall or nothing, I had hold of you. Prospect's bringing a cage so we can get you checked out."

Her brow creases as if she's trying to remember, and I see the moment she does. She sits up so sharply her head must start swimming as she cups it in her hands and groans.

"Stay still. You want anything? I'll get it."

She's waving her hands toward my cut. "The tests. Give me the other tests."

"You've already taken two, you won't have enough pee for more."

"I need to take them." She sounds frantic.

I kneel in front of her, taking both of her hands in mine. "We'll get you to the emergency room. Doctors will do the tests there. That way you can be certain." I place my hand over her stomach. "But I know, I feel it. You've got my baby growing in there."

Looking down at my hand, she places hers over it. "It's impossible, Heart. I'm sorry. I don't know why, but somehow the tests are showing a false positive. I've heard that can happen. Maybe I've got something wrong with me."

"There's nothing wrong with you. You're going to have my child." I don't know why I'm so certain, I just am. Then the implications hit me. "Amy will have a brother or sister." We haven't spoken about a relationship, haven't talked at all for two months, but I'm going to be right there beside her. Coming here today, seeing her again, has made me realise a piece of me has been missing. Our time apart caused by my anger had been fuelled by my reluctance to admit how much she means to me. I don't want her to have crept into my heart, to have kicked that organ back into life, but somehow she has. It's time now to man up and own it.

Resting my chin on the top of her head, my thoughts are whirling. How the fuck is this going to sort itself out? I'll have to leave the club, or she'll have to leave her job. One way or another, we *will* make this work. If she's having my miracle baby, then something must have guided me that night. Before Crystal, I always gloved up. I could say I'd got out of the habit when she went on the pill, but it's more than that. *Fate, or...*

For the first time I don't feel like I've been punched in the gut, but instead I get a warm feeling when I think of the wife who I lost. *Crystal, you guided me so fucking often, reckon you might have had a hand in this too.* Bound me to the ideal woman to be my old lady. Today being the kick up the backside to make me realise exactly what I want.

Now I've just got to persuade her. But I'm in a good place. Everyone already knows she's my old lady. I'll kidnap her if I have to and take her back to the compound. *But she's a cop.*

She's softly crying. I put my arms around her and hold her close. "Will you come with me to the hospital? I don't want to be alone when I find I've got cancer or something."

I laugh quietly. "You haven't got cancer, babe. You're having my baby." But she still won't fucking believe it.

"This is one day I should never have gotten up."

"Darlin'," I gently raise her face, "I'm so fucking sorry I came in the way I did, for the things I said. I didn't mean to hurt you. I wasn't thinking this through."

She grasps my cut with her hands and sniffles into it. "It's not just you, Heart. I'm home early because I lost my job."

What? I might not like her profession, but I know she was good at her job. *Why would they let such a dedicated cop go?* I want to hear everything that happened, but doubt now's the right time, so I settle for a few inadequate words. "I'm so sorry, Marc. So damn fuckin' sorry."

I hear a truck pull up. Before I can get up to open the door, Hyde lets himself in. *The fucker's got a key?* His eyes go to Marc, and he sees she's been crying. He pulls back his shoulders and prepares to square up to me. *Oh fuck, not again.* Before he can make an attack, I sweep Marc up into my arms, making her give a startled gasp.

"We'll talk about this later," I warn him. "For now, let's get her checked out."

Marc's prodded and poked, made to pee *again*, and has blood taken. She explains to anyone who comes near her she can't be having a baby, and to test for whatever else it could be. Eventually, a doctor appears.

"Hmm." Doctor Cassidy is a middle-aged woman. She has a glint of humour in her eyes as she regards the woman sitting next to me, who's biting her nails. She nods slowly, then smiles. "Marcia, you are definitely pregnant."

Marc goes still, the blood rushing from her face, leaving her looking so white I'm worried she might faint again. The doctor must be concerned too, as she immediately stands and gets her a drink of water before sitting back down and asking in a concerned tone, "Are you alright?"

"Yes, no. I don't know. I can't be." As alternating expressions of confusion and joy come over her face, I pat Marc's hand, and as the doctor meets my eyes, we exchange amused glances.

"I take it this is good news to you both."

A few hours ago my answer would have been different. Now I beam and answer what I hope is true for us both. "Yes."

She studies Marc carefully, picking up a pen and rolling it through her fingers. "Okay, so this is what we do. I can see you still need some convincing, Marcia, so I'd like to do an internal ultrasound in a moment. But first, please tell me why you were so certain it was impossible?"

I watch as she gives herself a little shake and tries to pull herself together. Again I reach for her hand, this time to squeeze it, knowing it's still hard for her to talk about, especially after this already emotional day. After clearing her throat she begins. "I was in a bad car accident, eight years ago. A piece of metal pierced me, here." She points to her lower stomach where I already know she has scarring. "It ripped across and caused internal injuries." Marc stops and gasps. "If I'm pregnant, what if I can't carry a baby to term?"

"Hmm. I'd like the details of the hospital where you were treated, and then I'll get your notes. How old were you?"

"Eighteen."

"Okay. Let's see what I can tell about what we're dealing with. We'll get you undressed and on the table, and I'll call the technician in. I will need your full records to see if there's any extra care that needs to be taken until you're at term."

I help her undress, put on one of those despicable gowns, and then lift her onto the bed. She gives me a look, saying drily, "Apparently I'm pregnant, not dying. I could have gotten up myself."

"My baby." I tap her stomach and then tap her forehead. "My woman." I turn away to hide my smile at the incredulous look she gives me. *You're mine.*

The technician wheels a machine in, and I wince and turn away as the invasive procedure begins. Marc clasps at my hand, and I give her both, holding hers between my palms. She's staring at me, but my eyes have been caught by the screen.

"There's the baby," the doctor says, pointing to a tiny bean-like shape. She fiddles with a knob, and a sound fills the room—a fast thumping, swishing noise. But the doctor's not smiling, she's frowning instead.

Seeing her expression, Marc's hand grips mine so tightly she almost cuts off the blood circulation. "What's wrong?"

"Hmm?" The doctor, having been intent on the screen, now turns her attention away and catches the expression on Marc's face. "Well, I don't know if it runs in your family, but I can see two gestational sacs. That means there are two babies. Congratulations, my dear. You are going to have twins."

Fuck me! Amy was enough to look after on her own. Two babies? At once? Now it's my turn to feel faint. Marc, once again, has gone white as a sheet.

I help a stunned Marc to sit up. While the doctor's making some notes on a tablet, Marc doesn't say a word, just sits completely shell-shocked, and I admit I'm feeling the same. When the doctor has finished, she looks at Marc.

"I can see why your doctor thought you'd have difficulty conceiving. Your fallopian tubes have clearly suffered major damage, and you've had one of your ovaries removed." She rubs her forehead. "In fact, I'm surprised you conceived at all. At the time, the doctor you saw was quite right to warn you. I'd probably have said the same thing myself. But somehow, it's happened. You're definitely pregnant, no doubt about that. And, with twins."

So that's it, confirmed. She didn't lie, hadn't misunderstood what she'd been told. *Fucking miracle babies.*

Marc's gone completely pale with the news that not only is she carrying one baby she never expected, she's carrying two. Her voice is quiet as she responds, "Now I've conceived, what are the chances of me carrying the babies to term?"

The doctor nods as though she's asked a pertinent question. "That's why I need your full notes to be sure. From what I've seen, there shouldn't be any problems, but you've clearly had surgery, so I want to check how invasive it was."

Marc looks down as if she knew this is too good to be true.

"Now, Marcia. I think the likelihood of you having a normal pregnancy is quite high. We'll just monitor you carefully. What I must warn you both is, if you want to extend your family, that might not happen. As I've said, there was major damage to your tubes. So we'll be extra careful about this one."

What she's saying is this could be Marc's only chance to have a child. I squeeze the hand I haven't stopped holding. The woman by my side seems incapable of saying anything at all, and it's me who pockets the card for her next appointment and takes the prescription for prenatal vitamins.

She's still in a trance as she gets back into her clothes and remains that way when I walk her out.

Hyde's waiting by the truck and steps forward, giving one look at her, and addressing himself to me. "She alright?"

A wide grin splits my face. "Better than fuckin' alright."

A glance at her, and then at the smile on my face. "Goddammit. I was right, wasn't I? She's fuckin' pregnant."

I shoot him a look of caution, but I can't bring myself to deny it. He slaps his hand on the truck. "Fuckin' hell." He looks as happy as if he were the father.

"I'm taking her home."

"I'll follow you. Want me to stay?"

I laugh like a loon. "Nah, she's not going back to that fuckin' insecure house. She's coming with me. *Home.*"

At last he gets my intention, and slaps me on the back, nodding as though I've done something he approves of. Well he might, but I'm not so sure what Drummer's reaction will be.

It's not until it's obvious that I'm not heading toward her house that Marc comes out of whatever reverie she's been lost in. "Heart," she squeals. "Where the hell are you taking me?"

"The compound."

Her face turns to me in horror. "I can't go there!" she exclaims.

"Ain't got a choice, babe. Not having the fucker Hyde babysit you anymore. That house you've rented isn't secure enough for my woman on her own, and certainly not now you're carrying my kids."

"Heart, look, we need to talk about this."

"Nothing to say."

She turns to look at me, her mouth dropping open. Then she lets me have it full blast. "Nothing to say? Nothing to fucking say? You had plenty to say to me earlier. In fact, you spat it at me, didn't you? What happened to you thinking I was going to steal your baby girl from you? Oh my God." Her hand covers her lips and her eyes are wide. "You don't want me. You want what you think I'm carrying."

"Are carrying," I correct her. "Look…" Knowing what precious cargo I've got with me, I keep my eyes on the road but reach across and put my hand on her thigh. Although she tries to pull away, I hold on firmly. "You are pregnant. There's no denying that now. And yes, as the father, *and your ol' man*, I'm involved. I said some shit, I can't deny that." I break off, trying to analyse it all in my head in just a split moment of time. "I'll put this a way you can understand. I've been lost in my head, babe. Gonna take more than a minute to get you to understand that, but this?" I touch our clasped hands to her stomach. "This has put me straight."

There's silence for a moment, and then she says, "I don't understand what you're saying."

"We've got a lot of talking to do, and much more than that. We're not going to put things right if we're apart."

"I don't like this, Heart. I don't *trust* you. After the way you pushed me away. You showed me another side of you, and one I didn't like. Said some cruel things—"

"I was a fool." I speak over her. "Couldn't see further than my own fuckin' nose. Thought there'd never be room for anyone other than Crystal. But she's gone, I've accepted it. She's never coming back, and I'm done with pushing you away. I want you, babe. Want—"

"Stop! Stop the truck."

What?

Her free hands pointing to a car that's just pulled off the shoulder, and says desperately, "Heart, stop the truck, now!"

Wondering what the fuck's going on, and whether she's intending to run, I pull over. *Perhaps she needs to be sick?* Her seatbelt's unfastened and she's out of the damn truck faster than I can get down my side. She's running back along the hard shoulder. Incensed that she's trying to get away, I run after her. I've got longer legs, but she's fitter than me. I'm closing the gap slower than I want, when she suddenly drops to her knees, her hand reaching out.

"Here, fella. Here, boy. Or perhaps you're a girl." Her cajoling tone catches me off guard.

"Oh come here, you poor little thing." As she hears my footsteps crunch in the gravel, she shoots out her arm, her hand held up warning me to stop. I do and then see where she's pointing.

It's a puppy of some sort. She must have seen it being dumped out of the car we'd seen pull away. Marc with her cop's sharp eyes had seen it, but I'd been too focused on getting her home.

It's a grey bundle of scraggy hair, some sort of mutt, only a few months old by the look of it. Slowly Marc inches closer. The thing's shaking, but looking at her with trusting eyes. *Yeah, even a dumped puppy knows it can trust her, while I accused her of so much she didn't deserve.*

She's close enough now. The little pup reaches out its nose, touches her hand, and then, on its belly, inches cautiously closer. When she scoops it up into her arms, I see the enormous paws attached to a very small body. *Christ, that thing's gonna grow big.*

Slowly, Marc stands. She holds it away from her and examines it carefully. "Doesn't seem hurt, and it's a boy. Looks like a wolfhound mix."

Hell, what do I do now? I'm still getting my head around the fact that I'm going to be a father again. I wipe my hands through my hair, then decide, "Okay, bring it along, we'll find a shelter to take it."

"What the fuck, Heart? Not going to give him to somewhere that might kill him if they can't find him a home. No, I'm going to keep him." Her determined eyes meet mine in challenge.

I'm looking at her face, seeing she's already set on it, and suddenly I'm laughing, rolling back my head on my shoulders while her eyes stare wildly, as if wondering what I'm finding amusing in all this. It's only then I've noticed Hyde, who I had to trust to bring my bike back to the compound, has parked up behind us. It's he who puts into words precisely what's making me lose my shit.

"Prez is gonna go crazy, Heart. You returning with a pregnant ol' lady and a fuckin' dog as a pet."

"Grunt."

"What?"

Marc seems more able to accept that she's gained a puppy than the knowledge she's carrying twins. She looks up to me and her eyes sparkle. "You want me to come back to the compound, Heart? Well, Grunt's coming too. That's my condition."

CHAPTER THIRTY-ONE

*M*arc…

This day started out like normal. Then I went into work and found I no longer had a job. Then the last person I expected arrived at my door today, the man I hadn't laid my eyes on or spoken to for two months, though I hadn't been able to expel him from my thoughts. While Hyde might have joked about using my vibrator to thoughts of Jax Teller, he'd been far from the truth, and it was another blond biker that had fuelled my fantasies.

But never had I imagined I'd see him how he appeared this afternoon, his face twisted in such rage I was almost frightened… Until he threw those ridiculous pregnancy tests at me. *How could any man be so cruel?*

But with the result, it appears that I'm pregnant. *With twins.*

Still unable to accept the impossible, it seems easier to accept I seem to have acquired a dog which I never expected or knew I wanted. But as soon as I'd seen him dumped out of that car, I knew he was mine. His name? Well, if he's going to be on the compound among bikers, he might as well have a name to match. His little sniffling sounds as he snuggles up to me sound as though he's grunting. Grunt. It fits.

"Grunt, eh?" Heart's stopped laughing, his arms around both me and the pup. As I glance up into his face, it's to see a depth of emotion I never thought I'd see directed at me. *He thinks I'm pregnant. With his babies. It's them he wants, not me.* A sudden chill goes through me of what I might be walking into, but once again, it seems I don't have much choice. I've no weapon to threaten with, and two bikers outnumbering me.

Holding Grunt close, I walk back to the truck, only releasing him for a moment so I can climb inside, and then Heart hands him back.

Soon we're pulling off, back onto the road, and I accept I've committed to returning to the compound with no idea what reception I'll receive. I'm not even sure I want to be with the man beside me, unable to forget the malicious words he'd thrown at me.

I would be trembling were it not for the calming presence of the pup in my arms. Suddenly I realise I don't want to face the inevitable questions or accusations that will surely be thrown, at least not until Heart and I have thrashed everything out.

"Heart?"

"Yeah, darlin'?"

"Please don't tell anyone. About the… you know."

"Babies?"

"Yes. Look, it's really early. Anything could go wrong." And probably will given my medical history. I should be elated. This should be the best day of my life, but I can't allow myself to get excited. It's one last joke life's going to play on me, giving me hope and taking it away. I don't think I'll survive it. Right now, the parentage of the babies I'm carrying is the last thing on my mind. I'm too scared I'm going to lose them.

"Nothings gonna go wrong." Heart tries to reassure me. "But we'll keep it to ourselves for now, okay?"

I didn't expect my reappearance to be welcomed, but to top off my day, the clubhouse is crowded when we arrive. I reckon all the brothers are there, as well as their old ladies. All conversation stops as Heart leads me inside. I hug Grunt to me as though he's a shield, even though he's already a big pup and heavy.

Brothers part, allowing us free passage, looks of distrust on their faces. Heart's arm is holding me protectively into his side, his chin raised. We've just reached the bar when there's a loud shout.

"What the fuck is *she* doing here?" Drummer pushes his way through the milling throng, his eyes sharp with suspicion. He looks at me, at the bundle I'm holding, and then gives a death stare to Heart.

Heart's not fazed. He leans against the bar and turns me around, still holding me tightly, my back to his front. His arms go around me, one hand holding me and the pup, and the other resting on my stomach. I can't see his face, but hear the challenge in his voice. "I'm claimin' my ol' lady, Prez. And this time it's for real."

Drummer looks shocked. I doubt much takes him by surprise, but he doesn't appear to have seen this in the cards. He looks at me, then Heart, then at the dog who's stopped wriggling in my arms as if sensing his future lies in the balance.

"What the fuck?" he repeats. "Heart, we need to talk about this." Drummer's narrowed eyes land on me. "Nothing against you personally, darlin'. We've given you protection, and I'll continue to do that while there's a risk to you. But having the likes of you on the compound is a fuckin' mistake. You're a cop."

"No, she's not," Heart corrects, nuzzling my head, his lips on my hair. I haven't experienced demonstrations of affection from him before, but I don't have the strength to object.

Drummer's looking more and more perplexed, and there's a rumble of low voices around. If it wasn't for Heart's strong arms around me, claiming me, I'd feel scared.

"She lost her job today, Prez. She was sacked."

Drummer takes a moment for the news to sink in. "Still don't know where her loyalties lie. You been let go, darlin'? That seems a strange fuckin' coincidence to me. Reckon there's something more to it than you being a crap cop."

There is, and Drummer's sharp enough to know it.

"Even an ex-cop is not someone we can trust." Peg's come up alongside to support his prez. "Heart, think about this. She could be a plant."

I move and open my mouth, but Heart shakes his head and tightens his hold. "She stays or I go." Now it's Heart who's surprised me. "Not giving up my ol' lady, Prez."

"Because she's pregnant." A triumphant voice blurts out what I didn't want anyone to know. Hyde couldn't keep his mouth shut.

The stunned silence is broken by Drummer's direct question to me. "This right? You're not leading a brother on?"

Heart chuckles above me. "It's Marc who doesn't believe it. She's still in denial, but I made sure she got checked out by a doctor." He rubs my stomach. "What she's got in here is mine, and I ain't gonna have anyone questioning it."

I twist my head around. "Heart."

"Shush, hon. Everything's gonna be alright."

"Hate to tell ya this, Brother, but that right there isn't a baby, it's a fuckin' dog."

There are shouts and hollers as the biker at the back yells out his joke. Stunned as I am, even I feel a small smile playing at my lips.

"Shut the fuck up, Joker," Heart growls.

Drummer's old lady steps up beside him, her brow creased, and for once she doesn't sound friendly. "You said you couldn't have children."

"Sam," Heart says sharply.

At the same time, Drummer admonishes his old lady, "Darlin', leave it for now, okay?"

There's an air of tension, an atmosphere you could cut with a knife. "That staying too?" Drummer points at the bundle in my arms.

"Yes." It's the first time I've spoken.

Drummer rolls back his head, the ceiling appearing to have answers, then brings his head back down and says, "You and I need to have words, Marcia."

Heart's arms tighten. "She's had a fuck of a day, Drummer. Can we leave it tonight, get her rested?"

Again, I turn my head to Heart. While I feel safe as he keeps me close, I can't easily forget or forgive the hateful things that he's said, both today and that evening two months ago. I promised myself I'd never get close to anyone, and he's only confirmed what happens when I weaken and let someone in. I don't, can't, depend on him. I don't know if I'm still in danger now I'm not able to investigate anymore, but if there's a risk, there's apparently more than just me to think about now. I might be safer here on the compound, or at least continue to have the protection of a prospect. And for that, I need Drummer on my side. Let's face it, there's no one else.

"I'm alright, Heart. I'll speak to Drummer."

"Want in on that, Prez."

"No." Drummer sounds adamant as he refuses Heart's request. "Wraith. You come with." Still, they're being careful about talking alone in front of even an ex-cop.

As the president continues to stare at Heart in challenge, at last Heart's arms loosen around me. Stepping forward, I immediately miss the warmth at my back.

"Leave…" Drummer seems at a loss for words as he jerks his chin toward the bundle I'm still holding.

"Grunt."

"Well fuck me." The first grin comes to his face but slides away just as quickly. "Leave Grunt here."

Heart takes the pup from me, his nod and the way he's rubbing behind the pup's ears tells me I can trust him with my new dog. As Drummer turns and Wraith steps up to his side, I follow them into the president's office.

Drummer shuts the door behind him and takes his seat

behind the large desk. My eyes look behind him to the large Satan's Devils' logo hanging on the wall, ensuring I can't forget where I am. A shiver runs down my spine. As far as they're concerned, I'm a cop, in the office of the president of an OMG.

Those piercing grey eyes seem to see right through me. "What do you know about our club?" His tone is chilling, no comfort there.

I raise my shoulders then lower them, understanding what he's asking. "Not a lot." I pause, but it will come as no news to them. "The police think you should be disbanded, but otherwise I haven't learned anything at all. Apart from slurs on your characters, and a general warning to look out for you, there's no particular interest in the Satan's Devils."

I haven't told them anything they don't know already. Exchanging glances with Wraith, Drummer's attention turns back to me. "Okay, time for a bit of a history lesson. Club was started in the early seventies by my old man and a few of his friends after they came back from the Vietnam War. They were young, disillusioned, had seen war at its worst and the kickback against it here. They didn't return to recognition as heroes, and had no support for the PTSD that they suffered, as was usually the case back in those days."

It's a common story. I nod. Even the fallen weren't honoured until the end of the decade.

"Society didn't want them, so they settled into living outside of your citizen ways." Drummer's mouth twists as he remembers. "I was born into the club. Prospected along with my brothers, earned my place as a member. A few didn't make the grade. Things were more violent then. We earned money different ways. Whatever you learned of *OMGs*," Drum spits the term law enforcement uses, "in your training applied more to the sort of club my father, as president, ran. Drugs, guns, and prostitution. Something needed to change, no doubt about that. The original members began to die off, some from old age, some from bullets.

"I and a few of my brothers wanted change from within. The

new generation started to build slowly. We were making good progress until a new member arrived."

I start to get a feeling I'm not going to like what he says. There's a reason he's going over old ground.

"The sting operation was a long one. Smart, his name was. He'd shown from the start he had some intelligence, college degree and all." Drummer taps his fingers against his mouth. "I was beginning to think once he patched in that I'd get him on the side of the reformers."

Now he stands up, as though the memories are too hard to talk about sitting down and relaxed. I say nothing to interrupt him.

"Once the fucker got his patch, we brought him to the table. Let him in on every fuckin' thing we were doing."

"He was a plant." It's obvious.

"Yeah. He was a fuckin' snitch." His eyes meet mine, and not in a good way. "We got word something was going down at the strip club, the one we owned before Angels. Me and some of the boys, Beef, Digger, Peg, Dollar, Viper, and Tongue, who was still a prospect then, had gone to see what was going on. Fuckin' cops were all over it, pulling it apart. Pulling *us* apart once we arrived. But we'd all had clean records and permits to carry concealed. Apart from our affiliation with the club, there was nothing to hold us on, but we spent a few nights in your jail while they tried their hardest to pin something on us."

Wraith also stands, as if to give his president support.

"When we got out, well, we found a few changes. They'd raided the compound. Fuck knows what really went on. Three brothers arrested, eight others dead, including Bastard." He pauses and looks straight at me. "Bastard, my father." There is another second of silence. "The clubhouse was burned to the ground."

Oh my God. My hand covers my mouth. No wonder they don't like the police. It's surprising they even let me on to the compound. "When was this, Drummer? Have you still got members in prison?"

I swear his eyes glisten as he turns to me. "It was fourteen years ago, now. And no, they were got to and murdered. All the old-timers are gone, except for those of us who went to sort out the strip club." He stops speaking and rubs his eyes. "Some of the sweet butts were caught in the crossfire. When we had brothers still alive, I visited them in prison, heard the story. My mother had tried to protect her ol' man."

Christ. It was a massacre. "You just carried on?"

His fist hits the table. "We didn't just fuckin' carry on. We had nothing. No home, zilch. All we had was each other. We'd all lost family, by blood or by brotherhood. Took us a while to reassemble again. Couple of us bunked down at the strip club, and gradually the others came back, and that became our temporary home. Then, at last, this place came up. Dollar and Viper had a construction business, and it came in handy doing this up. Rebuilt the chapter piece by fuckin' piece. Cleaned up the club, wrote new bylaws. Got the other chapters on board. No one wanted another raid like that one."

"And all because they had a rat in the club." Wraith spells it out to me, in case I'd missed the point.

There we have it. Last time, they didn't know they had brought an undercover cop into the compound. No wonder they're suspicious about me.

"I'm sorry about your parents, Drummer. And the other men who were lost. But I'm not a cop any longer, and I'm not here to spy on what you do." I think about the situation for a moment. "If the cops wanted to infiltrate you, don't you think they'd send in a man? I know you don't divulge your business to the women in the club."

Again his hand raps down on the table. "If you stay in the club, you'll hear things that you shouldn't. Yeah, we protect our women from the worst of it, but stuff does get out. I run a clean club, Detective Hannah, but the way we go about it is different than in your world. Anyone, any-fuckin'-one crosses us, then we put them in the ground."

It's a dire warning. The cop part of me wants to arrest them, but there's a piece of me attracted to the idea of swift retribution and not letting the bad guys walk. *Like the truck driver who took my family from me.* I'd dreamed about taking him out, but as a law-abiding citizen, that was beyond me.

"I'm not a detective. I don't carry a badge anymore. I mean no harm to the club." But I would say that, wouldn't I? How the hell can I convince them.

Drummer takes his seat. He must have been young to take on the president's role, no wonder he's tough. Having lost so many brothers in his past explains how intense he is now. He stares at me, his gaze unwavering. "Smart thought that no one had suspected him. That he'd gotten away clean. But then I met Mouse, and he found him."

Mouse, their computer expert. I nod, realising how this story is going to end. "You took him out for what he'd done to your brothers and family."

He doesn't admit it, but his silence tells me a lot. If I'd been a man brought up in a violent way of life, that truck driver wouldn't still be breathing.

"So tell me, Marcia Hannah, how come you say you're unemployed? If you're going to be staying on the compound—and at the moment, I tell you, that's the last risk I want to take—you're gonna have to give me something so I can trust you." His tone is guarded.

I swallow, going back over everything I know about outlaw motorcycle gangs. Of course they're afraid of being infiltrated by the enemy. What better cover than to come back as an old lady, pregnant with a brother's child? If I was in his position, I would be skeptical too, particularly given what the club had experienced. Whatever Heart feels about me, however friendly I had become with the women, I'm sitting in front of the man who holds my life in his hands. *And now it's not just me.*

"Why did you allow me to stay before?"

His head tilts to one side. "We had you locked down with Heart. It was only temporary. While you were here, we made sure to keep our hands clean. But from the look on my brother's face, he wants this to be permanent. And that's far more dangerous." He sits up straight. "Not planning on breaking the law, but who knows what's around the corner? We protect our own with everything we've got."

And I'm not one of theirs. My hand rubs my stomach with the little miracles inside. *How can I convince him?* I could try telling the truth. "You want to know why I've lost my job?"

He leans back and folds his arms. "I'm listening."

"You've heard of the case of the missing children in Tucson?"

He gives a slight jerk of his chin to show that he has.

"That's the case I've been working on." I swallow again as a bad taste comes into my mouth. Heart had turned up before I'd had time to process everything that happened to me this morning, and I still barely understand it myself. "I was partnered with Garza and, well, he set me up. Made it look like I leaked information, when he'd told me himself I should give it to the press. He denied it, of course. Sergeant Reynolds had been looking for a chance to get rid of me, and he took it."

"Seems a bit weak. One mistake and you're out?" His eyes blaze into me, full of mistrust.

I nod in agreement. "Garza's apparently been providing reports about how bad I am at my job. All trumped up. I am, was, a good detective."

"Sounds like you could fight it. If you're telling the truth."

I raise and lower my head. "I could. I could get the union involved. I do good work, Drummer. That's how I got my promotion to detective. But you're already aware both Garza and Reynolds have had it in for me, and my suspicions that they're not straight. However I try to justify myself, they'll cook something up to make me look bad. Best I could expect is to be demoted, and I don't want that. I worked hard to get where I am." I close my eyes briefly then open them again. "And of course, there are the attempts on my life." I sigh and wipe my hand over my face. "They wanted me out of the way, which would confirm I've been looking in places they don't want me to go."

"You think Reynolds and Garza are the ones trying to kill you?"

That I can't be certain of. "Probably not directly, they wouldn't get their hands dirty. But I think they're feeding information to the people who are."

Now his VP enters the conversation with a direct question. "So where have you been looking? What have you found that they don't like?"

I should be keeping my mouth shut, not telling them anything. I look from one to the other before coming to a decision. I won't be dropping this case, even though I'm now unemployed. And maybe, just maybe, there's a way to get the outlaws on my side. With a sigh I start talking. "As I said, I'm looking into the cases of the missing children, trying to find a pattern, looking for something which they weren't spotting. Oh, watching the TV, you'd think the police are doing everything they can. But they're not."

"According to you."

"According to me," I agree.

"You think they're covering for someone?" Drummer's sharp eyes get straight to it. "You think they're getting paid? And kids are going missing and they're doing fuck all to stop it?"

At my nod, Drummer pushes back his chair and rests his foot against the table. His eyes go to Wraith's, and after a second they come back to me. "Okay, if I buy the story that you've been dismissed under false circumstances, where do you go from here? You gonna be trying to get back your job?"

I haven't thought that far yet. Too much else has happened today. "I don't know," I reply honestly. "But whether I'm working or not, whether what happened was unfair, dismissal doesn't hide the fact there are kids out there hurting. That's what I want to stop, Drummer."

My impassioned plea seems to get to him. His eyes gentle, his hand waves to my stomach. "And, what's all this about?"

My hands seem to move of their own accord, covering the place where babies are supposed to be. "Another shock," I admit. Tears come to my eyes as Drummer's eyes sharpen. "I was told after my accident that I'd never conceive." I try to put the events of the afternoon into words. "It sounds so stupid, but I've been tired, nauseous in the mornings. I put it down to the stress of my job."

"When did you tell Heart you were pregnant?"

A laugh escapes my lips. "I didn't. Hyde must have noticed something. He didn't speak about it to me, but must have said something to Heart. First thing I knew about it was Heart throwing pregnancy tests at me." Tears come to my eyes as I remember the awful things that he'd said. "If Hyde hadn't blurted it out, Heart had agreed we wouldn't have said anything. If I really am pregnant, I don't know…"

"If?"

I take the photo out of my purse. "That bean there, that's shows I'm supposed to be." I trace the shape then slide the picture over the desk. Drummer looks at it carefully before sliding it back. Reverently, I place it back in my purse. I haven't admitted to an educated eye, it shows twins, still convinced I'll lose one or both of them. "Drummer, it wasn't my idea to come back to the compound. That I'm apparently pregnant and that Heart is the father wasn't planned. And…" I pause, wondering how to say this. "The whole thing's ridiculous. Heart's not the man for me."

"He seems to think that he is."

Shaking my head, wondering how the man who's got a Jekyll and Hyde personality toward me could ever be a permanent fixture in my life, I refute it. "It's what I'm supposed to be carrying he wants, not me."

"You don't know much about Heart, do ya, darlin'?" I think I know all that I need to, but before I can answer he continues. "Heart changed when he lost Crystal. Did things I'd never have expected."

I can see, *understand* that. I'd been a part of his life for almost a year.

"Thing is, darlin', I've not seen the man that I knew before his accident reappear until tonight. That man, his arms around you and that fuckin' mutt? That's the real Heart right there." He breaks off and again studies me. "Something's happened, like a switch being thrown. It's been more than a year now since he lost his wife. A man can't grieve forever. He offered to choose you over the club—that means one fuck of a lot in our world. But I don't think you've seen too much of the man that he was. Glimpses, perhaps, but not the whole package. If I allow you stay on the compound, I think you should give him a chance."

That's not what I expected him to say, and I'm not sure it's what I want to do. "It's better, Drummer, after everything you've told me, if I don't stay. Easier for you and for me." I swallow a couple of times, knowing they owe me nothing. "I won't take Heart away from the club, but I'm scared. Especially now." I glance down at my stomach then back up. "I'm asking you to consider continuing to provide protection."

Another glance at his VP. Wraith hasn't said anything, but has been following the conversation carefully. He raises his chin at Drummer, as if answering an unspoken question. Drummer nods back and changes the direction of the conversation without saying whether he's going to help me or not.

"Thing is, Marcia, we've got things in common. This case of the missing children ain't settling well with me either." He replaces his foot on the floor and pulls his chair forward. "Your cop friends ain't helping ya, or letting you follow your head. You got thoughts on what's going on… Well, I want to hear them."

That again, is not what I expect him to say.

With a heartfelt sigh, Drummer places his steely gaze on me

again. "Far as I can see it, there are two choices. Either we take a risk and let you stay on the compound, working with us to put this fuckin' case to bed and find those kids, or if nothing else, find out what's happened to them to give their fuckin' parents some closure. Or, we cut ties, send you out, and you fend for yourself."

That's no choice. If they're going to be looking for the children, I want to be there alongside them. But there are problems with staying here. "Heart?"

Drummer shrugs. "He's claimed ya. You're his ol' lady whether you like it or not. On the compound or off by the sound of it."

That's a rather misogynistic approach, and it makes me bristle. I take a moment to think. He is the father of my babies, and together or not, we *will* need to sort through how this will work. I'd never stop a man from seeing his children.

Drummer sees my indecision and adds more to persuade me. "If we let you stay, you'll be protected. Safe to assume you've got folks still after ya, 'specially if you keep working the case."

Another shiver runs down my spine, my thoughts repeating themselves. *It's not just me anymore.*

Wraith looks at me, his expression almost as chilling as his president's. "I'm leaning toward believing what you're saying, but the club learned from what happened with Smart. We don't trust easily."

"Darlin'?" The word might be an endearment, the tone it's delivered in means it's not. "Staying here carries its own risk. Cross us, and they won't find your body."

I don't intend to cross them. Not knowingly anyway. My hands rub my stomach, my head still not quite believing, but what started as a fuck-up of a day is ending in ways I could never have predicted. It's those missing children that I want to help, knowing Drummer's concerned too—and seemingly more than the cops—and in the end I know what option I prefer.

I give a small smile then a nod. But there's one last thing to ask. "Okay, you've persuaded me. If you let me, I'll stay at the compound." Then I remember what else I've acquired, and add, "What about Grunt?"

"Fuck me. If we decide you can stay, that fuckin' pooch can too," Drummer grumbles, a small smile softens his face for an instant until he returns to looking stern once more. He jerks his head toward his VP. "We've got things we need to think about and discuss. Stay close to Heart tonight, and we'll let you know our decision when it's been made."

CHAPTER THIRTY-TWO

*H*eart...

Watching Prez and the VP take Marc into the office, I wonder what the fuck they're going to say to her, hoping they don't do anything to increase her already highly charged emotional state. Today's thrown so much shit at her, I'm not sure how much more she can handle. Knowing she's carrying my babies only increases my anxiety. *I don't want her upset.*

Babies. Fuck. I'm still trying to get my head around that. Trust the fucker Hyde to spit out she's pregnant, but that it's with twins we'll keep to ourselves. Listening to that doctor, there are a lot of hurdles in the way until she gives birth. Whatever she believes, I'm going to be right by her side every step of the way. And if the worst happens, and she loses them? I'll be there to pick up the pieces.

Even if it's not here. I don't want to leave the club, but it's obvious neither Drummer nor my brothers want a cop permanently on the compound. While we don't often discuss members lost during Bastard's days—the majority of us having come to the club long after they went—their spectre still hovers above us, the way they died hanging heavy as a warning.

"You know what you're doing, Brother?" Viper, one of the

originals, has come up to me, moving quietly for such a big man. "You really want this? Want her?"

That's one thing I'm sure about. Fuck knows why, but now I've realised I can't let her go. And it's not just because she's carrying my kids. I like the woman, missed her like fuck when I couldn't talk to her. "Put it this way, Viper. If I have to turn in my patch, so be it. Don't wanna live in the civilian world, but she's the best thing that's happened to me since I lost Crystal." There, I've said it. Mentioned her name aloud. What I don't tell him is this feeling inside me that's convinced me my lost wife has had a hand in bringing us together.

As Sam comes up, Viper puts his arm around her. Out of all of us, he should know how much I want to be part of these children's lives and not just get to know them when they're adults. The prez's old lady looks concerned, even annoyed. She smacks her lips together and then makes an observation. "She tricked you, Heart. Oh, I know you must have fucked her, takes two to tango and all that. And you could have gloved up, but apparently didn't. If she got pregnant on purpose—"

"Shut the fuck up." Although I'd been feeling light-hearted since hearing the news, having seen Marc today, having witnessed her breakdown, I know Sam's so far from the truth with her suggestion I've been trapped, it's laughable. Some of my anger of the past months returns as I stare at her. "You don't know what the fuck you're talking about."

Now, she's joined by Sophie. "Heart, why did she lie?"

"She didn't, alright?" I snap, then noticing Viper's glaring at me, realise I have to tone it down. Fuck, their reaction is only the same as mine when Hyde dropped his bombshell. "Look, when she lost her family, she was badly injured herself. Fucking doctors made a call, told her she couldn't have kids. She was rightly convinced she could never conceive." My eyes go to the door of the closed office, and I hope Drummer isn't being too hard on her. She doesn't need any more shit to worry about, not today. I sweep back my hair, then turn to the two women. "I heard it today myself from the doctor. Fact is, it's a fuckin' miracle she got pregnant. And if anything happens, chances are she might never be able to again."

"Hey, you got super sperm or something?" Joker's hand slaps my back.

My anger starting to fade, I flash him a quick grin. "Seems that way."

"You got twins in your family?" Lady, never far from Joker's side steps up. "Might be lucky and get two at once." I look at him sharply, then understand he's just joking. *We hadn't said there were two.* Some things are best kept to ourselves. We'll be lucky if she carries one to term, let alone two.

Frowning, I realise what a long fucking journey this will be, for me and for her. I answer Lady's question, leaving it open.

"Fuck if I know, man. Never knew my folks." Again, my gaze goes to that door. I don't want that for my kids.

I realise, if I'm staying, I want my brothers' support. "Truth is, we weren't going to say anything. Can we not make a big thing of this? Just in case things go wrong? Her injuries might mean she loses it."

Sam, quiet since I admonished her, has her hand over her mouth, sympathy shining out from her eyes. Her fingers press into my arm. "We're here for you, Heart."

Sophie, still relatively new to our world, goes one step further. "For both of you."

My insistence that I haven't been trapped eases some of the tension out of the air. Now, Dollar switches to the other subject.

"She really lose her job?"

"Yes, Dollar, she did." I believe her, have every faith in her. Today proved she's never lied to me before, and for some reason I don't think she would.

Grunt makes a whimper, and I realise the pup probably needs to go outside. Thinking fast and sliding my belt out of my pants, I fashion a makeshift slip collar and lead and make my way to the front of the clubhouse. Good dog that he is, he soon does his business and I take him back inside.

Tongue's eyeing him up. "Looks like he's got deer or wolfhound in him. Doubt if he's a pure breed, not if he was discarded." He squats down to examine him and ruffles his hands through the grey wiry hair. "Probably only a few months. Cute little fucker." He's rewarded by a lick.

"Prospect!"

At my shout, Fergus, who still works part time as a bouncer at Angels, runs up. He's always eager to please, but even his mouth drops open as I send him to get food, bowls, and all associated paraphernalia that goes with having a pup. He goes off muttering under his breath, but that's what being a prospect's all about. In truth? If I'd seen him thrown out of the car, I'd have taken the mutt myself. If I ever catch up with the person who threw him away like a piece of garbage, they'll have breathed their last breath.

I can't wait to introduce him to Amy. *And where is my daughter?* "Where's Amy?" I call over to Sam.

"Jayden's babysitting all the kids up at our house. You want her to stay with us tonight?" I think about her offer, it will give Marc and I some space to talk. Tomorrow will be soon enough to introduce Amy and Grunt. As I'm thanking her, the office door opens, and the woman who's occupying most of my thoughts steps out.

She looks tired and worn. As her eyes catch mine, she gives a half-smile and makes her way over to me.

Drummer follows her out and hollers, "Peg, Blade, and Dollar. My office, now."

An officer meeting. Well, without me. But as I'll be the subject of their discussion, I can't argue at that. I watch the sergeant-at-arms, enforcer, and treasurer as they walk toward the prez, then guide Marc toward the bar. Now she's here, with me, and I've made a commitment. I'm nervous. I get a beer for myself, and a soda for her.

I take a deep breath, and ask, "How did it go in there?"

She makes a seesaw motion with her hand. I take it no decision's been taken, or not one that's been communicated for now. I lean on the bar and stare unseeing at the bottles behind. Will I have to make good on my promise to leave the club if my brothers don't trust Marc to be around? Until Drummer gives us his verdict, all I can do is play a waiting game.

"You feeling alright?" She looks tired and drawn.

"Honestly, Heart? My mind's in a whirl. I don't know which way is up at the moment." She's relaxing against me, as though she's got no fight left in her.

It seems natural to put my arm around her, and her head rests against my shoulder. I can't help glancing down to her stomach, still finding it hard to believe she's carrying my babies in there.

We stand like that, in silence. When the office door opens again, it's as if everyone in the room stands to attention. Marc presses herself back against me.

Prez marches out and stands in the middle of the room. He doesn't have to call for quiet, all eyes are on him. "Heart's ol' lady stays."

I let out a breath in a whoosh. *Thank fuck for that.* I'd have done it, but I didn't want to leave the club, go out into the world with no brothers at my back.

Prez hasn't finished. "Heart takes responsibility for her." His eyes find mine. "I'm sorry, Brother, but I'm still not sure if this can play out permanently. Leopards can't change their spots, and once a cop, always a cop. But for now, and until the current situation is sorted, this is where she'll be."

So our future isn't certain. Except, I can't see anything other than being with her. I nod my thanks to Drummer while knowing Marc and I need to have that talk. If she does anything the club takes an objection to, it won't just be her that ends up dead. It will be me too.

Formalities over, I put my arm around my old lady, take the

lead of our new dog, and walk them both up to the suite. She makes a move to go to the door of the room where she stayed before, but that's not going to settle with me. Tightening my hold, I pull her into mine instead. I free Grunt from his leash and take him to the crate Fergus had bought and set up, settle him inside, and give him a bowl of food to keep him occupied. She stands and watches me.

When I've finished, and clearly to her satisfaction, she shakes her head. "Heart."

"Don't talk."

I twist my hands in her hair and angle her head, then my mouth comes down on hers. It's the first time our lips have met. The first time I've kissed since the last I shared with my wife. The first time my mouth's touched that of another woman in years.

Her hands bat at my chest, trying to push me away, but now's not the time for conversation. I've claimed her, for real. Time enough for words later, but now I want to cement our relationship the biker way. *She's mine.* The suspense of waiting for Drummer's pronouncement, the expectation of having her back in my arms, I'm not giving her any opportunity to escape.

My lips press so tight to hers with almost enough pressure to bruise, and at last her arms drop to her sides and she opens for me. As my tongue makes its invasion, a little gasp escapes and her hands rise again, this time to touch me, her fingernails curling into my biceps.

She matches me, giving as good as she takes as I grasp her hair tighter, her tongue duelling with mine. Her taste, slightly sweet from the soda she'd consumed, acts like a drug invading my veins. My damn cock's so hard, it's pressing against my zip. This is no gentle exploratory kiss, this is a meeting of animals, two creatures preparing to rut.

But there's something else as well—pent-up emotions and longings. Her response to me suggests I'm not alone in admitting my feelings at last.

I'd enjoyed passion with Crystal, but never like this. She'd take what I wanted to give, responding almost politely in a lady-like manner. Marc is trying to take control, but I'm not going to let her. My tongue dives in, hers pushes it back, sweeping into my mouth. I retaliate in kind. Releasing her hair, I place my hand on the back of her head, pressing her to me, not allowing her to break away until we're both gasping for air.

Slowly I pull back, then lean my head to her forehead. "You're mine."

"Heart, we need to talk about this," she gets out in between pants.

"Nothing to talk about, darlin'." Too impatient to wait, my hands go to the top of her blouse, taking hold of each of the sides and ripping it apart. Buttons fly left and right and ping to the floor.

"Heart!" she gasps. "We can't do this."

Yes, we can. It's not like we haven't done it before. What she's carrying in her belly bears witness to that.

I unclasp her bra and release those amazing tits, nipples already erect. I need to taste her, this woman of mine. With one hand on her back, I imprison her, pulling her closer so I can lower my mouth.

"Heart." There's a hitch in her voice as my tongue traces her aureole and then my teeth nip at her teat. *Soon she'll be nourishing my children here.* The thought makes me even harder, and I have to loosen my jeans. At least I don't have a belt to undo.

With my free hand, I undo the button and take down the zip. As my hands free it from its confines, I can't remember my cock ever feeling so much like steel. Now I've eased my immediate discomfort, I move my hand the few inches and next tackle the rest of her clothes. Soon my fingers are pushing the fastening aside. Due to my administrations to her breasts she doesn't notice until her dress pants slide to the floor.

"Heart." I grin against her chest. All she seems able to say is my name. At least she knows who she belongs to.

Sweeping her up into my arms, I turn to the bed and lay her gently down on top of the covers. Her eyes are wide open as she stares at me, bewildered.

Without giving her time to protest, I'm sliding off her underwear, and now she's naked, lying spread out as though she's a feast, and I can't wait to partake. Quickly, I dispense with my jeans and shirt and then kneel between her legs.

"We can't do this," she rasps out. "Heart, stop. We need to talk."

But the scent of her arousal is driving me crazy, and the glistening between her thighs shows she's just as turned on as I am.

I don't want to talk, don't want to pause to make conversation. Putting a hand on either thigh, I force her legs further apart, and then my mouth's there, on her most private place. The taste just as good as I remember.

Her hands twist in my hair, at first trying to pull me away, but as I find her clit her back bows, and now she's holding me close. My tongue sweeps inside that channel which will give birth to my kids, so tight it seems it will be an impossible feat. I use my hands and thrust my fingers inside, working her clit with my tongue and my teeth.

She's pushing up toward me, and still my name keeps coming out of her mouth. "Heart, Heart. Right there. Oh God, that feels good. *Heart.*"

One hand comes up to toy with her nipple. As I pinch it hard, I feel her whole body tense. Her thighs and her hands now keeping me trapped, I couldn't move away even if I wanted. And right here and right now, that's the last thing on my mind.

She's shaking, her muscles visibly rippling, and then she goes still, and a wail comes from her lips. "Heart." My name extended as though it has more than one syllable.

I continue to lick, to lap up her cream. That taste of hers I know I'm already addicted to. My cock's leaking pre-cum onto her thigh.

"This is gonna be fast, darlin'." I start to move up the bed when she suddenly moves and I find myself flipped on my back.

"Fair's fair." I didn't expect her to flash that grin toward me. Nor for her to slide down and before I realise her intention, she sucks my cock into her mouth. She can't take it all, but uses her hands on the shaft.

"Not going to take much, sweetheart." I give her fair warning, watching her mouth over my dick, the way her tongue's lapping up my pre-cum as though it's the best thing she's ever tasted, that look of concentration as she works me. I'm enraptured the way her cheeks hollow as she takes me inside until I'm hitting the back of her throat. She raises her head, takes a breath, then sinks back down, this time taking more and swallowing around me. Then she repeats her actions, pausing to lick at that sensitive spot under the head. My balls draw up, and I'm close, so close…

"Sweetheart. Marc. Now goddammit."

But she's ignoring my instruction to pull away, and I can't hold back my release as I come into her mouth.

She swallows it all, licking her lips and then licks me clean. When she sits back, she's wearing a wide, satisfied grin as she wipes the back of her hand over her face.

I sit up sharply, my hand curling around her neck, pulling her to me. As our tongues meet, I taste me on her, and her on me, the combination driving me wild all over again. Her cheeks are flushed, her eyes sparkling. What fucking magic she's working I don't have a clue, but my cock is already swelling and ready to go once more.

This time it's me who tosses her over, first onto her back, then manhandling her until she's on her hands and knees. She's trying to get me where she wants me, but I give her no chance to take charge. We're fighting for dominance in my bed, but I'm going to win this, no question of that.

Lining myself up, I slide home in one thrust.

"Heart! Oh my God, Heart!"

I only came a minute or so ago, but the feeling of her tight cunt squeezing me shows it barely took the edge off. She's no passive lover, she's an active participant. I fucking love it. As I hammer in, she's pushing back against me, trying to take all I've got to give. It doesn't take long before I feel the telltale signs. Reaching around, I press the heel of my hand to my dick to give me more time and then move my fingers to her clit and pinch it. That's all it takes, and she's coming all over me, my poor cock being strangled as her muscles contract. Thank fuck I've already come, else I'll have lost it again.

While she's coming down I pull out, turn her over, then hoist her legs up over my shoulders and drive in once again, this time even deeper. Her whole body's flushed red now, covered in a sheen of sweat, and I wipe a drop from my own brow. This is no civilised union, we're each giving as good as we can get.

Raising my hand, I encircle her neck. Her eyes go wide, but she doesn't protest. I'm letting her know exactly who's in charge here, and it's not her, it's me.

I'm lunging in and out as though the devil is after me, driving hard into that sweet, tight cunt. Suddenly, I need to see her joining in.

"Touch yourself, babe. Come for me."

She starts rubbing her clit, circling that button. She's so fucking beautiful. Her head's thrown back, my tanned hand a contrast against the skin of her perfect white throat. I tighten it slightly, not much, just seizing a little more control. It's enough to send her over again, and this time she takes me with her.

My cock seems to explode, more cum than I thought possible shooting out of me. Filling that cunt until it leaks out onto the bed.

Slowly I take my hand away from her neck, helping her take her shaking legs down off my shoulders. Her body is quivering, small aftershocks still running through her. As I sit back, my own lungs heaving, I take a moment just to watch her, realising

I've never experienced anything like this, and recognising sex with my old lady will never be boring.

Our combined juices have made a mess. While she's still dazed, I leave the bed, go to the bathroom and clean myself up, then collect the nearest thing to hand, and bring a towel back to the bed, wiping away all trace of our union. Well, apart from the growing damp stain on the sheets.

As her breathing returns to normal, her slightly unfocused eyes meet mine. "What the fuck was that, Heart?"

"That was me claimin' my ol' lady." Even I can hear the tinge of pride in my voice.

"Next time I get to claim my old man. You hear me, biker?"

I chuckle as I lay down beside her, already realising our bed will be a battleground. And fuck me if that thought isn't arousing.

She's had a hard day, and I've not treated her carefully. As I pull her close to spoon her, she twists out of my hold and turns to face me, laying her tired head against my chest. It's an unfamiliar sleeping position for me, but it means I can watch her, see her bleary eyes close, and the slowing of the rise and fall of her chest.

My last waking thought is that tonight's conversation certainly hadn't gone the way she'd expected. Come to that, I'd been surprised by the way the impulse, my *need* to claim her had overtaken me.

CHAPTER THIRTY-THREE

arc...

Waking in strange surroundings can always be momentarily disorientating, but couple that to waking to a warm tongue giving my ear an enthusiastic wash I'm left completely flummoxed for a moment.

Then everything comes back to me in a flash, thoughts tumbling through my head one after the other. Losing my job, Heart's unexpected visit, coming back to the compound, finding Grunt—the little devil who's now moved on to licking my face. And then that final recollection, the one I've been trying to avoid. The fact that I seem to be pregnant.

Using both hands to push the boisterous pup away, I open my eyes in time to see Heart exit the bathroom, a towel slung low around his waist. Too low. It brings back memories of the way the previous night had ended. Inadvertently I lick my lips as I remember. *Christ, that man knows how to fuck.*

As soon as he sees I'm being attacked, he comes and lifts Grunt away. He sits on the side of the bed and strokes him between his ears. "Who's a good fella then?" Then, as he too gets Grunt's morning ablations, puts him down on the floor with a laugh. "Better take him out for a quick walk."

"I'll do it. I insisted we bring him with us." I go to get up, then realise I've slept naked. Although he's already seen everything I've got to offer, I still don't feel comfortable exposing myself. "Give me some space, Heart. Do you know where my clothes are? I'll get dressed."

"No need to get dressed on my account, babe." Reaching across, he first cups his hand behind my head, then pulls me in for a kiss. To my shame, I don't even object. It's nothing like the kiss that banished all my restraint last night, it's gentle, almost loving. A kiss full of affection.

After a second, I move his hand away and compose my features into a serious expression. "Heart, we need to talk."

"Not sure we do, darlin'. Why not just take things as they come?"

I pull the sheet around me so I can sit up. "Heart, I've got to deal with the idea that I'm pregnant for one thing." Suddenly I'm worried. "Last night, wasn't it too rough?"

His hand moves toward me again. He touches my chin. "Hey, sex can't hurt the babies, they're well protected. Babe, hate to remind you, but I've been here before."

"I'm glad one of us knows what they're doing." I smile to show I mean it.

His fingers move slightly to cup my cheek, and something makes me lean into his touch. "I'm sorry, Marc. Can't deny that I had an ol' lady."

Moving back, leaning against the pillows to put some distance between us, I reassure him. "Heart, even if this was going anywhere between us, it really wouldn't matter. Crystal's a big part of your life, and I wouldn't ignore it or want to take her place. She'll always be with you." Stretching out my arm, I place my hand over his heart. "She'll always be in here. It doesn't matter that you've seen and done things before. We all come with baggage and things that will live with us forever."

Heart's shaking his head, but smiling. "Always with your

compassion and understanding, babe. You know, that blows me away."

I bite my lip. He's taking things where I don't want, can't afford, them to go. "Heart. We'll have to work something out about the babies. I'd never want to keep a child from its dad. But you and I, well, it just won't work, you must see that."

He rears back. "I see nothing of the fuckin' sort."

I've got a temper to match his, and right now it's rising. Gripping the sheet tightly, I kneel up. "For fuck's sake, you're the last person I should need to explain this too. You know better than anyone. Let someone get close to you, depend on them for your happiness, and it destroys you when they leave."

I'd misread the signs, he isn't getting angry. Instead he says calmly, "Your family didn't leave you, Marc. Same as Crystal didn't leave me. They were torn away. And me? I'm not planning on going anywhere. Not leaving my kids, or you."

"You can't say that. Anything could happen."

"You were eighteen, darlin'. An adult, yes, but far too young to lose everyone you loved. Yeah, it fuckin' hurt when I lost Crystal, still does. I'd give my right arm to have her walk through that door. But you know what? I loved her, and in here," now it's his hand that covers his heart, "I always will. She made my life richer for being in it. She gave me Amy, and I truly believe she led me to you. I'll never wipe her out of existence, or wish I'd never met her, or fucked her and left her instead of making her mine."

I stare at him, unable to move my eyes away from his face set so earnestly.

"Hey, tell me something about your brother. Bet he teased you mercilessly when you were growing up?"

My eyes widen.

"And your mom and dad. Were they overprotective? If your dad was still around, would he be after me with a shotgun?"

Wherever he's going with this, I'd prefer him to stop. I don't want to think about them, it hurts too much. I shake my head, but he's not going to be put off.

As I try to look away, he grasps my chin and turns me toward him. "Tell me about them, Marc. Explain what amazing people they were. Give them a memorial in your memory, share what they brought to the world. Don't lock them away letting dust dull your recall. Keep them alive by letting them live in your heart."

"I can't," I protest, as I feel my eyes leaking.

"You can. Loving someone, missing them when they're gone, is all part of being alive. Yeah, it hurts, but never letting anyone in, in case you lose them again, means you're not alive, you're just existing. Take some of that advice you offered to me."

"If I don't let you in, you can't hurt me."

As if sensing I'm weakening, he moves a little closer. "If we don't try, we'll never know what we could have. And while it hurts like a bitch to think about Crystal, I'd never wish a moment of what we had together away." He pauses, then laughs. "You and Crystal couldn't be more different, you know? The way you look, your mannerisms, fuck, the way you're so aggressive in bed. You're not a replacement, in any shape or form."

Me? Aggressive?

"You're asking too much, Heart." My voice comes out as a whisper.

"I wasn't a man who believed in a God and a hereafter, Marc. I never thought there was life after death. But when I was on my road trip, little things would happen, and I'd swear Crystal was with me. Maybe it was just a memory of things she would do or say, but I heard her voice in my ear, and her touch on my arm." As I'm wondering where he's going with this, he continues, "Hadn't felt that since I came back to the compound. But yesterday, I sensed something when we found out about the babies. I think she's happy for me to have found you, and if there is something that happens after we're dead, that she had a hand in this miracle." His hand touches my stomach and his eyes meet mine. "Wouldn't your family be disappointed if you didn't grab something like what's between us in both hands? Would they really want you to go through life alone?"

One tear escapes from my eye, followed soon by another. And then a torrent begins. Heart closes the distance between us, taking me into his arms, and lets me cry like a child. As my sobs come, some of what he's said starts to sink in. My mom, dad, brother, and all of my lost family would be devastated to know I was only going through the motions in life. I do owe it to them to live the life they couldn't, and that means taking hold of some happiness for myself.

But with Heart? As my tears dry, I pull away from him. "Yesterday, Heart, I hated you. The things that you said…"

He lets me go and sits with his legs apart, his hands clasped between his knees. "I was in shock when Hyde suggested you were pregnant. It's no excuse for the cruel words I threw at you, I know that. I felt if you were, and the baby was mine, you'd tricked me into betraying Crystal."

A glance my way, and then he continues, "When I saw how upset you were, I knew there was no trickery involved. Your reaction to being told you were pregnant—it was as if veils had been removed from my eyes. Suddenly I fuckin' knew Crystal wouldn't want me to mourn her forever. And if I'm going to move on, it has to be with the woman who's somehow taken up residence," again he places a hand over his heart, "alongside Crystal in my heart."

I swallow, realising how significant what he's saying is. "It's me, not just the babies?"

A serious look, and then a dip of his head. "You, Marc. And I know there's a long way to go before the babies are delivered safely, but whatever happens, I'll be here by your side, whether our family grows or it doesn't. Now, you gonna pick up what I'm offering?"

He's offering himself. A man with flaws, but for whom my

attraction has been slowly growing over the past months. A man who's been there for me as much as I've been there for him. Tentatively, I reach out my hand and touch his face. "I don't know how good I'll be at having a relationship, Heart. This is new ground for me."

A smile plays at his lips. "We'll take it one day at a time. You and me, together." A scratching at the door has both our heads turning and reminding us both we've got a new responsibility. Heart chuckles, then stands and picks up the leash. "I'll take Grunt out, give you some space to get ready. Then we'll go down and introduce Amy to the mutt."

Yes. "She's gonna be so excited. What little girl doesn't want a pup?"

He grins, then takes Grunt out to do the necessary. When he returns, I'm dressed in jeans and a t-shirt, ready to do the pleasurable chore of seeing Amy's reaction to the dog. Wrapping a mantle of confidence around myself, ready to face the reaction I'll get from his brothers.

Predictably, Amy squeals when she's sees the pup, and her joy when she realises it's *her* dog can't be described. Soon the three of us are rolling around with Grunt on the floor until I come to my senses and suggest we should be careful until we get him checked to make sure he hasn't got fleas or worms, and make sure he has all his shots.

"You know, that fuckin' pooch," a gravelly voice comes from behind me, "he's found the right place. Looks like a fuckin' misfit like the rest of us."

Peg's right.

I'm just about to tell him that I agree, wondering whether the word misfit works for me too, when my phone rings. Curious to see who might be calling—I've no friends or people who would check up on me—I take it out, and am not surprised when I don't recognise the number. I stand, ready to take it outside.

Peg's hand stops me, his eyes, which had softened while watching the dog and child interact, now glare with suspicion.

I stay where I am, but answer the call. The room's suddenly gone quiet around me.

"Hi."

"Reed? Why are you…"

I listen carefully as my ex-colleague explains exactly why he's calling me.

"I don't think that would help."

"You did?"

"Oh my God. Really?"

"*Now?*"

"What's the charge?" I grow cold.

"I'll tell them. And you'll be behind? How long?"

"Got it. Okay."

While I've been talking, Drummer, Peg, Wraith, and Blade have come to surround me. Knowing there's no time to waste, I turn to Drummer. "You need to hear this." I place my phone on a table and hover my finger over a key. "As soon as I knew who it was, I recorded the conversation."

"Who were you speaking to?"

"Detective Reed. I work, worked, with him. Not as a partner, but he's been around a long time. He's sort of a fixture in the department."

Drummer's eyes narrow at my answer. "Better hear what he has to say."

The whole phone call's repeated.

"*Hi.*"

"*Hey, Hannah. It's Reed.*"

"*Reed? Why are you…*"

"*Look, there's a few of us not comfortable about what went down yesterday. Might not have worked closely with you, but I could see you did good work. You'll get support here if you want to take it further. Up to the lieutenant or even higher…*"

"*I don't think that would help.*"

"*Park that for now, there's something I need to tell you. I overheard Garza and Reynolds talking together.*"

"You did?"

"Fucking morons were plotting in the men's bathroom. I was in a stall and they didn't even check. I'm pretty certain it won't come as news to you that they're dirty—hell, everyone here suspected it, but no one could prove anything. But what they let drop was very interesting. They talked about you, and how they needed to shut you down for good. Kicking you out wasn't enough. They mentioned getting their instructions from one Alonso Herrera. He's paying good money to see you dead."

"Oh my God. Really?"

"They know where you are. Had you followed when you left yesterday. They know you went to the hospital with the bikers, and where you went after. They're on their way to the compound with a warrant for your arrest."

"Now?"

"I've rounded up a few cops I can trust, and I'm taking this to Diaz as soon as he comes in. I recorded the conversation as soon as I got the gist of what they were plotting. The lieutenant can't fail to act on this now, so hopefully we'll be right behind them.

"I know you're with Drummer, and I reckon you can trust him. We might be on different sides of the law, but as far as I'm concerned, nowadays, he runs a clean club. You need him to stop Reynolds coming on to the compound, and for Christ's sake, don't give yourself up when you see that warrant."

"What's the charge?"

"That you're an informant working for an OMG. But Hannah, Diaz is coming in now. I'll go straight to him. Finch, is rounding up a posse. Hopefully I'll get the go ahead to arrest Reynolds and Garza, or at least, bring them in for questioning."

"I'll tell them. And you'll be behind? How long?"

"As soon as I can make it. Reynolds and Garza haven't left yet. They're still fluffing about in the office, maybe having delays getting the warrant. If I can convince Diaz before they leave, I'll stop them here. But, Hannah, if they get there, it could get bloody. They get paid when you're dead. Let Drummer know you'll need the protection of his

boys. Keep out of the line of fire, won't you? Hey, I like you, girl, wouldn't want to next see you in the morgue. Don't give yourself up and don't give them a chance to say you were resisting arrest."

"Got it. Okay."

The whole room is silent. Drummer's staring at the phone. "You record all your calls, or just ones meant to put you in the clear?"

"I am, was, a cop, Drummer. When I get a call, I usually record it so I can reference exactly what witnesses have said. It's a natural action for me."

"Whether or not it's a setup, Prez, sounds like we've got a fuckload of police heading for the compound. How do you want to play it?" Blade's glaring at me, but he doesn't have to say anything. It's my fault.

If Reed hadn't warned me they'd kill me on sight, I'd give myself up and try and get it sorted from a cell. But clearly their end game isn't to take me in.

"Hyde. You keep Marcia here and out of sight. Tie her up if you fuckin' have to, but she ain't coming anywhere near the gate. Blade, Peg, Wraith, Heart, you come with me, and we'll make sure they don't come onto the compound."

"Drummer—"

"I'm in charge here, Marcia. Don't want no heroics about you giving yourself up. If," he points to the phone, "this Detective Reed was telling the truth, the fact that you're here with us could be enough evidence that you've been playing both sides. I don't care for your chances if you go with them."

My thoughts exactly, but, "I don't want anyone hurt."

"Ain't our first rodeo, darlin'."

CHAPTER THIRTY-FOUR

*H*eart...

Chills as cold as ice ran through me when I heard that call, the detective's warning and the death threat he'd overhead. We've got to protect Marc. I haven't just claimed her to lose her now. There's no fucking way we're giving her up to dirty cops looking for a chance to get her permanently out of the way. *Alonso Herrera.* That's the same name that Susie spouted with what she hadn't known was one of her last breaths. How has Marc crossed him? Why does he want her dead so badly? What's he got over the cops who are risking their jobs to take her out? They must know what they're doing is chancy, and that's why they won't risk taking her in. She must know too much.

Drummer's deep in conversation with Wraith and Peg, hopefully working out a game plan. I take my gun out of my waistband and check it over, patting my pocket to make sure I've got enough ammunition, hoping like fuck we can avoid a firefight, but needing to be prepared. It wouldn't surprise me if Reynolds and Garza intend to force their way onto the compound.

As I'm replacing my weapon, a hand grips my arm. "Heart, I can't let you do this. It's me they've come for, not any of you."

I gaze at her staring up at me intently, then put my arms around her and pull her in close. "I thought we'd established how much you mean to me. Not gonna let you walk into a bullet. It's not just you, now, Marc. Think of those babies you're carrying."

"I still can't believe they would hurt me."

"Your friend, Reed, sounded pretty certain they would." Placing my finger under her chin, I turn her to face me. "Can't take the risk. And, I need you to look after Amy." Again I move her head so she can see my daughter playing with Grunt, pleased to see the pup seems quite tolerant as she pulls at his ears. "I want you to take her and the dog up to Drum's house. Sam, Jayden, and Sophie will be there with the kids." It's one good thing that the other old ladies who have homes off-site haven't yet come in today, or are working.

"I need a gun. If…" her voice breaks. "If something happens, I need to be able to protect them."

She's got a point. A quick word to Drum, a cautious look in her direction, and then she's given a Glock, which she checks over and seems to know how to use. Oh fuck, who am I kidding, of course she knows, she's been trained as a cop.

Prez has given it to her himself, along with a few words. "Sam's armed, she's a good shot. If they get through us, then the two of you will give them a run for their money."

Marc shakes her head. "If they get that far, I'll give myself up, Drum. Not going to risk women and children."

Prez looks at her sharply then follows that up with a pat on her arm. Though she doesn't realise it, it's a silent acceptance, his way of showing she's now one of us. No longer a cop, but a biker's old lady.

I tell her goodbye with a kiss, not drawing it out, not giving her any idea that it might be a final parting. She's scared enough as it is, for me, for herself, for everyone here, and for our babies.

We don't know how long we've got, they could already be

approaching, so following Drummer we go to the gates. Prez might just have wanted the officers with him, but as we mill around waiting for instructions on how to greet our unwelcome visitors, all of my brothers have come with us.

Prez steps into the centre. "We're not supposed to know that they're coming, so I don't intend a show of force to greet them. Slick, Viper. Look like it's any normal day and man the gate, will ya?" Both men nod, giving him chin lifts, not even complaining that's normally a prospect's job.

"The rest of you, get into the shop. When they start waving that warrant, Peg and I will come out. Won't raise suspicion. Wraith, you and Blade stay back out of sight. If it sounds like we need backup, come out with the rest of the boys, armed, and form up behind us."

"Got it, Prez."

"Don't you want me to go out first? Keep you in reserve?"

Drum tosses a glare at his VP, that one expression showing why he's got the respect of the club. He'd never ask anyone to do what he's not prepared to do himself.

As Wraith shrugs, looking like he thought it was worth a try, the sound of sirens approaches us.

"Prez, I'd like to be here. She's my ol' lady after all."

He considers it, then nods. "Don't think they know who you are, so okay, you tag along when Peg and I come up. Now scat, everyone. Why the fuck they're coming in loud I don't know."

"Intimidation," Peg suggests as we walk to the shop.

"As if that's gonna fuckin' work," Blade shouts back.

Yeah, but it might if we hadn't been warned and only had a green prospect like Fergus on the gate.

The sirens get louder, and then the engines cut off. I'm trying to estimate the number of cars—definitely more than one, probably three. Reed was right, they've come with full backup, and all just to pick up one female ex-cop.

There's shouting outside, an exchange I can't quite make out, and then Drum gives the signal, and I follow him and Peg out, walking the fifty or so feet to the gate. Slick and Viper are arguing with a man in uniform, beside him is standing a man in a suit, and behind them eight other cops.

"What's going on?"

"Prez, the cops here have a warrant."

Without getting close to the gate, Drum asks, "What is it? Not a good time to look around the compound. We ain't got any guided tours running today."

Ignoring Prez's attempt at levity, the uniformed man steps closer. "I'm Sergeant Reynolds. I've got a warrant for Detective Marcia Hannah."

That's interesting, he's given her her title. Does he not remember yesterday he gave her the sack? But I keep my face impassive, giving nothing away.

"Not sure I know anyone of that name. And why you think we'd have a cop on the compound, I've no fuckin' idea."

"She's here," Reynolds states, and then startles as the man at his side pops his gum loudly. A brief twinge of disgust, then his attention turns back to the prez.

Drum's grinning, only those that know him realise he's not amused. "You saying I'm harbouring a cop? And if there's a warrant out for her arrest, one who's walking my side of the law?" He shakes his head, and his gaze takes in me and Peg. "You seen any cops here?"

Dutifully we smirk. Remembering she lost her job, we're not even lying.

Drummer takes a step forward. "There is no cop on the compound," he repeats, as he rolls his shoulders.

Reynolds exchanges glances with Garza. Garza moves closer to the gate. As he does so, he spits the gum out of his mouth. Another job for the prospects to clear up. I, for one, don't want that shit stuck in my treads.

"Look, Drummer, I know she's here. I don't know what story she's given you, but she's playing both sides. Telling you things she shouldn't, and feeding back facts to us about the club."

No she fucking hasn't. I'd stake my life on it.

Reynolds swings around and makes a gesture to the cops who'd arrived with him. All of a sudden, they're all holding guns. Peg whistles, and Wraith, Blade, Dollar, and all my brothers come out and stand at our backs. I watch Drum's hand, it's held palm down, our own weapons stay firmly out of sight. Safer that way, one trigger-happy cop could kill the first man who goes for his piece.

"Unless you've got a search warrant, that's as far as you come." Prez sounds reasonable as he explains, "My brothers and I have a right to protect our property. Any attempt to force open the gates, and you'll be illegally trespassing. Don't give a fuck as to the reason you're here, but you're not coming inside."

For a moment it's a stalemate. They'd love us to take out our guns and threaten the cops. It would result in a firefight which they wouldn't win, and I really don't feel like burying bodies today.

"Could do with the dirt track being extended."

Road's low mumbled comment behind me makes a few men give strangled laughs.

Drum silences him with a look that could kill all by itself.

It's quiet for a moment, both sides waiting for the other to make a move, the peace broken by the sound of yet more engines. As they're obviously cars and not bikes, Reynolds and Garza share a look of concern.

The new police cars park sideways across our drive, making sure the vehicles in front can't get past them. The cops turn around and start greeting colleagues, wide-eyed at the interruption. Reynolds swings about and goes to meet the uniformed Hispanic man getting out, alongside another plain-clothes detective.

"What the fuck are you doing here, Reed?" he snarls out. *Ah, so that's who Marc was talking to.* He's an older man, obviously been in the force for years. Then the sergeant looks more respectful as he greets the uniformed man. "Lieutenant Diaz? What brings you here?"

The lieutenant looks on wearily. "You've got some explaining to do, Reynolds. And Garza too." He pinches the bridge of his nose, then gives the instruction. "Take all of them in, we'll sort it all out at the precinct."

Suddenly cops are being handcuffed by cops. Several of those first to arrive look bemused. A couple of others object and put up a half-hearted fight.

As we stand watching our entertainment for the day, I almost miss Garza taking out his gun and pointing it at the prez. Diving for Drummer and pushing him aside just as it fires, I feel a burning sensation in my arm. *Fuck, not again. Haven't I been injured enough?* Clasping my other hand to the wound, I feel blood dripping out.

Garza's been overpowered and taking down by his own. When the presumably clean and dirty cops have sorted themselves out, Lieutenant Diaz steps up to the gate and points at me. "You alright?" His voice sounds weary, as if this was a day he didn't expect.

Peg's by my side and answers for me. "He'll live. He'll have to see his best friend, Doc." Yeah, I've been seeing far too much of him over the last few months.

Diaz then focuses his eyes on the prez. "Drummer. Heard some things today. It's going to take time to sort out. Detective Hannah appears to be under your protection." He wipes a hand over his face. "These are strange times. I don't know what's going on, but what I have heard, I don't like. Think it's best she stays here for now, but she will need to come down to the precinct once I've questioned Sergeant Reynolds and Detective Garza. Tell her I'll be in touch."

Drum acknowledges him with a lift of his chin, and then we watch as the police get back into their cars and drive away. No one's surprised when the next word out of his mouth is,

"Church." But I don't expect him to add, "And bring Marcia along. Reckon there are a few things we need to discuss."

And that's how an ex-cop takes the unusual step of taking a seat at the end of the table. She's biting her lip as she sits down, so I throw her a smile. Doc's already been and put a couple of stitches in my arm. As Peg thought, the bullet just grazed me, though it hurt like a bitch. When I see her eyes fall on the bandage, I shake my head to dismiss her concern.

"Let's get started. Marcia, you missed all the fun." There's a rumble of laughter, which prez waits to fade. "Your man Reed was right. Your sergeant and partner definitely had the hots for you. Lucky for you that detective managed to raise the alarm and get the lieutenant on his side."

She raises her hand, and when Drummer nods, casts her eyes around everyone sitting there. "Thank you, all. I don't like asking other people to fight my battles for me—"

"You wouldn't have won this one, darlin'. They were intent on taking you in. Came in heavy enough to show that. And, as Reed predicted, I don't think you'd have arrived at the precinct."

She's looking flummoxed. "I've just been trying to do my job."

"I suspect you were doing it too well." Wraith nods at her.

Prez jerks his chin toward Wraith. "And I think that's what we're dealing with here. Thing is, what do you know? What is it that makes two experienced cops risk themselves like that?"

"It wouldn't have been a risk if Reed hadn't found out." Again, her teeth worry her lip. I notice she's gone a bit pale as she realises how close she'd just come to ending up dead. "He mentioned Alonso Herrera. He's either paying them or holding something over them."

"Or both. This didn't start yesterday. If they've been working for the Herreras for some time, no doubt there's plenty of stones that could be turned over."

Blade points his knife directly toward Marc. "What is it? Just what do you know?"

"And would you tell us?" Drummer asks succinctly. It's a short question, but what he's really asking is whether she's going to throw her lot in with the club. My thoughts confirmed as he continues, "Lieutenant Diaz referred to you by rank. I suspect your job is still yours."

She drops her head into her hands, and we give her some space. When she looks up, she catches my eye and the corners of her mouth turn up. "I became a cop so I could put the bad guys away. Trouble is, I don't even know who they are anymore. And now I think I need to re-examine what I want out of life. There are two things I know. I want to give what's between Heart and I a chance. And the other, I can't give up searching for those missing kids, finding out what's happened to them, and preventing any more going missing."

As I feel a warm glow inside as she publicly admits she's going to give our relationship a try, Drummer cocks his head to one side. "There's more than one way of doing that." He nods at Slick and me. "We've got a vested interest in trying to keep our girls safe."

"You're saying the club will help me investigate?"

"You want to put the bad guys off the street? Seems we're both on the same side."

Now her tongue's licking her lips and eliciting a most inappropriate reaction from my cock in church as I remember her mouth around me last night. As I adjust myself under the table, I try to concentrate on her words.

"I can't have Heart and my job. And I'd never ask Heart to leave the club. So whether or not my lieutenant thinks I'm still a cop, consider me unemployed." She looks at me and smiles.

There's a ripple of relief around the table, a couple look more reserved, but much of the tension has been relieved. Slick gets out his smokes, offers one to Blade, and they light up.

"So, what have you got to share?"

Marc leans back in her chair. "I've been thinking. Reynolds threw out my report on Archer. I thought it was because he didn't want his reputation tarnished, possibly working on instructions from the Herrera family." Again she's biting her fucking lip, and I wish she'd stop drawing my attention to her mouth as I'd prefer not to keep experiencing very inappropriate flashbacks. "What if I was on the wrong track? What if I hadn't done enough digging? What if there was more to Archer being in the house that night? What if he'd been working with someone else?"

"What do you mean?" Drum asks sharply.

"We had information that house was used to molest kids. I didn't like working with Archer, he acted inappropriately toward me and other women, and some of the things he said… Well, it wasn't too far a stretch for me to assume he took part, if not in the grooming, in benefitting from the results." Now she sits forward. "But what if there was another sideline?" She pauses, then focuses her eyes on Drummer. "What if he had closer links with this Alonso Herrera than I'd supposed?"

Mouse puts up his hand. "Alonso's one of the new lieutenants Javier promoted when he took over from Leonardo."

How the fuck he found out while tapping at his keyboard I've no idea, but the information comes in useful now. Drum's staring at him, smoothing his hand over his beard, then gives a brief nod of acknowledgment. Alonso's far enough up the food chain for Javier to be involved. We still don't know what we're dealing with.

Marc's savvy enough to allow a pause for the news to sink, then tells us, "I found a report on Jayden Greenway being a missing person. Archer had written it up, but it was unusual that there was no interview with her mother."

Drummer looks at Slick, who thinks for a moment before he nods. "You tell this to anyone, and you're fucking dead." He waits for that to sink in. "Jayden was part of the child grooming ring."

I watch the pained expression on Paladin's face and then

glance back to Marc. She's connected the dots. Her hand's gone over her mouth. "That poor kid," she gasps.

Drummer nods. "And you already know about Amy. We happen to know the Herreras were behind it. Thought the ring had all been taken out." He doesn't go so far as to admit we were responsible.

But Marc's not stupid. "Tucson has a lot to thank you for." No one acknowledges her words, so she fills the silence. "I don't think all who were involved were killed that night, and that those who were left have taken it a step further. Not only grooming, but moving on to taking and selling underage kids."

I think we've all reached the same conclusion. Prez pushes back his chair in that familiar stance which shows he's thinking, one foot perched against the table. After a moment, he lets us in on his thoughts. "Archer was behind wanting to take Amy. Maybe the idea came to him then. Okay, so they got money from the customers sexually abusing the kids, but maybe the payoff is bigger if they can sell them."

"And it's less messy," Marc adds intelligently. "Instead of keeping the kids controlled by threats and hoping they work, this way is a quick in and out. Snatch them, then find a buyer to take them. Less trouble all around. Let's face it. The reason we know kids were groomed to go into that house was because on one occasion at least, their threats didn't work."

Mouse looks up. "That's been the business of the cartel, not the Herreras. What if we've got Los Zetas in town?"

Marc shakes her head. "There are too many from one place in quick succession. It smacks of something local to me. The cartel is too clever to concentrate the abductions in the same town."

Peg clears his throat then adds to the conversation. "Seems very convenient that the head of the family has been deposed."

"I agree with you, Peg. Mouse, any word on what happened to Leonardo?"

"What you thinking, Prez?"

Drum cups his beard with his hands. "I'm thinking we helped out the cartel. Maybe it's time they helped us."

"You don't think they know what's going on?"

"Javier Herrera's still breathing."

"Perhaps he doesn't know what Alonso is up to?"

Drum shrugs. "Or perhaps he's behind it."

CHAPTER THIRTY-FIVE

*M*arc…

Sitting at this table is a bit like watching a sociological experiment. There's no doubt there's some hierarchy, with Drummer's word being final, but all men here can, and are encouraged to have their say. Some irrelevant points might be greeted with amusement, but when an observation is made, it's examined carefully.

Having said my piece, I'm happy to sit back and watch what's going on. I'd thought I would have been dismissed after they'd questioned me, but either they've forgotten I'm there, or have, at last, begun to trust me.

As the debate flows, something occurs to me. I lift my fingers in a small wave. Drum gives me permission to speak. "If the cartel takes out the Herreras, how are we going to find those kids?"

Tongue jerks his chin toward me, his stud glinting in the overhead lights. "Good point there, Prez. We want to make sure our kids are safe, but it doesn't settle with me there are others out there. I think we can safely assume they're going through hell."

"As must be the parents," Lady throws in.

He's right. I've met some of them.

"They could be out of state by now. Fuck, out of the country." Drummer's frowning down at the table. He raps his hand on the desk, and then his steely gaze rises to settle on me. "What I can't understand, is why the local police thought they could handle it. Surely they should have called in the FBI?"

I've no idea either. "Above my pay grade."

"It's been in the press enough," Lady observes as Joker nods at his friend.

"But only in the last couple of weeks when a parent went to the press and others stepped forward. And 'we'," I use my hands to demonstrate I'm putting the word in quotes, "worked on the basis that they were runaways at first."

Drummer's looking intense and raises his eyebrow at Wraith, who shakes his head in response. "We've had the FBI around this table before. Not keen on inviting them in again. Right, we've been going around in circles. Here's what we're going to do."

I sit and listen as he hands tasks out, counting them off on his fingers. Almost everyone ends up with something to do. I'm to put my head together with Mouse and go back over what I do know are the facts of the case. Some of the brothers are going to see if they can get the parents to talk, and Drummer, himself, is going to see if he can try and track down Leonardo Herrera. If he's still above ground.

It's a positive meeting, and I come away with the thought that maybe, just maybe, I'm now on the right side.

As we're dismissed, I wait for Heart in the hallway.

"Let's go get Amy," he says. "I need some loving from both my girls."

I follow him up to the top of the compound. We collect Amy, then go back to the suite, Grunt in tow. As soon as we enter, Grunt finds his bed and settles down to sleep. He looks worn out for a pup.

Heart's got a thoughtful expression on his face as he looks around the room. Then he crouches and speaks to his daughter. "Hey, Amy. Think you're big enough for a big girl's bed now. How about we give you the bedroom next door? You're too old to be sleeping with your dad."

She looks at him, and then at me. "Where's Marc gonna be sleeping?"

"In here. With me."

Amy pouts. "But she's older than me."

I have to put my hand over my mouth to smother my laugh. "I don't mind. And it will be nice for you to have your own room."

I'm almost knocked off my feet as she runs over, reaching her arms up around my waist and cuddling into me. "You're the best, Marc."

Heart tilts his head to one side, his wide smile making him look so handsome I'd welcome some alone time myself. He gets to his feet and comes over and puts his arm around my shoulder. "Need to ask you, Amy, how you feel about Marc being part of our life? We'll get a new house off the compound and become a family. What do you think about that?"

I realise a year's a long time in a little girl's eyes when her face beams and she asks, "Are you going to be my new mommy?"

I don't want to upset either of them, or lead her on. But looking at Heart, and knowing I'm carrying, at least for now, his two children, I know, now I've let him in, I'd like to give our relationship a damn good try. If I ever lose him, well, I'll just have to cope.

I'm uncertain how to respond to Amy, but Heart nods to encourage me. At first I'm uncertain what he expects me to say, but the warmth in his expressions lets me know the response he wants. Now it's my turn to crouch down to bring myself to her level.

"If that's what you want, honey. I'll never want to try to replace your real mommy, but I can be there for you."

This time she really does knock me over as she flies at me so fast and takes me by surprise. I suppress a sob, wondering why it's taken me so long to open my heart to others again, but then the answer hits me. *I was waiting for Heart.*

After taking Amy into her new room and getting it arranged with her toys and clothes, Amy's exhausted from playing all day and doesn't object when Heart suggests she has a nap.

Alone with Heart, I go to him, put my arms around him, and rest my head on his chest. We stand like that for a few minutes.

"Lieutenant Diaz wants to see you."

"He can stuff his job."

Heart chuckles, the sound reverberating through me. "You sure you've made up your mind?"

"I think I had before, but the way you work… Well, let's just say I've got more faith in the way you get things done than the police." I think about what Diaz might want me for. "I suppose he might need to interrogate me about what's been going on with Reynolds and Garza. If he's taking them into custody, it must be safe for me to go in. And while Reed will have filled him in, there's a lot he doesn't know."

"Not happy about you going there. Even if they're locked up. What if someone else is working with them?"

"Whether they are or not, I'll need to show my face, Heart."

Heart's phone rings, stopping our conversation. He answers it without moving away. I can hear Mouse on the line, but not clearly enough to distinguish what he says. When the call ends, Heart explains.

"You're not going anywhere today. Mouse has been doing some digging. Wants to talk to you, okay?"

I'm eager to know what he's found. "Yeah. I'll go down."

"I'll stay here with Amy."

I cock my eyebrow. "You're allowing me to walk down to the clubhouse unattended?"

He smirks. "I think you can find your way. And I know I can trust you." As I go to move away, he pulls me back and cups his face with my hands. "Don't overdo it, Marc. You're looking tired. Remember you're carrying twins."

How can I forget? "I'm fine, Heart. I'm pregnant." Those words still don't seem real. "I'm not ill."

"You're mine. I'm gonna watch out for you." He lowers his lips and meets mine. A moment when we express with our mouths the depth of our feelings toward each other, and then I'm stepping out the door and going down to the clubhouse. Unescorted. Alone.

As I walk down through this adapted ex-vacation resort, I realise it already feels more of a home than any place where I ever stayed since I was eighteen.

Walking into the clubroom, I get chin lifts and nods from the men as I make my way through. I have to ask Viper which office is Mouse's and follow his directions. I enter a room with blacked-out windows and an assortment of screens. It must be their security hub as well as his den. The strong smell of cannabis hits me almost like a physical wall. As he acknowl-edges me, he takes a drag on his joint.

"Thanks for coming, Marcia. I wanted to pick your brain. Tell me where you got to with this. Can you remember names and addresses?"

I frown. "I need my files for that."

His fingers fly over his keyboard. Then he looks up. "You're one of us now, right?"

Not sure why I have to confirm it again, but I nod.

He grins. "These the files you were after?"

As he turns the screen around, I inhale sharply. He's hacked into the police database, and into my account. "How did you do that?"

He taps the side of his nose. "Ain't giving all my secrets away." Then he gets up, grabs a spare chair, and pulls it around his side of the desk, indicating I should sit beside him.

We lose track of time. I point out the relevant info from my files, and he uses another computer to check out the names, explaining he's using the dark web to see if there's any chatter about any of the missing kids. He's delving deeper, and while doing so making sure he's covering his tracks. At one point, he places an international call to an Arab country and gets some advice, then he's back to tapping again.

"Fuck." His quiet utterance interrupts my thoughts. He points at something on the screen. "We need to get Drummer in on this. And fast." Wasting no time, he takes out his phone and sends a quick text.

A couple of minutes later we're joined by the president, who listens carefully to what we have to say.

"Well, fuck me." Drummer leans back on the chair, one hand stroking his beard. "If you're right, that could be good news. We might be able to find those kids after all."

I try to suppress my excitement, not wanting to get my hopes up too soon. "And bring them home." My optimism has been growing since Mouse found the information.

Drummer nods slowly, then recaps on what he's been told. "An underground auction, to be held in five days. Hmm." He suddenly sits forward. "Reckon the likelihood is that they'll be held together prior to that."

"One option is to find out where they're holding them." I think for a moment. "Would it be possible Reynolds might know? I may be able to get some time with him."

"I doubt it. He was probably just a pawn, just paid for looking the other way or providing misdirection. Something like this, they'll keep close to their chest. Any idea of where this auction is to be held, Mouse?"

"Arizona," Mouse tells him. "A fuckin' big search area. They'll narrow it down and give coordinates just before the auction starts. That's the way these things usually work."

"Can we get an invite?" As I ask, Drummer raises his eyebrows at Mouse.

Mouse grins. "That's why I got Cara involved. She's trying to get an Amahadian on the invite list. A rich Arab won't arouse suspicion in any way. Of course, he'll appoint a representative to attend on his behalf. One of us."

I'd earlier heard that Sophie's best friend is now married to an emir, and one of his brothers has a wife who's a renowned hacker. Yes, no one would be surprised at a sheikh wanting to buy a young girl at auction—they have a certain reputation which means that wouldn't be unexpected. And likely as well that though he might be the customer, he wouldn't attend in person.

Drummer's gone quiet, his hand stroking his beard, something I've seen him do before when he's deep in thought.

What Mouse and I have found out is terrifying, and my gut churns at the thought of how those kids are being kept, their conditions, and how frightened they must be. Taken from their families to face an unknown future, and one probably filled with torture and pain. We've got to do all we can save them.

"I'm sorry, Drummer, but I think this is too big for even the Satan's Devils to handle. We've got to involve the police and the FBI."

Brought out of his reverie, the president views me. "I need to make a phone call." Then his stare turns to a glare. "Marcia. Give me some time to explore some options and don't go running back to your cop friends. It might go deeper than Reynolds and Garza. We, you, don't know who to trust. This information is like dynamite—put it in the wrong hands and they'll change the arrangements and go deeper underground. The kids will be lost forever."

I study him as sadly I realise the truth in his words. In such a lucrative business, one word out of place and they'll move mountains to make sure we lose their trail. "All I ask, Drummer, is that you keep me in the loop. I'll need to go down to the precinct and make my statement, and that means I'll be hiding things, lying to my ex-boss. But the number one priority is reuniting those kids with their families."

Drummer lifts his chin toward me. "I know a man I can trust. Just need to have a conversation."

CHAPTER THIRTY-SIX

$\mathcal{H}$eart…

After spending time cooped up with Mouse, I make Marc rest for a while, seeing she's emotionally, if not physically, exhausted after everything that's happened over the past couple of days. After her nap, we head back down to clubhouse, and the first thing I spy is Sophie grinning from ear to ear. From what Marc had told me, Mouse has been in contact with his hacker friend in the Arab state of Amahad, and I suspect has given Sophie a message from her friend, Zoe. Those two were so close, their friendship being the reason why Sophie lost half of a leg and ended up here under our protection. A biker's old lady and the wife of an emir—it's a strange alliance.

Memories come back of happier times when Crystal, Amy, and I, along with many of my brothers, were invited to attend Zoe's wedding in Amahad. Fuck, that was a laugh. Bikers rubbing shoulders with politicians and celebrities, but strangely seeming to fit in along with rough desert sheikhs. Mouse still harps on about how he beat the desert dwellers in the bareback horse race. I smile as I remember and then frown.

Marc had told me everything that Mouse had found out.

My woman might be rested but remains distracted, her heart

torn in two worrying about those kids, and I feel powerless to help her. While I trust Drummer to come up with a solution, Marc doesn't know him well enough yet, and is having difficulty suppressing her natural leanings to get the authorities involved.

She's quiet as we eat, ignoring conversations around her, only sparing the odd smile for Amy and Grunt. Prez doesn't appear, so she gets no more answers. I start to think how I can take her mind off things later tonight. Hmm, I might be able to come up with a thing or two.

As she automatically puts food on her fork and raises it to her mouth, my cock starts to twitch. Though I'm loath to compare the two women, Crystal was satisfying, but not adventurous in bed. Marc, I believe, will be up for something different. And tonight, I'll be the one in control.

A sudden movement beside me brings me out of my thoughts. Marc has put down her fork and is pointing at Amy.

"Amy, sweetheart, I can see you. Don't keep feeding Grunt. He's got his own food and doesn't need to eat yours."

Amy looks far from chastised. "But, Mom, he's hungry."

Marc grabs at my hand and glances at my face. She's got tears in her eyes, and while I'm going to have to get used to Amy using that handle, I find I'm proud as fuck that I've found a good woman to give back my kid some normality in life. Two parents. Sure, Crystal should never have been taken away, but all she'd want is for her daughter to be brought up right. And two parents, a mom and a dad, would form a big part of that. As I watch Marc swipe away a tear, I reckon Crystal would approve of my choice of old lady.

Amy's comment hadn't gone unnoticed. Conversation has stopped around the table, but I smile and give Marc's fingers a supportive squeeze, letting her know what Amy has said is no problem for me.

She swallows, clears her throat, and then gets back to the subject at hand. "Dogs eat dog food, Amy. There are some things we're able to eat that could make them ill. So either give him nothing, or ask first, okay?"

Amy stares at Marc, then slowly nods. The reasonable explanation seems to have sunk in. "Okay, Mom," she says quietly.

But fuck me, looking around the table, there are a few guilty looks from my brothers. Reckon Grunt's had more than enough to eat today, which leads me to say with a scowl, "And that goes for the rest of you assholes."

"Ain't giving him any of mine."

All eyes turn to Beef, who's sitting in front of a huge plate piled high. Yeah, that greedy fucker is unlikely to share with anyone.

"Yes, Mom and Dad," Joker has to add, causing a laugh.

I put my arm around my old lady's shoulder. A year ago, I could never have dreamed I'd ever be this happy again.

A couple of hours later, Marc takes Amy to get her ready for bed while I stay a little longer to talk to Slick before making my way up to join them. I read my daughter a story, explain that no, Grunt can't sleep with her, and then turn out the light and leave her to sleep.

Returning to my, *our*, room, I find Marc just standing, staring out at the balcony, but I doubt she's admiring the view.

"I don't know how to cope with this, Heart," she starts as she hears me. "What those kids must be going through."

Approaching her, I wrap my arms around her, and she leans her head back and puts it on my shoulder. "There's nothing you can do tonight, darlin'. Prez will come up with something."

"I feel so useless. And what's worse, I keep thinking I should be out there, trying to find them."

And there's another difference. Crystal would have relied on me and my brothers to sort matters out, content that we'd do everything necessary. Marc wants action and is frustrated there's nothing she can do.

"They won't hurt them, Marc. Not if they're going to auction them."

"But they'll be so frightened."

"Worrying about it won't help. Here…" I turn her around so she's facing me. "You need to let it go for tonight." My hands move down to the hem of her t-shirt, my intention clear. "Let me help take your mind off it."

She lets me slide her shirt off, raising her arms to make it easier for me, and doesn't complain as I remove her bra. "I don't think you can, Heart."

"Trust me."

Undoing her zip, I push down her jeans, automatically her feet lifting as I kneel and slip her shoes off, then remove the rest of her clothes. Placing a kiss to her mound, she shivers, showing she's not immune to my touch, even if her head's still elsewhere. I want her to stop thinking, to switch off, cease worrying about things over which she has no control.

Standing, I pull my own shirt over my head, then take a scarf from my back pocket and raise it to her face.

"What's that?"

"I'm gonna blindfold you."

Her head tilts in question, and I just wait. Then she nods, clearly curious. "Never done this before."

"Trust me," I repeat. Not telling her this is a first for me too, but Slick had some good pointers.

When her sight's taken away, I guide her to the bed. "Lie down, babe. Put your hands over your head and keep them there, okay?"

Goosebumps appear on her skin, but it's not from the cold, as she gives a little laugh.

"You haven't got your handcuffs with you, have you babe?"

She gives a shake of her head and a surprised giggle now. Fuck, that's a good sound. She's getting into this now.

I take my time just looking at her body. She's in amazing shape, obviously keeps herself fit, not an ounce of fat on her, her muscles clearly defined. A perfect hourglass shape, her waist I could span with both hands. Her stomach, for the moment so flat, but which will soon grow with the babies she's carrying, is marred by old scarring, which does nothing to detract from her beauty. Her gorgeous breasts, are thrust out by the position of her arms, and so tempting.

My cock throbs just at the sight, but I keep my jeans on for now. *This is for her.*

She wriggles, uncomfortable with the delay. I smile and swap the item I'm holding from hand to hand. I'd found a feather on the track up to the suite, and I make good use of it now. Her body jolts as I circle it around her breasts, teasing the nipples so lightly it barely touches her.

"Heart?"

Then I move it down her stomach, gently moving it down, for a second tracing those silvery scars, then evading the place where she most wants me to go, moving it down her right leg, and then the left. Taking it off her skin for a second, I then stroke the sole of one of her feet. Smartly she pulls up her leg.

"Ticklish?" I grin.

"Just a bit," she agrees.

Judging by her reaction that's an understatement, but I move on to the next stage. Taking my knife out of its sheath, I warn her. "Stay very still, babe." Now it's the cold metal of the sharp blade gently tracing her skin, not pressing enough for it to hurt, just skimming her lightly.

"What the fuck, Heart?"

She's fighting to obey me, her body tensing in her effort not to move. Her concentration on the implement I'm using, and thank fuck, not the thoughts in her head. Now I'm using both the knife and the feather, alternating the sensations so she doesn't know what's coming next. I slide the knife up between her breasts and rest it against her fragile neck, while at the same time lightly circling her clit with the feather.

Hardly daring to breathe, she doesn't know whether to react to the arousing touch or the threat. I take both implements away and leave her not knowing what's coming next.

Silently I go to the fridge, open the freezer and take out an ice cube. She's still, her whole body flushing as she waits. When her arms start to come down, I bark out, "Don't move."

Melting ice in my mouth, I lower my head and put my lips on her. She gasps at the cold touch on her clit. My hands grab her hips to stop her pulling away and use my cold tongue to roll the ice against that sensitive button. Fuck it if she's not wetter than I've seen her before, her arousal weeping from her cunt.

"Oh my God, Heart," she cries.

I plunge two fingers inside her, curling them around to find that soft spot inside while licking and nipping her clit, which doesn't seem to know whether to evade the cold touch or come out to play. At the same time, I pinch first one nipple, and then the other. Her thighs trap my head, her body tightens, and she writhes as she tries to push against me when my touch is too light, pulling away when I firm it. But I'm in control.

"Keep your hands where they are." I rumble another warning, suspecting she's about to disobey.

The vibration of my voice, together with my tongue and fingers, has her tensing up, and then she can't hold back.

"Heart, I'm…"

I pull away. "Stay still." I move the knife back.

Immediately the cold steel touches her. She stills, but is unable to control the rapid rise and fall of her chest. Her fair skin is covered with a sheen of sweat.

"What are you doing?"

What I'm doing is trying to remove any thought in her head other than what I might be doing next. Dropping the knife, I pull her up with both arms and turn her over. "Head to the bed, babe." I pull her ass into the air. I spank one cheek, and then the other, my cock jumping as I see the red imprint of my hand.

"Fuck it, Heart."

She starts turning her head, but I spank her again.

"Heart…"

If she tells me to stop, I will. "Go with it, babe."

I'm not hitting hard enough to bruise, just to arouse her. My hand meets her ass again and again. And fuck me if she doesn't start leaning toward me. When my hand reaches the point it's starting to sting, and her buttocks are glowing red, and she's panting and squirming on the bed, I part her legs and slap her straight on her clit.

She's so aroused she comes with a scream.

I hold my breath, hoping there'll be no sound coming from the other room. But luckily Amy stays sleeping.

While she's recovering, I take off my jeans. She's dripping wet, and so swollen from her orgasm I have to work my way in. Having this independent woman giving me total control is a massive turn on, and my cock seems to have grown twice its normal size.

I start with slow strokes, ramping up both my own arousal and hers. She's close, thank fuck, because I'm not going to be able to last long. With one hand on her nipple, and the other rubbing her clit, I pick up the pace and start hammering in, feeling that tingling down my spine and the tightening in my balls as she clenches around me.

As she orgasms again, my thrusts lose their rhythm, a few last punishing strokes as I empty myself in the cunt of my old lady.

Fuck, does it get any better than this?

She's collapsed onto the bed. As I spoon around her, gently removing the blindfold and pulling her back against my chest, she's totally relaxed.

"Hmm, Heart. What the fuck was that?" Her voice sounds slurred as if she's on the edge of sleep.

"Just getting you out of your head, babe."

I get no response as I smile against her hair. *Thank you, Crystal, for bringing us together.*

The wind outside blows up, and the windows gently rattle in their frame, and I swear I hear a whispered, *"Be happy, Heart,"* before the sound, as quickly as it started, dies away.

CHAPTER THIRTY-SEVEN

*M*arc…

If I'd been asked, I would have said with everything swirling around my head, I wouldn't have slept a wink last night. Instead, I don't stir until it's morning. As I turn over in the arms of my man, I realise my ass is feeling sore, and I start to remember exactly what he did to me. I'm not ashamed to admit how much I enjoyed every single thing he did. While normally I'd prefer to be a more active participant, he'd given me precisely what I'd needed last night, the chance to turn off my thoughts. But now, along with the light of day, they all come flooding back.

He's staring at me with a slightly amused smile on his lips. "You okay, babe?"

"More than okay."

"Hey," his hand touches my cheek, "what's that frown for?"

I rub my hands over my flat stomach. "Before I came here, Heart, I was feeling queasy in the mornings. I was sick a couple of times. But now…"

"Babe, some people don't get morning sickness at all, and it's still early days. If you're worried, we can go back to the doctor.

But you've got no bleeding or pain, have you? Just go with the flow. If you're not feeling sick, view it as a good thing."

"I know it seems crazy, but if I were suffering, I'd feel more like I was pregnant."

He reaches over the side of the bed and pulls his wallet out of his jeans, takes something out and passes it to me, his hand curling around mine so I end up clutching it. "This says you are, babe. Concrete evidence." It's the sonogram picture.

How is it that this man knows exactly what to say and do?

He slaps my already sore backside, making me jump. "Come on, get up now. Already had a text from the prez. Church at eleven, and you've got an invite."

"Invite or instruction?"

"Take it whichever way you want, darlin', but if I were you, I'd be there."

Nothing would stop me. "Where are Amy and Grunt?"

"You were sleeping, so I didn't want to wake you. Jayden's got Amy, and Tongue, fuck knows why, wanted to take the dog for a walk. Reckon the pup's already picked up a few fans here."

Two hours later, I'm taking the same seat as last time, greeted with a few chin lifts and even a couple of smiles. As the brothers come in and the chairs become filled, Hyde walks in with another and we all shift along to make room. Drummer's the last to enter, and he's not alone.

The stranger is a dark-haired man, his most striking feature a scar running down his face from the corner of one eye to the side of his mouth. If it wasn't for that, he'd be quite handsome. As it is, he looks terrifying.

That the men know him is confirmed by the nods they give to him. That his presence is a surprise is shown by uplifted eyebrows and tilting of heads.

"I don't need to introduce Devil to most of you. Devil, meet Marcia, she's an ex-cop who was working on the kids' disappearances." The man gives me a nod before taking the seat beside me. "Devil flew in overnight after I filled him in on our little problem."

With a slap on Devil's shoulder, Drummer walks around to take his seat at the head of the table. All eyes go to him and then swing in the other direction as it's the newcomer who starts talking without preamble.

"As I've already told Drummer, I don't see how you can avoid involving the FBI. Though after what happened last time, I understand why you're not enamoured of the idea." His voice is cultured, and he's got a UK English accent. I wonder how the Satan's Devils and he are acquainted, and what he's referring to about their previous dealings with the feds.

"I agree with Devil." Drummer casts his eyes around the table and puts up his hand to forestay the round of objections. "We won't be inviting them onto the compound, and the liaison will be through Devil. Mouse. Give us an update."

Mouse is looking tired, his eyes rimmed red as though he'd been working all night. "Our ruse worked. Sheikh Nijad has got himself an invite to the auction."

"I've got a man who's managed to secure a place too. One of my team." Devil inclines his head toward Mouse. "Sean, my chap, is coming in from England. Nijad, as you know will be staying in Amahad and appointing someone, one of your men, to attend on his behalf."

"We know the auction will be in Arizona, and the when, but not the precise where." Mouse takes over again. "They had to at least release which state it was going to be in so international travellers won't have to travel too far on the day."

"So, what's the plan, Prez?"

"That's what we're here to agree on, Peg." Drummer raises his chin toward Devil. "Firstly, we need to choose who will be Nijad's representative. It will be one of us. Who wants to volunteer to get dressed up in a posh suit?"

"Got to be someone clean-looking."

All eyes seem to focus on Lady, who shuffles awkwardly in

his seat. Joker gives him a worried look and then speaks for him. "Fuckin' dangerous going into a place like that. They suspect anything, a bullet to the head would be the least of his worries."

"I'll do it." Lady nods at the man beside him. "I'm about the only clean-shaven one out of all of us here, and I don't look like a fuckin' bodybuilder."

Joker doesn't look convinced, but everyone else is nodding.

"So, we'll have a man on the inside. Devil will brief you on what to expect."

Devil's peering over at Lady as if making his own assessment of whether he'll be able to play the part. As a crooked smile slowly emerges, it seems that Lady will pass. "I can give you a rundown. I've been to auctions like this before. Can't show my face now as I'm too easily recognised."

Mmm. It would be hard to disguise that scar on his face.

"Sean, my man, will be inside too. Two chances to get information out." Devil's taken over again, but no one seems to object. "He's bringing his wife with him, Mouse. You know Nessa?"

"Yeah, I've worked with both her and Cara before. She's a good fuckin' analyst." Mouse frowns. "They leaving the kid behind?"

Devil nods. "Sean's mother is looking after Mollie. I thought Nessa would be useful. Now, what you all want to know is the rest of the plan." Nods and chin jerks greet that statement. I'm bobbing my head enthusiastically too.

"The way these people work is to move their," he pauses and grimaces, "product around. Even if we found the location where they're keeping the children, it's probable they'd move to a different place before we could get together a team. They contact high rollers and put a discreet advert on the dark web, as you've found Mouse." He pauses and looks at me. "I've spoken to Sheriff Evans, you'll be the liaison with the police, Marcia."

My eyes open wide. He's spoken to the man at the top of the police department? My mouth drops open. Devil notices. "He wants you to go in and meet with him and his top team. Of course, the location might be beyond the jurisdiction of Pima County, but he'll be keeping his colleagues in other counties up-to-date. What you tell him will be determined by us." Devil points to himself, and then to Drummer.

"I'll be the one talking to the Human Trafficking Taskforce. I've made contact briefly, and they're willing to work with me. Agent Haughton you all probably remember." That statement's greeted by jeering and sneers. "I know you have reason to distrust him, but he's good at his job. And he knows I am too." No false modesty here, I can tell. "The FBI will also be trying to get the information, but as we've got people already invited, they won't be trying to get a man of theirs in." As there are a few curious looks, he explains, "The organisers will be ultracautious over who gets an invite. The sheikh was easy, they'll have no difficulty believing he might want to stock his harem with underage girls."

I'd been in the room when Mouse had spoken to the sheikh's wife, and I suspect, in reality, nothing could be further from the truth. I don't know whether to believe it, thinking it might have been a joke, but I'd overheard them laughing that Nijad's harem had been turned into a BDSM dungeon.

"Sean too. Well, Nessa's managed to rewrite his history. He's now got a reputation as a rich man with particular appetites. The FBI is playing catch up. It's too late for them to produce a credible plant."

He glances around as if to ensure everyone's following him. They all are, each man rapt as they listen to the plan. "Once we know the location, I and Marcia will inform the police and FBI. They'll mobilise and get men on the spot. We'll have it surrounded."

"We going to be any part of that?" Wraith wants to know.

Drummer's fists thump down on the table as he thunders out, "Ain't gonna leave a brother with no one at his back."

There's uproar around the table. Devil's voice is even louder than Drummer's. "Quiet. I've addressed that." Gradually, the objections die down. He attempts a grin, which doesn't work because half his face doesn't move. His contorted expression, though, suggests he's trying to convey amusement. "When I spoke to the sheriff, I explained he wouldn't be able to keep you out of it. Your man inside will have all of you at his back. He didn't like it, but could do with the extra numbers. He's agreed to have you work alongside the cops for the night."

Now there's an incredulous silence. "Well, fuck me," Drummer says, showing this was news to him too. "No tricks?"

Devil shakes his head. "They'll be grateful of all the manpower they can get. And as you say, you want to keep tabs on your man, and for my part, Seth and Ryan, two Grade A protection officers, will be flying out to have Sean's back."

"Hey, we going to be deputised or something?" Tongue's stud flashes as he jokes.

"Not in a fuckin' western, Brother."

"Do we get cop medical cover if we're hurt?"

Peg's not looking amused. "Not going to try to arrest us if we have to take action?"

Choosing to answer the sensible question, Devil raises his chin at him. "Complete amnesty. You'll be on the same team as the cops. Not going to try to pull the wool over your eyes. This will be dangerous, and bullets will fly. What happens at the auction will be sanctioned. Soon as you leave, you'll be on different sides again."

Most of the men around the table are having difficulty getting their heads around it, and comments fly about law enforcement and bikers working together. As Drummer and Devil wait for it to sink in, and the laughter and jokes to fade, I can't keep quiet. "I want in on this too."

"No you're fuckin' not." Heart's glaring at me. "You're gonna keep well away from any action."

Devil raises his eyebrow at Heart, then addresses me. "You will be. You're the liaison with the sheriff's team. You'll be attending meetings, setting it up, and feeding the plans back to Drummer." He sends a look of apology toward the president. "Sheriff wouldn't go so far as to allow a biker in on that, but Marcia, he'll accept."

I'm happy with that. Overjoyed to be included, but, "I want to be there. At the auction."

"And you will. But you'll stay in the background with Mouse, providing information."

I sit back and fold my arms. A raid is something I've been trained for, and I'm not happy sitting on the sidelines while my man puts his life on the line. That he'll volunteer, I'm already certain. There's no point arguing now. The only female among these misogynistic overprotective men is not going to be given a fair hearing.

"What exactly is the plan, Devil? We wait until we know the location, surround it…?"

Devil gives another of his twisted grins. "Once we know the location, we'll get into position. First thing will be to take out the guards on the outside. That will have to be done quickly and cleanly. Ryan and Seth are both ex-SAS, like your SEALs, and will take that on. They won't see them coming. Then we wait on the information from your man, Lady, and Sean. We want everyone focused on the auction, and not who's sneaking inside." He suddenly sits forward. "I want all the sick bastards. The organisers, people who've watched over the kids, and all the sick buggers who wanted to buy them. We round up every bloody one of them."

"Round up? Or kill?" Blade's still speaking for his brothers.

Devil shrugs. "I don't much care, but the feds will want someone left to question. This probably won't the first time this group will have done something like this. There may still be people in the background they'll need to catch up with."

For a moment, no one person can be heard. There are many different conversations going on in the room. The one I hear most clearly is taking place beside me.

"You sure you want to do this, Lady? Don't like you putting yourself at risk." Joker's speaking quietly, and I wouldn't catch his words were I not so close.

"Of course I fuckin' do, Brother. And I'll have you watching my back."

A range of expressions are crossing Drummer's face—pride in his men, worry they might not all come back, and disgust that he's been caught up in this. It's not too much different from being in a detective's briefing with a lieutenant concerned about what he's leading his men into.

When the furore dies down, the prez nods toward Mouse. "Don't think anyone needs any further incentive, but do you want to tell us the fuckin' rest?"

The computer nerd looks down at his laptop, and then his eyes rise over the top. "There's a fuckin' catalogue for the auction, so buyers can be prepared with their bids. There are fifteen items listed for sale."

I frown. "There's only thirteen missing children. Are they expecting to take more?"

Mouse continues as though I hadn't interrupted. "All items are fully described. I've matched thirteen of them to the kids that are missing. There are two descriptions in addition with crosses against them."

That gives us a lead, we can tell people to keep kids who match safe.

"One's a fifteen-year-old teenager who's apparently already been broken in, the other listed as a three to four-year-old girl."

You could hear a pin drop in the silence. Then Slick and Paladin are on their feet, and Heart's pushed back his chair.

"What the fuck? *Jayden?*"

"Not Amy. Fuck. They're not getting their hands on Amy."

"Sit down and shut the fuck up!" Drummer's on his feet, his voice shouting over their protests.

That's why Archer was interested in Jayden Greenway. I knew he was mixed up in something bad. And Amy. My eyes go to Heart, and my heart bleeds for him.

"No one," Drummer states each word slowly and clearly. "No one is getting their hands on Jayden or Amy. They'll be guarded all the time and not allowed off the compound."

"What if I take Jayden away?" Paladin asks.

"You're not taking her fuckin' anywhere," Slick roars back.

"No one's going anywhere," Drummer, still standing, states firmly. "That auction will go ahead with two empty places. There's no way anyone's getting close to those girls."

CHAPTER THIRTY-EIGHT

*H*eart...

I feel sick, bile rising into my throat as Mouse finishes his update. As my eyes meet Marc's, I see horror in her eyes. The room feels too hot, and my hands start sweating. My heart's beating so fast I feel it thumping in my chest. No one, especially these sick bastards, are getting their hands on my daughter.

I hardly hear Devil as he starts speaking again. "From the reports that I've read—particularly yours, Marcia—I think their chance has passed." I see Marc's mouth drop open as she must be wondering how Devil has gotten hold of and absorbed so much information in such a short time. He's still speaking to her. "I agree with your summation that there was something extremely suspicious that Archer prematurely reported Jayden as missing."

Marc frowns. "But that was a year ago."

"Leads me to believe this isn't the first time this has gone on. Maybe not with kids missing from Tucson, they may have been taken from somewhere else. And of course, they tried to take Amy at the same time."

"You think they're going to try again?" Wraith's asking the questions Slick, Paladin, and I are too stunned to voice.

Devil raises his shoulders. "Can't say. We can't be certain what the crosses mean. But time's getting on if they're going to include them. Drummer and I both feel they're sufficiently protected here, on the compound. The crosses might mean they're no longer available, or, the other option we can't completely take off the table, is that they take interested bids on the night and provide the goods at a later date."

Again I glance at Marc, she's biting her lip. But Devil's words have made me feel slightly easier. "You're saying, if we take this group out we can ensure the girls will be safe?"

"That's what I hope, Heart. As long as we get all the ringleaders and can shut this thing down."

"I still want to take Jayden away." Paladin's glowering at Slick. "I don't want to risk anything happening to her again."

As Slick starts to growl, Drum holds up his hand. "It's an option to consider, Slick. Paladin could transfer to another chapter. Hellfire, for instance, would keep him in line. He's got kids of his own."

Slick considers the prez, then gives a slow nod. "Don't know what Ella would have to say, but I'll think about it. As long as the asshole can keep her safe, that's what's important."

"We'll park that for now. No one's going anywhere until this thing's finished." Prez studies all our faces. "Now, it's a fuck of a lot to take in. We're proposing entering a fight we've no real part of, except for the tenuous link to two of our kids. We need to take a vote on this. Devil, you got anything more to say?" Devil's head moves side to side, and Drummer nods. "Okay. We're voting to go along with Devil's plan and stand up alongside the feds and the pigs." His lips curve slightly as he says the latter, as if he can't quite believe what he's putting to the vote.

I'll be voting aye with no hesitation. I have to do what I can to reduce the risk to my daughter. My eyes catch Slick's and know it will be an easy decision for him too.

I realise the voting's started. Wraith's given his affirmative, and Blade's looking confused, but then adds his agreement. One by one we vote around the table—except for Devil and Marc, who, not being members, stay silent.

At last I'm writing in the decision book, not quite knowing what I'm recording, but I scribble sufficient sentences to sum up this bizarre meeting.

Then we're dismissed, and there's only one place I'm going to be—beside my daughter and my old lady.

A couple of hours later, while topics we discussed in church are still whirling around in my head, I'm sitting and watching my girls. Marc's sitting on the floor, playing with Amy. They're dressing fucking Barbie dolls. Grunt's in there as well, trying to steal the clothes. Even with all the shit going around, the normality of the scene brings a smile to my lips. *I can't lose this. Any of this.* Losing Crystal darn near killed me. Losing my daughter, or my new woman would destroy me and I'd never recover. My smile fades.

Glancing up, Marc gets to her feet. A quick peek behind shows Amy's engrossed, so she raises her eyes to meet mine. "It could be old news, Heart. They might have forgotten about Amy. Have you heard from her grandmother lately?"

"Susie Clyde's dead." I'm surprised she doesn't already know. "Died of an overdose or some bad shit."

She huffs in a breath and puts her hands on her hips, her eyes searching my face, then surprises me. "Couldn't have happened to a better person." She glances back down at Amy and, without missing a beat, checks in. "You alright there, sweetheart?" As Amy nods without looking up, I'm thinking what a good mother Marc makes. She does it so naturally, doesn't even know she's doing it. And with that Glock no one's taken back off her yet, I know she'd protect my daughter with her life.

"My gut feel is that they are no longer after Amy. They can't use the grandmother, so would need to take her by force. They wouldn't stand a chance getting onto the compound."

"They listed her as a three to four-year-old. Why would they do that? She's four now…"

"Perhaps they never knew her exact age. Doubt Clyde kept any note of her birthday. She was probably spaced out at the time."

"We can't afford to be complacent." I shiver as I recall the name Susie had dropped. Alonso Herrera. We still have no idea whether the new head, Javier, is on board with his plans, but the less Herreras left breathing, the happier I'll be.

"I agree." She taps the gun at her belt. "Either you or I will be with Amy at all times, Heart." She pauses to grin. "I reckon Paladin's got Jayden covered."

"What worries me, Marc," I pause, thinking how I would never had had this type of discussion with Crystal, "is that Jayden and Amy are the ones who got away. Or in Jayden's case. Thank fuck they never got close to Amy."

"You think it could be some sort of grudge?" Her eyes narrow. "You could be right, these are sick fucks we're dealing with. Only thing I can see is to go through with the plan. Take all of them out and remove the risk to the girls."

Knowing she's right, I curl my hand around her neck, pulling her to me, and take her lips. Fuck, how did I get so lucky to find this woman? There can be no doubt in my mind that Crystal led her to me. She's fucking perfect.

It's torturous waiting for the next few days to be over. Drummer keeps calling us together, going over the plans again and again. As soon as we know the location, we'll be saddled up and riding. Slick and Viper will be staying with Fergus and Jekyll at the compound, just in case anyone comes for the girls, but we're mostly agreed, if they haven't taken them by the time of the auction, it's unlikely they'll choose that night to pounce. They'll be more about getting the dollars in for the victims they've already got. I'm torn between wanting to protect Amy and being close by in case my woman decides to become a hero—in her role as liaison between us and the police, there's no way anyone can make her stay behind. In the end, I'm persuaded that Amy will be safe enough here, and decide I'd rather be there with my brothers in case Marc needs me.

It's when we're discussing needing the crash truck along in case any of us are wounded that I realise just what I'm heading into, and that not all of us might be coming back.

Devil's colleagues from Grade A Security arrive, Seth and Ryan, tough ex-service men who I can immediately relate to. They're given a couple of the rooms at the back of the clubhouse to use, which they seem to find sufficient. Serious men, Ryan in particular is a man of few words, but what he says is always pertinent to the situation. They spend most of their time pouring over the information provided by Mouse, and by Nessa, who'd arrived with them. Mouse quickly made room for her in his cave after greeting her like an old friend.

And it's her who's currently walking across the clubroom, making the journey between kitchen and Mouse's retreat yet again. "Hey, Nessa, isn't it?" Blade eyes up the redhead as she emerges carrying refills of coffee.

She glances over in passing and grins. "I'm taken," she says drily, making us laugh.

"Your man doing okay?" I frown. Sean, her husband, is staying in an upmarket hotel in Phoenix, and like Lady, will be the first to put his head on the line. Sean's building up his back-story by acting out his role as a successful businessman with money to burn.

"He's living it up and drinking champagne from what I can hear." Nessa purses her lips.

"He'll be fine, Nessa." Ryan, her colleague, has obviously been listening to the conversation. He points his index finger toward the enforcer. "Unlike you, Blade, if you hit on his woman." He glances over at his colleague and cheekily adds, "His *pregnant* woman."

A brief moment of relief as chuckles and congratulations echo around, and then the now blushing but very happy looking Nessa's disappeared once again.

"What d'yall think?" Lady strolls in, modelling his custom-made suit, hastily put together by a tailor whose eyes lit up with the money he was offered to do a quick job. A professional haircut courtesy of Carmen, and I hardly recognise my brother.

"Wouldn't have known you," Peg calls out. "Just remember to keep your mouth shut."

Yeah, we'd tried to give him a lesson in how to clean up his language, and when that failed, instructions to remain dumb unless absolutely necessary in order to maintain the image as a representative of a sheikh. Lady's colourful language is hard to curb, but on looks I reckon he'll pass.

Marc flops down into the seat beside me, Hyde hovering behind. She looks tired, and I'm worried for both her and our babies. Surely so much stress can't be good at this time.

"How did it go?" She's been to yet another meeting down at the precinct, Hyde close behind just like the days before we got together.

"Garza and Reynolds still aren't talking."

Grimacing, I realise that was probably a hard meeting to have. It's not the first time she's been involved in interrogating her former partner and boss, and even on the other side of the table, they're still acting as though they've got the upper hand.

Her eyes narrow. "Sheriff himself was in the main meeting today." As much as I wish she didn't have to be involved, I'm proud as fuck as how she's holding her own, and particularly when she told me they pressed her about Satan's Devils involvement in the Herrera killings last year, the one that Archer got caught up in. She'd kept her mouth zipped tight, pleading ignorance. She's on our side, no one now has any doubt about that.

Tired though she is, after a quick kiss she's on her feet again. "I've got the paperwork confirming we're working with the cops tomorrow, and there won't be blowback for anything that goes down. I need to give it to Drummer." As she goes off to find him, there's laughter and smiles at the strange thought we'll be fighting alongside law enforcement, but the amusement fades quickly, as the seriousness of the situation catches up with us. What we're heading into will be dangerous. Probably we'll be going up against the Herreras, but it could be the cartel. Or both.

That last night before the auction, I make love to my old lady. There's not any other word for it. We don't fuck, instead taking our time learning each other's bodies, climaxing together, and then falling asleep in each other's arms. I hold her so tightly, thinking the universe wouldn't be so cruel as to take her away from me. It would kill me for certain.

A few months ago I felt I had nothing to live for and would readily have given up my life. Now that's all changed. I've got my daughter, my woman, and two babies on the way. I'll be taking no risks tomorrow, my recklessness has left me. I want to come back, for all of them.

That final day it's subdued in the clubhouse. Weapons are cleaned and checked, ammunition stored safely away. Blades are sharpened. Devil is at one table along with Seth and Ryan, who're now keeping to themselves. Not because of any aloof-ness, but because their sole focus is on the task ahead. They will be the first to move in. Their job is to take out the guards, silently taking them unawares. Knifes will be their weapons of choice, or their bare hands.

Drummer walks in, pausing to exchange a few words with Devil, then comes over. Some brothers are drinking beers, others abstaining to keep a clear head for the night ahead. Prez leans his back against the bar and surveys the room, his eyes landing on each man in turn.

Mouse appears out of his cave, stretching his arms up high then rolling his head on his shoulders.

Drummer beckons him over. "Any news yet?"

"Nah, nothing."

"Should have heard something by now. Any chance it's not going ahead?"

"No need to worry yet, Prez. They'll leave it right to the last minute. Just enough time for people to get there, and not enough to involve the feds."

Except, thanks to Mouse, the feds already know.

"They're cutting it close," Drummer grumbles.

The door that Mouse just exited through opens, and a woman's head pops out. "Mouse, I've got something."

As Nessa disappears back into the room, Mouse is there like a flash, Drummer and Devil hot on his tail. Only seconds later, they both come back.

"Right." Drummer's waving a piece of paper in the air. "Got it."

A phone dings and Lady waves his. "Got a text, Prez." They compare notes. Then Lady stands and brushes off his smart suit. As I'm turning back to my old lady, out of the corner of my eye I see Joker hugging Lady to him, holding him a fraction of a second longer than I would have expected. The pair had transferred from Vegas together. I suppose that forms a special bond.

Drum yells, "Let's give Lady a moment to get moving, then we'll get rolling."

A wave of emotion sweeps through me as I draw Marc in close, kissing her deeply, trying to imprint the memory of her taste and feel on my brain. When I pull away, I rest my forehead against hers. "Don't take any risks, darlin'. Promise me you'll look after yourself. Remember the babies. Need to go into this with a clear head and I won't if I'm worrying about you."

"Same goes for me, Heart. I love you, you know that. I need you to be here, for me..." She places my hand on her stomach. "For us."

"Love you, babe. Fuckin' love you."

Her eyes look watery, and her hand rests on my chest. "I love you."

I wished I had longer to savour the first time we declared our feelings for each other, but I've no time at all.

"Heart!"

"Coming." One last look and I'm on my way. The last thing I see is her in conversation with Devil.

Then I'm putting on my bulletproof vest and throwing my leg over my bike, firing up the engine and kicking it into first gear. Prez is in the lead, the VP and sergeant-at-arms behind him, then Dollar and Blade, me and Mouse, and the rest of the boys behind with Joker bringing up our rear, and following him, the crash truck driven by Hyde with Marc accompanying him.

I'm nervous tonight, knowing how much I have to lose. The ride passes with none of the normal thrills or exhilaration. I'm trying to concentrate on the fact if together with the feds and the cops, we bring this group down, Amy and Jayden will be freed from any fear of abduction.

But apart from the location and the time, even the feds haven't gotten wind of what exactly we're riding into. Until Lady and Sean get inside and start feeding back info, we'll know nothing of how many adversaries will be inside. As I keep a careful eye on my brothers in front, and in the mirror, those behind me, riding in formation, keeping a steady distance apart, the dour thought comes to me, and I hope it won't be any of our blood that will be spilled tonight.

Lady is off on his own now, well in front and out of sight of the bikes, heading off to do what he has to do. He's wearing no wire, but he's got one of those tiny devices in his ear which will let him hear Devil's instructions, and us what's going on around him. An undetectable earpiece that won't be found even if they search him, and search they will. With the nefarious activities taking place tonight, the organisers won't be taking any chances.

I admit to being worried about my brother, frowning as I ride, hoping the feds know what they're doing, and that his earpiece really won't be found. That he won't do something stupid and draw attention to himself. Out of all my brothers, I tend to know least about Joker and Lady, they keep to themselves.

With the truck following behind us, we meander our way

through the night. My hand clenched on the throttle, I keep my place in the pack.

Eventually it's time to leave our loud bikes. At the hastily arranged rendezvous, we meet up with a large police contingent, and another of feds—funny to think of them as brothers-in-arms tonight. I admit it gives me an uneasy feeling that for once we're all on the same side. As my eyes watch Marc going to join her former colleagues, I also take in the various trucks and vans parked around, and notice medics talking together in quiet voices.

After a brief conversation, Drummer comes over. My brothers shift uneasily as they clearly recognise the man who's accompanying him.

"Agent Haughton, you'll probably remember." Prez keeps his voice impassive as he introduces the man we all know. He's the fed who set the club up for a fight he didn't expect us to win. We've got no love for him.

"Your main job," Haughton begins without hesitation, "is to concentrate on getting your man out. We're going in heavy. The bidders won't want to be taken, and the organisers will want to get away clear, but we do want some still alive to question. You hear me?"

There are various growls and nods. Far as I'm concerned, I want everyone involved in this disgusting trade dead. And if any of my brothers are in danger, I won't give a fuck about leaving anyone breathing.

"We don't know what we're facing in there, but as soon as we find out where the kids are located, I want a group together to be part of that." He turns to Drummer. "Okay if some of you join them?"

Drummer raises his chin, and with a last nod at us, Haughton walks away, joining the group of police next.

Now it's Devil who approaches us and starts handing out earpieces, larger than Lady's. I manage to hook it over my ear.

"I'll be turning the receiver on and off and will be in control of what we're transmitting. Don't want Sean or Lady to be distracted by voices in their heads until we start giving them instructions. Got it?"

We indicate we do. Anything to keep our, and Grade A's, man safe.

He goes back to the control truck, and a hush descends as the ear piece in my ear starts transmitting. Now I can hear what's going on inside. It feels weird to hear voices in my head, but I can tell Lady's already inside, and it sounds like Sean's just entering. Lady's been offered a glass of champagne which he readily accepts, and Sean's polite enquiry about when the auction will get underway is answered, giving us vital information we need. The last of the guests are expected shortly, and they expect it to start within the hour.

Seth and Ryan dressed all in black, along with a few feds, are getting ready to leave. Devil gives them one final instruction and then sends them off to take out the guards as soon as the outer doors are closed and locked.

Blade offers me a cigarette. I'm tempted to take it, but with one look across to Marc, I shake my head. As he walks off, another brother approaches.

"I fuckin' hate all this hanging around."

"Me too, Tongue. Me too."

"Just want to get on with it and get back to the compound. Promised Allie I'd show her a good time when I get back."

"I bet you will." I grin, knowing I'll be relieving the stress of the night not in the arms of a sweet butt, but those of my old lady.

Beef's shifting from one leg to another. Rock is surprisingly looking composed, until I see a tick at the corner of his eye. All of us impatient to get moving. Looking over at the other men milling around, the waiting doesn't seem easy on anyone.

According to Sean's voice in my ear, things are starting. I watch two black figures ease away from the group and start making their way to the building that's still out of sight. Seth and Ryan are getting themselves into position.

Now I hear Devil's order. As soon as the guards have been dealt with, we'll have to move fast. We've already been over this. When the organisers lose radio contact with their men outside, they'll become suspicious. Sean's got the task of trying to locate the head of security and keep him occupied to give us more time. From the tinny conversation echoing in my head, he's already managed that task.

Now after a few more moments of stomping our feet, shifting impatiently, wanting to get moving, we're given the sign. I nod to Marc, who's talking to one of her cop colleagues, hoping she'll be sensible and stay safe, and back here, out of harm's way.

Then acting on the information Sean's managed to get and transmit to us, we divide into our groups and approach the three entrance points into the building. One at the rear close to where they're keeping the children, and the prez has assigned myself, Blade, and Peg to go with the police and some feds with one instruction—get the kids out and away from the fighting and bring them back here to get whatever medical attention they might need.

I seem to be walking in slow motion, my brain racing at such a fast speed, mentally examining whatever could go wrong. My gun is in my hand as I move forward. No one speaks, everyone intent on the mission in hand.

The larger group, the remaining feds, police, and bikers will be taking the main entrances as soon as the auction begins. All wearing masks, they're armed with tear gas cannisters, hoping to take the bidders and ringleaders by surprise.

We're in sight of the building now and crouch a little way back from the rear entrance. A couple of police come to the front, carrying a battering ram which will gain us entry. My free hand keeps opening and closing, ready for the fight.

Through my earpiece I hear from inside the noise starts to die down, the music is turned off, and an auctioneer can be heard from the stage.

"On my count." Devil's voice comes over clearly. Then, as he's obviously switched Sean and Lady's earpieces onto receive says, "We're coming in five. As soon as we come in, cover your faces."

On "Two" the police prepare, on "One" they're swinging the battering ram. On "Go" the door has burst open, and we run inside. Blade signals to where we can hear high-pitched voices, even over the sounds of screaming, shouts and shots coming from the main room.

We rush into a room where there are a number of children, scantily clad, crying and looking so scared it breaks my heart. Two men guarding them are taken by surprise and are shot by the feds as they're reaching for their guns.

"This way." Two cops have gone to the children and have started corralling them together. "We're rescuing you, understand?"

Cautious nods, one child is so disbelieving, he doesn't move. The big cop picks him up and carries him, and now we're outside.

A guard has been missed, or had been hiding. Whatever, he's quick to raise his weapon and shoot before anyone can stop him. I fire a shot and he goes down. Glancing behind me, I see one of feds has fallen. I run to him quickly. He's still alive. Knowing I have to get him out of here, I throw the fed over my shoulder in a fireman's lift and then follow after the others and the children, their short legs slowing us down. The poor kids are screaming now as shots ring out into the night. Blade picks up one, Peg's arms are around another, encouraging them away from the fight behind us and down to safety.

Our hearts in our mouths, we get them away. A quick count up shows our timing was perfect, before the auction commenced, which means they were still held together and we've got all of them out. Apart from the man I'm carrying, none of us seem injured unless we're powered by adrenalin and can't feel pain. Most of the fighting seems concentrated in the main arena where the auction was held, as bidders try to protect their identities and the organisers try to get away without being caught.

At last we're back at the ambulances. Medics quickly take charge of the children and the injured man I'm carrying. As I give the fed over into their charge, his hand comes out and clasps mine. It's a weak grip, but his eyes looking intently into mine, show me he's thanking me. I nod and go off to find Marc.

She's nowhere in sight. Fuck it. When Mouse raises his hands indicating she's not with him, I just know she's joined in with the other cops. I run around the front, feeling so fucking helpless, but Blade holds me back.

I try to fight him. "Marc's inside," I yell. "She's fuckin' gone in." I struggle to get out of his hold. "I need to find her."

"You've got no gas mask. She's trained for these situations, Heart. Trust she knows what she's doing."

But all her knowledge and training won't stop a bullet flying her way. Shit, she must have planned this from the beginning, to fight alongside her colleagues. I realise now she's not one to back down. Fuckin' stupid bitch. She can't leave me. Not now she's given me back the reason to live.

Blade's not releasing me. All I can do is wait, hearing shots and screams in my ear, trying to analyse the voices, hoping to hear hers, but among all the shouting and shots I can't distinguish her voice.

It seems like forever until people start to emerge. Cops, feds, and even bikers pushing men handcuffed in front of them. I see Drummer, Dollar, then Beef and Bullet. But no Marc. Then I see Mouse, Shooter, and even fucking Paladin and Road. One by one all my brothers emerge. Shooter's got his hand around Rock, who seems to be limping. Knowing we didn't all get away unscathed, I start to push forward.

Drummer grabs me by the shoulder. "It's done, it's over. Did you get the kids?" His voice sounds grim.

"Yeah, Prez, they're all safe with the medics. But I've got to go in. Marc's disappeared, she must be inside."

"She is, but last I saw her, she's fine. Let her do her job."

"I can't, Prez." Blade's grip has loosened, and I manage to push past him, but Peg's quick to take his place, and now it's him who holds me back.

"For fuck's sake, Heart. It's contained and controlled. She'll be out in a minute..."

What the fuck is she doing?

But even before he finishes speaking, the most wonderful sight in the world comes into view. Marc's emerging, her blond hair escaping from her bun and cascading around the mask she's only just removing. Still held back, all I can do is wait until she comes up to me, my eyes examining her for any sign of injury.

As she draws closer, her shoulders are slumped, and she barely acknowledges me. Instead she's looking at Drummer and shaking her head, wiping a tear from her eye. Even as I'm reaching for her, she takes my hand absentmindedly. Then she speaks the words I didn't want to hear. "Tongue didn't make it. I'm sorry, Drummer. I tried..."

As police lights come on illuminating the scene, I can see blood on her clothes.

"Are you hurt?" I ask sharply.

"It's not mine," she explains, her hand coming up to wipe her eyes, and again her attention goes back to Drummer. "I stayed with him, held his hand, but he slipped away."

Conflicting thoughts run through my head—the pain of the loss of my brother, and anger that my woman had entered the fray, putting her life, and the life of my children in danger. I don't know whether to kiss her or put her over my knee. In the end, I decide later I'll do both.

My brothers are gathering around, all now hearing the news about Tongue. Fuck it. He didn't deserve to lose his life. Tongue, who's not now going to be ending the night fucking Allie. I shake my head, unable to believe I'll never see my brother again.

"We need to get him out, Prez." Blade's eyes are wet, shining in the floodlights. I realised I've unashamedly got tears on my cheeks.

"Anyone else hurt?" Drum asks sharply, looking around, seeming to count us all up. It seems it's only one of us that had taken a bullet tonight.

Shooter waves around, drawing our attention to who's missing. "Rock took one in the leg. Beef was helping him down to the medics."

Devil strolls up. He nods at us all, clearly making his own assessment, then shakes his head. "I'm sorry you lost a man."

Prez lifts his chin. "What's the count?"

"Just two on our side, a cop and your man. A few with minor injuries, nothing too serious. They weren't expecting us so we had the element of surprise." He pauses, then carries on. "The ringleaders are dead or rounded up." His scar and his permanent scowl give him a furious look. "A good night's work, all the kids are safe. Heart, hear you brought out a fed. Good work."

I just nod at the recognition, and at last Marc draws close to my side, allowing me to put my arm around her. I allow myself to relax for the first time in hours.

"You okay, Detective Hannah? You took that man down hard." A man steps up in police uniform. "Thought I was a goner until you stepped in."

Fuck! "Marc?"

She puts her hand on my arm. "I'm fine, thank you, Lieutenant."

"I want you checked out." My voice is clipped.

She looks at me, then nods slowly. "I'm okay, Heart, but I will if the medics aren't too busy." She turns back to the cop. "And I'm not a detective. I was sacked, if you remember."

The lieutenant stares at her. "You realise you made all this happen? That the kids are going home tonight is down to you.

You'll get a promotion for this. We need dedicated cops like you in the department."

But her features are set, determined. "That's not what I want." She snuggles closer. "Not anymore."

He waits for a moment, then after telling her to contact him if she changes her mind, he walks away.

Then all we can do is wait until the body of my brother is brought out. No one wants to go and leave him behind. But as he fell alongside his cop brothers tonight, he's being treated as reverently as though he was one of their own. We follow the stretcher and watch as he's loaded into an ambulance and taken away into the night.

Only then do we go back to our bikes. Tongue and Rock's are loaded onto the crash truck—being injured, Rock will be going back with the prospect and Marc. Rock had refused to go to the hospital, the bullet a through and through. We'll get Doc to stitch him up at the club.

At last sorted, we make the sad journey back to the compound, keeping a space in our ranks, our brains still unable to register that one brother will never be riding with us again.

CHAPTER THIRTY-NINE

Marc…

"Well, I'm pleased to say all looks normal." Doctor Cassidy nods to the ultrasound technician who starts to wheel the machine out of the room. We know the routine now. This is the third time we've been here.

"You're over twelve weeks along now, and I'm pleased with what I'm seeing." The doctor sits back and smiles. "Your notes, as you know, showed extensive scarring from the accident, and I wasn't sure how that would affect you having a normal pregnancy. But from what I've seen today, your womb has been unaffected, and everything looks as it should be. The babies are growing and are exactly where they should be at this time."

"That's great news." Heart glances at me. I'm still trying to take it in. I'd been convinced I'd lose the babies, even more worried after I'd had to take down a man in a fight, landing hard on the floor. It took awhile for Heart to stop being angry with me for that. As I remain speechless, it's my man who continues talking for me. "Any idea of the sex?"

The doctor laughs. "It's too early to be sure about gender, but we'll keep doing scans as I want to monitor this pregnancy very carefully. If you want to know what you're having, then we'll probably be able to tell soon."

I'm quite happy with that. If this is really the only chance I'll have at having children, I won't be taking any more risks, and I couldn't give a damn whether they'll be boys, girls, or one of each. Having put myself at risk, and knowing how much that affected Heart, it was easy to remain strong in resolve not to return to my job. Anyway, there's more than one way to get bad guys off the street.

Devil had stayed for a few days after we'd freed the children, and he's offered both Mouse and I a job working remotely with him and his team, a sort of unofficial US base. We'll be following leads picked up on the dark web. As soon as we get a sniff of anyone targeting kids, we put it together, and Devil feeds the info to the feds. I won't get any recognition for what I do, or any payment, just the sense of satisfaction that I'm righting wrongs in this world. It's more than enough.

Bringing myself back from my mental meanderings, I manage to pull myself together enough to stammer a thank you to the doctor. Once I'm dressed and we're out in the corridor, Heart pulls me into his arms, and his lips find mine in a, for him, chaste kiss.

When he draws back, it's to tell me, "I love you, Marc. And these babies." Looking into my eyes, he continues, "How about we make it official now? Tell everyone."

Everyone already knows I'm pregnant thanks to Hyde having blurted that out, but no one but us have a clue that I'm having twins. Because of the uncertainty surrounding me being able to successfully carry the babies, Heart clamped down on anyone that's been talking about it, and even Amy doesn't yet know she'll be getting siblings. It scares me to bring it out into the open, but he's right. Now is the time. "As long as we discuss it first with Amy."

Heart grins. "She's gonna be thrilled. She's asked me for a baby sister for Christmas."

I laugh. Yes, I'd heard that. I think it was along the lines of, *Now I've got a new mommy, can I have a sister?*

"Anyway, you won't be able to hide it much longer." He caresses my stomach as he adds, "Two little ones in there, you're already showing."

Only just. But of course he'd notice. He particularly likes the changes in my breasts. But he's right, it won't be long before others do too. Two big biker babies are already making my stomach swell, even though I'm barely past my first trimester.

"Come on, let's get back. My brothers could do with some good news right now."

I nod. He's right. It's been a sombre month on the compound. Tongue was given an amazing send off, the funeral cortege including brothers from other chapters, patriot riders, and even the police were there not just to make sure things didn't get out of hand, but to escort the coffin as well. Everyone he fought beside, and lost his life for that night, stood up for him as he was lowered into the ground. Tongue died a hero, but that doesn't go to make any amends that he's no longer with us. I swear even Grunt misses him.

The sweet butts took his death hard, he was one of their favourites, liking to use the ornament in his mouth. So much so they wanted his special talent mentioned in the eulogy, but Drummer put a stop to that.

Apart from the brief respite at the funeral, after that night, cops and bikers resumed their chosen roles. And now I am ostracised by my former colleagues, but it doesn't bother me. I've been accepted into the club, and now this is my life, alongside my old man. Some people might think I'm now walking on the wrong side of the law, but I happen to believe I'm on the right one.

Heart walks to the passenger door and opens it.

"Allowing me to drive?" I smirk.

"No fuckin' chance." I don't argue, his answer was as

expected. I might have been given police driving training, but my man won't ever let me take the wheel when he's there. After the first few protests, I've learned to give in, saving my breath for things worth fighting over. And there are a few of those. I couldn't have found a better man for me had I tried.

As we walk into the clubhouse, Drummer's walking out. He pauses, looks at us both, having known we'd had a doctor's appointment. "Everything alright?"

Heart squeezes my hand. "We're going to make an announcement later."

Drummer grins, slaps Heart on the back, and then continues past.

Inside, Ella and Jayden are giggling, Amy's sitting close by, and Carmen and Sandy are shaking their heads, each with a baby on their lap. Something's up, I can tell. I've learned to read my fellow women here well. A smile plays at my lips as I wonder what they're plotting.

"Amy." Heart seems oblivious to whatever the women are up to, just calls his daughter over to us. She comes running, followed by Grunt. Dog and child have become inseparable.

She hugs first her dad, and then me, and happily comes with us, chatting nonstop as we pass the other blocs housing the other brothers' suite. Once we reach our own, Heart sits her down.

"Amy," Heart starts, glancing at me. We're both slightly anxious how the news will be received. Despite her off-the-cuff remark about wanting a sister, she's been an only child for all of her life.

Her little face looks up at him, her hazel eyes shining with intelligence. "Daddy?"

A small grimace crosses his face, and he wastes no time. "Sweetheart, how would you feel about having a brother or sister. Or both."

Her face meets mine and then looks back at Heart. For a moment she doesn't speak. Then she throws herself at me. "It's what I asked for, for Christmas! I wanted a baby sister." She's grinning and laughing. "Can I have a sister?" Her face falls. "I don't want a brother. Yuck."

"Hey, hang on a minute, squirt." Heart's lips have turned up, his brow that had been furrowed is now smooth. "You might get a sister. Or a brother." His grin widens. "Or both."

Now she's looking confused.

"Amy, sweetheart. I'm going to have twins."

Her little eyes widen. "*Two* babies?"

Putting my finger to her lips, I try to explain. "If all goes well, Amy, yes, in six months I'll be having two babies. And you'll have to help me look after them."

"And you'll have to help me take care of Mommy until they're born."

Her arms, which were tight around me, loosen. Suddenly the news sinks in. She pushes away from me, stands in the middle of the room, jumping and squealing, her face scrunched up. "I'm going to have a brother *and* a sister!" she screams.

"Hang on," Heart says laughing, "you might end up with two brothers."

For a second her grin fades, then she's smiling again. "But I'm the oldest. So they'll have to do what I say."

Then Heart's on the floor tickling her, telling her not to be bossy. I just sit back enjoying my family until Heart says it's time. With Amy holding both our hands, and walking between us, Grunt following at his own pace, sniffing at, then cocking his leg and watering the shrubs on his way, we go back down to the clubhouse. It looks even stranger now. Ella and Jayden have been moving tables and chairs, making space in the corner. Brothers are milling around, asking what they're doing. They just laugh in response, telling them they'll see shortly. More than a few brothers are exchanging glances and looking concerned.

There's a commotion outside, and then Sophie and Sam appear, holding the door open as Fergus struggles inside, carrying an enormous Christmas tree. Grunt shoots over and starts barking and growling at the alien object being brought into the club. I start, never having heard him bark like that before.

Running over, I try to pull him away, but even with my hand on his collar he won't be appeased. The sound brings Drummer out of his office.

"What the fucks going on?" he yells, then moves closer to the offending object. "What the fuck is this?" Right now it's harder to tell who's barking louder, man or dog.

"A Christmas tree," Sam says proudly, and a bit unnecessarily. "Thought with all the kids around, this year we'll celebrate in style."

As she's speaking, Fergus has undone the tree, and it's now on its stand. It must be one of the biggest trees I've ever seen, reaching to the ceiling and taking up all the space in the corner that they'd cleared. Sophie steps forward with a box in her arms and empties a pile of decorations on the floor, which starts Grunt off once again.

"Well, fuck me." Drummer seems stunned. He looks at Grunt, who I'm still holding back, then guffaws and bends over laughing. "Fuckin' good guard dog we've got there. Never barked at anything before, now he's losing it at a fuckin' tree. We're all safe, boys. If anyone comes in covered in foliage, we'll know all about it."

That starts the rest of us off. I look around for Heart, but he seems to be missing. I'm wondering where he's gone, and a cold hand reaches out and touches me. *Oh shit. Does the tree remind him of Christmases with Crystal?* My mind flits back twelve months. He'd had such a hard time of it last year, hiding away, trying to avoid the celebrations. *Is this too much for him?* Just when I'm considering going to find him, the door of the clubhouse opens again, and he steps inside. Immense relief goes through me as I see that he's got a wide smile on his face.

He walks to the bar, shushing Grunt as he passes, and *my* dog sits on his haunches and quiets down. *Damn him. How does he do that?* Then my attention turns back to Heart, who's climbed onto the bar and is now standing up straight and yelling for quiet.

At some point every brother must have come in. Well, it's Friday night and they've assembled for church. As all eyes go to Heart, he starts speaking.

"Marc and I, well, we got some news today that we'd like to share. You know Marc is pregnant, miracle baby for fuckin' sure, and that there was a chance she could have problems."

A hush falls over the room. A few glance at me as if to check whether it will be bad news or good.

"Well, we've seen the doctor today, and everything seems to be well. Looks like we'll be having two more baby bikers soon."

"Two?" Drummer's eyes have gone wide.

"Twins? Fuck me!"

"Nah, Beef. I prefer my old lady."

"Boys?" Rock yells as he limps in, his leg still not quite healed.

"Nah. Don't know yet."

"We'll start a book. One of three options," Blade yells. "Who wants to join in?"

"Four options," Beef's loud voice corrects, and incredulous eyes find him. He just shrugs, "Boy, boy. Girl, girl. Girl, boy. Boy, girl. We'll include the order they're born in."

That cracks me up, and also everybody else. Heart shouts for silence again.

"It's been over a year now since I lost my wife. Been a fuck of a long journey to get where I am today, and I wouldn't have made it if it wasn't for Marc." He throws me one of his beautiful, love-filled smiles. "But I'd just like to take a moment for us all to remember Crystal. Crystal loved Christmas." I feel slightly awkward as those around me agree, and a few anxious glances come my way. But I don't mind Heart talking about his dead wife, she'll always be part of our lives.

Heart's continuing. "You know I'll always love Crystal, and

she'll hold a place in my heart. But one thing I've learned is that love can expand and include others." He points to me, then curls his finger. Holding tight to Amy's hand, and bringing her with me, I go and stand at the bar, looking up at the man that I love. "I reckon Crystal would be happy that Marc found me, saved me, and I'm beyond lucky she's in love with me. As I am with her."

He jumps down from the bar and puts his arm around me and leads us both over to the tree. Brothers part like the red sea, allowing us through, giving him curious looks, not sure what he's doing. Once we're in front of the green monstrosity, he brings something out of his cut, then turns to face everyone again.

"Each year, Crystal would buy a new ornament for our tree. Last year, when I set out on my journey, I bought one on her behalf. At that time, I didn't know why, and my last thought would be that I'd ever be putting it on a tree. In all my travels I carried it with me. It was even brought back with my stuff from the fuckin' Demon Sons' clubhouse. So it seems the right time to celebrate the end of my journey which brought me full circle, back here, and to Marc and Amy.

"It also seems right that we all take a moment to remember Crystal and celebrate her life, and her love of this season in some small way. I'd like this to be the first decoration. For her, for Marc, and for my old and new family." Hearing no objections, he leans down, picks up Amy, hands her the snow globe, and points to the centre spot. As Amy hangs it in pride of place, everyone gives her a round of applause.

"Now all you fuckers grab a drink and raise your glasses in memory of Crystal, and in celebration of the new lives which will soon be swelling our ranks."

There's a brief rush to the bar, and those who've not already got beer in their hand get drinks from Jekyll and Fergus. Then a loud noise goes around the room as toasts go up to Crystal and my babies.

I stare at the ornament hanging from the tree. It's fitting we remember the woman who, like Heart, I believe brought us together. I'm one of the first to raise my orange juice in the air. "To Crystal."

Thank you, I whisper under my breath.

CHAPTER FORTY

*H*eart…

Last Christmas, I didn't think I'd be here this time the next year. Hurting so much, I couldn't find the strength to carry on. It was this woman beside me who saved me, who gave me what I needed, who showed if I opened up my heart there was room for more than one woman inside.

As Marc and I receive congratulations, my mind's going back over all the talks that I had with my woman on my long journey, and when she had told me about the stages of grief and helped me through every one. Well, now I've reached the end of that process, and as she'd once so wisely explained, I've reached the final stage. Acceptance.

I'll never forget Crystal, she'll always be with me, not least in the shape of the amazing daughter she left me. Amy will always be there as a reminder. Marc won't replace her, no one could do that, but she's offering me something more. Something I never thought I would find, or even wanted to look for. Life can be strange. I've lost one soulmate, only to find another.

This last year has changed me, and the woman who's absolutely right for me now is standing with me. I couldn't ask for anyone better to ride through life at my side, and it helps she's got her own bike—I'm never going to replace that single seat on mine. I'd never have found anyone like her if I went looking. I'm the luckiest motherfucker in the world to have had the love of two such amazing women, as different in every way they could be, but each one in their way perfect for me.

Apart from the ornament, I'd brought something else down with me. I reach for the bag I'd left on the side and then whistle loudly to get everyone's attention.

"What's this?" Marc's looking surprised as I put the brown paper-wrapped package into her hands.

I gesture to show she should open it. "Club took another vote, babe. Not like the first when they voted you in so I could keep an eye on you, but a proper one this time. You've earned all their trust. You're officially my ol' lady."

Her beautiful head tilts to one side, and then she takes out a brand-new cut. Turning it over, she sees 'Property of Heart' written on the back. Her eyes open wide at the physical consolidation of our relationship, and I see tears glistening as she realises how much this means. As unlikely as it seems, an ex-cop's been formally accepted into the club.

I'd never thought another woman would be wearing my cut. As she slips it on, I feel a light touch on my shoulder, and a gentle squeeze. *I hope you approve, Crystal.*

Another squeeze suggests she does.

The door must be open. A breeze makes the tree rustle, and then the air stills again and the brief clenching of my heart tells me Crystal has gone, and this time, won't be coming back. A quick frown, then I realise I'm all right with that. She'll always live on, in my memories and our daughter.

Smiling again, I barely hear the women cooing over Marc's new rag, or feel the slaps of my brothers on my back. I only have eyes for the woman, my leather around her.

"Fuckin' love ya, darlin'."

She's so emotional, she can't get out the words to say it back, but the reciprocated emotion shines out of her eyes.

I can't wait. Putting a hand either side of her face, I lower my head and take her mouth, my tongue sweeping inside, then my arm drops and I cup her sweet ass, squeezing her cheeks. And fuck me if her fingers don't find their way to my backside, kneading my flanks, making my cock immediately swell.

She's forgotten where she is, grinding against me. Fuck, I don't think I can make it back to our suite.

"For fuck's sake, get a room."

As I raise my middle finger toward Blade, I realise that's exactly what I'm going to do.

I'm gonna fuck my old lady. Or she'll fuck me. One way or another, fuck cares who's in charge.

Marc's mine. And I'm hers. That's all that counts.

READING ORDER

Turning Wheels
Drummer's Beat
Slick Running
Targeting Dart
Heart Broken
Peg's Stand
Rock Bottom
Joker's Fool
Mouse Trapped

       Paladin's Hell (Colorado Chapter #1)

Blade's Edge

       Demon's Angel (Colorado Chapter #2)
       Devil's Due (Colorado Chapter #3)

Truck Stopped

       Devil's Dilemma (Colorado Chapter #4)
       Amy's Santa (Next Generation #1)

Ink's Devil (Colorado Chapter #5)
Devil's Spawn (Colorado Chapter #6)
Coming Soon
Being Lost (San Diego Chapter #1)
Hawk's Cry (Next Generation #2)

Note 1:

Each book can be read as a standalone, but to get the best reading experience for the Satan's Devils, read the books in the order above.

Note 2:
While the Blood Brothers series is completely separate to the Satan's Devils series, there is some crossover. Turning Wheels continues the story of a minor character who appears in Second Changes, and some characters appear in both series.

OTHER WORKS BY MANDA MELLETT

Blood Brothers – A series about sexy dominant sheikhs and their bodyguards

Stolen Lives (#1) Nijad and Cara

Close Protection (#2) Jon and Mia

Second Chances (#3) Kadar and Zoe

Identity Crisis (#4) Sean and Vanessa

Dark Horses (#5) Jasim and Janna

Hard Choices (#6) Aiza

Satan's Devils MC - Arizona Chapter

Turning Wheels (Blood Brothers #3.5, Satan's Devils #1) Wraith and Sophie

Drummer's Beat (#2) Drummer and Sam

Slick Running (#3) Slick and Ella

Targeting Dart (#4) Dart and Alex

Heart Broken (#5) Heart and Marc

Peg's Stand (#6) Peg and Darcy

Rock Bottom (#7) Rock and Becca

Joker's Fool (#8) Joker and Lady

Mouse Trapped (#9) Mouse and Mariana

Blade's Edge (#10) Blade and Tash

Truck Stopped (#11) Truck & Allie

Satan's Devils MC - Colorado Chapter

Paladin's Hell (#1) Paladin and Jayden

Demon's Angel (#2) Demon and Violet

Devil's Due (#3) Beef and Steph

Devil's Dilemma (#4) Pyro and Mel

Ink's Devil (#5) Ink and Beth

Satan's Devils MC - Next Generation

Amy's Santa (#1) Wizard and Amy

GLOSSARY

Motorcycle Club – An official motorcycle club in the U.S. is one which is sanctioned by the American Motorcyclist Association (AMA). The AMA has a set of rules its members must abide by. It is said that ninety-nine percent of motorcyclists in America belong to the AMA

Outlaw Motorcycle Club (MC) – The remaining one percent of motorcycling clubs are historically considered outlaws as they do not wish to be constrained by the rules of the AMA and have their own bylaws. There is no one formula followed by such clubs, but some not only reject the rulings of the AMA, but also that of society, forming tightly knit groups who fiercely protect their chosen ways of life. Outlaw MCs have a reputation for having a criminal element and supporting themselves by less than legal activities, dealing in drugs, gun running or prostitution. The one-percenter clubs are usually run under a strict hierarchy.

Brother – Typically members of the MC refer to themselves as brothers and regard the closely knit MC as their family.

Cage – The name bikers give to cars as they prefer riding their bikes.

Chapter – Some MCs have only one club based in one location. Other MCs have a number of clubs who follow the same bylaws and wear the same patch. Each club is known as a chapter and will normally carry the name of the area where they are based on their patch.

Church – Traditionally the name of the meeting where club business is discussed, either with all members present or with just those holding officer status.

Colours – When a member is wearing (or flying) his colours he will be wearing his cut proudly displaying his patch showing which club he is affiliated with.

Cut – The name given to the jacket or vest which has patches denoting the club that member belongs to.

Enforcer – The member who enforces the rules of the club.

Hang-around – This can apply to men wishing to join the club and who hang-around hoping to be become prospects. It is also used to women who are attracted by bikers and who are happy to make themselves available for sex at biker parties.

Mother Chapter – The founding chapter when a club has more than one chapter.

Nomad – In an outlaw MC a **nomad** is typically a member who's been given permission/instruction by the national president to enforce the laws of the club at other chapters.

Patch – The patch or patches on a cut will show the club that member belongs to and other information such as the particular chapter and any role that may be held in the club. There can be a number of other patches with various meanings, including a one-percenter patch. Prospects will not be allowed to wear the club patch until they have been patched-in, instead they will have patches which denote their probationary status.

Patched-in/Patching-in – The term used when a prospect completes his probationary status and becomes a full club member.

President (Prez) – The officer in charge of that particular club or chapter.

Prospect – Anyone wishing to join a club must serve time as a probationer. During this period they have to prove their loyalty to the club. A probationary period can last a year or more. At the end of this period, if they've proved themselves a prospect will be patched-in.

Old Lady – The term given to a woman who enters into a permanent relationship with a biker.

RICO – The Racketeer Influenced and Corrupt Organisations Act primarily deals with organised crime. Under this Act the officers of a club could be held responsible for activities they order members to do and a conviction carries a potential jail service of twenty years as well as a large fine and the seizure of assets.

Road Captain – The road captain is responsible for the safety of the club on a run. He will organise routes and normally ride at the end of the column.

Ronin – A biker who travels alone, sometimes wearing a patch denoting he's Ronin. Not affiliated to any club, but often bearing a token which will help ensure safe passage through territories of different clubs.

Secretary – MCs are run like businesses and this officer will perform the secretarial duties such as recording decisions at meetings.

Sergeant-at-Arms – The sergeant-at-arms is responsible for the safety of the club as a whole and for keeping order.

Sweet Butt – A woman who makes her sexual services available to any member at any time. She may well live on the club premises and be fully supported by the club.

Treasurer – The officer responsible for keeping an eye on the club's money.

Vice President (VP) – The vice president will support the president, stepping into his role in his absence. He may be responsible for making sure the club runs smoothly, overseeing prospects etc.

ACKNOWLEDGMENTS

Heart Broken

Author's Ramblings and Acknowledgments

From the beginning it was always going to be difficult to write Heart's story. Heart and Crystal were a thread running through the previous books, introduced as a loving couple in Turning Wheels and Drummer's Beat. In Slick Running. Crystal was killed, and Heart was in a coma. During Targeting Dart, when Heart regained consciousness he came back a changed man, destroyed by the loss of his old lady and soulmate.

A man so deep in grief, how could I ever introduce him to another woman who would take a place in his heart alongside that reserved for Crystal? How could such a story be credible? And what was I going to do about his daughter, Amy?

Heart wasn't going to fall for the first woman he came across, he needed time to grieve. I knew I had to move his story along in time, and the answer was given to me in a suggestion made by the wonderful MariaLisa Demora (if you haven't read her Rebel Wayfarers series I suggest you do). Heart would become Ronin, and disappear for six months.

So I had Heart undertaking a road trip, incidentally the same one that I undertook many years ago the very first time I came to the States. My personal experience, I hope, has injected some flavour into the descriptions. Along with my husband and (then young) son, I travelled from San Diego to Tucson, to Flagstaff and the one place Heart didn't detour too, the Grand Canyon. From there we went to Las Vegas, where I was struck by the sounds and lights followed by the stark contrast of the silence and peace in Death Valley. Heart's sinus headache in the highest parts of Yosemite was the same pain that I suffered. I went to San Francisco, rode on a cable car and saw the Golden Gate Bridge (but no Hell's Angels). Then the Winchester House, and oh my, is that place creepy.

I also ate snow crab at Monterey, and watched the otters eating fish in the sea.

I think Heart would have enjoyed his ride down the Pacific Highway a little more than me, it was a long journey, particularly with a four-year-old repeatedly asking the typical question, when are we going to get there? But unlike Heart, we did make it safely back to San Diego. It was a great trip, and one that's stayed with me. If my memories faulty in any part, that's down to me and I apologise.

I felt Heart needed someone who understood what he was going through, and liked the idea that two broken people could mend each other. Marc, well, there's a little bit, maybe a lot, of her in me. I often fall back to some extent on my own life experiences when writing, but this book includes more than most. When you lose your parents as a child/teenager/young woman it comes as an incredible shock after having grown up with the expectance you'll have your family around forever. Shunted out of a safe cocoon, nothing can be viewed the same way again, no longer looking at the world with confidence, and constantly wondering when is the other shoe going to fall.

It also took me six years longer than I hoped to fall pregnant, Like Marc, I, too, avoided looking at pregnancy tests afraid it would never happen. It makes me even more thankful to have my son now.

I think Heart's been my favourite book to write of the series so far, but it was hard. And I hope Heart's emotional journey isn't too painful to read, particularly for anyone who has lost someone close to them. You never forget, but it does become easier, and if it's a partner, I hope, like Heart, everyone gets their second chance.

I hoped I was on the right track with this story, but having doubts I was being too self-indulgent with Heart's road trip and too downbeat as he went through his suffering, I invited several wonderful people to beta read for me. I have to admit, my beta readers were fantastic, and I think I've incorporated all their suggestions into the book.

I'd like to thank Mary, Danena, Sheri, Colleen, Terra, Zoe, Vikki and a special mention to Alex who saved me from making a mistake at the eleventh hour, showing she knows my books better than I do. I'm so very grateful to you all for working through an unedited copy and giving me your advice, suggestions and encouragement. Y'all make a really great team.

As always, thanks to Brian Tedesco my editor who tries his best to keep me speaking American English and manages to keep up with my short timescales and punishing schedule.

Lia Rees, what can I say? As usual you've outdone yourself with the covers and interior design. Thank you so much.

Massive thanks to Maggie Kern who's re-edited this book, making it so much better than it was before. Really appreciate your help, Maggie.

Last, but not least, thank you to everyone who's taken a chance and picked up and read one of my books. It's your reviews and encouragement that keep me writing. You can't know how much it means when I get feedback saying how much you like my style or my stories.

STAY IN TOUCH

Email: manda@mandamellet.com

Website: www.mandamellet.com

Sign up for my newsletter to hear about new releases in the Satan's Devils and Blood Brothers series.

Facebook reader group: https://www.facebook.com/groups/mandasbadboys/

facebook.com/mandamellet

twitter.com/manda_mellett

Manda's life's always seemed a bit weird, starting with a childhood that even today she's still trying to make sense of, then losing her parents in the late teens. Going from the tragic to the bizarre, who else could be unlucky enough to have had two car accidents, neither her fault, one involving a nun, and another involving a police woman?

There isn't enough space to list everything that's happened to Manda, or what she's learned from it. But by using the rich fabric of her personal life, psychology degree, varied work experiences, and amazing characters she's met, Manda is able to populate her books with believable in-depth characters and enjoys pitting them against situations which challenge them. Her books are full of suspense, twists and turns and the unexpected.

Manda lives in the beautiful countryside of Essex in the UK, the area's claim to fame being the Wilkin's Jam Factory at nearby Tiptree. She can usually find jars of jam which remind her of home wherever she goes. As well as writing books and reading, Manda loves walking her dogs and keeping fit. She lives with her husband of over 30 years, who, along with her son, is her greatest fan and supporter.

Manda is thankful that one of the more unusual, and at the time unpleasant, turns her life took, now enables her to spend her time writing. Confirming, in her view, every cloud has a silver lining.

Photo by Carmel Jane Photography